Angels of Justice

A Circle Sleuth Mystery

Titles by Betty Lucke

FICTION

Circle Sleuth Mystery Series
Circle of Power
Family of the Heart
Secrets of the Past
Angels of Justice

NONFICTION

Festival Planning Guide:
Creating Community Events with Big Hearts and Small Budgets

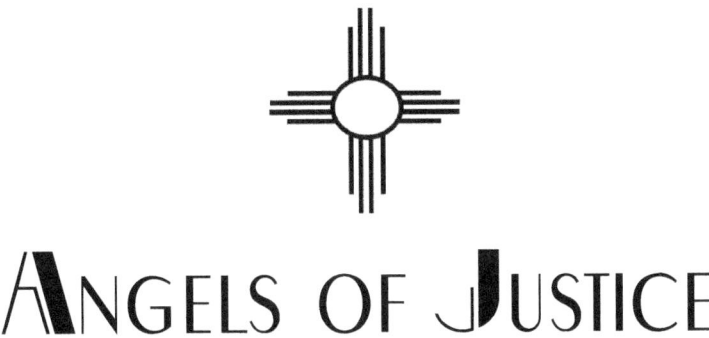

ANGELS OF JUSTICE

A Circle Sleuth Mystery

Betty Lucke

Spearmint Books

Angels of Justice
A Circle Sleuth Mystery, Book 4

Published by Spearmint Books.

© 2020 by Betty Lucke. All rights reserved.

No portion of this book may be reproduced, stored in a retrieval system, or transmitted in any form or by any means—electronic, mechanical, photocopy, recording, scanning, or other—except for brief quotations in critical reviews or articles, without the prior permission of the publisher.

This novel is a work of fiction. Any references to real people, living or dead, business establishments, places, organizations, or events are intended only to give the fiction a sense of reality. These references are used as background in which the fictional characters live, move, and have their being. The fictional law enforcement entities portrayed in this book may or may not reflect how their real-life counterparts function. All other names, places, characters, and incidents portrayed in this book are the product of the author's imagination.

To contact the publisher, please email: spearmintbooks@gmail.com.
Editor: **Wendy VanHatten**
Cover Design: **Tara Baumann**
Cover Photos: **Emily Brown, Jo Pemble**

Library of Congress Cataloging-in-Publication Data

Lucke, Betty, Author
Angels of Justice: a circle sleuth mystery / Betty Lucke
First Edition   Spearmint Books, 2020
Library of Congress Control Number: 2016910487
    ISBN 978-0-9884631-6-5

1. Schultz, Pete (Fictitious Character)—Fiction
2. Mystery—Detective—New Mexico—Santa Fe—Fiction
3. New Mexico—Santa Fe—Fiction
4. Dogs—Terriers—Airedales—Fiction
5. Kidnapping—Fiction
        FIC LUC   813.6 DD   PS – LCC   1. Title

Printed in The United States of America

Acknowledgements

I wish to thank the following for their expertise and encouragement. The journey with Pete and his friends in the Circle of Sleuths—exploring the characters, bouncing ideas back and forth, and digging deeply into the world of writing fiction has been challenging and rewarding. This mystery is dedicated to the Fiction Writers' Coffee Klatsch folks. Thanks to all who welcomed Pete and Hoot into their lives and helped the story come alive.

Draft and Beta Readers: Cheryl Potts, Emily Brown, Jean Norrbom, Joann Helmus, Lauren Filarsky, Laurie Rawlinson-Evans, Mark Helmus, PJ Loomer, Page Frechette, Peggy Lucke, Rachel Lewis, Scotti Butler, Sierra Janisse, Su Schlagel, Susan Walsh, Tom Markle, the Fiction Writers' Coffee Klatsch, and the members of the Town Square Writer's Group.

Consultants: Cheryl Potts, Don Bestwick, Dotty Schenk, Jean Norrbom, Kelly Hess, Lauren Filarsky, Laurie Rawlinson-Evans, Marty Markovitz, Peggy Lucke, Su Schlagel, Steven Carey, Syl Bestwick, Tom Markle, and Vince Nadasdy.

Editing: Wendy VanHatten

Cover Photos – Emily Brown, Jo Pemble,
Cover Design – Tara Baumann
Airedale on the cover: "Ch GlenRoyal Highland Piper, GlenRoyal Airedales, Stephentown, NY.

Circle Sleuth Families and Law Enforcement Personnel

The McCreath Clan
    Cliff McCreath. 29. Married to Lou. Father of Dougie.
    Lou McCreath (nee Schultz). 29. Oldest child of Pete and Akiko. Married to Cliff, Mother of Dougie.
    Johnny McCreath. Kidnapped twenty-five years ago when he was six. No trace was ever found of him.
    Andrew McCreath. Father of Johnny, Cliff, and Erin.
    Lynn McCreath. Mother of Johnny, Cliff, and Erin.

The Schultz Clan
    Pete Schultz. 53. Married to Akiko. Father of Lou, Rick, and three other children.
    Akiko Schultz. 51. Married to Pete. Mother of Lou, Rick, and three other children.
    Alarik (Rick) Schultz. 14. Youngest child of Pete and Akiko.

The Bjornson Clan
    Anton Bjornson. 34. Lives with his fiancée, Skyla; his mother, Karen; and his daughter, Krista.
    Krista Bjornson. 11. Anton's daughter.
    Karen Bjornson. 56. Widow. Mother of Anton, grandmother of Krista.
    Skyla Van Dyken. 30. Lives with her fiancé, Anton.

The Martinez Clan
    Sam Martinez. 29. Married to Farah. Has an adopted daughter, Leyla. Is the grandson of Domingo Baca.
    Farah Martinez. 29. Married to Sam. Mother of Leyla.
    Leyla Martinez. 11. Farah's daughter, adopted by Sam.
    Domingo (Dom) Baca. 70. Widower. Sam's grandfather.
    Steve Martinez. 14. Youngest of Sam's siblings.

The Stewart Clan
   Ross (Hoot) Stewart. Married to Melody. Father of a son,
      Matti, and a daughter, Bonnie.
   Melody Stewart. Married to Hoot. Mother of Matti and
      Bonnie.
   Marilyn Stewart. Grandmother of Ross Stewart.

Law Enforcement Personnel
   Hiram Brower. Captain, New Mexico State Police.
   Selwyn Cannon. Officer, Southwood Precinct, Denver PD.
   Leroy Grover. Chief of Police, Santa Fe PD.
   George Isaacson. Commander, Southwood PCT, Denver PD.
   Cheveyo Loloma. Detective, Santa Fe PD.
   Sam Martinez. Detective, Santa Fe PD
   Yvonne Novak. Pete's Administrative Assistant. Married to
      Vassily Novak.
   Elena Ruiz. Detective, Santa Fe PD.
   Pete Schultz. Lieutenant in charge of Detectives, Santa Fe, PD

Airedale Terriers (with significant roles) and their owners
   Beowulf (Wulf) - Pete Schultz.
   Gandalf - Cliff McCreath.
   Twitch - Anton Bjornson.

PART I – WHO AM I?

PROLOGUE

May 19, 1991

Through the blue Montana sky, the de Havilland Beaver amphibious plane flew over the national forest toward its destination on Flathead Lake. A little boy with red curly hair and tear-streaked cheeks slumped dejectedly in the passenger seat. The big man at the controls scowled at the child.

"You will be living with your new grandparents," he said. "If you ever tell them that you aren't Ross Stewart, they will tell me, and you'll be sorry. I will kill your father. I'll kill your little brother and your mother. It will be your fault, because you told. Your fault. Do you understand?"

"I want my daddy. I want to go home." A wailing sob rose.

"I'm your daddy now," the man said. "Quit your bawling."

"You're not my daddy!" Johnny screamed at him.

The pilot's hand left the yoke to backhand the boy. The blow landed ineffectively, glancing off the yellow life jacket he wore. Johnny shied away toward the window, cowering in his seat, still sobbing.

The engine noise of the plane droned on. Mountains with rocky slopes gave way to thousands of trees as they descended. Sometimes he saw cars; they looked smaller than ants. Occasionally he'd seen rooftops, snaky roads, and funny green circles against the endless brown of open space. The mountains in the distance were white on top. The shores of a big lake came into sight. The plane came down closer, and he saw the darker blue of the water.

The door felt cold as he leaned against it. He grew quiet and curled up in a ball on the seat, bringing his feet up and awkwardly hugging his knees. He rocked back and forth on the seat. Maybe when they landed this time, he would jump out and run into the airport. Maybe he could find a policeman or somebody who knew where his mommy and daddy were. Or maybe he'd just run and run and run until he got home.

The big, mean man picked up a thermos and poured some coffee. He set the thermos between them on the floor. "What's your name?"

The boy said nothing. He was Johnny. But saying that only made the man angry and hit him.

"What is your name?" the man yelled.

"Johnny."

Slap!

"What is your name?"

"Ross." Tears blurred his sight.

"Ross what?"

"Ross Stewart."

"Finally. Stop that damn crying. How old are you?"

He was only six. The man wanted him to say seven. He bunched up his lower lip mutinously. He hated lying, but that was the only way the man would stop hitting him. "Seven."

"Where do you live?"

"S-Santa Fe."

Slap.

"Where do you live?"

"Denver."

"Who am I?" The mean man glared at him.

"You aren't my daddy." Johnny started to cry again. He couldn't help it.

"WHO AM I?"

"Daddy, I want my daddy." He ducked as the hand came at him again, catching him on his nose. He tasted blood on his lip.

The plane lurched to the side. "Damn it. See what you made me do. Now, who am I?"

"Daddy."

"What happens if you tell?"

"You gonna hurt my daddy." He was so tired, so scared.

"Whose fault will it be?"

"Mine," Johnny whispered.

"Promise you won't tell."

"I promise."

"Who are you going to stay with?"

"Grandma and Grandpa."

"What will they do if you tell them the truth?"

"They will tell you."

"What happens then?"

"You hurt my daddy."

"So bad your daddy will die, and it will be your fault."

"No, no. I hate you. *I hate you!*" The hand came at him again. The boy lashed out, kicking with both feet, drumming them on the cockpit panel. He screamed, "No!"

"Not another word. We're here. We're landing. You remember what I told you. You can't *ever* tell."

The boy curled against the window again. He would run away from him. He'd run as soon as the door opened. The blue of the water came closer and closer to the big things underneath the plane which the man called pontoons.

What? This was different.

Weren't they going to land at an airport like they'd done before? Could they land on water?

He couldn't look away. The pontoon touched the water. Spray came flying back. Suddenly white spray was everywhere. Johnny jerked forward. The thermos flew into the window. Johnny's world somersaulted as the plane flipped over. The groan of wrenching metal and the gurgle of water were the last sounds he heard.

3

CHAPTER ONE

November 1, 2016
Santa Fe, New Mexico

Lynn McCreath uttered a soft cry as she spotted the stuffed Koda toy on a shelf in her son Cliff's home office, where the family had gathered after dinner. Koda's bright eyes stared back at her from a merry face, framed with white curls peeping out from a traditional, Sami four winds hat. Lynn picked up the doll, smoothing his blue and red Laplander costume and touching the lantern he held.

This little fellow tugged at her heartstrings every time she saw him. Johnny had loved him so. She closed her eyes and drew the figure close to her chest, as though she could fill the ache within and somehow send her love to her missing firstborn child.

Was he still out there? Would they ever find him?

Her eyes opened to see Cliff watching her from where he stood with his dad, wife, and in-laws by his desk. Lynn took pride in Cliff's accomplishments as an author, but she found herself near tears at not knowing who Johnny might have become or if he even survived.

"Mom? You okay?" Cliff left the others debating the merits of the book cover for his forthcoming young adult mystery and crossed his spacious study toward her.

She nodded, her finger caressing the gold-rimmed glasses Koda wore. "I'm glad you kept him."

"Me, too," said Cliff. "Johnny talked to him, and he said Koda listened. Even now, grown with a child of my own, I find myself telling Koda what I wanted to tell Johnny. He's heard everything."

Another of the group joined them. Lynn smiled at Pete Schultz affectionately. Over the years, Pete and his wife, Akiko, had become good friends of Lynn and her husband. Originally, they'd been drawn together because their children were classmates and members of the same Celtic music group. Now, since Cliff had married their daughter, Lou, they were family. Pete and Akiko understood moments like this coming upon the McCreaths unpredictably. They, too, felt the longing for the one who was missing.

When Johnny had been kidnapped on that long-ago, horrific day, Pete had just started his career with the Santa Fe Police Department. Though Lynn hadn't been aware of it for years, Pete was the bulldog-stubborn officer who refused to let Johnny's case go cold and forgotten. Now he was a lieutenant and head of one of the detective divisions. He was the one who kept them in touch with any leads. Caring, persistent, with a droll sense of humor—that was Pete. They were lucky to see his sensitive, sometimes emotional side, but in his police mode, she knew he was a fierce, eagle-eyed, screw-around-at-your-own-peril type of guy.

"That Koda was his, wasn't it?" asked Pete. "Johnny's kidnapping has indeed been a painful journey. I'm still hopeful that someday we'll get a break and be able to bring him home."

Akiko joined them, slipping her arm around her husband's waist.

Andrew McCreath set the book cover back on his son's desk and moved over to his wife. "I remember when we finally made the decision to pack up Johnny's belongings. Cliff wouldn't let go of Koda." He sighed. "It was one of the toughest moments I ever faced—putting away Johnny's things and confronting the fact I might never see him again."

"I have to believe we will, Dad," said Cliff. "Every day, I wonder, will this be the day?"

Andrew took Koda from his wife. "He's always in my heart."

Lynn picked up a framed photo from the shelf. She studied her younger image captured for eternity, hugging her two sons—blue-eyed, ginger-topped imps. When had her hair lost its brightness? It used to be just like theirs. "Andrew took this. I don't remember what we were laughing at, but we were so happy."

In Lou's arms, little Dougie cried, "Ahhh, b-b-buh." Lou wet her fingers and tried to give some semblance of neatness to her son's wild, dark hair.

Cliff laughed, draped his arm loosely over his wife's shoulder, and tickled the baby's tummy with his other hand, making a playful sound. Lynn smiled at the three of them. Lou had made such a wonderful difference in Cliff's life. Lou—artist, musician, and a sweet, loving woman—was dear to her and Andrew. A year ago, Cliff's home had been functional, but cluttered and uninviting. Now it showed Lou's influence, treasures grouped with warmth and pleasing color schemes. Baby paraphernalia lay scattered—a pacifier, a brightly colored rattle, and a cloth diaper ready at hand for catching spit-ups and drool.

Her eyes rested on her grandbaby. Dougie could hold his head upright on his own now. She smiled as Cliff and Lou talked to him. He was growing so fast.

Akiko's voice drew her attention back to the photo in her hand. "I've always liked how that picture captured feeling so incredibly well."

Andrew toggled the switch for Koda's tiny lantern. "It still works," he said in wonder.

Through the sheen of moisture in her eyes, Lynn saw the glow of Koda's lantern light her husband's face, showing the mark of his years.

"I always keep a fresh battery in it," said Cliff. "You never know. Maybe that light will be important. Silly thought, isn't it?"

"Not silly at all." Andrew smiled at Cliff. "You're looking at parents who have kept the porch light on for Johnny every night for twenty-five years." He shrugged, and his smile withered. "Maybe someday. That's what hope is."

CHAPTER TWO

Almost eight o'clock. Would that detective be at work yet?

The morning sun flooded the bay window of Marilyn Stewart's mobile home in the rural town of Pecos, New Mexico, warming her as she sat with her tea. A phone and a worn business card lay on the table. She'd put this off too long. It was already the second of November.

Should she make the call? Or leave well enough alone?

Distracted by a noise next door where her grandson and his family lived, she looked out to see her great-grandson running to his dad's white car carrying his schoolbooks, his red hair shining in the sun. Ross, ready for work in his National Forest Service uniform, walked behind, his hair a darker, burnished version of his son's.

How proud her husband had been when Ross followed in his footsteps and began working as a forester. She felt Dwight's death keenly, years later. She longed to share her burden with him now.

Before the car could drive away, Melody, Ross's wife, stepped out and called, "Matti!" She held up a lunchbox. The seven-year old ran back, took it, and lifted his face for his mother's kiss.

As Ross drove away down the lane, Marilyn picked up her tea, savoring the heat against her hands. Thoughts nagged her as she sipped. Thoughts unbidden, unwanted by day, and keeping her from sleep at night.

Dwight must have been uncertain. Had he kept those papers from her on purpose? Had he lived with the same agony she was experiencing now?

He wouldn't have torn apart their world unless he was positive of his facts and convinced it was the right thing to do. Marilyn sighed. Going through the boxes of papers she'd avoided for so many years had become a mixed blessing.

She closed her eyes. Maybe she could start by asking the detective an innocuous question or offer the box of papers if he showed interest. Depending on how her overture was received, she could cross the line of the unimaginable.

Opening her eyes and setting aside her tea, she called the number written on the card.

◆ ❖ ◆

In his office at the Santa Fe Police Department, Lieutenant Pete Schultz answered his phone, pushing aside the morning's stack of case files on his desk and the work of his detectives he'd been reviewing.

"This is Marilyn Stewart," came an uncertain voice. "You met me and my grandson, Ross, several months ago at St. Raphael's Care Center when I was recuperating. Do you remember?"

Mein Gott. How could he forget? The resemblance was uncanny between Ross and Cliff, the kidnapped boy's brother, who was now Pete's own son-in-law.

"I do remember. Your little great-grandson looked remarkably like a child who was kidnapped from here years ago."

"I've been going through some old papers." Marilyn paused. "I'm not sure, but . . . I think you should see them." She gave a trembly sigh before continuing. "Oh, dear. This is difficult."

"Mrs. Stewart, would you like to meet with me and talk about this?"

He heard an intake and release of breath before she agreed.

After they'd made arrangements, he called to a detective in the bullpen and took the well-worn McCreath kidnapping file from a drawer. When he opened it, light from his big window fell upon the photo of the six-year-old boy with red hair.

How many times had he looked at this picture? Any kind of media exposure brought a flurry of leads. Very seldom did they yield anything of importance, but to discern good from bad, they all must be followed. Would this bear fruit?

In the course of that care-center conversation, Ross had told him he'd been injured in an amphibious plane crash on a lake in Montana in 1991. The dynamics changed rapidly when the young man learned why Pete was there. He showed signs of distress and developed a headache. Further attempts by Pete to pursue the matter had met with stiff resistance.

Hearing a knock on his door, Pete looked up and smiled in welcome at Sam Martinez, a dark-haired man with the patrician features of his Spanish ancestors. Sam was his division's newest detective, but Pete had known him and his family for a long time.

"What's up, Pete?"

Pete gestured toward the round table near his desk. He picked up his coffee and joined Sam there with the case file. "I'd like you to look through this. Maybe a new set of eyes will see something we've missed."

Sam began flipping through it. "Being Cliff's friend, I know this story, but not from a police perspective. Why your interest now?"

"It was the first police case I had any real involvement with. It became more personal when my daughter married into the McCreath family. Just now, Hoot Stewart's grandmother called. I'm meeting her tomorrow morning."

"Marilyn wasn't at Anton and Skyla's engagement party, was she? She missed that moment when Hoot came face to face with you and Cliff."

"The air crackled!" Pete remembered. "I had no idea this guy, Hoot Stewart, you and Anton talked about all the time, was Ross."

"Hoot didn't expect to see you there either."

"He certainly made it clear he didn't want to be around anyone who thought he might be that missing child." Pete leaned back in his chair. "I have hopes for this visit with his grandmother. She's troubled about something."

"Did she give a reason for her call?"

"Says she may have some papers I'd be interested in." Pete took a sip of his coffee. "I've always wondered how the hell Johnny was whisked away with no trace so quickly. Now there's Hoot. Startling resemblance. Dates fit. Amphibious planes are unusual here, yet one flew out of Santa Fe that day." He frowned at his cup. "Must be a reason for his reaction."

"Wouldn't Hoot remember if he'd been kidnapped? How could one forget something that traumatic?"

"That's just it. If Hoot is Johnny, he got hit with two traumas— the kidnapping and the plane crash. Could it be PTSD? Amnesia?"

"How could someone kidnap a child and give him to their parents to raise? Wouldn't they know it was the wrong kid? If they were bamboozled into thinking he was their grandchild, what happened to the real grandson?"

"Good questions, Sam." Pete took another sip, then set down his cup. "Blegch."

"What's the matter? Something get in that battery acid you call coffee?"

"It's just not the same as when Rosie made it."

"How is our new administrative assistant? She's certainly efficient."

"True. She doesn't waste time socializing."

"There's a reason for that. Have you noticed she doesn't make friends easily?"

Pete looked sharply at Sam. "She should have many friends in the police department. She's been in the traffic division as long as I've been around, maybe longer. It's only to investigations that she's new."

Sam snorted. "I've never met a person who's so insecure, and yet, at the same time, tells everyone how to do their job."

Pete grimaced. "There is that."

"How did she end up here?"

"Immediately after Rosie announced her retirement, Yvonne Novak marched to the HR desk, slapped down her resume, and asked to be transferred from Traffic to the Criminal Investigations Division as my admin."

Sam chuckled. "Maybe she has the hots for you."

Pete scowled. "Watch it, youngster. I only have eyes for my angel."

He looked up as the admin, a pudgy woman in her fifties, entered. "Yvonne, this coffee tastes funny. What'd you do? Clean the pot?"

"It's decaf, Lieutenant." She smoothed back her thick gray hair.

"I don't do decaf, Yvonne."

Yvonne shrugged and put some messages on his desk. "You should call this top one first. It's from Captain Brower about that antiquities-looting case you just finished." She strode out.

Sam was right. There was something off-putting about her. Her bossiness made one want to run in the opposite direction. "Now, where was I?"

"Talking about Hoot's grandmother. She may be the only person who can tell you about Hoot's going to live with them."

"Right." Pete sighed.

Sam looked up from the binder. "I'm due in court soon. I'd like to study this."

"Just ask Yvonne for it, if I'm not here." Pete arose. "By the way, Tuesday is Election Day. If you plan to vote, best do it ahead of time. You never know what'll tie us up that day."

"Voted by mail already. Dom would never forgive me if I didn't."

"Your grandfather is a wise man."

"Farah's very concerned about this one."

"Your wife has reason to be concerned. I mailed my ballot last week. You going to the gym tonight?"

"Yes. I'm picking up the kid brother. You?"

Pete nodded. "It's one way Rick and I can carve father-son time out of our schedules. I like to see what the kids are doing in their parkour class." He took the file from Sam and put it away. "Where'd the name 'Hoot' come from, by the way?"

"He got it working his way through college as a lumberman. Guys who had to get out there at dawn were called Hoot Owls. They couldn't use their machinery in the forest after the humidity dropped. The name stuck with him, and he likes it."

"I'm wondering what happened to Hoot's mother. He says his parents died—plural, but he only mentioned father in relation to the plane crash. And how many years passed between when the grandparents last saw Ross and when he came to live with them? I'll ask Marilyn."

That evening at the gym, Pete watched his fourteen-year-old son, Rick, and Sam's brother, Steve, practice their parkour moves with other teens. One after another, they ran, leaped into the air, extended their arms, rolled, and came up ready to run again.

Pete grinned at Sam standing next to him. "I find it funny that I learned this stuff back in my air force obstacle-course training. Now they give it the glorified definition of moving through the environment, running, climbing, and jumping in a way that your body uses your momentum and absorbs the impact, so you don't get hurt. Then it gets a fancy French name, and suddenly it's the rage and something cool teens do."

"I didn't know you'd ever done parkour."

Pete shrugged. "It's been useful a few times when I found myself in a tight spot. I told Rick to forget it if he just wanted to impress his friends. Then I put the fear of God into him about learning it right and practicing. Told him I didn't want any emergency room visits." He glanced at his watch. "We'd better get to our workout. Days aren't long enough."

CHAPTER THREE

The next morning, Thursday, Pete arrived at Marilyn Stewart's single-wide trailer, about a forty-minute drive from his office in Santa Fe. Fences to discourage deer surrounded what used to be a vegetable garden. Killing frosts had wiped out the marigolds in flower beds. Behind the trailer and Hoot's home next door, trees grew thicker, and he heard the Pecos River flowing lazily by.

The white-haired woman he remembered opened the door.

"Lieutenant, welcome. I have some questions, and I wouldn't mind hearing more about that kidnapped boy who looked so much like Hoot's son. Would you like coffee?"

"I'd appreciate it," Pete said.

She hustled to the kitchen. Good lighting, an open layout, light walls and cabinets banished any dark, claustrophobic feeling he associated with the stereotypical mobile home. On the wall hung a framed watercolor—forests and mountains reflected in a lake. Pete wondered if it were Flathead Lake in Montana near where the Stewarts had lived until just a little over a year ago.

Marilyn waved to where the morning sun shone into a dining area. "Do you mind if we sit here?"

Pete smiled and sat at the table. "Is it okay if I record our conversation?"

"Fine by me."

"What would you like to know, Mrs. Stewart?"

"Call me Marilyn, please." She took cups and saucers from the cupboard. "You told me before, but when was that little boy kidnapped?"

"May 17, 1991."

She stood perfectly still for several seconds and then turned to face him. "My son, Gordon, brought Ross to live with us on May 19, 1991."

She handed him his coffee and sat down with hers. The sunlight formed a nimbus of her white hair. Marilyn sighed and leaned back. "I want to find out what happened to Gordon's wife, Winona."

Pete nodded. Just what he wanted to know. Was that question her excuse for involving him? An undercurrent which was hard to interpret swirled around Marilyn. "I'd be glad to share with you what I learn."

"I've started going through boxes of papers belonging to my son and to my husband." Marilyn frowned. "Melody, Ross's wife, is helping me. Friends from our church traveled to Denver and cleaned out Gordon's apartment after he died. They saved the papers, the photos, and the personal items for Dwight and me. I should have gone through them years ago, but I just couldn't force myself to do it. Now it's time."

"What can you tell me about your son?"

She looked down with a grimace. "Gordon was not a nice person. Dwight and I tried to instill good morals in him, but he was a rebellious child and ended up in the wrong crowd. We learned to expect lies from him."

"You said he was bringing Ross to live with you. How long had it been since you'd seen your grandson before that?"

"At least four years. He'd been just a toddler. A couple of months before Ross came, Gordon asked us for money, as he often did. A huge sum, forty thousand dollars. Dwight and I offered him a proposal. We would take it from our savings and give him the money, this one last time, if he and his wife signed over custody of Ross for us to raise."

Pete's eyebrows shot up in surprise.

14

Marilyn smiled at his reaction. "We never got along with his wife. She was on drugs. Maybe it was sinful, our asking for custody, but we wanted our grandson out of that situation. We said when he brought Ross to us, we would give him the money."

"Were his parents willing to sign the custody papers?"

"At first Gordon said there was no way. But several days before the plane crash, he called and said he'd changed his mind. He would fly Ross in to us. He said his wife had died of an overdose months earlier. I was shocked. He had never said a word before about her death."

"Months earlier?" Pete's voice echoed her shock.

Marilyn nodded. "I asked who was taking care of Ross. He said another family was, but they couldn't long term. We had already had a lawyer draw up papers so we could formally adopt him. He faxed them to Gordon, and then faxed us the signed copies. We had the cash ready for him."

"Do you still have the custody papers?"

"Yes."

"Tell me about the day Ross came to live with you."

"We were already at the fire lookout where we lived every summer. Dwight worked for the forest service. Winters we spent in Kalispell. That day we came down to Flathead to visit friends at the lake and pick up Ross. Gordon called us from Butte. He said the trip was too long to do all in one day, so they'd spent the night there. He cautioned us about Ross. Said he was going through a rebellious stage and behaving badly. He hadn't accepted his mother's death. She'd been seeing another man and poisoned the boy's mind. Gordon said Ross would yell at him and say he wasn't his father. He would tell lies and get angry. This wasn't the same story Gordon had told us before—we didn't know what the truth might be. I weep for what that child must have gone through."

A heavy sadness descended upon Marilyn's face.

"Is that when the plane crashed?" asked Pete.

"It was a beautiful sunny day. We were standing with our friends watching them fly in. The water was calm and so blue—how could we know it would turn deadly? The plane crashed because the landing gear was down. You can't land an amphibious plane on water without first bringing the wheels up into the pontoons. When the plane was about to land, Dwight saw the wheels and knew what would happen. He ran to his friend's speedboat at the dock, and they started for where the plane was coming down. The wheels touched the water. Suddenly there was spray everywhere and the plane flipped over. When the water quieted, we saw the pontoons sticking up high and those ripples. I can still see those ripples—spreading. Relentless."

Marilyn blinked rapidly. "The cabin was upside down and sinking. Gordon may have behaved badly, but he was still our son." She wiped a hand over her cheek.

"They got to the passenger side of the plane very quickly. Dwight dove out of the boat, forced open the door, and got Ross out. But Gordon . . . the plane had crumpled, pinning him. He drowned before they could extricate him."

Marilyn closed her eyes, and she shook her head slowly. "Dwight brought Ross to shore. Ross looked so small, so hurt. He was breathing on his own, but he wasn't conscious. Someone called an ambulance. The medics worried about his head injuries, and he had several broken bones. All I could do was pray. He was in the hospital for three months, and I stayed by his side. Dwight came whenever he could."

"Thank you for sharing that, Marilyn. I know it's still difficult." Pete patted her hand. "If you'll allow me to see Gordon's papers, I might be able to help. Look for their marriage certificate, and his wife's death certificate. If you're okay with my tracking down individuals and asking them about Ross's mother, I'd be glad to. Police have resources available that private citizens don't."

She pointed at a banker's box between their chairs. "I was hoping you'd offer. Some of those documents are here, if you'd like to take it today."

"Certainly. I'll go through these papers." Pete lifted the lid on the box and glanced briefly at the contents. "I'll make copies of anything that will be useful in our search and get the originals back to you."

"Lieutenant, I . . . There's a blue folder in there with papers of my husband's I'd never seen before. I don't . . . They made me wonder if he had tried to find out something." Her voice dropped to a whisper. "I don't think he ever received answers. And by then—" She set her cup carefully in its saucer. "Life gets very complicated."

As Pete headed back to Santa Fe, he reflected on what he'd heard. She was troubled about the kidnapping. He realized she'd been testing him. So far, he'd passed. The prize? The box of papers and the cryptic comment about the blue folder.

But the bombshell was a motive for her son to kidnap a child. If the boy the Stewarts had raised was Johnny, now the question loomed larger than ever.

What happened to the real Ross Stewart?

CHAPTER FOUR

Yvonne crossed the stage to the podium as thunderous applause arose from those assembled in the standing-room-only city council chambers. Her husband stood in the front row, a broad smile on his normally stern visage. He clapped loudly. With a regal nod, she acknowledged him.

Addressing the crowd, Lieutenant Schultz spoke of how she, Yvonne Novak, because of her clever thinking, had solved a case which had stymied him and many detectives over the years. Police Chief Leroy Grover shook her hand, then pinned a star on her lapel. Schultz handed her an award, a fancy Lucite plaque with her name engraved above those of grateful officials. She smiled as cameras flashed, capturing the moment for newspapers and television.

The award rang.

Odd, but nice. An award that drew attention to itself.

"Yvonne! The phone."

The assembly and the award vanished. Her eyes popped open to see the plain walls of her office and Detective Elena Ruiz, standing in the door with an annoyed look. Feeling hot color rise in her face, Yvonne picked up the phone.

◆ ❖ ◆

Yvonne smiled as the last detective left for an interview or whatever it was they did. Schultz had gone to Pecos to see someone.

She'd discovered patterns in behavior and knew when the detectives' bullpen would be all hers for a while. Too bad she only worked mornings. This was much more exciting than the traffic division—here she had access to the inner workings of cases.

She'd show those who scoffed at her. She went into the lieutenant's office and took the McCreath case file from the drawer where he kept it. Her boss would worship at her feet if she could solve that old kidnapping. That case might be her best opportunity to shine.

Yvonne always kept some legitimate work with her while snooping—scratch that word—*researching* the case she was interested in, making copies of papers and tucking them into her oversized purse to study at home on her own time. It wouldn't be proper to do it on police time. She ignored the fact that making copies was strictly forbidden, an act made even more heinous by her smuggling them out of their secure area. After all, she was *helping*!

Her brother, Curtis, known even to family by his last name, Hayle, would be coming this afternoon. She enjoyed his visits, a change from Vassily's silence. Hayle often took time off and drove down from Denver to stay with them. He used to be a cop, but now owned a security company.

She'd wanted to be a cop, but that wasn't something women in her family were encouraged to do. Pity. She could ask Hayle questions about things which eluded her understanding. She picked up her purse, checked to make sure the papers were safely hidden, and turned off the light in her office.

In Yvonne's small home in an older, quiet Santa Fe neighborhood later that afternoon, Yvonne, her husband Vassily, and Hayle sat in the living room, watching an old episode of *Colombo*. Ten minutes into it, she announced, "The blonde did it."

Hayle stuffed another pretzel into his mouth, even though it would be dinnertime soon. The fabric on his shirt stretched between the buttons and gapped over his increasing girth.

He let out a snort. "No way. The way he was killed was clever. Women use poison. That's their weapon of choice."

Yvonne smirked. "I can figure these things out."

"In your dreams," her brother said.

"You're just a dime-a-dozen secretary," said Vassily.

Yvonne felt her face heat. "You just wait. I read lots of mysteries and pay attention on CSI. One of these days, I'll solve a crime that cops haven't been able to, and they'll appreciate me." She glared at her husband. Small, meticulous, stingy with praise and generous in criticism.

Vassily grunted.

"Whatever." Hayle tossed the empty pretzel bag aside and wiped the sweat from his balding head.

The TV drama continued to unfold.

"Damn. The blonde did it. Lucky guess," said Vassily. "It's four. Time to walk. You coming, Hayle?"

◆ ❖ ◆

Hayle got his jacket and followed his brother-in-law out the front door, leaving Yvonne behind to make dinner. The route Vassily walked wound through the working-class neighborhood, along the weedy edge of a wide arroyo, and back past a dreary collection of coyote fences and adobe walls.

Hayle looked at the sun, hanging low in the sky. "How about if we take another route today? Don't you ever get tired of going the same way?"

"Routine is healthy."

"So's giving up booze. That doesn't mean I'm going to do it."

"We'll go my way." Vassily marched off.

"Whatever." Hayle fell into step beside him. "So, Yvonne still thinks she'll be the world's greatest detective?"

"She's always studying those papers she brings home. That woman couldn't detect her way out of a paper bag."

"What's got her attention now?"

"Some kidnapping. Happened right here back in the nineties. I remember it."

"She could get in trouble for bringing file notes home, Vassily."

"She ain't that stupid. Makes copies. Originals stay put."

"Maybe we should help her. Read the notes, drop hints. We could have her thinking she's getting close."

"Don't encourage her."

"That's mean, Vassily. She's been wanting to solve a case ever since she discovered the Hardy Boys and Nancy Drew. Do you know where she keeps her papers? I'd like to see them."

"Sure. I know what goes on in my own house." Vassily walked on.

Hayle smiled. He was certain Vassily would show him her papers.

They walked on in silence. Hayle bent and picked up a rock. Several steps later he collected two more.

Vassily looked back at him. "What's holding you up? You looking for something?"

"Rocks. Shooter marble size. Round, smooth."

"What the hell for?"

"Practice."

"Practice what?"

"Juggling."

"Juggling? You any good?"

Hayle selected two more rocks and set all five flying one after another, keeping them aloft for a minute before missing one and letting the others drop. He bent, picked up one, and tucked it into his pocket. "I like this one. Feels good."

"How'd you learn to do that?"

"There's a vendor at shows we do security for, who sells juggling items. We shoot the breeze and play around with what he sells—all kinds of skill-type merchandise, like catapults and slingshots. I always learn stuff from him."

"Slingshots?" Vassily snorted. "Kids' toys."

"Some are, but his are serious. You'd be amazed. I got one right here." Hayle pulled a slingshot with a contoured-steel handle and a yellow band from his jacket pocket.

"What's it for?"

"Gives me good hand-eye coordination practice." Hayle flexed the band. "This is no toy. It's a weapon. See that soda can up ahead in the weeds?"

"You can hit that? It must be thirty feet away."

"Piece of cake." Hayle fitted a rock in the center of the pouch, stretched the band back, aimed, and let fly. Almost immediately, there was a bang, and the can went flying through the air to clatter off an adobe wall.

"Good God. That was something."

"Want to try?" Hayle handed the slingshot to Vassily, who turned it over and over in his hands. "I'll set up the can."

As Hayle turned from positioning the can, he saw that Vassily had picked up a rock and was stretching the slingshot band out.

"Jesus." Hayle scuttled quickly to the side. "Don't do that while somebody's in front of you. You could hurt them."

"Ain't likely."

"Here—I'll show you how to aim it."

"Yah, yah, yah. Just let me at it." Vassily pulled back and let go of the pouch. The band snapped his wrist. The rock landed a few feet away. With a yowl, Vassily dropped the slingshot and grabbed his arm. "Damn it, that hurt. You knew what was going to happen, and you just let it. This ain't fun. Stupid toy. We're going to be late." He strode down the path, rubbing his wrist. "Damn good thing I'm wearing a jacket."

Hayle picked up his slingshot, made a face behind Vassily's back, aimed at him with an empty pouch, and let go. With a smirk he tucked the gadget back into his pocket and hurried to catch up with the furious strides of his companion. His brother-in-law was too predictable. He might be complaining now, but he'd go buy a slingshot and try to outdo him. Jerk.

CHAPTER FIVE

Friday morning at seven, Sam knocked on Pete's office door. "Could I see the McCreath file again?"

"Sure. By the way, Marilyn Stewart is giving us more boxes of Gordon's papers. Looks like she didn't throw anything away. I'd like your help sifting through them." Pete popped a little cup into a coffee machine and started it.

"Son of a gun, he's making his own coffee."

Pete smiled. "I liked the machine Lou and Cliff got me for my birthday, so I got one for here. Yvonne can't sneak me any more decaf." He opened a drawer and handed the binder to Sam.

Sam sat at the round table. "I can help with boxes. I've been wondering how Gordon became aware of Johnny, and I remembered this." He pointed to a photo accompanying a newspaper article about a zookeeper's visit to a kindergarten. Johnny was pictured clearly, in full color, admiring a hedgehog.

"That ran just before he was taken," said Pete. "It was the most recent photo of him."

"What if this picture was the reason he zeroed in on Johnny? It says where he goes to school. He could stalk and discover where he lived."

"*Heilige Scheisse*! Why did Gordon need him? What happened to the real Ross?"

"Maybe Gordon did something stupid, and Ross died," said Sam. "He was scared he'd be caught."

"And if Gordon hadn't been able to take Johnny?"

"Then he wouldn't have called his parents to say he'd changed his mind," said Sam. "But he did call."

Pete pursed his lips and nodded. "If Ross had never been reported missing, just taken out of school to transfer, but never showed up at a new school . . . Ross wasn't on anyone's radar." He dug into the banker's box and pulled out the blue folder. "There's something I want to show you. Marilyn raised my curiosity with a cryptic comment about this."

Pete took two pictures from the folder. The first showed a red-haired toddler, dressed up, his hair slicked back. The second was a redhead of about thirteen, his hair in a buzz cut. "It took me a while. There's maybe ten years' time between the photos."

Sam studied the two shots in silence. Pete settled back in his chair with his coffee, watching the play of emotions on the young detective's face. He chuckled when he realized Sam had spotted the clue.

"It's the hair line. The little kid's is straight. The teenager has a widow's peak."

Pete nodded. "I've never seen pictures of Johnny without hair falling down over his forehead. Have you ever seen Hoot's hairline?"

"Never that short, nor slicked back. I have no idea if he has a widow's peak or not."

"These are Dwight's." Pete handed Sam a sheaf of handwritten notes on widow's peaks and heredity. "He must have wondered, but never said anything. What an awful dilemma."

"Anything else in that folder?"

"Copies of letters Dwight wrote in the late nineties inquiring about lost or missing boys in the Denver area. No replies."

"Man, this is big." Sam tapped the binder. "Where the hell is Ross? I hope that if he'd been killed, his remains have been found."

"I'll talk to Marilyn again. Grandparent DNA might show Ross as possible or not in comparison with a set of remains, but it wouldn't be conclusive." He collected the papers back into the blue folder.

"Stroke of luck, that we got the Denver location for our seminar. Are we going to do some poking around where Gordon Stewart used to live?"

"You bet. And it wasn't luck. I saw Denver and convinced Chief Grover that we needed this seminar to meet our certification requirements with interrogation techniques. He knew what I was up to."

Sam stood up. "That was cool Wednesday night."

Pete was already thinking of the next step in his investigation. "Wednesday?"

"The gym. Parkour demonstration at the end of their class."

Pete smiled. "Rick was pleased when the coach showed you and me some tricks afterward. He cracked up when you tried rolling and coming up pretending to have a gun in your hands. I didn't know you were such a show-off."

"Got to keep the kid brother in line somehow. You didn't do badly yourself."

"I only tried a few low rolls. Even though I work at it, the body doesn't want to do now what it did at thirty." He flexed his shoulder. "Kids are doing pretty well, aren't they? I was damn proud of mine."

CHAPTER SIX

Pete spent Saturday morning knocking items off his "honey-do" list. Several of them were maintenance chores for the casita next to their home. When his parents were alive, they'd stayed there. Then Lou and Mika, his two oldest kids, had taken it over. No one called it home at the moment. Lou and Cliff had their own home, Mika was working in Albuquerque, and Zumi and Heidi were off at college.

Pete stowed his toolbox in the utility room and glanced at the clock. Time for coffee.

He called out to Akiko. "Want to go to Books and Bearclaws with me?"

She came into the kitchen carrying her market bags. "Wish I could. Errands."

"What errands? Where will you be? When will you be back?" Oops. At the look on her face, he winced, knowing what her response would be.

"Why do you do that?"

He closed his eyes and counted silently to eight. "I care about you. I like knowing where you are."

"Being forced to tell you where I'm going and how long I'll be there, makes me feel like you don't trust me."

"I trust you," said Pete. "But how can I protect you if—"

"Stop. You've taught me to be aware of my own environment. And Rick, too. It's extremely off-putting. The other day he complained to me, 'I'm a good kid. I don't do stupid stuff. Why has Dad got me on such a short leash?' It's hard on a teenager."

"It's a parent's job—" His phone rang.

"Work calling?" asked Akiko.

"My cousin." Saved by the bell, he thought, pressing the answer button. "Karl, what a surprise. Everything okay?"

Akiko blew a kiss at him and left. He knew he'd hear more later.

After a few minutes of back-and-forth family news, Pete asked, "What's up? You never just call out of the blue."

"A strange dude showed up on our doorstep the other day. Told me he was an old friend of yours from the Air Force, went through basic with you at Lackland. Wanted to know if you still lived in New Jersey. Said he was traveling through the eastern states and decided to get in touch with his old buddies."

"Strange how? What was his name?"

"Jason Miller was the name he gave. Intense, nervous. He made me uncomfortable."

"Did you tell him anything?"

"Hell, no. I know better than that. That would have been the end of it, but today, I saw him again. Sitting in his car down the block from our house."

"Can you describe him? Or his car?"

"Looked ex-military. Erect posture, arrogant attitude. Dark eyes that looked right through you. Bit older looking than you. Drove a newer model Toyota sedan. New York plates."

"Appreciate your heads-up, Karl. Be careful out there. You might tell the police, just to get it on record." As he tucked his phone in his pocket, Pete shrugged. Jason Miller—didn't remember that name. Then again, it had been a lifetime ago. He grabbed his keys and set off.

Fifteen minutes later, Pete walked into Books and Bearclaws and joined the line at the counter. The lady ahead of him ordered a latte, and Pete watched the barista creating the latte art. Soon a bear emerged in the foam. He'd try that and have a bearclaw, too.

Books and Bearclaws was one of his favorite coffee places in Santa Fe. A third of the area was filled with small tables where customers could sit and chat while they enjoyed their coffee and pastries. The rest was bookstore.

As Pete waited for his drink, he smiled and waved at Domingo Baca, Sam Martinez's grandfather. Dom was a retired history professor and at seventy, was the oldest in their group of friends called the Circle Sleuths.

When Pete's latte was ready, Dom beckoned him over to where he sat with a gray-haired man.

"You remember my roommate from the care center, Oliver Wright?" said Dom.

Pete chose a seat where he could see people entering and shook Oliver's hand. "*Ja*, retired from the Denver PD, as I recall." He took a sip of his latte and licked the foam off his lips. "Amazing. Way better than that swill our new admin tried to pass off as coffee."

"New admin?" asked Oliver.

"*Ja*. Just mornings—knows her stuff and works hard, but she decided I shouldn't have caffeine and kept on sneaking decaf into the pot. Now I make my own with a single-cupper machine." He took a bite of his pastry. "Sam and I have a seminar in Denver soon, and a trail of clues leads there for a cold case I'm working on."

"What kind of cold case?" asked Oliver.

Pete told him the story of Johnny McCreath's kidnapping. "I'm investigating a young man who might have some answers. It's complicated. He was raised by his grandmother. I want to know more about his parents."

"Have you asked the Denver PD to run the names?" asked Oliver. "To see if there were any arrests or convictions on them?"

Pete nodded. "The mother had several brushes with the law. What precinct did you work at?"

"Southwood."

Pete perked up. "That's where the leads take me. Two DUIs in 1989 and '90. She died of an overdose in 1990."

Oliver snorted. "Super old case. I don't suppose you saw the names of the arresting officers?"

Pete pulled out his little notebook. "Cannon and Hayle."

Oliver broke into a smile. "Cannon is a good friend of mine. He's still there, but you're talking eons ago. Doubtful he'd remember anything."

"How about Hayle? Recognize that name?"

Oliver made a face. "Hayle quit the force after about five years and went to work for a security company. Both Cannon and Hayle went through police academy with me. I wasn't sorry to see him leave. You should look Cannon up if you have a chance."

"I'd like to. We're flying in a day early."

◆ ❖ ◆

On Sunday afternoon, Yvonne stripped the bed Hayle had used and piled the sheets into the washer, wondering how long before he visited again. While the tub was filling, she sorted clothes, checking the pockets for tissues. She hated when one sneaked by and left white stuff everywhere. As she picked up Vassily's jeans, she frowned. Now what had he left in his pocket?

She marched out to where he was watching TV. "Vassily, I'm doing the wash, and I found rocks in your pocket. Do you want them?"

"Your brother was showing me how to juggle and use a slingshot."

"Are you feeling okay?"

"Stupid question."

"It's not either. A slingshot? Little boys use them to torment people."

"It's good for maintaining hand-eye coordination."

Yvonne turned away, then spun back. "You're not trying to hit animals, are you? I don't like this, Vassily."

"Mind your own business, woman. Next time I see a dog crapping on the trail, I'll get him."

"Vassily, no! You could get in trouble. Get sued."

"How could somebody sue me if their dog wasn't on a leash, which is the law, and when they don't clean up their messes, which is also the law? They'd never win."

"Please—"

"Enough. Go do your damn wash. Don't you dare throw anything away from my pockets."

"Then clean your pockets out before you put clothes in the laundry." Having managed to get the last word in, Yvonne hurried away.

CHAPTER SEVEN

On Monday evening, Hoot Stewart heard the car doors slam in front of his home in Pecos. The guests had arrived.

"Twitch is here!" Four-year-old Bonnie jumped up and down by the window, her flame-red hair flying.

Hoot got up from where he'd been helping Matti with his arithmetic. He shook the hand of the tall, dark blond Anton Bjornson and gave Anton's fiancée, Skyla Van Dyken, a warm hug. Over the din of delighted squeals from Bonnie and enthusiastic barks from the year-old Airedale pup, Hoot joked to Anton. "Bonnie's excited about Twitch. You don't rate."

Anton grinned. "Ah, but I'm his chauffeur." He handed Twitch's leash to Bonnie.

Hoot's wife, Melody, set salad dressings on the table and came forward to give them hugs. "Skyla, I wish you were still close enough to pop over for tea."

Marilyn followed her from the kitchen area, wiping her hands on her apron and smiling as she took their jackets.

Skyla sniffed the air. "Marilyn, you baked bread. What a treat."

Hoot took the bottles of wine that Anton offered and opened one. Soon they were all seated at the round oak table, enjoying chicken tortilla soup, salad, bread, and wine.

♦ ❖ ♦

After dinner, Hoot suggested they move to the family room where sectionals and stuffed chairs surrounded a coffee table. He counted on Anton's willingness to talk about gadgets. Hoot was loaded with questions from the drone magazines Anton had lent him and pulled them both into a world of techy wonders.

If only all of Anton's friends were as affable.

Bonnie startled them all with a screech. "No, Twitch. *My* Foxie!"

"Twitch, leave it," said Anton. The Airedale looked at Anton, dropped the plush toy, and came over to him. "Where's your collar?"

Hoot spotted it by a chair and picked it up, still attached to the leash. He handed it to Anton.

Bonnie snatched up her fox and hugged it. "My fingers couldn't do that thingy on the weash, so I took off his collar."

"Is Foxie okay?" asked Skyla.

Melody took the white fox. "Just a little dog spit. Bonnie, let's put it out of his reach, okay? Then you can roll a ball for him, so he'll forget about Foxie."

Bonnie nodded and was soon giggling as she and Twitch played roll and fetch.

"God forbid something happens to Foxie," said Hoot. "She left him in my car one day. I had a late-night meeting and came home to a disaster. She wouldn't go to sleep and had been crying for hours. Nothing would get her mind off that fox."

"She was utterly impossible," muttered Matti as he plunked down on the floor and dumped out a box of Legos.

Hoot looked over Matti's head at the others. He could tell they were trying to keep straight faces.

Anton chuckled. "That's quite a statement, coming from a seven-year old."

Hoot grinned. "He hears it a lot from Melody and me."

"Where'd he get the nickname Matti?" asked Anton. "It's unusual."

"He was christened Matthew, that was Grandpa's middle name, but ever since the first time we read *Koda and the Sami* to him, he's

32

wanted to be called Matti like the boy in the book. One of these days, I reckon, he'll decide he wants to be called Matt."

Anton set his coffee mug down, and picked up a rectangular box made of smooth, striped wood of dark hues.

Hoot watched as Anton hefted the gleaming box, which was easily big enough to hold a six-pack of pop cans. An oval cutout on the top showed a layer of lighter-striped wood underneath. Knots in the grain of the lighter wood formed two eyes peering out from the lower layer. A carved wooden hand appeared to be emerging from the inside, grasping the rim of the oval in the dark wood.

"This is interesting," Anton said. "Clever, the way the knots become eyes. Reminds me of Gollum. Look at that hand." He touched the spatulate fingers. "It looks like there's a creature in the box trying to get out."

"Grandma and Melody have been going through my grandfather's and my father's things," said Hoot. "They found that puzzle box. I'd never seen it before."

"I think it's cool," said Matti as he began to build a tower.

"How does it open?" asked Skyla. "I don't see any hinges."

"I've tried all the obvious stuff. Haven't figured it out," said Hoot.

"Intriguing." Anton held it near his ear with both hands and shook it. "Don't hear much. It's much bigger than most puzzle boxes I've seen." He handed it to Skyla.

She ran her hand over the satiny finish and curled a finger under the wooden hand holding on to the oval opening. "Beautiful wood." She gave it back to Anton.

"It's zebrawood," said Hoot, "from a tree that grows in Africa."

Hoot grinned as Anton fiddled with the box, trying all of the things he'd already tried. The longer sides of the box came up above the two-layer lid with the oval cutout and the hand. The hand did not move, but there was some play in the lid itself as it slid back and forth between the sides. When Anton tipped the box, a small metal pin on one end slid forward. He pushed it back and tipped it out again. He turned it. "Wonder what this pin does. It's not spring-loaded or anything."

"I haven't gotten further than that," said Hoot. "But it's addicting. I keep coming back to it."

Anton set the box back on the coffee table. "You might try going online. Must be dozens of videos on puzzle boxes."

"Is Bonnie reading already?" asked Skyla. "She's not even four yet."

Hoot looked over at Bonnie, seated on a fat cushion on the floor and leaning against the wall. A picture book was open in her hands, and she was chattering away to Twitch, lying with his head on her legs.

Melody laughed. "She just looks at the pictures and makes up a story as she goes along. Sometimes it's uncanny how close it is to what's printed."

"That's because every picture book we have has been read to her dozens of times," said Hoot, smiling at his youngest child. "She knows some by heart."

"Does she still need the hall light on because of the monsters when she sleeps?" asked Skyla.

"God, yes," said Melody. "She screeches if we forget and turn it off."

"Do you have plans for Thanksgiving?" asked Skyla, switching the topic.

"We'd like you to celebrate it with us," said Anton. "Marilyn, you, too."

A tingle of alarm shot down Hoot's spine.

Melody spoke up eagerly, "We'd love—"

"Who all's going to be there?" Hoot interrupted, trying to sound casual.

Melody gave a squeak of dismay. She grabbed his forearm and squeezed, but he ignored the pressure of her fingers.

Anton raised an eyebrow as he regarded Hoot. "Just Mom, my daughter, Krista, Skyla, and me. And of course, Maria and Diego. Maria came to work for us when I was in high school, and Diego has been with us even longer than Maria. They're part of our family."

"I know what you're thinking, Hoot," said Skyla. "Pete and Cliff won't be there."

He felt the heat rising in his face. "Sorry. It was rude to ask. It's just that they think I'm Cliff's long-lost brother. I'm not."

"Please say yes," said Skyla.

Hoot felt the pressure from Melody's fingers increase. "We'd love to come. I've told Grandma about your spread with the alpacas and horses." Melody's hand relaxed.

"I'd love to be there with you," Marilyn said. "The children will want to show me the animals."

"We'll count on it then," said Anton. "Hoot, we want your family to join us for our St. Nicholas celebration, too. All of the Circle Sleuths will be there then."

"Who are the Circle Sleuths?" asked Marilyn.

Anton chuckled. "There's quite a bunch. Take notes." He winked at her. "I'll pass out the quiz later. The Circle Sleuths formed after Krista was kidnapped a little over a year ago."

Geez, thought Hoot. Kidnapping again. What was it? An epidemic?

"Krista escaped. Cliff found her, and you can believe it was super important to him to bring her home and prevent another family going through the pain his has gone through."

"I can't imagine anything worse than to have your child stolen," said Melody.

Hoot covered her hand with his where it rested on his arm. Dang, that's all he needed to hear. Cliff, the great hero.

"It was agony," said Anton. "Pete, the detective in charge of Krista's case, spearheaded our group to uncover who was behind it all. Yes, that same Pete. He's married to Akiko, who raises and shows Airedales. We got Twitch from her."

"Have Anton tell you about Twitch sometime," said Skyla. She tossed a mischievous look at Anton. "Twitch adopted him, not the other way around."

"He's a smart dog," replied Anton. "Let's see—the rest of the Sleuths. The heart of our group is my mother, Karen. She's made our home a welcoming spot for the Sleuths. Krista, Maria, and Diego are part of the group."

Skyla flashed a grin at Melody. "You and I talked about how scary it could be for me, moving into a household with a stepdaughter, a mother-in-law, and a housekeeper. We've had our challenging moments, but I love them dearly."

"Cliff is part of the group, of course," said Anton. "And his wife, Lou, who is Pete's daughter. There's also Sam Martinez. Hoot and Melody know him."

"I've met him, too," said Marilyn.

"Sam recently transferred from patrolman to detective with the Santa Fe PD. You'll get to hear him play his guitar on St. Nicholas. Sam's dad owns a ranch here in Pecos where they raise Andalusians—you know, the Spanish horses that are so great at dressage."

"When we were first exploring Pecos," said Marilyn, "we drove by there. I remember beautiful dapple grays."

"Those folks were the first Sleuths," said Anton, "but we've welcomed others since—members of Sam's family. Dom, Farah, Leyla, and Wilma."

"Farah is Sam's wife," said Marilyn.

"Yes," said Anton. "Leyla is her daughter and is in Krista's class at school. Wilma is Leyla's nanny."

Anton swallowed the last of his coffee and put the mug on the table. "Dom is Sam's grandfather. He's become the patriarch for our group in more ways than one. Dom and my mom have fallen in love. I don't know if they'll ever get married, but I love him like a father. I'm sure you'll see him Thanksgiving, at least for part of the day. Dom is at our house as often as he is at Sam and Farah's which technically is his home."

With her hand by her mouth, coyly pretending to block her voice from Anton's hearing, Skyla leaned closer to Melody and Marilyn. "Actually, Anton is just glad to have another someone with testosterone around. Poor guy is outnumbered. He says he's going out to his workshop to work on prototypes for his drone company, but we know he just needs to get away."

Anton rolled his eyes. "There have been moments." He took Skyla's hand. "You are well-acquainted with our most recent addition to the Circle Sleuths." He raised her hand to his lips. "My soon-to-be-wife. It was at our engagement party that Hoot discovered Pete and Cliff were among our close friends." He looked at Hoot. "I'm sorry they made you uncomfortable that day."

Hoot was sorry they'd been there, too. He couldn't think of anything to say, so he nodded briefly.

"Marilyn, there you have it. *Uff da.* Lots of people to sort out, but you'll not find a more supportive and fun group anywhere."

"Life doesn't often give you friendships like that," said Melody. "I envy you."

Hoot turned to her in surprise.

She glanced up at him. "Well, I do."

Hoot wasn't even sure the others heard her next soft words. "That's been the hardest thing about being a stay-at-home mom and moving to a new place. I need friends, and now Skyla's moved to the other side of Santa Fe."

Ouch, he thought, troubled by the longing he heard. He closed his eyes. It was inevitable. He'd have to put up with Pete and Cliff at the St. Nick thing. Marilyn's voice drew him back to the others.

"Thank you," said Marilyn. "I'll be happy to put faces to all those names."

"Glad you'll be joining us for Thanksgiving. I hope you can be with us on St. Nicholas, too." said Skyla. "Right now, we'd better be on our way."

◆ ❖ ◆

A little later, Hoot walked his grandmother over to her home. When he got back, he slumped down on the couch. He looked up to find Melody gazing at him, her brows drawn together and a tenseness to her posture.

"Skyla is my best friend. Why don't you want to be a part of this group?"

"I'm sorry. I don't like to be around Pete and Cliff."

"I hate it when you avoid people just because you might run into those two. It's not like they jump on you and nag you about that kidnapped boy. They were just struck with the resemblance. I can see it, too. It's no big deal. As they get to know you as Hoot, they'll stop." She sat down next to him.

"Anyhow, Pete and Cliff won't be there for Thanksgiving," she continued. "I want to go. I want you there, not reluctantly, but to have some fun and enjoy yourself."

"I said we'd go." Hoot leaned forward and picked up the puzzle box, touching the hand on the lid. He wished she'd drop the subject, but no such luck.

"I want us to go on St. Nicholas, also. Can't you just get over it? And we *are* going to Skyla and Anton's wedding. Pete and Cliff will be there, too."

Unwilling, yet, to make a verbal commitment that they'd go, he fiddled with the box, feeling a connection to the being whose hand reached from the opening.

"You know, sometimes I feel like there's something in my mind, trying to get out like this creature. I see glimpses. But they won't show themselves long enough for me to identify anything. And then my headache starts. Whatever's there is just out of reach. I get a strong feeling of danger—like I should avoid whatever it is." He hoped that she could understand how important this was to him. "It frightens me to death. Have you ever had that feeling?"

"No. When I try to remember something, it's only annoying. No danger." She reached out to him. "Have you always had that feeling of something trying to get out?"

"More this past year." Absently, he rubbed the scar on his head from that long-ago plane crash. "God, I'm bushed, and it's only Monday."

Soon he was lying on their bed. Melody rubbed his neck and shoulders for several minutes and then moved her fingers to his head, brushing over his widow's peak. "You're about due for a haircut."

"Mmmm." Pure pleasure filled him. Her strong fingers rubbed rhythmic patterns on his scalp. He shut his eyes, allowing his tension to drift away. The pleasant woozy darkness of sleep clouded the corners of his mind and crept closer.

"I should tuck in the kids," he murmured. Like a cube of butter in the sun, the definitive edges left his body and softened. "Your hands . . . magic."

He felt her lean forward and drop a soft kiss on his head. His body couldn't move as she drew the blanket around his shoulders.

"I'll check on them. Sleep, Hoot, honey."

CHAPTER EIGHT

Karen Bjornson leaned her head back in the cushioned window seat in her sitting room, cuddled in a plush throw against the chill in the wee hours of November 9. She drew up her knees, tucked her slippered feet under the folds of the throw, and let the heat from the mug warm her hands.

In her darkened bedroom beyond, Dom slept on. It was good he'd stayed over tonight. When she'd slipped out of bed, unable to sleep after watching the election results, she'd tried not to awaken him. She'd gone to the kitchen for hot chocolate and come back to sit and think. There'd been no need to turn on a light. She'd lived in this house for more than thirty years, had seen it change and grow with the needs and wishes of her family, and walked it confidently.

Her window looked out over their ranch on the outskirts of Santa Fe. The moon shed faint light on their backyard and the piñon-covered hills beyond. The vista stretched to the Sangre de Cristos, especially now that the tall trees in their yard were bare of leaves. No sound or light, other than from the moon, broke the deepness of the night. Even the great-horned owls were silent outside—all still, unlike the turbulence of her mind.

She set the empty mug aside and pulled her hands inside the throw. Idly, her fingers smoothed the nap back and forth. A deep sadness brought moisture to her eyes, as thoughts wove themselves in and out of her mind. So many people she loved would be affected by the outcome of yesterday's election.

Probably the most distressed would be Farah, an immigrant from Syria. In June, Farah had married Sam. His was the kind of leadership Karen admired—a true role model to follow, making a positive difference in people's lives. As a policeman, Sam lived justice. He was good at helping people understand each other's stories and helping them work together to solve problems. When Leyla had been bullied at school, before Sam had even known Farah, he'd intervened and had cared enough about the young bully to change his life for the better.

As the light gradually began to color the eastern sky, she heard Dom. He came into the sitting room, tying the belt on his robe.

"Want some company?"

"Please."

He arranged more cushions on the window seat, kicked off his slippers, and sat opposite her, pulling another warm throw over himself. He nudged her slippers off with his toes, tipped them over the edge of the seat to land with soft thumps on the floor, and found her feet with his under the overlap of their throws.

She smiled and returned the play with her toes against his.

"Do you want to talk?"

"I wish I had some answers, Dom." They were so attuned he would know exactly why she was awake and in a blue funk. She loved his mind and treasured hearing him talk about thoughts and ideas. Even when they were both absorbed in their own activity—reading, drawing, or listening to music—there was a connection, a comfort in the other's presence.

"Sometimes it's okay just to be forming questions," he said.

"How did this happen? What happened to our values and love your neighbor as yourself?"

"Why did people vote the way they did? What were the needs and fears that motivated them? I'm sure the historian in me will eventually put it into perspective. I do know we're seeing a phenomenon that is not unique to our country."

41

"I was at a conference for nonprofits once," said Karen. "I got into a discussion about backing candidates for office. This one guy said that it was all in the packaging. He said you don't want the voter to think. You want them to react emotionally. React to sound bites, code words. And fear. Self-interest and fear. Now there's a combination."

"Labeling is not new. Look at the Jackson presidency with its manifest destiny claims of Divine Providence to justify their actions of self-interest."

"Do you believe education is the answer?"

Dom chuckled. "You're talking to a teacher. It's part of the answer, not the whole answer. I've gotten skeptical about some aspects of education at my age. Who is financing it? Who is writing the history texts? What are they including, and what is left out?" He paused, then let out a hmmpf. "Just look at how my own ancestors are shown in the history books. Glowing stories of conquistadors conquering new territory for Spain, bringing Christianity to the natives. They tell you very little about the brutality, the slave labor, and the chicanery." He lapsed into silence.

The growing pre-dawn light brought more definition to her sitting room, showing the curved chimney lines of the kiva fireplace. Across from her, Dom's dear lean, sculpted features grew clear; the light found his tousled silver hair. She moved her toe under his foot to tickle his arch. He flashed a grin and moved his feet to capture hers. As their feet stilled, warm, skin-to-skin, her thoughts drifted on.

A light came on in the kitchen in the center part of their home, shining out on the portal. Anton and Skyla's suite lay on the opposite side of the sprawling, two-story, H-shaped adobe home. Krista, her eleven-year-old granddaughter, had a room near theirs.

Karen heard the faint swoosh of the family room sliding door, followed by the happy barks of Twitch and Shadow, the Airedales, as they raced around the yard. Daylight stole into her sitting room. Shadows faded, and colors emerged.

One of her prize possessions almost glowed in the sunlight on the wall opposite the window, a small tapestry woven by Maximo

Laura, her idol when it came to weaving. It showed two birds bathed in light, with colors of deep cobalt blue, vibrant reds and golds. Her own tapestry, a Viking ship with its dragon prow cutting through waves of blue and green, graced another wall. Her goal, even as she'd done that early piece, was to use some of the mythology of her own Norwegian ancestry and weave a thing of beauty and light.

A low growl interrupted her thoughts. She chuckled and turned to Dom. "Your tummy is telling us it's time for breakfast." Karen stood, stretched, slid her feet into her slippers, and welcomed Dom's hug. "Thank you for being here."

In his embrace, she felt his hand smooth her blond hair behind her ear. She smiled into his eyes.

"We'll find a way to make a difference, Karen. I don't know what it will be yet, but we will find a way to be a light on the hill, a way of treating others like we want to be treated."

"St. Nicholas this year . . . I'm wondering if we can begin there. It fits, don't you think?"

"What did you have in mind?"

"Nothing . . . yet."

"I love you, *mi corazón.*" His fingers stole into the opening of her robe, covering the beat of her heart and spreading over the curve of her breast. Her lashes drifted shut, and she raised her lips to meet his. Dom's being lifted her spirits and energized her.

A shining example of what life could be like, she thought, when people were kind and worked together to make the world better for all. A light on the hill.

CHAPTER NINE

In Denver later that same day, Hayle waited in the lobby of the Southwood Police Precinct for someone to escort him to Commander Isaacson's office. He rolled his eyes at the interchange between the bored officer at the window and a complaining woman. Too bad the officer couldn't tell her to get out of his face and go to hell.

Smartest move he'd ever made, quitting the Denver police force. He remembered it like yesterday. The bullies in blue on his shift hazing the new guy on their detail. No big deal, said his supervisor, shrugging it off and laughing. So what if they ripped your name and made fun of your birthmark. That SOB had no idea of the shit his men were involved in.

Bastards! All of them. In those days, Officer Curtis Hayle III had hated his name. Curt Hayle. Curtail. Cut it short. Make it less.

Well, he'd quit and taken a job with a private security company. He saw possibilities, learned the ropes, and rose steadily in their ranks. Now he owned his own security business, and, in defiance of those who'd belittled him, he'd made a bold gesture and named it Curtail Investigation and Security. He liked the sound of it.

And that birthmark, which had earned him taunts of Rabbit Man? Years later, he'd learned of new technology to erase port wine stains. His mark had responded to laser treatments when he finally could afford them. The procedures had been damned uncomfortable to go through, but now the stain stretching from his neck up onto his cheek was gone.

A volunteer appeared to escort him to the office where Isaacson, his friend, greeted him with a sour look on his pinched face.

"Whatever happened, it wasn't me," joked Hayle. "What did you want to see me about?" He'd known this guy from police academy, and they understood each other. Isaacson had stuck it out, though not always like the public or the higher ranks assumed.

"Sometimes I wish I'd bailed like you. Being promoted higher in this rat race just means you have more rats and a bigger cage."

Hayle laughed. "You wouldn't leave it. Too many of those rats are forced to share their cheese with you."

"Well, a big dirty rat is messing where he shouldn't be. I heard from a Santa Fe detective, a lieutenant, no less. He's coming here to poke around in a kidnapping cold case. Or so he says."

"Santa Fe? Where Leroy Grover, your old nemesis, is chief?"

"Grover and our chief were always tight. Now suddenly, here comes this lieutenant from Santa Fe all the way to my precinct. I think they know something about what we used to do. I wouldn't put it past them to try and get me fired and screw up my pension."

"Even before I got out, you were setting up your own retirement. And what do you mean, 'used to do'? Still happening, bro."

Isaacson frowned. "Something's screwy. Why would a lieutenant be involved in a cold case? He's in charge—he can delegate somebody."

"Santa Fe's a Podunk force. Denver is ten times bigger. Maybe there ain't nobody else to do it."

"Still doesn't make sense."

"You want me to see what he's up to?"

"Yes."

"You say a kidnapping?"

Isaacson nodded. "Back in '91. Some boy. And this is interesting. He's checking on Gordon Stewart, the same Gordon you used to go hunting with."

"Gordon! He's been dead for decades. He never had anything to do with a kidnapping." *Damn. I don't need this.* "Whatever. Ain't nothing to do with me." Hayle pulled a small notebook from his shirt pocket. "Tell me this lieutenant's name."

"Schultz."

"You've got to be kidding. You're in luck, bro. My sister works in that PD and just took the position as Schultz's admin."

"No shit. Can you find out anything for me? And when Schultz gets here, I want to keep tabs on what he does, where he goes, who he sees. Should I spread the idea he's up to no good? That stalling him will make the chief happy?"

"You're a conniving bastard." Hayle laughed. "Just hope the chief never finds out."

In his stately Victorian mansion on a suburban Denver estate, Wit Wysocki, a tall, suave gentleman, entered his study where a fire burned cheerfully, warming his paneled, ground-floor domain against the chilly afternoon of Thursday, November 10. He sat at his desk, opened a drawer, and slid the contents around, looking for his jeweler's loupe.

He opened a small metal box, spotting the magnifier inside next to a flat, M-shaped object. His hand hovered over the loupe, but picked up the M-shape instead. Flipping it into the air and catching it, feeling the cold iron in his hand, Wit wondered why he kept this key. For decades there'd been no hint of the puzzle box it went with.

The box had been a showpiece—part of his father's collection. Made of unusual wood, it had a carved wooden hand that seemingly belonged to some human-like creature stealthily escaping from inside. His father had shared with Wit the secrets of opening all the levels of that puzzle box.

The box had been stolen from him twenty-five years ago, just after his father died. Still, he wasn't ready to let the key go.

For years, he'd been afraid of the items he'd hidden in the box resurfacing. Why hadn't he just chucked them all that night as soon as he'd driven away from the reservoir?

He'd planned to, but the letters he'd grabbed from Tonya's purse included two from other people. Better to wait until he was home, had light to read them, and could be certain there were no loose ends. That fabulous necklace had already been hidden in his car. Planning to hide it, he brought it into the house along with everything he'd taken from Tonya. He opened the puzzle box, then heard his wife come home early. Quickly he stuffed everything inside and closed it up. He would take care of it on Monday when he could get to the bank and his safety deposit box. There was no rush. No one else knew how to get in the box.

How could he have foreseen it would be stolen over the weekend?

God forbid those items should ever show up. The contents of that box could ruin his life, turn his world upside down, and tear his family asunder. He'd be facing a murder charge.

Wit put the key back, took out the magnifier, and closed the drawer. He swiveled his chair toward the life-size wooden cat crouched on the corner of his wide desk and caressed the patina, remembering his father doing the same. He'd loved wood carvings and had collected spectacular pieces, including this cat, poised to leap, one paw slightly lifted, and its muscles tensed. The carver had given it a beautiful sense of balance.

The hawk above the credenza had been another of his father's favorites. It seemed to be captured in motion, its wings partially open, like it was hunkered down before springing into flight. The eyes were keen, intent upon some imagined prey, its whole attitude fierce.

Those wooden sculptures, in a way, seemed more lifelike than his own trophy heads, hanging above the massive fireplace. Once those creatures had lived, but now they were static, eternally fastened to their mounts, gazing through dead glass eyes—an elk from Montana, an oryx from New Mexico, and a moose from Alaska. He chuckled. What an absurd thought. Those beasts had been brought down by him—proof of his power.

"Daddy, are you busy?"

Wit looked toward the door and smiled. "Come on in, baby. You look stunning. Are you home for dinner tonight, or will you be off with that handsome fiancé of yours?"

She crossed to his desk, her stiletto heels silenced by the rug. He stood and kissed her cheek.

"We're meeting some friends for dinner. I'm so happy. He's a dream come true."

"He's a lucky man, sweetheart. He couldn't do better than to have you by his side."

"He so admires the work you do. Just about all your candidates won this year."

Wit smiled. Success bred success.

"Mother wants to know if you've gone over the guest list yet. She thought you'd want to before we address the invitations."

"I'll look it over before tomorrow."

"Thank you, Daddy."

She left, a subtle hint of perfume in her wake. Wit turned to the window, lost in thought, only half-seeing the vista of Denver in the distance and the blue of the mountains rising in the other direction, set off by snow-dusted slopes where a few short weeks ago yellow aspens had reigned.

Could he hope that puzzle box with its wretched contents had been lost forever? Nothing should threaten his daughter's happiness. When had she grown up and gotten so beautiful? Though she was in her twenties now, she would always be his little girl.

Later that evening, a double knock sounded on the outside door to Wit's study, a slight pause and then two more knocks. Good, he thought. Jed was here. He pressed the electronic switch to unlock the door.

A tall, muscular man in his twenties came in, along with the November chill, and closed the door quietly behind him. Wit nodded approval at his appearance. Classy overcoat, suit and tie, shaved head, unsmiling face, leashed energy, erect posture. Just the right attitude of power and intimidation.

"What can I do for you, sir?"

Jed's voice was unexpectedly deep for a young man. It went well with the image Wit wanted his employees to project. Few would dare to cross this man.

Wit looked the young man in the eye. "Wilcox usually handles these situations for me, but lately he's been slipping."

Other than one eyebrow raising slightly, Jed's face showed no emotion.

"I'm trusting you to deliver this letter for me immediately. Make it clear that we won't wait longer. We take action tomorrow."

"Yes, sir."

Wit handed Jed the envelope and buzzed him out the door.

Jed had been a useful find and had responded well to training. Wit had first noticed him as a college student hired on for security at a political rally for one of their candidates. He'd picked the young man for more responsibilities to be handled under Wit's own close scrutiny, and later promoted him to trusted-bodyguard status.

Recently, he'd discovered Jed's aptitude for digging up secrets and dirt on those who dared oppose Wit. He was pleased—this guy could deliver results. Jerome Edward Hawkins had no idea he was being made ready for bigger and more sensitive jobs.

CHAPTER TEN

On Friday, Pete headed to Marilyn Stewart's home again. Supposedly this was the last day of his work week, though more often than not, he was called out on the weekend. Marilyn had two banker boxes of her son's papers for him to pick up. He was welcomed inside to find Melody there, helping her daughter at the sunny table. Bonnie bent over a coloring book, crayons spread out around her.

Marilyn invited him to sit in the living room area. "I told Melody I'd asked for your assistance in finding out what happened to Gordon's wife." She scribbled something on paper and passed it to Pete.

He glanced at her note. It read that she'd rather not discuss the blue folder today. Pete caught her eyes, and she motioned with her head toward Melody. He nodded and tucked the note away. He'd talk with her later.

Melody left Bonnie happily coloring and singing to herself. As she sat by Marilyn on the sofa, she looked at Pete. "My husband is not comfortable in your presence or Cliff's. Marilyn knows that. Surely you can see that there is no way Hoot could be the lost boy you are looking for."

"Not lost, dear," said Marilyn before Pete could respond. "Kidnapped. And that little kidnapped boy has been much on my mind as we've gone about this task." She stood up to fetch Pete a cup of coffee. "Melody, the other day you were asking me if Hoot ever had a baby sister. I think you should tell the lieutenant that story."

"I'm sure he wouldn't be interested."

"I would like to hear it," Pete said. The undercurrent flowing between the two women was almost palpable.

Melody frowned. "Oh, all right. It was simply that Hoot and I had been talking about my stepsisters. Hoot said, without really thinking, he remembered when his baby sister was born. But then he stopped, all confused. He doesn't have a sister. We wondered if there'd been another baby who'd died, so I asked Grandma."

"I never heard Gordon mention another child." Marilyn glanced at Melody, before speaking to Pete in a tentative voice. "Did this child, Johnny, have a sister?"

"*Ja*, the McCreaths had three children, each two years apart. Johnny was four when she was born."

"Oh, dear, I thought so."

Melody turned to Marilyn in surprise. "What're you thinking? You didn't say anything before."

"I know. But it's heavy on my heart. It's not just that I want the truth about what happened to my daughter-in-law. I keep coming back to Ross's front teeth."

"Front teeth?" The jump in topic surprised Pete.

Marilyn picked up a school photograph of a red-headed boy with a gap-toothed grin. "This is the last picture we had of Ross before he came to live with us—it was his kindergarten picture. His front tooth was missing, like so many other six-year olds."

"Matti lost his first tooth at six," said Melody.

"Just so," said Marilyn. "But when Ross came, he had all his front teeth. Then he lost one—that same tooth as in the picture, just before his eighth birthday. I thought it might have been loosened in the accident. Soon after that, he lost the other front tooth. But they grew in again. That's rather old to be losing those baby teeth. I remember being amazed, but thankful the good Lord saw fit to grow them again after the plane crash. I told that to the dentist a few years later, and he said I must be mistaken. That's not how teeth behave."

51

She looked at Pete. "It has started to frighten me. I don't know why his teeth grew back." She shut her eyes. "Or maybe . . . dear God, maybe I don't want to know why."

"Grandma!" Melody looked startled.

Pete sipped his coffee and considered his next question. "Looking back on those first months with your grandson, was there anything else? A feeling that something wasn't right?"

Marilyn was quiet, downcast, twisting her handkerchief in her fingers. Finally, she looked up with a tormented expression. "Ross was small for his age. But then, I had no respect for how his mother cared for him. I thought he hadn't gotten the right foods. Winona didn't even want Gordon to talk to us. We tried to visit, but about the time Ross started school, she refused to let us see him anymore or talk to him. It hurt, unimaginably. Gordon backed her up."

She looked at her twisted hanky and set it on the table next to the couch.

"When he was in the hospital, he would cry so pitifully for his mommy and daddy. I'd say over and over again, 'It will be okay. Grandma will take care of you. Later when we had told him his father died, he was heartbroken. He whimpered something about not telling."

"Not telling?" asked Pete. "What do you suppose he meant?"

"He said it was his fault. He didn't mean to. I wondered if he had touched something on the plane. Moved some lever or pushed a button that he shouldn't have. I told him it wasn't his fault."

"How awful, if he felt responsible," said Melody.

"For a long time, when someone asked him about the plane crash, he would just clam up. He was confused and forgetful, too. Quite a while later, he asked what happened to the man who was flying the plane. I said, 'We told you, Ross. Your father died.' Such anguish. We began to avoid any talk about it. We didn't see the angry, rebellious child Gordon had warned us of, just a very sad, quiet one."

"What did the doctors tell you about his memory?" asked Pete.

"They said his skull fracture and the trauma had made him lose his memory of his earlier life."

"How did he do in school?"

"He knew how to read, but not well. He was behind other kids—didn't know what you'd expect for a child his age. I blamed his injuries. I was with him when one of the aides at the hospital asked him to print his name. She said, 'Come on. You can do it. First an R, an O, an S, and then another S.' He refused, began to cry, and another headache came on. I thought he was frustrated because he couldn't remember how to do things. But later, I saw him writing with no problem. He liked to draw and write."

Pete shook his head as the story unfolded from Marilyn's lips. His thoughts centered on his theory of a small boy, ripped from everything he knew and thrust into the role of a stranger two years older.

"We home-schooled him quite a bit. He loved learning. Dwight and I would take him out and talk about the plants, the animals, the trees. When he finally was able to go back to school, he caught up well."

"Did you keep any of his schoolwork?" asked Pete.

"There is some in these." Marilyn gestured at the boxes. "Now that I've started, I'm surprised. One saves the good things, so the task is full of happy memories."

"I'm not a great fan of elephants in the room, Lieutenant," said Melody, glancing over at Bonnie. The little girl was still singing softly as she scribbled away.

"There's a big elephant here now," she continued. "I will not do anything sneaky to get around my husband's wishes. I'd prefer it if the St. Nicholas celebration could be just that—a celebration with friends. I don't want Hoot badgered or getting a blinding headache."

Pete met Melody's look with one of his own. "I admire you for saying that. Cliff and I will keep this out of the celebration. But I will also say I'm a detective. This case has haunted me for twenty-five years. I have not and will not stop investigating leads that might solve it or provide answers to a family desperately searching for them." Their gazes locked in silence.

"I think Hoot should take a DNA test." At the sound of her soft voice, two heads swiveled toward Marilyn.

"Grandma!"

Marilyn raised her chin. "Then we'd be sure."

"As much as I'd like to see that happen," said Pete slowly, "it cannot be coerced. It would be best if Hoot makes that decision and chooses when the time is right on his own."

"Amen to that," said Melody.

In the wee dark hours of the following morning, Pete turned onto his side and tried to think of something else. As happened all too often, he'd awakened, and his mind wouldn't turn off. This time, it repeated the loop of what he'd heard yesterday in his conversation with Marilyn. Sleep wouldn't come.

He turned onto his back and tried again. He pictured his grandson sleeping quietly, chest rising and falling, breathing in and out. He concentrated on that monotonous rhythm, but the mental picture only reminded him that the missing six-year old would be his grandson's uncle.

He glanced over at Akiko, lying next to him, her hair dark against the pillow in the dim light from their digital clock. Careful to not disturb her, he arose, grabbed his robe and slippers, and went downstairs. Beowulf, his Airedale terrier, padded after him. Experience told Pete he'd get more sleep by getting up and breaking the routine now before going back to bed.

Should he have coffee? When he couldn't sleep? What the hell, he wanted some. He used his birthday-present coffee machine to make it, sat on the couch in the family room, and leaned back. Beowulf stretched out at his feet.

Pete turned his head as Akiko came in. He held out his hand and smiled when she sat next to him. "I'm sorry I woke you, Angel."

"You didn't. I just woke up, reached out my hand, and you weren't there. Something troubling you? One of your cases?"

"Hmmpf," he grunted. "Should have been a bridge-toll collector. Work my job. Go home. No thoughts, no worries. Wouldn't wake up with puzzle pieces all jumbled in my brain."

"You'd hate it. It sounds deadly dull. And the gas fumes. You'd be gagging every time a diesel truck drove past."

"You're right." He sighed and took another sip of coffee. "The McCreath kidnapping bothers me."

"Pete, why now with this case? Has there been a development?"

Pete told her a little of his interview with Hoot's grandmother. He didn't mention the blue folder. "If he is Johnny, why doesn't he come home?"

"I can think of two reasons," she said. "Either he is ashamed of what happened to him, or he doesn't remember. Do either of those fit with the facts you know? He seemed like a nice young man when I met him. I liked his wife, and their children are adorable."

"I haven't sensed any shame. But when the Johnny situation is mentioned, he stubbornly refuses to even consider the possibility. The phrase 'first your father died' brought a physical reaction—paleness and a headache."

Akiko leaned her head against his shoulder. "You got another idea from this last conversation, didn't you? What is it?"

Pete smiled. "Ah, Angel, you know me so well. Yesterday, Marilyn said he talked about not telling. She thought he'd touched something on the plane and caused the accident. But I don't think so. If my theory is correct, he's Johnny. It's not uncommon for kidnappers to control victims by threatening to harm their family if they tell anyone or don't obey. It's evil, convincing the powerless victim that it will be their fault if their family is hurt or killed."

"What do you know about PTSD in children who have suffered trauma?"

"You got to that conclusion, too." Pete put down his coffee cup and patted his legs. Akiko sat on his lap, turning to kiss his bristly cheek. He fingered the strap on her short nightgown and ran a hand over her arm. "You're cold." He pulled the fleece throw from the back of the couch and draped it over them and heard her contented sigh as she cuddled with him under the warmth.

"Johnny was only six," he said. "We don't know what the man did to the child during those days."

"If Hoot is Johnny." Her voice trailed off as she thought. "How many days went by between the kidnapping and the crash?"

"He was kidnapped on the seventeenth. Santa Fe to Denver to Butte, where Marilyn said they spent a night, and then to Kalispell, Montana. Crashed on the nineteenth."

"You have no idea if there was verbal, physical, or sexual abuse—or all three."

"The kidnapping itself is a trauma, being stolen from all you know and love. All alone. Then to follow that with a plane crash. Good reasons for a child not to remember. The brain can go to extraordinary measures to protect an individual."

"Even now, he may be coping. At some unconscious level, he might hear voices saying, 'Don't let that pain come to the surface. You don't want to live it again.' " She tipped her head back to look into Pete's face. "Or even more extraordinary. That courageous little six-year old may have decided *never* to talk about it."

"That's a helpful thought."

"Thank you for confiding in me," said Akiko. "I like to know what you're thinking."

"I don't want to burden you with my work, Angel." He saw a slight frown appear on her face and brought a hand from under the cover to smooth it out. "You don't need that."

♦ ❖ ♦

Under the softness of the blanket, held against his warmth, Akiko was now the wide-awake one, even as Pete's breathing began the regular rhythm of sleep. So close, and then he backed away again. What if she wanted to know about his work, wanted to understand what he felt? She didn't need to know details, but she wanted more than the typical 'How was your work?'

'Fine.'

She could tell it wasn't fine. He bottled it up.

When they'd met and become friends in Japan, she knew more of what he did then than she did now. With her and her dad, he talked for hours about ideas, differences in culture, and how those affected harmony. If it hadn't been for those talks, she never would have known the significance of what she overheard those officers talking about, and he would have been killed.

His sharing anything, like he'd done just now, was rare. She understood he had to keep confidentiality, but it seemed his reasons for not sharing had more to do with keeping her separate from his world. That had chafed in all the years of their marriage.

It was so frustrating. When she became a wife, Pete had assumptions that she couldn't shake him loose from. She didn't want to follow three steps behind him, safe and protected. She wanted to face the world by his side. That's how she thought Americans viewed marriage. Facing difficulties together, side by side.

CHAPTER ELEVEN

Pete laid his napkin beside his plate and glanced around the table at their dinner guests, Lou and Cliff, Karen and Dom. "Your sauerbraten was delicious, Angel. Just right for a nippy Sunday night. Shall we have our coffee in the family room?"

Soon Pete had flames dancing in the kiva fireplace. He heard the dishwasher begin its cycle and saw Akiko check on their grandson, sleeping in a crib in a corner of the family room. Then she sat down with them and put a plate of brownies on the coffee table where everyone could reach.

"I wanted to say something while it was just the six of us," said Karen. "Anton has invited Hoot and his family to our place for Thanksgiving. He said Hoot was leery about coming if Pete and Cliff might be there."

"Good grief," said Cliff. "I don't understand why he acts the way he does. Anyhow, we're not going to be there."

"But you will on St. Nicholas," said Karen. "We've invited them for that, too."

"What are you asking, Karen?" said Pete. "To make Hoot feel welcome, we won't talk about Johnny?"

"Yes, that would help."

"That still irks me," said Cliff. "Why won't he just do a DNA test?"

"Because he's not ready," said Akiko. "Even if Hoot is Johnny, how can you know the pain behind his reluctance?"

Cliff glared at Pete. "Aren't you frustrated? So close, but not knowing?"

"I *do* want answers, but I need his cooperation. Let him work it through," said Pete, seeing his son-in-law's frown.

"Bloody hell. Writing is easier than real life. I'd be able to write some plot twist, a need to know his genetic background and voilà."

"How is your new book coming, Cliff?" Akiko asked.

Cliff brightened. "I'm trying a mystery for adults for a change. Maybe you could help with some ideas for a character. He wants to be a good leader, but he's floundering in the task. He seems to lack focus or vision, and something happened to him when he was younger that gave him psychological scars."

Dom settled back on the couch, brownie in hand. "You mean like a kid failing at something and his father telling him he'll never amount to anything?"

"Exactly. That could be part of his struggle."

"Some things, ingrained in us when we are very young, keep coming up again," said Pete. "For example, my mother was told girls weren't good in math. It became a self-fulfilling prophecy."

"Stories that challenge those stereotypes are important for children," said Akiko.

"Like *The Little Engine that Could*?" asked Karen.

"My father told me stories like that when I was little," said Akiko. "He told me to reach for the stars."

"I see you as a strong and independent woman, Akiko," said Karen. "Do you suppose the stories made that difference?"

"I hadn't thought of it, but maybe yes."

"There's one story I've wanted to hear for a long time," said Lou. "The story of why Dad calls you his Avenging Angel."

Akiko glanced at Pete. "It's your father's story to tell if he wishes."

Pete met her gaze and finally nodded. "It's not a happy story, and it left my spirit wounded—a hard lesson which still gives me pain."

"What happened?" asked Karen.

Pete reached out to take Akiko's hand. "You all know I was stationed in Japan. Akiko and her dad both worked on base. I spent a lot of time at their home, talking about cultures and ideas. She and I knew we had something special going, but we hadn't thought of marriage yet."

"He hadn't thought of marriage yet." Akiko smiled. "I knew what I wanted."

"My partners and I discovered some of our guys were stealing weapons and selling them to arms dealers, raking in thousands of dollars. I was appalled. It never even occurred to me that our own would betray us like that."

"That's terrible," said Cliff.

"I was a lot more naïve and idealistic back then," said Pete. "My partners, Ryan Davies and Cowboy Olson, and I figured out their scheme. We took it to our superior officer and, in secret with him, planned to bust them. The trap was set to spring in this huge warehouse. Ryan came in on one side, and Cowboy and me the other."

He closed his eyes briefly, remembering the pain. "But it went horribly wrong. Turned out the officer we'd confided in was in cahoots with the dealers. He set us up, and Ryan got killed. I knew then our expected backup would never show. I thought it was over."

Still unbelieving, Pete shook his head. "Akiko happened to be off base somewhere and had overheard the officer talking and realized what was about to happen."

"I was at a nearby table with other girls," said Akiko, "speaking Japanese. The men didn't recognize me or worry that someone might be listening. When I overheard what they planned, I was so angry. How dare they look to harm my friends, let alone betray their country?"

Pete picked up the tale. "Akiko told her dad, and he told an officer, high enough in rank to get the job done. But this Avenging Angel couldn't wait and came barreling around the corner and into the warehouse in some kind of delivery truck. She hollered at us to get in and blazed out through another door followed by gunfire. She had called the police, the fire department, the softball team, hiking club, knitters anonymous, and Lord knows who else. The place soon teemed with people."

"I'm sure I didn't call the knitters. Your list gets longer each time you tell the story."

"Seems like you must have," said Pete. "I'm positive they were there." Then he grinned wickedly. "Actually, it was the grinding truck gears that startled the bad guys, giving us enough time to escape."

"I knew how to drive a stick shift, but I'd never driven anything like that truck. Help was coming. All they needed was a few more minutes. I was scared to death."

"Did they capture the one who killed your partner?" asked Lou.

Pete nodded. "Eventually. It took a long time to sort it all out. That scumbag had destroyed a lot of evidence and manufactured fake evidence to put the blame on Ryan, Cowboy, and me. But we had the forethought to make backup copies of what we'd discovered. We'd documented everything, and we hadn't shared all of what we knew with the officer."

"Good thinking," said Karen. "Did the dealers get closed down?"

"That particular operation did. But greed is hard to stamp out. You whack it down in one spot, and it pops up somewhere else."

"Whack a mole," said Cliff.

Pete frowned. "Indeed. Even today, I wonder sometimes if a mole from that episode won't poke his greedy head up again."

Dom helped himself to another brownie. "After the death of your partner, why didn't you quit the idea of law enforcement? Why did you make it a career?"

Pete thought as he sipped his coffee. "We'd worked hard on that case. It was the right thing to do. I discovered I had an aptitude, even a passion for the pursuit of justice."

"This left you with lessons," said Dom, licking a chocolate smudge from his finger. "Lessons that were positive for your life."

"I'm sure Akiko will tell you I'm a slow learner when it comes to some lessons."

"Like being overprotective and always shielding me from danger."

"I'm a man." Pete's voice challenged her. "Protect, provide, and procreate. It's what we do."

"I'm a mother," said Akiko, her dark eyes flashing. "I will protect my cubs *and my mate* as long as I have breath."

Pete threw up a hand. "See what I mean about the lessons? This one seems to come up with some regularity."

Lou laughed. "That's true. I can't tell you how many times I've heard this, growing up."

"I became slower to trust people," said Pete. "I dig deeper into what looks innocuous. That's contrary to what used to be my nature. I have to keep reminding myself to not take innocence for granted."

"Interesting concept, since our whole system says we are innocent until proven guilty." Dom turned to Cliff. "Maybe your character needs to go back. Examine what happened and come up with a positive vision. Study the dark corners of the human soul. Find and follow those who have the light and those who inspire hope. Those are the folks who keep you buoyant on a sea of darkness."

"That's poetic." Lou raised her cup to Dom.

Cliff reached for another brownie. "That helps. At different times, my book character can visit the dark again. Each time, he might see it with new light."

"We all need mentors to give us hope and lift us up," said Pete. "Too much negativity paralyzes your soul."

Karen leaned forward, a look of happiness on her face. "This is exciting! I love hope, rather than fear, being chosen as the vision. It brings people together rather than building walls between them. We all have light within us. It needs to be seen. It needs to be shared."

"Your light on the hill," said Dom with a smile.

CHAPTER TWELVE

As Pete was checking his weekend's accumulated messages, he found a voicemail from Marilyn and called her.

"Lieutenant, I've found two items that I believe will be useful to you."

"What are they?"

She hesitated. "I need to show you and to talk about the blue folder. Thank you for not mentioning it when Melody was here."

"I'll be there about ten thirty." When he'd cleared the work on his desk, he tucked the blue folder into his portfolio and walked out to his car. A chilly breeze swept a swirl of dust into the air. Another thing for his to-do list. His white car collected dirt and needed to go through the carwash again.

After Marilyn welcomed him into her home, she handed him a drawing done in crayon.

Pete studied the art—two boys and a gray cat near a tree. Why had Marilyn thought this was significant? Was it the boys' red hair? The work certainly didn't show the best talent. Everything was lined up with no regard to proportion. The name Ross was penciled in childish printing in a corner.

Then he sucked in a breath.

"You saw it," she said, handing him a magnifier.

He looked closely. Under the name, some of it erased into oblivion so thoroughly that a tiny hole had appeared, impressions remained from letters J, O, and H. *"Mein Gott."* His eyes met Marilyn's desolate expression.

He pulled out the blue folder and laid it between them. "Dwight noticed the differences in hairlines, didn't he?"

"He must have." She sat quietly, her elbow resting on the table, fingertips covering her lips. Then, blinking rapidly, she reached for a small, yellowed envelope and handed it to him. "I found this tucked in Gordon's baby book. They are his."

He peered inside at two baby teeth and said, "I thought to ask if you'd be willing to do a DNA test, but a father's is far better, more conclusive."

"Lieutenant—" She swallowed. "How can I even say it?"

Pete reached to cover her hand resting on the table. "You're thinking the unthinkable. That the child you loved and raised wasn't Ross at all."

She nodded, tears slipping down her cheeks, before whispering, "I'm afraid you're right."

Later Pete entered the bullpen with a spring in his step. For a Monday, it was going extremely well. Progress, of any kind, was encouraging. He stopped by Yvonne's door. "Messages?"

She finished transcribing a line into her computer with brusque efficiency before lifting her head. "On your desk, sir."

"Excellent. And I need a FedEx envelope."

He went to his own office, made a cup of coffee, and sat to check his messages.

"Here's the envelope." Yvonne plowed confidently in and set it on his desk.

"Thanks." He filled out paperwork for CODIS, the national DNA database, and sealed a protectively wrapped tooth inside.

He finished his coffee, picked up his portfolio, and stopped by his admin's office with the envelope. "Yvonne, please see that this gets sent."

Pete walked down the hall to see Chief Grover and tell him about Marilyn's revelation, the discovery of Gordon's baby teeth, and her concern about the real Ross. He ended by saying he'd sent one tooth off to CODIS.

As Pete spoke, Chief Grover absently stroked his walrus mustache.

"I've an idea," said Grover. Humor lit his pale hazel eyes. ""You still have the second tooth?"

Pete nodded.

"Didn't you tell me last week that you wanted to meet Cannon when you got to Denver? I remember him. Good man. I'll call the Denver chief and see if he can arrange for you to meet Cannon at Southwood."

Pete felt his smile grow at the twinkle in Grover's eyes. He was up to something. "That would be appreciated, sir. I envy Denver their crime lab with its DNA testing facility. Could they be convinced that processing this tooth might actually move one of their own cases forward?"

Grover laughed. "Nicely put. Maybe Cannon can expedite this. Give me the information on those remains that are possibilities. I'll see what I can do."

Later before going home, Pete cleared off his desk. As he tucked the drawing into the case file, his mind turned to Marilyn. She must be torn apart. No one to confide in. She needed someone like Karen.

His brow lifted as he tossed the used cup out of his coffee machine. A Starbucks stood near where her charitable foundation office was.

Coffee. It often solved problems.

Curiosity filled Karen as she turned away from the Starbucks barista, latte in hand. Pete had called her last night and asked if she were available this morning. He said Hoot's grandmother was going meet him at Starbucks. And if it wasn't too much to ask, could Karen make it seem like she'd run into him accidentally? Pete thought Marilyn needed a woman to talk with.

As she heard her name called, Karen managed a surprised look. She smiled when she saw Pete beckoning her to a corner table where he sat with a white-haired woman.

"Please join us. Marilyn Stewart, this is my good friend, Karen Bjornson."

"Marilyn, Anton tells me you'll be joining us for Thanksgiving."

"Thank you for inviting us. We're looking forward to it."

Pete smiled. "Marilyn met me here to deliver some papers."

At the mention of the papers, Marilyn's smile faltered.

Pete held up a fat manila envelope. "Before we forget, was there anything special you wanted to tell me about what's in here?"

Marilyn flicked a glance to Karen.

"It's okay to talk in front of Karen." Pete leaned forward. "Marilyn, forgive me if I'm out of line, but it must be hard. You can't talk with Melody or Hoot. Karen's a good listener. I know you've just met, but I would trust her. She will keep our confidence."

Marilyn's lips trembled. "Gordon's address book is in there and a few more papers. Please, if you can . . . find out what happened to my grandson, Lieutenant. I think maybe . . . my son did something unforgiveable. That he stole—" Tears welled in her eyes. She set her tea down and pushed back from the table. "I'm sorry. I'm making a spectacle of myself. Pete's right. I'm a mess inside."

"If I can help by listening," said Karen, "I'd be glad to. My foundation's office is just a few doors down. No one is there to see or overhear. Maybe you and Pete would like to go there with me now."

"I wish I could, but I have an appointment," said Pete. "Marilyn, it would be good for you to talk it all out."

Marilyn blinked back the tears. Amidst the curious looks of the other customers, they gathered their drinks and left. Outside, Pete hugged Karen and whispered a thank you in her ear before driving away.

Karen led the way to her office, ushered Marilyn through the small lobby dominated by a colorful tapestry, past a board room with a large table, to comfortable chairs in a corner of her own office.

Marilyn sent an anguished look to Karen. "It's awkward, the thought of confiding in a stranger. Yet, it seems right, even easier than it was to talk with the lieutenant. Where do I begin?" Marilyn sipped her tea. "Lately I've learned some things that made me think that the boy my husband and I raised as our grandson is not really him. It appears my son kidnapped the McCreath boy and lied to us." She broke down sobbing. "There. I finally said the words aloud."

Karen sucked in a breath. "Hoot is Cliff's brother? But that would be miraculous."

Marilyn sniffed, blew her nose, and struggled with her composure. "Yes, except it would turn Hoot's life upside down. That's the first thing. He refuses to consider it. He's a strong person, but he hides pain inside that must be crushing." Marilyn dabbed at her eyes with a tissue.

"And then the second thing follows. Hoot, Melody, and their children are my life, but if Hoot is . . . Johnny . . . where is Ross? Where is my real grandson?" She put her fingertips over her lips and took a long, shuddering breath.

Karen put an encouraging hand on Marilyn's arm. "Is Pete looking now?"

"Yes. He's been wonderful." The older woman turned to her. "Being unable to tell anyone has been horrible. If it's true, my grandson's been missing all these years, and no one even knew to look. Did we accidentally abandon him to death or worse?"

Karen listened as all the troubled thoughts poured from Marilyn. The shame she felt and her mixed feelings about Dwight's questions. Karen's own eyes grew wet as the story unfolded.

"I feel like I've gone through a wringer," said Marilyn when they finally left the office, "but I needed that."

Karen pulled her into a hug. "We all need someone to listen. Anytime you want, call. And if anyone can find your grandson, Pete can, and he won't give up."

CHAPTER THIRTEEN

District Commander George Isaacson of the Denver Police Southwood Precinct sat a bit straighter behind his desk. He took great satisfaction that his high-powered visitor, Wit Wysocki, a multi-millionaire and political promoter, had agreed to meet with him on such short notice. Another rung on the ladder Isaacson was climbing.

Isaacson had been disappointed recently by the poor showing of the police-backed candidate running for city council. He hoped by starting on November fifteenth their candidate for next year, Dale Brown, would win. If he could get Wysocki behind him, surely Brown was as good as elected, and it never hurt to have a well-placed politician beholden to you.

Wysocki uncapped a wooden pen and opened his notebook. "It's essential that your candidate be supported by a wide base in Denver if he is to win."

"Others who might run for that council seat won't be nearly as tough on crime as our Brown is," said Isaacson. "Certainly, you can understand why we support him. Brown will make Denver much safer."

"You have said two very important things." Wysocki smiled, making his face even more handsome.

"I did?" Not that Isaacson cared much about his appearance, but sometimes he was conscious of his own narrow, plain face petering out with a receding chin. He could have used some of that rugged, outdoor look.

Wysocki laughed. "Tough on crime, and safer. Those are, in our business, buzzwords. Politics is all about marketing. We give the candidate the right code words to say. We make sure he's seen with the right people. For example, if we can convince Pastor Powers to endorse Brown, you'll win the evangelical vote. We are successful because we find out what the political base wants to hear and package our man to play to it."

"That's how it works?"

"I'll tell you an inside secret. You get a candidate to use the right labels—like family values, tough on crime, safe streets, job creators, lower taxes—and you'll have a happy base that will come out in droves to support him. Then you make sure the candidate labels his opponents with a different set of buzzwords. Big government, activist, liberal, socialist. Doesn't matter if any of it is true or not. You want to stoke the fears that all people have deep down. Fears of what will happen if the other guy wins. It's us versus them. *They* are different. *They* will take over. *They* will take jobs, money, rights that should be *yours*. And if you don't act now, *they* will be in control."

"That's impressive."

"Voters don't think. Push the right buttons and they react emotionally. When the candidate is elected, he can do as he likes, just as long as he keeps in mind that reelection comes around again quickly."

"I'm a little confused. I understand that you sometimes back liberal candidates."

"One politician is much like another. We just use a different set of buzzwords and labels if we're backing another party's candidate. Both sides play the same game. Hiring our firm will be your best move." He handed Isaacson a glossy folder of information. "We produce winners."

"Our group is meeting with Brown tonight. We'll look this over and get back to you."

Wysocki rose and shook his hand.

The intercom on Isaacson's desk buzzed. "Mr. Hayle is here to see you, sir."

"Please send him in." Isaacson laid the folder on his desk. "Can we call you tomorrow?"

"That will be fine. I'm sure you'll make the right decision." Wysocki turned to leave.

At that moment Hayle came through the door almost colliding with the other man. Hayle's face went pale before he ducked his head.

When the door closed behind Wysocki, Hayle hissed in a breath. "What the hell was he doing here?"

"We're looking for his support for Brown, our council candidate. What's the matter with you?"

"He startled me. I told you about that long-ago business Gordon and I did with him."

"That was ages ago. He would never recognize you."

Hayle seemed to regain his composure as he unzipped his briefcase. He took out a thick, plain envelope and handed it to Isaacson. "Here's your cut."

"Thanks." Isaacson looked into the envelope and thumbed the bills before putting it in his pocket. "Have you heard anything from your sister about Schultz's trip here?"

"No. He's coming to some seminar plus looking into that kidnapping. Their plans were probably made in the chief's office, and she has no papers to see or file."

"Our chief called me. Wanted me to arrange for Cannon to meet with Schultz tomorrow."

"Cannon? Mr. Brown-noser? Can you bug the room?"

Isaacson grinned. "Already done."

CHAPTER FOURTEEN

Later that evening, Anton Bjornson watched the flames from blazing piñon twigs lick at the bigger logs in his kiva fireplace as his family and Sam's family gathered after dinner. His daughter, Krista, opened the sliding glass door for the dogs, before sitting with Leyla at the counter where their painting materials were spread out.

"Brrr," said Sam. "That wind is freezing."

"Anyone want more wine?" Anton made the rounds before sitting next to Skyla.

Dom sipped his wine. "Should we talk about our St. Nick plans? I checked with everyone, and they're fine with celebrating it on Sunday, the fourth, rather than the sixth."

"It'll be hard to beat last year." Sam grinned at Farah. "Ginger cookies, for sure. I'll always associate the smell of ginger with one of the best days of my life."

"I'm sorry I missed it," said Skyla.

Leyla looked up from her drawing. "I loved the *Smørrebrød*— open-faced sandwiches. We had foods from all the nationalities represented in the Sleuths."

"What will be special this year?" asked Anton. "Should we look at other St. Nick traditions?"

"In Holland they put presents in the shoes," said Skyla. "But from what I've heard, your emphasis isn't individual gifts."

Dom squeezed Karen's hand. "You have something to say."

She looked fondly at him. "I'm still reeling from the presidential election. I've been looking for how we can move forward in a positive way—to find our light on a hill."

Sam exchanged a look with Farah and interlaced his fingers with hers. "You know that day's results were a blow to us. But I don't know if I want politics brought into our celebration."

"Not politics per se, Sam," said Karen, "but attitude, a way of looking at it."

"More of what would have pleased St. Nicholas?" asked Dom.

"Yes. Look at who all will be here. We have power. We can speak. We can affect the people we deal with daily by example. I don't like what I see happening in this country. What will make people respond with the best of themselves, rather than reacting with self-interest and fear? Whatever happened to tolerance and the Golden Rule?"

"Wow, Mom," said Anton. "This really has you going."

"You're darn right."

Farah spoke up. "I find it alarming. I feel like they are watching me, waiting for an excuse to send me back."

"You sound worried," said Skyla. "Do you feel like your future citizenship is threatened?"

"Yes," said Farah. "People twist what you say and turn it against you."

"That's just wrong!" Karen sat up straighter. "Is this what we've come to?"

"*Uff da*. It's a celebration. Keep it in perspective," said Anton, wishing she'd get off her soapbox.

"It's more than that," said Karen. "It's an opportunity."

"Mom—"

"It can be both," said Dom. "A fun time, enjoying our friendship. Affirming that Farah and Leyla have found a place to belong. Celebrating our differences while coming together to accomplish a common task. And I see opportunities, too. Hoot and his family need our friendship. Pete and Sam, and Farah, too, for that matter, need this time to enjoy friends, away from the stress of their work."

Sam nodded. "You got that right. I remember thinking last year— Pete and Diego. Trading puns and working together. It hadn't been that long since their relationship was police officer and suspect."

Karen sat back with a smile. "I thought that might work."

"That was sneaky," said Anton.

Dom chuckled. "My heart, you see? Your light on a hill happens wherever you are."

Krista seemed to follow the conversation closely from the counter, her head swiveling back and forth between the speakers as if she were following a ping-pong game. "Sam, what about what you told us when you were helping that boy in my classroom after he bullied Leyla? Telling our stories, listening to each other?"

"Good question, Krista," he responded. "You can make a difference one person at a time."

"Our teacher in school talked about random acts of kindness," said Leyla.

"Would that work?" asked Krista.

"How could it not?" said Dom. "Especially if we make it a lifestyle, not just one act and you're done for the week."

Sam's brow furrowed in thought. "Listening to each other's stories and trying to understand someone by looking at it from a walk in their shoes was the whole point with that bully."

"We should be able to compromise or be respectful, when we don't agree with someone," said Karen. "Work together on the things we do agree on. Acts of kindness is a wonderful idea. It's contagious, too. People pass it on."

"How about," said Dom, "putting the random acts of kindness before the Circle Sleuths as a challenge? We could make sure everyone knows about it before our St. Nick gathering, so they can be thinking."

"I love it," said Karen. "Thank you, Leyla, Krista."

The girls beamed at her.

CHAPTER FIFTEEN

Pete looked away from the snow-covered mountain panorama below them and settled back into his seat, coffee in hand.

"Pete, what are your hopes for this trip?" Sam handed his coffee cup to the flight attendant and put his tray in its upright position.

Pete sipped. "It's important to establish that Ross was still in Gordon's custody after Winona died. It negates any possibility Gordon needed a ringer because she'd taken Ross away somewhere."

"What else?"

"Marilyn was told Ross was cared for by another family after his mother died. Can that be corroborated?"

Sam pushed the button to recline his seat a bit. "What's the plan?"

Pete swirled his remaining coffee. "The school district is expecting us. We've located his second-grade teacher. She's recently retired."

"I'm impressed you found her. It'd be remarkable if she remembers one particular kid from that long ago."

"First we'll go to the Southwood precinct to view files I requested last week." He frowned. "It's odd. We both know requests from outside police agencies happen all the time, but I felt a distinct lack of cooperation. It was like they were stonewalling me."

"Or too lazy to dig back that far. What else?"

"We meet Oliver's friend, Cannon." Pete grinned. "On Monday Grover paved the way for us to deliver that second tooth of Gordon's to the Denver crime lab."

The flight attendant interrupted with the obligatory preparation-for-landing instructions. Pete handed off his coffee cup and adjusted his seat. "Also, on Thursday before our seminar starts, I've set up a meeting at the old airport where Gordon kept his plane. I lucked out in finding a group of old codgers—plane enthusiasts and retired pilots—who hang around there. Groups like that have good memories—especially for any kind of unusual plane."

♦ ❖ ♦

Denver was downright chilly. Pete zipped up his jacket and looked toward the west as they waited for their rental car. Rather than the clear sunlit mountains he'd been hoping to see, there was only haze. He took a deep breath, coughed at the slight jet-fuel smell that hung over the airport, and longed for the piñon-scented Santa Fe air.

At the Southwood precinct, he and Sam waited in the lobby after giving their information to the officer at the window. Tired of sitting, Pete walked around, glancing at the forms available for the public and the notices posted on the bulletin board. He checked his watch. So much for having an appointment, but he knew how chaotic an officer's day could be. Finally, a thin volunteer with mascara-caked eyelashes escorted them into the commander's office. She waited inside near the door.

Commander Isaacson gave the impression of height, partly from his ramrod-stiff spine. Closely set eyes peered out from behind glasses in a face devoid of warmth.

"What brings you to Denver, Schultz?" asked Isaacson.

"Seminar and a new lead in one of my long-time cases. We have other appointments as well."

His intercom buzzed. Isaacson picked up his phone. "Sure. Send him in."

The door opened and a balding man with a burly build walked in, wearing a security guard uniform complete with a sidearm.

The commander shook the man's hand before turning back to Pete. "Curtis Hayle, owner of Curtail Security and Investigation. Hayle, meet Lieutenant Schultz and Sergeant Martinez from the Santa Fe PD. They're here investigating new leads on a cold case."

"What kind of case, Lieutenant?" asked Hayle.

"A kidnapping in 1991. We're checking a link to Denver."

"That's not a cold case; it's frozen solid." Hayle chuckled at his own wit.

"I'm surprised you haven't got a flunky that could research that for you," said Isaacson. "Of course, Santa Fe is pretty puny compared to Denver."

Pete raised an eyebrow. No solidarity among men in blue here.

Isaacson scowled. "I'm sure you gentlemen want to get on your way." The commander nodded to the volunteer. "Take them to Records first to view the files they requested from the central department. Then they're meeting with Cannon in Room 356."

"This is Records," said the volunteer, after leading them through several halls. She fumbled with her ID at a door control.

Pete and Sam sat at a desk in the reception area to go through the requested files. Pete was disappointed to see that there was not one on Gordon, but Winona's gave him useful information. It included a summary sheet of her autopsy. She had died November 3, 1990. Pete noticed that the cause of death was listed as an overdose and the manner of death was noted as 'undetermined.' To him that meant that the coroner had been unable to discern intent. It could have been homicide, suicide, or accidental. He wrote down the address where she'd lived.

The volunteer leaned over his shoulder as he perused the file. Pete straightened quickly in his chair, crashing into her and making her step back.

"Sorry," she said, her hand to her breast where he'd bumped her. "These cases interest me." She sidled away, the hot color receding in her face.

Pete turned to the files of the three juvenile John Does found in 1991 and after. One in particular captured his attention, looking more promising than the other two. In 1993, hikers had discovered scattered remains near a road in the mountains outside Denver. There was enough of the skeleton and clothing to tell them it was a young boy. Though the skull showed trauma, possibly from a bullet wound, the cause and manner of death were again listed as undetermined. He remembered hearing about this find way back, and they had checked Johnny's DNA against it at the time. The results had come back negative for Johnny.

"Poor little guy," said Sam.

"We'll request a copy of this one and Winona Stewart's," Pete said. "When I get home, I'll ask for the full autopsy reports."

Pete made the request of the officer at the counter and was told that they were backed up, but their copies should be ready by the afternoon. The volunteer escorted them to Room 356 before she disappeared.

◆ ❖ ◆

In his office, Isaacson watched the computer screen as Cannon entered Room 356 and introduced himself to the visitors before setting his notebook on the table.

Good, Isaacson thought. Perfect camera angles. Clear sound. He had set up the room with only three chairs around the small conference table.

Isaacson angled the monitor so Hayle could also see and settled back in his chair. Now maybe they'd find out what the lieutenant was up to.

Before the men in 356 sat down, Schultz spoke up. "Cannon, is there somewhere nearby to snag a bite to eat and get some coffee?"

Martinez smiled. "Those mini pretzels on the plane don't keep body and soul together."

Cannon gathered his things again. "I know just the place. Follow me."

The computer screen showed the door shutting quietly and an empty room.

With an expletive, Isaacson stood, sending his chair rolling back to crash against the credenza. At the sound of Hayle's laughter, he rounded on him. "You won't think it's so funny if they're on to our scheme."

Laughter fled Hayle's face as he rose to face him. "I don't work here. How could I have known that police moonlighting as my guards were also being paid by the city for special detail?"

"And your clients charged top dollar." Isaacson glared at Hayle. Some days he hated him, wished the slob realized how ridiculous he looked, buttons straining over his growing beer belly. "If I go down, you go down."

"Then we'd better hope my trailing is better than your bugging."

Pete enjoyed the easy-going Cannon. He was about Pete's own age, and like Sam, had the build of a runner. His agreeable nature and the laugh lines around his eyes spoke volumes as to why Oliver and their chief talked highly of him.

Over lunch, at the soup and salad chain he'd brought them to, Pete talked about the files with Cannon. "What can you tell me about the area the Stewarts lived in?"

Cannon stroked his neatly trimmed, gray beard and glanced at the address. "That's a dead end. All those houses have been torn down and those little streets are gone. That whole area is a huge business complex now."

"Could the Hayle we met this morning be the same as the officer who responded to the Winona Stewart call in '90?"

"Easily. Wonder why he was here."

"An S. Cannon was listed as the arresting officer on at least one of those DUI calls. That you?"

"Yes, but that's way too long ago to remember. Sorry."

"It was worth asking."

"I do remember being glad when Hayle quit."

After they finished lunch, Cannon drove them to the crime lab. Since they were expected, the details were handled quickly, and Pete was told he could expect the results before the end of November.

When Cannon brought them back to Southwood to retrieve their car, Pete turned and looked up at the building. A man stood at a second-story window. As Pete watched, he turned the blinds.

"The corner window on the second floor. Whose office is that?"

"Commander Isaacson's," said Cannon. "Why?"

"Either he was having blind trouble or didn't want to be seen."

"Schultz, you're paranoid. Your sixth sense is working overtime. I'd better get back. Give my best to Oliver and Grover."

They got into their rental car, and as Sam drove away, Pete noticed in the side mirror a small black sedan turn and follow them. His sixth sense had saved his butt more than once. It was working just fine.

CHAPTER SIXTEEN

In the school district office, Pete and Sam were met with efficiency and courtesy. Pete checked Ross's file, noting the date of his last attendance—the day before the beginning of the 1990 Christmas vacation. He nodded in satisfaction—one question answered. The last notes on the file indicated that the father had notified the school that the child was going to be living with his grandparents out of state. The request for records from Kalispell, Montana, came in the fall of 1991.

Pete handed the file back to the clerk. Then they left for their appointment with the teacher.

As he got in the car, Pete glanced down the street to the left. A small black sedan was parked about fifty yards away.

The teacher's one-story home sat back on a wide expanse of snow-covered lawn in a well-kept residential area. Lois Dillsburg met Pete and Sam at the door and welcomed them into a light, airy home. She moved briskly, bypassing the living room with cozy-looking chairs and an area with bookcases and two desks with laptops. Knickknacks of owls and apples were grouped on shelves. She motioned them to a dining table. Several photos peeked out of a file, labeled 1990-91.

Pete spotted three coffee mugs next to a plate of small, rounded cookies. The tantalizing scent of their baking still hung in the air.

"Would you like some coffee?" she asked.

Pete's gaze met friendly brown eyes in a face framed with salt-and-pepper hair in a no-fuss style. He was certain that she hadn't missed much in her classroom. She reminded him of one of his own long-ago teachers who'd kept his lively curiosity challenged. "That would be appreciated," said Pete. "Have you been baking *Pfefferneusse*?"

"Pepper what?" asked Sam.

Lois laughed. "German spice cookies." She brought the pot over and filled their mugs before she sat. "I thought with a name like Schultz, you might enjoy them. My maiden name was Bergermeister. This is my family's recipe."

Lois smiled broadly as Pete bit into his cookie and relished the spicy flavor.

"You said you were interested in a former student of mine, Ross Stewart? I had to dig deep into the past for him. Glad you knew the year. I have kind of a haphazard journal for every year and kept notes for each student, mostly funny and touching stories. I took photos of some of the special projects and parties. If I can, I like to keep track of my students and see what kind of adults they turn into. If I ever want to write a memoir, this would back up my memory."

She pulled out several photos from the file folder. "I'm sure Ross is in some of these. I wrote their names on the back."

Pete wiped his fingers on a napkin and picked up a photo of several little boys posing around a batch of stretched-out slime. "This was an interesting science project."

"That was about Halloween time. Kids love that stuff."

Pete pointed to a skinny boy with red hair and a Teenage Mutant Ninja Turtle T-shirt. "If I'm not mistaken, that would be Ross." He turned the picture over. In neat printing, there among the names was Ross Stewart.

"Did you ever meet his parents?" he asked.

"I don't remember meeting the mother, but I do remember her death in the fall—just a few days after that Halloween party. A hard thing, to lose your mother when you're only seven. I don't recall the father, either."

Pete browsed through more of the photos and passed them on to Sam.

"The child stands out more, of course. I went out of my way to give him more attention because of his mother. Some children tug on your heartstrings. Some you remember because they are so precious. Another year, I had one little girl, a first grader. The class was taking one of those standardized achievement tests—the math part. I saw her counting on her fingers, clearly frustrated that she didn't have enough. So, she quietly took off her shoes and finished her figuring on her toes. It was all I could do not to laugh."

Sam chuckled. "A good problem-solver. I'm sure she did well in life."

"She became one of Denver's first female CEOs."

"I understand," Pete said, "that Ross was staying with another family for a while after his mother died."

"If that was true, I don't remember. There's nothing noted, but my journal was mostly anecdotal." She pulled another photo from the stack. "Here he is at our party just before Christmas."

Pete studied the photo. Something about this shot, a side view, puzzled him, but he couldn't think what it was. "How did Ross do in school? How about his writing? Art work?"

"Nothing stands out." Lois shook her head. "It's such a long time ago. So many children."

"You have been helpful. May I take photos of the pictures you showed me?"

"Certainly." She watched as he arranged them and snapped photos with his phone. "I'm curious. Why are you looking for him?"

Pete motioned to Sam.

"The family has lost track of him," said Sam. "There's an inheritance issue."

She seemed to accept that answer. Then Pete grinned as she came forward with two small containers of *Pfefferneusse* to take with them.

◆ ❖ ◆

82

"Nicely put answer to her question, Sam," said Pete as they got back in their car. "Have you noticed our tail?"

"I have. Not very clever."

"I'd say obvious. Dash-cam. Tinted side and rear windows. Doesn't strike me as a police vehicle, more like a PI. No tax-exempt plates or recessed flashers."

"Following two cops? Man, do they think we're dumb?"

"They have to know we'll spot them. What I want to know is why."

The sun was low in the sky as they returned to the station to pick up the copies they'd been promised. They weren't ready yet; the files were still sitting on the counter. A different man was at the desk.

"I'll wait," Pete told the officer. He picked a promotional flier for new recruits from a rack and idly flipped through it before putting it back. He drummed his fingers on the counter. "How long do you think it might be?"

"It'll be a while. This ain't Mayberry, you know. We're busy here."

"I can see that. Long lines." Pete waved his hand at the emptiness. The man shrugged and sat down. "Files here." Pete tapped the folders on the counter. "Copy machine there." He pointed at the nearby copier. "I'm sure you can fit it into your busy schedule."

The officer surveyed him indifferently and pulled out a report to study. Another officer came in and handed him a slip of paper. He pulled a file, made copies, and gave them to the woman who left.

Pete glanced at the clock and then at Sam before looking back at the bored officer. "I see your name is Saybeck, badge number 974. I hate to keep bothering you, but if I have to leave without these copies, my chief will want to know why. Good man. Leroy Grover. We just hired him. From Denver. Good friends with your chief. He'll certainly get a laugh and give his buddy a hard time about why it took one of his subordinates so long to fulfill such a simple request. From a lieutenant. A lieutenant who is good friends with

George Warstein. We go way back. That would be the same George who is the head of your oversight board."

The officer bristled. He picked up the files, made the copies, and slammed them down in front of Pete.

"Thank you. You are so kind."

"How the hell do you know Warstein?" asked Sam as they closed the door behind them.

"I don't. Never laid eyes on him. Saw his name in the recruitment flier."

Sam let out a bark of laughter. "Man, you're good."

Chapter Seventeen

The next morning as they left the motel and went out to their car, Pete checked around. No little black sedan roused his suspicions. He put on latex gloves, took a signaling mirror from his wallet, knelt by the car, and methodically checked the underside.

Sam stood by the driver's side, frowning at him. "What are you doing?"

"Our tail didn't show up. I wondered why." He slipped the mirror into his pocket, reached both hands under and tugged, rocking back on his heels, and clutching his prize, a GPS tracker with a strong magnet. "Interesting—not your typical over-the-counter tracking device. These're available on police equipment sites. Damned expensive. Shiny, no road dirt. Somebody was busy in the night."

"What are you going to do with it?"

Pete opened the cover and removed the battery. "I might have forensics at home see what they can learn from it. I'll check with the car rental company to make sure it's not theirs."

He pulled a plastic bag from his suitcase and zipped the tracker into it. The battery he bagged separately, then flashed a grin at Sam. "They'll wonder why it's not functioning properly."

They headed to a private airport on the edge of the city. In the small cafe, they found the group of retirees he'd made arrangements to meet. They were swapping insults and tales with the ease of longtime friends.

"I'm Lieutenant Pete Schultz from the Santa Fe PD. This is Sam Martinez. I'm looking for Floyd."

"Welcome," said one with thick white hair. "I'm Floyd. This here's Paul." He motioned to a fellow wearing glasses, whose nose was his most striking feature. "This grumpy-looking guy here is Stanley. This young whippersnapper is Glenn. I don't know why we put up with him. I don't think he's old enough to vote yet."

Glenn's eyes twinkled, and he laughed. "I'm still spry enough to fetch and carry canes and walkers for you sorry bunch of geezers, that's why."

"I'm working on a cold case that happened twenty-five years ago," said Pete as they sat down. "The trail leads to this airport."

"From Santa Fe?" asked Paul.

"Yes. Anybody here mind if I record this conversation?"

The four men shook their heads. "When you talked to me on the phone, you mentioned a pilot who flew a de Havilland Beaver," said Floyd. "Awesome little plane. They don't make them like that anymore."

"Wish they did. Good little workhorse," said Stanley.

"Do you remember one that was based here about twenty-five years ago?" asked Pete.

"I remember," said Glenn. "Belonged to that cranky guy."

"Came to a bad end. He crashed that sweet little plane," said Paul.

"That was Gordon," said Stanley. "He was a cocky pilot. Took chances."

Glenn stirred his coffee. "Aw, you say that just because you're the world's worst worrier. You were always double-checking stuff."

"My point, exactly," said Stanley. "I'm still here. He ain't."

Paul rubbed his nose. "Too careful to die."

"Paul, I've seen you do some fool stunts in your day," said Floyd. "Crop-dusters are crazy. Zinging around fields and playing do-si-do with the powerlines. God knows how you've lived this long."

Glenn took a sip. "Focus. That's what you have to do. Can't let your mind wander."

Stanley waved the toast in his hand. "Damn fool thing Gordon did—landing on water and not remembering to put his landing gear up. Lack of focus killed him. What was your question again?"

Pete settled back in his chair and gazed at the faces around him. "I wanted to know about Gordon and his son, too, if you remember him."

"Yeah, little red-headed guy like Gordon." Stanley chewed his toast thoughtfully. "Don't remember the kid well, but I did see him and Gordon the day before their plane crashed. That's the only reason I remember. I always wondered what happened to him. Heard he survived, that's all."

Pete asked, "What do you remember about that day?"

"Gordon must have come in late the night before," commented Stanley. "Don't see much activity here after dark. Most of us would rather fly in the daylight. His plane wasn't here when I left the night before, but it was in the morning. I remember because I was waiting for a charter group. They were going to Estes Park. Never did show."

"Did you bill them for it?" asked Floyd.

"Pardon? Speak up if you want answers."

"Stanley, listen up." Floyd raised his voice and spoke slowly. "Did you get paid? Why the hell aren't you wearing your hearing aids?"

Stanley's grumpy look turned grumpier. "I hate those damn things. Don't remember if I got paid. They sure as hell never got their deposit back. Some people got no consideration." He looked at Pete. "Gordon kept his plane next to mine. He was in a mood that day. He had ornery down even better than me, if you can believe it. In a big hurry. Hustled that kid on board. Kid was all upset. Gordon almost threw him up the plane steps. I asked Gordon what his problem was. He said the kid was going to go live with his grandparents and didn't want to. Then he yelled at me to mind my own damned business. Last time I saw him."

Ach du lieber. Had Stanley seen Johnny? "Just the two of them on the plane?"

87

"Don't remember anyone else."

"What kind of business was Gordon in?" asked Pete.

"Charters, from what I remember. Hunting trips. Flew all over the west. Mexico, Canada, Alaska. They'd go flying off to some wild place and the next thing you know they'd be showing up with some trophy head. Actually, I still have one of his hanging in my garage. My wife wouldn't let it in the house."

Pete nodded. This corroborated what Marilyn had said about Gordon's business.

"Those things gave me a few starts," said Paul. "I'd be working on my plane and he'd come hauling the head of some dead beast with antlers out of his plane."

"Who'd he hang around with?" asked Pete. "Did you know any of Gordon's friends?"

"Being friendly wasn't his thing," said Glenn.

"Gawd, do you remember that time you took that trophy head and put it in the loo?" Stanley asked.

All four of the men broke out in laughter.

"That I'll never forget. Almost split a gut laughing. Paul here rigged it so you come in the john and here's that thing looking at you over the stall. He even tied a scarf around its head. Used hair from an old wig to make curls dangling down by its ears."

"He was livid," said Stanley. "Gad, that was funny. Him and his cop friend went to the airport manager. He reamed us out, but it was worth it."

Pete's antennae focused on Stanley's words. "Cop friend?"

"Yeah, he hung around with this cop, the kind who likes to throw his weight around. Don't remember his name or anything."

"Wasn't too long after that that Gordon bought it," said Paul, sobering.

"I still have that head," said Stanley. "When I heard Gordon died, I contacted his father. Asked him what to do with Gordon's tools and stuff. He said to keep what I could use and give away the rest. Weren't nothing personal there."

Pete passed around his notebook for them to put their name and contact information. He handed each a card and said to call if they thought of anything else. He looked at his watch. They would have plenty of time to check into the hotel where the seminar was held before the opening session.

The speaker for this two-part seminar on Interview and Interrogations was one he'd never met, but had heard good things about. Psychology, reading body language, and planning productive approaches to use with each witness or suspect were key as they built their cases. He was ready to have at it.

After the close of the seminar, Pete settled back and watched Sam negotiate the Friday evening traffic to the airport. He found himself facing a barrage of questions of how the material they'd received that day fit in with Pete's experience in Santa Fe.

"I'm enjoying this," Sam said. "I have a lot to thank you for. A year ago, when I was waffling about staying on the force, what you said really made a difference."

Pete savored the comment. "Our department needed you, Sam."

When they turned in the rental car, Pete remembered the GPS tracker.

He held up the gadget, encased in its plastic bag, for the man at the desk to see. "I found this on our car. Do you ever track your customer's vehicles?"

"Never with a magnetic one, sir. Some may have hard-wired trackers built in that let the company retrieve a car by location."

"Thank you," said Pete, tucking it into his suitcase.

"Well done," said Sam. "Let's head for home."

CHAPTER EIGHTEEN

"Look out, kiddo." Hoot stopped short to avoid crashing into Bonnie. She'd halted abruptly as she ran into the Bjornsons' home on Thanksgiving. Her mouth dropped open at the sight of a lifelike reindeer. Its back was level with Hoot's waist, and its antlers soared higher than his shoulders. It stood on a base covered with cotton snow.

"This is Clyde," said Anton. "He just arrived to stay with us. After Valentine's Day, he'll go back to his own country."

"What country is that?" asked Melody.

"Storage. It's in the far north."

"I might have guessed," said Hoot, grinning at the twinkle in Anton's eyes.

Bonnie reached up to pat the soft gray-brown fur. "Is he real? Does he fly?"

"Clyde can't fly. He's made by a toy company."

"You can sit on him and pretend," said Krista.

"Can I ride him, too?" asked Matti as his mom took the kids' jackets.

"If it's okay with your folks," said Anton.

Hoot nodded, and Anton picked up Bonnie. She straddled the furry reindeer and reached forward to grasp his antlers. She giggled as her eyes followed the antlers to their tips above her head. Anton settled Matti behind his sister.

Hoot set down the bag he held and snapped several pictures on his phone, as did Melody and Anton.

Karen came forward and gave Marilyn a big hug. "Welcome to our home."

She took their coats. "If you want to come early on St. Nicholas and bring Christmas clothes for the kids, you can get some good shots with Clyde for your Christmas cards. Come on into the family room."

"What's in the bag, Hoot?" asked Krista.

"I brought along the puzzle box. I figured we might try to open it if we have time before the tryptophan sets in." He picked it up and showed it to her.

"Fantastic," said Anton. "I've been watching some puzzle-box videos online."

"What's tryptophan?" asked Krista.

"It's a natural chemical in turkey that makes us sleepy," replied Anton. "Some say it's why we feel like having an after-Thanksgiving-dinner snooze."

"Anton told us about this box," said Karen, taking it from Krista. "Oh, it's heavier than I thought. Is there something in it?"

Hoot grinned. "Can't tell you yet." He looked over to the kitchen and waved at Maria. Diego nodded at them, his hands busy with potholders and the turkey fresh out of the oven.

Warmth and the aromas of good food surrounded them. Conversation flowed. Hoot winked at Melody. It was turning out to be a great day.

◆ ❖ ◆

Anton eyed the puzzle box with anticipation as he ate the last morsel of pumpkin pie on his plate. Their numbers were complete now, as Dom had arrived from Thanksgiving dinner at his daughter's home just in time for pie and coffee.

Anton picked up the box. "How long do you suppose it'll take us?"

Hoot laughed. "I must have fiddled with it for hours already. You go first."

Anton manipulated the lid back and forth between its sides. "The only places with give are the lid and the bottom."

"And that crazy little metal pin on the end, which doesn't seem to connect to anything," said Hoot. "I don't see how that works."

"Let's try a logical approach. Stand it on end and move the lid back and forth." Anton's actions followed each direction. "Other end. Upside down. Side. Other side."

"Okay, that's not working," said Hoot.

Diego grinned. "Let me know if you want a crowbar."

Anton set the box on his lap. "It has to have something to do with the movement here in the lid." Twitch suddenly jumped up and plopped down beside him on the couch, knocking his hand. "*Uff da,* I didn't invite you— Hold on. Look! This end is farther open now. What happened?"

Twitch looked at him and licked his hand.

Hoot took the box and peered closely through the widened opening. "There's a cut-out in the lid. Hard to see. Something's in it." He wiggled the cover. "Oops. Now it's back where it started."

Dom leaned back, laughing. "Twitch, tell us what you did."

"How were you holding it?" asked Hoot, handing it back to Anton.

"I was wiggling the cover back and forth like this." Anton demonstrated. "He knocked against me and it tilted." He tilted it and kept on wiggling. "That's it! It opened a little again."

"Rotate it in the opposite direction," said Hoot. "Keep on wiggling it. I think I saw a video of a similar box."

Anton slowly followed his direction. At a certain point, he was able to slide the cover almost all the way off, revealing an empty compartment inside. About an inch from the box's edge, the cover stopped sliding. "Voilà!"

They looked inside. The compartment had a strange routed-out design on its floor.

"What did that little pin do?" asked Diego.

"Not a damn thing that made any difference," said Dom. "Maybe its only function was to mystify you."

"That's mean," Diego said.

"I thought it would be deeper," said Hoot. "The bottom is only about a third of the way down. And there are three funny holes lined up in the floor of this compartment. The end ones have curved tracks like they might allow something to turn." He positioned it to allow the light to hit the holes.

"I'd say you are only partway there," said Dom. "More puzzles to solve before it's all the way open."

"Let me see that design," said Karen. "Is it a rune symbol?"

Anton traced it with a long finger. "Something that fit in this depression, would fit in the holes. The distances match."

"I see where you're going," said Hoot. "What if it was a key? Grandma, did you find anything in the boxes of stuff that looked like it might be a gizmo shaped like this?"

Marilyn took it. "It's an odd shape. I don't remember throwing anything like that away."

Melody chuckled. "That's not one of your failings, throwing things away."

"My dear, you know me well. I still have more boxes to go through. Can you take a paper and trace that shape to remind me?"

Matti crowded next to his mother. "Can I see?"

Melody tilted the box for him. "Have you ever seen a shape like that?"

"Huh-uh," he said. "I'd remember. Looks like an M. Stands for Matti." He grinned triumphantly.

Anton traced the design for Marilyn and passed the box to Dom.

"What happens if Marilyn isn't able to find the key?" asked Dom.

"Hmmm." Anton took the box back and studied it. "Maybe I can recreate that shape. Then I can make a key on my 3-D printer."

"Is that possible?" asked Hoot.

"Quite often I make prototype parts for our drones that way when we're in the R and D stage of design for our business."

"If it involves a gadget, Anton can do it," said Skyla.

"Wow," said Hoot. "We're partway in. Maybe next time we'll see if there's anything inside."

"It's going to be a while until I can concentrate on it." Anton took Skyla's hand and gifted it with a kiss. "Only little things like the St. Nicholas celebration, our wedding, and Christmas to get in the way."

Skyla smiled at Anton. "Our wedding—only three weeks left."

"After the holidays is okay for the box," said Hoot. "I've never seen a 3-D printer work. I'd like to."

"I'm glad you mentioned St. Nick," said Dom. "Leyla had an idea for our celebration beyond making cookies."

"The cookies were great," said Anton. "Everybody—all ages—worked together."

"We're just adding another dimension," said Karen. "In keeping with the attitude of St. Nicholas."

Dom told them about the girls' random acts of kindness suggestion.

Hoot leaned forward. "Can we include our kids in that discussion?"

"Of course," said Karen. "It's their world, too, and we can learn a lot from them."

It almost made Hoot look forward to the St. Nick thing.

Almost.

CHAPTER NINETEEN

On the Saturday after Thanksgiving, Pete stopped by Lou and Cliff's home. He took three-month-old Dougie on his lap and soon had his grandson smiling and gurgling in response to his baby talk.

Finally, Cliff said, "You're stalling, Pete. You didn't come here just to play with Dougie. There's something on your mind."

Pete nodded. "I've been thinking about Hoot Stewart."

"Why does he resist finding out whether or not he's Johnny?" asked Cliff. "Wouldn't he remember?"

"The mind is a complicated thing," said Pete. "Think. Johnny was only six. There was the trauma and the terror of the kidnapping, then the plane crash that hospitalized him for three months. We have no proof he's Johnny, just suspicion. Give him time."

Cliff studied his father-in-law. "Okay . . . I guess. Bloody hell, can't we help him remember? I assume you won't stop investigating."

"You know I won't." Pete rubbed the back of his neck. "But we should back off. Keep St. Nicholas social and not confront him."

"I find myself drawn to Hoot," said Cliff. "Is it because I've searched so long, and I want my brother back? At the party, I almost wanted to grab him, shake him, and say 'Open your eyes.' When I cooled off, I thought maybe he's just a doppelganger. But—" Pain settled on his face.

Lou took Cliff's hand as he struggled with his next words.

"When I got old enough to realize what could happen to a kidnapped boy, it hurt to think of my brother being abused like that or killed. I wanted him to be safe. I want it to be over."

"We all do, son."

"Bloody hell, how can you be so calm? Can't you sneak some of his DNA and find out?"

"As much as I want to, that wouldn't solve the problem. He's not a criminal or suspect. He has rights, and without his permission, it's a non-starter. These are rules I can't break." He frowned slightly. "Cliff, I have a dilemma here. I want to keep you and your parents in the loop. Have you said anything to your mom or dad about him?"

"No. I thought about it, but I didn't want to raise their hopes and then have it fizzle out."

"Exactly." Pete sighed deeply. "But it's time to catch them up on the lead. I'd like you there when I talk with them. Now, if you have the time."

Cliff looked at his wife, who nodded. "Mom and Dad should be home. I'll call to make sure."

On their way up the walk, Pete glanced over at the park from which Johnny had been stolen, next door to the McCreaths. Twenty-five years hadn't brought many changes to this scene he remembered so well. Maybe it was so poignant for him because his own kids had been about the same ages as the McCreaths' kids.

In an hour or so the sun would set, and Pete knew the porch light would be on, reflecting Andrew's hope that the light would guide the way home for their elder son.

Cliff led the way inside, and they were greeted with curious faces. Andrew and Lynn set aside the student papers they were correcting and turned off the TV. They settled in the family room.

There was nothing Pete wanted more than to bring a happy ending to their desperate search. Over the years this couple had been strong for other families plunged into a search for a missing child. Lynn was wonderful at listening, at embracing a grieving stranger, and always seemed to extend hope. Andrew had taken his gifts of organization and had helped their support group, Families of Missing Children, working at the local and state level.

Pete accepted a cup of coffee from Lynn and took a deep breath. "The reason I'm here is to keep you informed. I don't want you to get your hopes up, but we have another lead."

Lynn let out a small cry and sat down abruptly next to her husband. He put one hand over hers. "How many times have I heard that?" she asked.

Pete studied Andrew's shuttered face and tense jaw muscles. He'd seen this same reaction many times. Andrew was protecting himself.

"We have met a young man," said Pete. "I don't know where it will take us."

"You mean he might still be alive?" asked Lynn. "It's gotten so that when I hear the word 'lead' I fear bones or a grave."

"Cliff met him at the Labor Day festival," said Pete.

"He certainly looked like he could be my brother," said Cliff, telling his parents about meeting the red-headed man.

After Cliff finished, Pete took up the tale, about his visit with the grandmother at the care center and her grandson. Then he told about the plane crash, the death of the pilot, and the injuries the boy suffered. Lynn drew in a sharp breath and leaned against Andrew.

"Understand," Pete continued, "that even if he does turn out to be Johnny, in all likelihood, he truly doesn't remember. The plane crash, resulting in a skull fracture and other injuries, appears to have blocked any memory of his life before the accident. He says he's thirty-three. But the timing works. This boy appeared in his grandparents' lives two days after Johnny was taken. I've seen the resemblance. This young man is married and has two children. The oldest, a boy of seven, looks remarkably like Johnny did when he disappeared. That could all be coincidence. The man still suffers headaches and physical distress when he tries to remember his life before the plane crash."

Andrew put his arm around his wife. "Is he willing to take a DNA test?"

"Cliff asked that, too, but not yet. In his mind, why should he? He knows who he is," said Pete. "I have two questions. They might seem off the wall and strange to you, but it might help put more pieces of the puzzle in place. Could I look through your old albums with Johnny's photos? And maybe make copies of a few?"

"Sure." Andrew fetched the albums from a bookcase.

As Pete flipped through an album, he asked, "I know Johnny was at the end of his kindergarten year when he was taken. Do you remember if he had learned to read at all?"

"Johnny had always been eager to read," said Lynn. "He devoured library books. I was teaching second grade at the time. He used to look at my readers and do some of the seatwork. I even caught him and Cliff playing school. He was teaching Cliff how to read."

Cliff chuckled. "Is that why I was bored in my reading group?"

"Thank you, Lynn." Pete's theory had just gained credibility—how young Johnny was able to cope even though he'd been forced to skip two years of school.

It didn't take him long to find what he was looking for. Johnny's hairline did have a widow's peak. Then he spotted the photo. A side view of Johnny—showing his ear with a free lobe—very unlike the photo he had on his phone from Ross's teacher with what he would call an attached lobe. Mounting evidence that Hoot was not Ross. He kept on flipping through the pages, reluctant to let his audience know what he was looking for. When he finished, he asked if he could make copies of four shots.

Lynn turned to Cliff and spoke with hurt evident in her voice. "This man you met. Why didn't you say something to us?"

"Mom, for years and years, every time I've seen a red-headed, blue-eyed guy that looked to be the right age, I would ask his name and tell the story. I thought this was just like all those times. There was no point in telling you. He told me his name, and I thought that was the end of it."

"What is his name?" asked Andrew.

Pete intervened. "I'd like to do more investigating before we share that. I ask that you be patient a little longer." He caught Cliff's eyes. Cliff nodded in agreement.

"I've seen a lot over the years we've been working with Families of Missing Children," said Andrew. "I've learned how children are affected by trauma. Sometimes miracles and sometimes heartbreak." He touched Lynn's face and smiled into her eyes. "We're overdue for a miracle."

CHAPTER TWENTY

Pete turned a page of the *Santa Fe New Mexican* and took another sip of coffee. Newspapers were so skimpy on Mondays. He glanced at his watch. Plenty of time before he had to leave for work.

Akiko made a soft cry of distress. He looked over to where she was looking at Facebook.

"What's wrong?"

"Arlene Olson posted that her husband was killed when he was out riding on their ranch."

"Aw, no, not Cowboy," said Pete. "What happened?"

"He was shot."

"Shot? *Mein Gott*. Why? Who?"

"They don't know. His horse came home without him, and they went looking. No witnesses."

"Such an easygoing, likeable guy. Couldn't wait until his tour was over so he could get back to North Dakota and work with his dad on their ranch. He loved it. Never saw him off-duty without that Stetson of his. If he could have worn it with his uniform, he would have."

"He'd just been elected sheriff last month."

Pete shook his head. "We talked a few times during his campaign. I never heard the result. Glad he was elected. I suppose their Christmas letter would have told us. He really liked police work and was good at it. Damn. That hurts."

Surely some of his sources could give him more particulars on the investigation. He'd kept in touch with Cowboy when they got out of the service. He and Akiko had even gone to North Dakota for Cowboy's wedding. Even though Pete hadn't talked with him often, when they did, it was like they'd never been separated. Some friends were like that, you just picked up where you left off.

Damn. He'd miss him.

♦ ❖ ♦

Late that afternoon, Pete sat at the round table in his office, suspended between numbness and discouragement. He'd been so hopeful that the juvenile John Doe remains found in the mountains near Denver would be Ross. The timing, the age, and size of the child fit. But the letter from the Denver PD crime lab on the table in front of him said Gordon was excluded as the biological father. Denver would send Gordon's DNA sample on to NamUS to see if there was a match in their system.

The sun set, yet Pete made no move to the light switch, just sat in the gloom, only illuminated from the bullpen. No one was out there now. He sighed. Usually he could bounce back, but this, following on the heels of Cowboy's death . . . this little mite, unclaimed, bereft of love, lost and alone, cried out to him. How the hell could a child have ended up like that?

A soft knock on his open door brought him back from his thoughts. Sam came in and sat next to him. Seconds and minutes ticked away, marking the silence.

"Pete?"

"The child in the mountains. I got the results. It wasn't Ross." He cleared his throat. "It's such a struggle, Sam. It shouldn't be like this."

"No, it shouldn't."

"So much evil in the world. So much selfishness and cruelty. And idiocy. I get tired."

"Because of what we and others like us do, some lost souls will find their way home." Sam leaned forward in his chair. "I want to tell you something Jesús Morales told me when I was a teenager.

Some things we can change, some we can't—even with our best effort. He would say to visualize this child's soul, like a little glowing ball. Imagine holding it in your hands, surrounding it with love. Imagine the glow getting brighter, and holding it as high as you can, setting it free, and watching it float away, rising higher and higher until it joins the stars in the night. All the way to God. When you look up, see all the stars in the sky, those souls alight, then you know they're in God's hands. They have found their way home."

Pete raised his head. "All the myriad stars in the Milky Way."

Sam's eyes widened a bit as they met Pete's in the gloom of the darkened office. "You heard him, too. Those were his exact words."

Pete sniffed. "Jesús Morales was a cop with the soul of a poet. He was a mentor not just to you, Sam. He's one of the brightest stars up there, don't you think? *Mein Gott*. I needed to hear that again. A little hope that gives the strength to push on."

Sam stood, grasped Pete's shoulder briefly. "I'm sorry, Pete, about the results. Grieve while you need to. Then go home and hug your family. I'll see you tomorrow. We have a child to find." He left quietly.

Pete sat in the darkness until he heard the detective room door close behind Sam. Then he closed his eyes, cupped his hands loosely on the table, imagining a ball of light cuddled within. He wrapped it with love and hope until it had reached a piercing brilliance. In his mind he held it up and watched as the unclaimed soul of the boy from the mountains slowly ascended on its way to join the myriad stars.

In the deep darkness of that night, Akiko awakened gradually out of her dreams to a gentle stroking that brought a smile to her face in the warm cocoon of their bed. She moved against her husband, turning to him, tracing her own fingertips over his skin. Heat began to rise as their strokes became more deliberate. Slowly, slowly surging. Lips and tongues affirmed, encouraged, challenged. Her world became the gift of his touch, his heart so close to hers. Hotter than the sun, she flew through a burst of feeling, flowing, ebbing, landing in the quiet of afterglow. As their heartbeats slowed, his fingers rested over her breast. She guided his face to hers for a lamborous kiss.

They lay, dozing until the faint pre-dawn light crept into their room. Vaguely, she felt Pete's weight leave the bed and another sudden weight shift the mattress. A familiar touch tickled her cheek, and a wet tongue washed over her eyes.

"Fritzi, stop." The bed shifted again as Hoshi, her other Airedale, plopped down against her hip.

She opened her eyes to find Pete sliding into his robe, struggling to keep Beowulf from tugging on the belt. She chuckled as Beowulf pulled the tie loose and darted over the bed with it, his tail wagging furiously.

"Take your time. I'll let the dogs out and make the coffee. Off the bed, guys. Come." Pete leaned down to kiss her cheek and left, followed by three wide-awake Airedales.

Akiko adjusted the covers over her shoulder and lay still. This man—playful, sensitive, who carried the weight of his role to protect and serve—she'd long thought the community had him by day, but the nights were hers.

She'd purposefully structured their bedroom and bath to reflect a calm Japanese setting, and she loved Pete's whimsical contribution of a large, sculpted-marble polar bear, lying in what he called the terrier sprawl and overlooking their soaking tub. Even their children respected this haven of wife and husband. Here there was beauty and serenity. The world was shut out.

But now she wondered.

It wasn't that Akiko wanted the outside cares intruding on their sanctuary, but she didn't want to be excluded or protected from such an important part of his life. Thinking back to the wee hours of the night they'd talked about Johnny, she realized how rare and precious were the times when Pete really shared anything from the world of his work.

That night Akiko felt he'd respected her ideas. Much of his work was confidential; she'd no quarrel with that. But ideas, hopes, even glimpses into personalities of his coworkers—those he could share.

Maybe it was an oversight of hers, having no structure in place to encourage that.

She'd noticed a pattern. After she confronted him, for a while he would share more, but all too soon, he'd pull back. He hadn't even told her about his inquiries into Cowboy's death. She wondered what happened that he hadn't told her about, for it seemed his barriers were on the rise again. He'd been quieter than usual last night, and a bit down, though he didn't say anything. She supposed that could have been because of Cowboy.

It made this morning's loving even more welcome—that they were able to comfort and nourish each other. More special, affirming, and life-giving.

CHAPTER TWENTY-ONE

Hoot and his family arrived early for the St. Nicholas celebration to take Christmas photos with Clyde. "We're not the first," he said to Melody. "Sam's car is here already."

Inside, out of the chilly, overcast day, the kitchen bustled with Sam, Dom, Diego, and Anton stirring cookie dough in big bowls, as Skyla and Karen measured and poured ingredients. Maria, Wilma, and Leyla chopped busily at the tabbouleh makings. Fresh mint scented the air.

"Hey, it's a princess from the far north!" Krista greeted Bonnie, who looked a little startled at three Airedales plus Dom's border collie. "There'll be one more dog coming, too. Gandalf, the daddy Airedale."

Hoot laughed as he took off his coat. "Bonnie insisted on wearing her red-haired princess costume from *Frozen*. It was utterly impossible to talk her out of it."

"When they're almost four, sometimes the only way to get them dressed is to let them choose," said Melody.

"That's a really nice costume with its red plush cape," said Karen. "And look at your blue skirt. Is it full enough to swish when you twirl around?"

The little girl obliged with a giggle.

"Where did you find your outfit?" asked Karen.

"Mommy made it," said Bonnie, holding up the long skirt in a clumsy curtsy.

"I've learned that kids insist on wearing their costumes again and again," said Melody. "If I don't want them looking tatty, it's best to sew them myself."

"I didn't know the cookie baking was starting this early," said Hoot.

"Dough works best if it's been refrigerated, so we got a head start." Dom came over, wiping his hands on a towel.

"It was sticky last year," said Farah. "This will help."

"More efficient," said Anton. "And we'll still make more. You haven't missed out."

"Look at Clyde!" said Matti. "He has bells on his antlers."

"Let's get the photos taken."

All too soon for Hoot, the others arrived—Pete and Akiko, and Cliff and Lou, their baby dressed in a little elf outfit. Hoot's sharp eyes saw the wide-eyed look that his grandmother gave Cliff before she looked back at him. He scowled and didn't say a word. Thankfully she didn't either.

He hung back a bit, but Karen soon had everyone divided up working on the cookie assembly line. Hoot found himself rolling dough and cutting out St. Nicholas shapes with Anton and Cliff. Akiko and Melody kept Bonnie and Matti busy with a special recipe to make stocking-shaped biscuits for the dogs.

His kids' eyes were shining. Everybody seemed to be in a good mood, and he relaxed. Sort of. The word must have gotten around not to mention the elephant in the room. In a way that annoyed him, too. What was he? Some kind of wuss?

A burst of laughter brought his attention to Pete and Diego, spouting puns and in fine fettle. "Rolling out the dough-ho-ho." Their job was to shuffle the dough along its route and be in charge of the ovens and timers. "Going with the flow-ho-ho."

"Karen," called Pete, "we should also take on the responsibility of quality control. Periodically, a cookie should be selected, broken and taste-tested."

"It's very important," said Diego.

"I believe, that as patriarch of this group, I should take on that responsibility," said Dom.

"Forget it, Dom. What about the matriarch?" asked Karen.

Pete exchanged a look with Diego. "We have a compromise solution. The patriarch and the matriarch will get dibs on any cookies coming off the sheets broken. After all, broken means at least two pieces. One for each. Then the quality control gets any remaining pieces." He winked at Diego. "I think you know what to do."

Diego grinned. "Yes, sir. Odd how these cookies break into fours all the time."

Soon their cookie baking was done. The breakfast room table was loaded with decorated cookies, waiting to be packed for the residents of St. Raphael's Care Center.

They cleared away the cookie mess and laid out the feast of *Smørrebrød* makings. Hoot listened as Karen pointed out what was what. Rye and other whole grain breads, smoked salmon and other types of fish, roast beef, ham, hard-boiled eggs—all sliced. Thinly sliced radishes and cucumbers, dill, watercress, fancy greens, and crispy bacon. Blue cheese, Jarlsburg, Gouda, and other cheeses. Slices of apple and pear. Roasted chopped nuts and more. Side dishes of tabbouleh and fat cubes of honeydew melon.

Everyone created their own open-faced sandwiches, tried new combinations, and came back for more. Hoot helped Bonnie make her *Smørrebrød* with buttered bread, pears, ham and blue cheese. Since she was mostly eating her collection of food as finger food, he helped with that sandwich by holding it together while she took bites.

Only once did his ears catch the word 'kidnapped', and he looked up, feeling his jaw clench, only to find that Krista was talking about her experience with someone else. No one was even looking at him.

◆ ❖ ◆

Dom sat back, enjoying the laughter, the food, and the friendship. He reflected on last year—how he, Sam, and Karen had come up with this idea to create a new celebration.

Then it was time for the story of St. Nicholas. Dom began by asking the girls to tell about their idea. It was obvious that many had given a great deal of thought to random acts of kindness. Some had even started their deeds.

They talked about little acts, too. Giving a stranger a compliment, shoveling the neighbor's sidewalk, letting somebody go first in line, and paying for someone's morning coffee.

Dom noticed Hoot made sure his kids got their say. When that happened, his eyes flicked to Karen. She was glowing.

"These are wonderful ideas," she said. "I couldn't have asked for a better beginning for our acts of kindness."

Sam began to whistle "Deck the Halls" and brought out his guitar.

◆ ❖ ◆

Hoot was amazed by the music the group made. He'd no idea that Anton played the piano that well and was blown away by Sam's guitar playing. Someone said to wait until someday when Lou had her violin and Cliff his bagpipes. That intrigued him. He tried to picture Cliff as a piper.

Singing was something he and Melody enjoyed. He suggested songs Matti and Bonnie knew to include them. At one point in a carol, everybody else dropped out, leaving himself and Melody, Lou and Cliff to carry the four-part harmony. He felt the heat in his face, but hung in there. There was applause when they finished. He thought they'd sounded good.

But Hoot couldn't shake the edgy feeling, like a cat in a room full of rockers. Everyone was behaving. No one was nagging at him. Everyone was just normal, having fun.

While they were singing, he was aware of Pete looking at him, but Pete didn't say anything. That annoyed Hoot, too. Another headache started to come on.

He noticed that Melody and Lou had hit it off and were chatting together throughout the evening. For some reason that irked him even more, though he knew that was foolish. Why shouldn't they get along? But he felt a bit betrayed. Then he felt guilty about that.

The hands of the clock seemed to be moving in slow motion. Finally, he noticed Bonnie's head drooping, half a gingerbread cookie falling from her fingers. Twitch snatched it up, and she didn't even notice. Finally, they could make a graceful exit.

They got their coats. He held Bonnie, fast asleep, her head resting on his shoulder. Melody and Lou hugged as they said goodbye. Why did that bother him, and why was he so cranky? He reminded himself that he was an adult. He went through the motions, smiling, thanking the Bjornsons.

At last they left, going into a crisp, star-filled night. He could tell Melody had enjoyed it, and he hadn't seen his grandmother that happy for a long time. He liked his kids being around people like that who treated others with respect and love. And him? He'd survived. Yes, he had fun. Well, his feelings were mixed.

CHAPTER TWENTY-TWO

In a downtown Santa Fe children's store a few days later, Melody held up a blue top for Bonnie to see. "How do you like this one?"

"Want the red one."

Melody sighed. "But this blue is really pretty. It's a princess blue."

"No blue. Want red." Bonnie's voice rose toward the screech level.

"Use your inside voice, please." She might have known. Well, why shouldn't redheads be able to wear red? When Melody was little, her mother steered her toward blues and greens, but she, a vibrant carrot-top, had always wanted the red.

"I thought I recognized your voices." Lou, carrying Dougie, appeared from the nearby infant wear section.

Melody laughed. "I hope you knew the screechy voice wasn't mine." She set the blue top back and found the right size of the red one. "Can you join us for coffee?"

"I'd love a break. Do you know Books and Bearclaws?"

"Yes. They have that big play cube. Bonnie loves it there."

In the bookstore, Melody spotted a table near the six-sided play cube with the beads and rollercoaster wires on top. Bonnie plopped down by the 'learn the alphabet' side.

"Look." Lou pointed at the *Koda and the Sami* merchandise displayed nearby. "Sneaky. Putting all that where they know kids will be playing."

"I think we already have most of it," said Melody. "I'll have to get that new coloring book for Bonnie's Christmas stocking."

"Cliff has already read the book to Dougie. I love it that he does things like that."

"I thought it went pretty well the other night," said Melody. "I'm glad Hoot and Cliff got along as well as they did. They're going to have to deal with each other—whether they turn out to be brothers or not."

"If they are, we'll be sisters-in-law," said Lou. "What do you think? Could Hoot be Johnny?"

"It's possible, I suppose. Even Marilyn wonders. It's almost like Hoot's afraid to find out. Usually he's very comfortable in his own skin. I've never seen him act like he does around Pete and Cliff."

"They have a lot in common—like hiking and loving the outdoors."

"I wish they could just enjoy each other's friendship," said Melody.

"Why don't you two come over for dinner some night?"

Melody paused to think. Did she dare push Hoot this way?

"They got along for St. Nick," said Lou. "Maybe another casual meal together would make them easier with each other."

"What does Cliff think?" asked Melody.

"Cliff's whole life has been affected by the kidnapping of his brother. It showed in how he felt about himself, about the power he felt he lacked to protect those he loves. And now, he wants so badly for Hoot to be Johnny. Not just for himself. He wants his parents to find resolution, too."

"What do you think, Lou? Is this maybe one of the acts of kindness we can do? Put our hubbies into a situation where they can get to know each other?"

"Let's do it. How about this Friday?"

"If this blows up in our faces . . ." Melody held Lou's gaze. "I really hope this works."

CHAPTER TWENTY-THREE

So far, so good, thought Melody as she and Hoot neared Cliff and Lou's home Friday evening. Grandma had been a surprising advocate, not that it had helped Hoot's mood any. She'd been all in favor of their having dinner with Cliff and Lou, and she was glad to babysit. When Hoot grumbled that he didn't want to be around Cliff, Marilyn had said point blank, "If they bother you that much, why don't you just get the DNA test done and tell them to take a flying leap?"

Melody had been watching his face. He flinched like he'd been slapped.

"I don't need a DNA test," he said. "I know who I am."

They'd looked at him. He rolled his eyes and threw up his hands. "All right. I'll go to the damn dinner." He turned and glowered at Melody. "This once."

Then he retreated into his stubborn shell. God, she hoped this would work.

Restlessly Cliff wandered into his study, finding himself drawn to the shelf where Koda sat. Everything was ready for their dinner. Hope refused to be tamped down, even though he'd been disappointed so many times over the years. He took Koda off the shelf and brushed the white curls away from the wise blue eyes.

"Koda, are you still listening? This might be Johnny coming. Will he remember you? If you could just—"

Lou appeared at his side, holding Dougie. "Cliff, thanks for being such a good sport about our idea. We don't want to pressure Hoot. Don't talk about a DNA test or Johnny. I'll be right back. Dougie needs changing."

He nodded automatically as she left, before giving his attention back to Koda. He toggled the switch for Koda's lantern. The light shone brightly. "Maybe, just maybe, Hoot agreed to come because he's ready to talk about it. I want it to be true—that Hoot is Johnny. I know I told Lou I'd behave myself." He turned the light off and set the toy back on the shelf. "But, somehow, I'll fix it so he sees you. Then we'll see what happens."

At first dinner went well. Cliff fixed the salad and opened a bottle of barbera. Lou had made Cliff's mother's recipe for lasagna, and he complimented her on how good it was. Everyone had seconds and generous portions of cheesecake for dessert.

Cliff was a little amused at how the conversation flowed. Obviously, Lou and Melody had planned several topics to facilitate their getting acquainted. How the couples had met, where they went to school, places they'd traveled. Music was a topic that he and Hoot had gotten onto without their wives' help. Though Hoot hadn't had much formal training, he'd been in choir in high school and college. He and Melody both enjoyed singing.

After dessert they started talking about hiking and hiking guides. Cliff said he'd written articles for several guides in New Mexico. He wondered if this might be a good segue to Koda, who sat on the shelf next to the books he'd written. Could Koda trigger a memory?

When they were all standing in his study and Hoot was making complimentary noises about the hiking guides, Cliff decided the time was right to bring up Johnny.

Hoot was quiet for a few seconds. When he faced Cliff, his voice sucked the warmth from the room. "You should know I didn't want to come here tonight, but Melody thought it would clear the air. I'm not sure it was a good idea."

"Hoot, I really am trying to understand," said Cliff quietly. "Why aren't you at least considering the idea that you might be my brother? You said you don't remember anything before the plane crash."

Hoot's voice had an edge. "I don't want to talk about it."

Cliff set the hiking guide back on the shelf. "I wish you would."

He felt a hand on his arm. Lou tugged at him. "Cliff, please. Not tonight."

He frowned, shrugged her hand off, and turned back to Hoot. "Looking at you is almost like looking in the mirror."

"We look alike. So what?" Hoot backed away from Cliff. "You just want to find your brother so badly, you're grasping at straws."

"Take the DNA test. If it comes back with no connection, then you'll know. Why do you resist?"

"Stop it, Cliff," Lou pleaded.

"I know who I am," Hoot said. "I don't need you butting in."

"Johnny was my brother. I loved him."

"Can't we talk about something else?" Melody sounded like she was ready to cry.

"Fine by me," said Hoot.

Cliff grabbed Koda from the shelf and held him out to Hoot. "Do you remember this?"

Hoot shrugged. "It's a Koda toy. There must be a million out there. What's that got to do with anything?"

"I believe it's yours. He was all I had left of you. Don't you remember me? I missed you every day of my life." Cliff felt an urgency, like if he just tried a little harder, he could convince Hoot to believe him. "I felt so guilty, so damn powerless when you were taken."

"I'm not your brother." Hoot's voice grew louder.

"Why won't you do the DNA thing? If you cared at all—"

"Damn it. I *don't* care. Get that through your thick head! I am Ross Stewart." His body grew straighter, more rigid; his voice cracked as it rose in intensity. "I can't tell you why I won't do the test. I can't tell! For God's sake, stop nagging! Just stop it!"

Gandalf got to his feet, stood stiffly by Cliff's side and began to bark at Hoot and his shouting.

"Bloody hell, I don't understand." Cliff's voice rose over the barking. "Are you afraid of the truth?"

"I can't *tell* you." Hoot's fists were clenched, shaking.

Cliff took a step closer to Hoot. "I looked up to my brother. He told me that Koda listens. I believed it. For years I've poured out my soul to Koda. Kept him safe for my big brother. Telling him all that I wanted to tell my brother who was *ripped* from my life."

Cliff suddenly hurled Koda at Hoot. Hoot caught it against his chest, stepping back with the force of the throw.

"Take it," Cliff yelled. "Get it out of here. I don't want it anymore. For twenty-five years I've prayed my brother would come back. I never gave up hope. *Never*. But no more. You aren't my brother. You're an asshole."

CHAPTER TWENTY-FOUR

As Melody watched in dismay, Cliff snatched up his jacket and strode out the back door with Gandalf at his heels. He slammed the door, rattling the glass in the French doors. In the light from the family room, Melody saw him kneel and pull Gandalf to him. His shoulders shook.

Melody looked at Lou's distraught face. Dougie began to cry in his bedroom. Melody reached out to pull Lou into a hard hug. Both of them were in tears.

"I'll call you. Maybe in a few days." Then Lou went to console the crying baby.

Hoot looked stunned, still holding Koda in his arms. He grabbed his coat and left without waiting to put it on. Melody picked up her coat and purse. She followed Hoot, shutting the door behind her, hurrying to catch up to her husband as he pitched Koda into the back seat of their car, threw on his coat, and got in.

He leaned his head against the headrest, shut his eyes, and began to rub his temples. Melody glanced at him as she started the engine. Why had she and Lou ever thought this would help? Hoot was already angry with her for arranging this dinner in the first place. Actually, she wasn't too happy with herself. Guilt ate at her. It was obvious he had a raging headache.

The miles unfolded in silence. They left the city lights of Santa Fe behind and merged onto the interstate. She knew in her heart that she hadn't been motivated by doing an act of kindness. She'd wanted the friendship of that circle of folks. And now, she'd made it more difficult. Why couldn't she have just smiled at someone for an act of kindness, or held a door for an elderly person? No, she had to take matters into her own hands and force it, even though she knew Hoot would be upset.

She blinked tears away and looked at her husband again as she took the turnoff for Pecos. He just sat with his arms folded, eyes shut, and a frown on his face. She'd put her foot into it this time.

When they got home, Hoot headed straight into the house without a word. She followed more slowly after rescuing Koda from the back seat. When she got inside, Hoot was pouring himself a glass of milk. He didn't look at her, just shook a couple ibuprofen tablets into his hand and settled into a chair in the family room.

Marilyn looked at Melody questioningly from the couch, where she held a sleeping Bonnie on her lap. A picture book lay next to them. Tears welled in Melody's eyes, and she shook her head at Marilyn.

Matti's excited voice startled her. "It's Koda. Can I play with him?" He reached out for the toy still in her hands.

Melody looked at Hoot. He didn't move, except to sip his milk slowly. She nodded, and Matti scampered off to his room, clutching his prize.

"Thanks for staying with them." Melody lifted Bonnie up in her arms. It was a good thing Bonnie hadn't been awake. The last thing she'd needed was the inevitable squabble that one Koda and two children would cause.

"I'll help you tuck her in. We can talk in the morning," said Marilyn.

◆ ❖ ◆

Hoot sat in his recliner, leaning forward, his head pounding. This headache was the mother of them all. His mind was in turmoil. He thought he recognized the Koda toy Cliff had thrust at him, but couldn't admit it. He was aware of Melody and his grandmother leaving, but just didn't want to move. Maybe sitting still would relieve the pain.

Melody came back, took the glass from his unresisting fingers, and started to speak.

Hoot held up his hand to stop her. "Not now. Leave me alone." Then he added, "please," to soften the rejection.

A roar filled his ears, and he covered them with his hands. Was he going crazy? Who was he? And it wasn't just that. The door in his mind was opening. A menacing threat to all he loved and held dear began to seep out—smoky, dark fumes of evil that couldn't be caught and pushed back.

A voice from a distant memory pierced him. *"You can't ever tell, or they will die."*

Where did *that* come from?

Concentrate. Take even breaths.

Gradually he calmed. The roar in his ears began to subside. He heard Melody talking quietly to Matti, putting him to bed. Hoot sat, numb and drained.

Melody left the kids' rooms and softly closed the bathroom door. He heard the water running. A little while later she came into the room where he sat. Hoot stood up and pulled her into a silent embrace. As they stood together, her warmth seemed to ground him; her heart beat steadily against his chest. He closed his eyes and let her quiet support flood through his being for several minutes before stepping back. Her eyes were wet when they met his. She leaned forward to press a kiss on his lips.

"I'm sorry," she whispered. Her fingers trailed from his shoulder down to his hand. He extended his hand as she backed away, coveting her soft touch until her fingertips glided from his. She turned and went into their bedroom, dimming the light switch partway as she passed it. How long he stood there in the darkened room, he didn't know.

Then Hoot went into Bonnie's room, pulled the blanket up over her shoulder. Her door was open to the hall light, to keep away the monsters. Oh, for such a simple solution to keep his own monsters at bay.

He went into Matti's room and stood looking at his seven-year-old son. Seven—just a little older than that stolen boy. Seven—so young, so vulnerable. Matti's arm was around Koda. The glowing light from Koda's lantern fell on the face of the sleeping child. It seemed to Hoot that Koda was watching him, that he knew his secrets. Hoot smiled ruefully at the thought.

Without thinking, he reached to turn off the lantern, then stood by his son's bed in the dark, arrested on the spot. His hand had gone unerringly to the switch. How had he known where to find it? Dear God, he knew because it was his, because that's what his father had done with him. The wisp of memory teased his mind.

He sucked in a deep breath. Was it true then? Why couldn't he remember? Why did he feel this overwhelming panic? If the McCreaths were his family, why couldn't he run to them and embrace them? Why was he so afraid?

His son sighed, turned over and slept on. His son. Part of himself, part of Melody, born of their love. If someone stole his child, he would never give up looking. Never give up hope.

Pete, Cliff, and even his grandmother wanted him to take the DNA test. Like a strike of lightning, the certainty slammed into him. *I must do the test*. His heartbeat quickened. That secret door in his mind loomed larger, the pounding intensified. The door wanted to open. But he must know. Only then could the menace be put to rest.

The pounding grew fainter as rational thought took over.

Of course, he wasn't Johnny. It was just coincidence. Pete and Cliff were mistaken, and they would go on looking. It would be a relief to remain Ross, to be sure. Yes. That would still the voices.

But what if? Dear God, what if?

He went into their bedroom and took his keys out of his pocket, reaching to put them in the tray on the dresser. His fingers rubbed the familiar shape of the Koda keychain Matti had chosen for him for Father's Day two years ago, a gift which had instantly resonated with him. His other hand grasped the dresser—he felt lightheaded. Was it only important because his son had given it to him? Or was there another reason?

119

Melody was still awake. He kicked off his shoes, tossed his shirt and jeans over a chair, and slid under the covers to lie next to her. Hoot pulled her, unresisting, into his arms. He felt tense, strung taut enough to vibrate, throat aching. He held her tightly, lying there.

"I need—" He took a big, shuddery breath. The door in his mind seemed to shake, looming larger. His resolve wrestled with whatever he feared behind the door, his voice challenging its threat. "I need to have that DNA test done. Will you go with me tomorrow?"

"Of course."

"Melody, who am I?"

"You are Hoot, the man I married. I love you so much. Nothing will ever change that." She whispered, "This man I hold in my arms, you are my mate, my love. Always, no matter what happens."

He lay in the darkness, surrounded by her love. She nestled against him, her head resting on his chest. Gradually the tension eased, awareness faded, and he finally slipped into slumber.

CHAPTER TWENTY-FIVE

When Pete got the early morning call from Hoot, he jumped at the chance to meet him at the police department. However it had come about, Hoot's decision filled Pete with elation. With Hoot being in such an emotionally charged state, he didn't want to allow time for second thoughts.

Gratified to see Hoot and Melody, waiting hand in hand, Pete led them in, snagging a patrolman to fill his complement of witnesses. He used a paternity test kit, which would assure results in days. He filled out the paperwork, got the signatures in place, and explained how it worked.

As Pete swabbed the inside of Hoot's cheeks, the young man radiated tension. Determined, yet fearful, was how Pete interpreted his attitude. His eyes went to Hoot's ears, and he was reminded of the pictures of Ross and Johnny. He nodded in satisfaction and secured the samples.

Deeply pleased, Pete breathed a sigh of relief. "May I ask, what made you change your mind?"

"We were at Cliff's house last night," replied Hoot. "He started to push. I'm afraid we got a little loud. He had this toy next to a photo. I didn't say so, but I felt I'd seen them before. I've got to talk to Cliff again—now, if I can." He looked at Melody, who nodded.

Pete wasn't going to let this opportunity slip by. This was his investigation, and damn it, he wanted to be there as it came to fruition. "I'll join you, if I may."

"Please," said Hoot. "I believe you have pieces of the puzzle that neither Cliff nor I do."

As Pete followed the Stewarts' car to Cliff's home, he could barely keep from shouting out a thank you to the universe. Hoot's former reluctance and animosity had frustrated him no end. But the pressure Hoot felt—what must that have been like? His whole identity was crashing down around him.

◆ ❖ ◆

Hoot's decision made and the deed behind him, he was filled with energy. He parked at Cliff's in the same spot they'd left less than twenty-four hours ago, got out, and went to the door, leaving Melody in a half-run to keep up. Pete was still parking his car.

Lou answered the door, her mouth an O of surprise. Cliff came out of his study. Instantly a wary look covered his face. Before Cliff could say anything or turn him away, words came pouring from Hoot. "Please, listen. I don't know who I am. Just now, Melody and I went to have the DNA test done. I need to talk with you."

Hoot looked over his shoulder at Pete, who followed them in, closed the door, and stood, not interrupting.

Hoot stepped forward. "Last night, Matti took Koda to bed with him. When I went to check on him, the lantern light was on. I reached to turn it off—"

Feeling overwhelmed, Hoot shook his head. It felt like his voice was clogged. "I remembered. That's what my daddy did with me. I remember. A bit. You had that fox. He would tuck you in, and then come to my bed and turn off Koda's light. I see twin beds, the light on in the hall, the bookcase in the shadow. It was the same every night. If we were still awake, he would say good night to us, and then good night, Koda, and good night— I think he said, 'Ro-ra.' "

Cliff's face changed; tears welled. "Bloody hell. You are Johnny."

"Oh God, I think I am. Why can't I remember?"

"Johnny, you *are* Johnny. No one else would know that name. I named my fox after the Northern Lights—Aurora. I called him Ro-ra."

Cliff opened his arms, Hoot rushed to meet him halfway, and brother clutched brother tightly.

◆ ❖ ◆

"Is our mother still alive?" asked Hoot.

"Of course. She and Dad still live in the same house. They never moved. They thought if you came home, that's where you would go."

"Dad?" Hoot was astounded. "But I was told my father died. I always thought . . ."

"Why did you think Dad was dead?"

"That man who took me told me that I could never *ever* tell. That if I did, he would kill my daddy. When I woke up in the hospital after the plane crash, they said my father was dead. I thought I must have told, and they killed him. And it was my fault." Hoot took a few panting breaths. "But he's still alive?" Hoot shook his head in growing wonder. "They said if I told, first he was going to kill my father. Then my little brother. I couldn't tell. That guy would come back and kill you. I couldn't tell."

Deep sobs welled up from inside him. Lou put her hand over her mouth, her eyes dark with emotion. Melody brushed at her wet cheeks.

Cliff guided Hoot to the couch and sat down with him, his arm around him, waiting until the sobs stopped.

"That man is dead," said Cliff. "He can't harm anybody."

"No, my father died. They never told me the pilot died." Hoot rubbed his head. "It's still mixed up. Nothing makes sense."

"Our father is alive," Cliff repeated.

Pete said, "Both your parents are alive and well. The pilot was Gordon Stewart and is indeed dead. He died when the plane crashed."

"There were pictures of Gordon around our house. I knew the Stewarts were my grandparents, and that Gordon, their son, must be my father, but it was unreal in my mind. I always had such a negative feeling toward him. No good memories. I thought it was because I'd been mistreated or something. I couldn't put together the feeling of missing my daddy . . . with him."

"Marilyn and Dwight Stewart really believed you were their grandson," said Pete. "They hadn't seen the boy for about four years. The last photo they had of Ross was from kindergarten. You were having a tough time recovering from your injuries. It makes sense now. You couldn't or wouldn't remember your name. Marilyn thought the accident left you with amnesia. Trying to remember used to give you headaches."

"It still does."

"The kidnapper said what he did in order to control you. It's not uncommon for kidnappers to say they will kill their victim's family to make a small child do their bidding. It's cruel. I believe to protect your brother, your mother, you refused to tell. You did what you had to do—pushed all those memories into a box in your mind and refused to open it. You kept your family safe. But now—it's okay. You can come home again."

Hoot struggled with emotion. "When can I see them, my mom and my dad?"

CHAPTER TWENTY-SIX

Lynn looked at her husband as he hung up the phone. "What did Cliff want?"

"He's on his way over with Pete. Just checking to make sure we're home."

"I'd better make a fresh pot of coffee," said Lynn. "Andrew, you don't suppose there's another lead? Maybe the fellow Cliff met at the festival?"

"He did sound excited."

"Hope. It's what we have left." She turned into Andrew's arms. "Without you, I don't know how I'd get through each day." Thirty-some years of marriage found comfortable familiarity in his hug.

A car door slammed, and she left Andrew's embrace to look out the window. "It's Pete. Cliff must be driving separately."

Soon Pete was inside and assured them that Cliff would be arriving shortly.

"What's up, Pete?" asked Andrew. "Something's happened."

"The young man we told you about? It looks promising. He's taken a DNA test. The results won't be back for a while, so we can't be certain. I told you he doesn't remember, but now his memory has started to return. He wants to meet you."

Lynn put her hand to her throat. "Meet us? He's coming? Now? Johnny?" She was aware of the sound of car doors closing. Her feet seemed rooted to the spot. She turned to their front door as it opened, and Cliff walked in. Behind him entered a woman with red, curly hair.

Then her eyes locked on a tall red-headed man.

She moved toward him as in a dream, her eyes searching his face, a stranger, yet so familiar. Blue eyes holding anxiety and hope met hers. Then she flew forward, throwing her arms around him. She felt Andrew's arms close tightly around them both. She felt the tears streaming down her cheeks, felt the fierceness of the young man's hug surrounding her.

Could it be? Was this man really her son? Somehow, even though she'd hoped for this day, it was always the exuberant child she'd envisioned hugging. Of course, she knew he'd change, but where was her son?

She pulled back, putting her hand to his face, looking for some semblance of the six-year old Johnny. Wet blue eyes looked down into hers. My God, he's taller than Andrew. He . . . he looks like Andrew used to. So much like Cliff does now.

"Johnny? Can it really be true? Are you Johnny?"

She pulled him to her again, feeling, just feeling. Feeling the muscled warmth of the body held so closely. After way too many years, was it finally over? Or would she wake to find it was a horribly tantalizing dream?

On the short drive over, Hoot had struggled with mixed feelings of eagerness and trepidation. Lynn and Andrew McCreath, Pete had said. Would he recognize them? He worried about what to say, but suddenly, when he saw them, the worry dissipated. His mom—wide blue eyes, light like his, filled with hope. His dad—nose and chin strangely similar to those he saw in his mirror every morning—like his, yet drawn with older lines.

Then he was pulled into an embrace, and he felt the tears streaming down. This he recognized—the warmth and the love—he was home!

"You're all grown up," Lynn said, leaning back again, putting her hands against his cheeks. "God, I've missed you. I never thought

I'd hold you again. I was so afraid you were dead, lying in some cold hidden place. That we'd never ever know. Oh, God."

"We never . . ." Andrew struggled with words. "We never gave up hope. To see this day is—" He raised his arm to include Cliff in their embrace. "My sons. Both our sons. At last."

Gradually Hoot calmed within the tearful warmth of the hugs. His eyes scanned the room, looking past the living room, the dining room, to the kitchen where the morning sun streamed through the window over the sink. He glanced down the hall. it was strange and yet, becoming rapidly familiar. He knew where their room with their twin beds would be.

He looked with wonder, taking it all in, until he saw Melody, a misty smile on her face. He stepped back from the embrace and held out a hand to her. "This is Melody, my wife."

"Oh, my dear," said Lynn, "my son home and now a new daughter-in-law. I'm so glad to meet you. They told me you have two children. Where are they?"

"Matti and Bonnie," said Melody. "He's seven, and she will be four next month."

"They're home with my grandmother." Hoot shook his head and smiled. "This is going to take some getting used to." He took a deep breath and plunged into the explanation. "Marilyn and Dwight Stewart raised me from the time of the plane crash. We all believed I was their grandson. Grandpa died a few years ago. But Marilyn, my grandmother, has loved me and cared for me for as long as I can remember." He paused, looking from his mother to his father. "I don't want her hurt because of what her son did."

Lynn lifted her hand to caress his cheek. "Of course, we understand. She must have been the angel God provided to look out for you."

Andrew nodded. "I look forward to meeting Marilyn. She kept you safe for us."

"All grown up," repeated Lynn. "I can't believe it. I wish Erin were here." She took hold of Hoot's hand.

"Erin?" asked Hoot.

"Our sister," said Cliff. "She was only two when they took you. She and Daniel, her husband, live in Pagosa Springs with their three kids."

"I have a sister." Hoot looked at Melody. "Remember that time—"

She nodded. "You remembered when your little sister was born, and then were all confused because you didn't have one."

Andrew spoke up. "Let's all sit. Pete, I'm sorry, we haven't even offered you coffee. Oh, God, after all these years. Johnny, when did you start to remember?"

Lynn broke in. "I want to hear all about your growing up. Where you went to school, what you like to do, where the two of you met, about your children. I want to see pictures. I think we need to pull out our old photo albums. Oh, my God, it's too much. I can't take it all in."

She began sobbing, sinking to the couch, not relinquishing her grip on his hand. He sat by her, with Cliff on her other side, his arm around her shaking shoulders.

Pete cleared his throat and remained standing. "I'll skip the coffee, Andrew. You have a lot of catching up to do. *Gott im Himmel,* my heart is full—" He struggled with his composure. "Before I go, there are a couple of details to look at. Andrew, Lynn, if you do a paternity test, that will be the fastest way of getting official confirmation. We'll know in days, not weeks or months. You know how long it takes to get DNA results back from police labs. And as soon as the word of this spreads, you're going to be besieged with reporters. It might help to plan how you're going to deal with that before you tell anyone."

"You're right," said Andrew. "Let's get the official results of the paternity test back, and then make plans. I'm assuming you came prepared?"

Pete pulled two testing kits from his portfolio and held them up with a smile.

Lynn suddenly let go of Hoot's hand and stood. Crossing to Pete, she threw her arms around him. "Thank you, Pete. Thank you for never giving up. Thank you."

Struck by the joy on Pete's face, Hoot began to get a glimmer of all the silence, the pain, the emptiness this family had endured for all those many years. While he'd been growing up in his own world, leaving childhood behind, falling in love with Melody and starting their family, forging ahead with his career, they'd been missing him, waiting, hoping. My God, what a day.

The door in his mind swung open. Nothing was in focus, but love surrounded him. The tension disappeared, and he knew it was going to be all right.

◆ ❖ ◆

That night, after the kids were asleep, Hoot went next door to his grandmother's home. He knew she expected the news, but it was still hard to deal with. Her shadowy shape moved in the dim light from her hallway.

"Grandma, are you okay? Why are you sitting in the dark?" He flipped the light switch on.

She raised her eyes to his. She'd been crying. He knelt in front of her and took her hand.

"How could my son have done such a thing?" she cried. "Oh, my boy." Her other hand fluttered out to him. "I'm sorry. So sorry."

"Grandma—"

"But I'm not—"

"You are. Maybe not by blood, but by all that matters. You and Grandpa surrounded me with love. You nurtured me, taught me. You are my children's great-grandma. That's not going to change."

"How can I ever face your parents? When I think of the agony they endured." Tears ran down Marilyn's face.

"They don't blame you. Instead, they call you my guardian angel. They're glad you were there to take care of me. You are part of my family, and they want to meet you."

"But I'm not."

"Listen to me. You are my grandmother."

"I don't even know what to call you. Strange. You aren't Ross, but John."

"Call me Hoot, just like always. That's a name I earned on my own. I like it. It has worn well."

"What will your children say?"

"We will tell them that I had been lost and separated from my parents long ago. But we've found each other. Kids might not understand family trees, but they know love."

Hoot saw Marilyn blink rapidly and her eyes fill with tears again.

"You've been found. But now . . . Ross, my little grandson. Where is he? What happened?"

Hoot looked at her in shock. "I never thought. No one was even looking. I'm sorry. We should talk to Pete."

Marilyn nodded.

"Come back with me and have a cup of tea. Please?" Hoot smiled and held out a hand to her.

Marilyn stood, and Hoot enfolded her in a hug. "We'll try to find out what happened to Ross. I promise. I love you, Grandma."

Chapter Twenty-Seven

Monday, the twelfth of December. How's that for a date to remember? Pete anticipated the congratulations from the bullpen about what certainly would be the successful end to the McCreath case. Finishing the knot on his tie, Pete came into the kitchen where Akiko was lingering over her coffee and reading her Facebook posts. She wore a somber expression. Uh-oh, now what? That look was a mood shifter.

"Pete, you should read this. You remember I told you two weeks ago that Cowboy was killed?"

"Sure. Did they find who did it?" He bent to look at the message.

"I don't think so. His wife just died in an explosion at their home. They're still investigating. Do you suppose it could have been gas lines, or a propane tank or something?"

"Ach, not Arlene, too." Pete sat next to Akiko and put a hand on her shoulder. "They lived way out on a ranch. I don't know that they would have natural gas available, and propane tanks don't explode. Theoretically I suppose it's possible, but highly unlikely. I'll go online and see what I can learn."

"Tell me if you find anything."

◆ ❖ ◆

"*Heilige Scheisse.*" Pete studied the news articles about Cowboy's and Arlene's deaths again. They had no person of interest yet. It appeared Cowboy had been ambushed and shot. And it hadn't been a natural gas or propane explosion that destroyed their home and killed Arlene, but a bomb. That had brought the ATF into the investigation and would help immensely, thought Pete. Surely, a small rural place like that wouldn't be able to mount an effective investigation like the ATF would. They had the resources, the experts, and were well-known for thoroughness.

Maybe he wouldn't say anything to Akiko. One of his greatest fears was that his work would bring his wife or his family into danger. He didn't even want to think that what happened to Cowboy and Arlene could possibly happen to those he loved most.

What kind of a sick person would target people who were just going on with their lives and meant no harm to anyone? He wondered if something as moronic as greed over mineral rights or a grudge over the lost campaign were to blame. Rather drastic, though, to murder two people. And why had the grudge extended to Cowboy's wife? Just a senseless tragedy.

◆ ❖ ◆

A couple of mornings later, Pete sat at his desk, typed in his password, and began going through his emails. One, with the subject line 'Paternity Test', caught his eye, and he made a pleased sound as he skipped to it. As he read, satisfaction grew. Finally. Confirmation.

He leaned back in his chair, set his glasses on his desk and closed his eyes. He hadn't even realized he had tiny residual doubts until he'd read the words in black and white. He took a deep breath and let it out. All those years. *Gott im Himmel*. We did it. Tears threatened as he reveled in the feeling of success.

"It's over," he whispered, rubbing the bridge of his nose.

Hoot Stewart was the son of Andrew and Lynn McCreath. Even though the unfolding events of the last few days had made it conclusive, here was scientific proof. To have a missing child come home—alive and well—rather than in a body bag. It was made even more special by how closely his own life was entwined with this extended family.

He printed three copies of the paternity test results and turned at the sound of a soft knock on his door.

"Sam," he said, handing him a copy.

A broad smile filled Sam's face as he read it and handed it back. "Congratulations, man. Good to have it verified. Been a long time coming."

"As soon as I finish here, I'm going to run over to Pecos and give Hoot a copy. When school gets out, I'll swing by Andrew and Lynn's." He put two copies into his portfolio. As he made short work of his messages, his eyes strayed periodically to the third copy. With each glance, warm satisfaction filled him.

Tired from his drive from Denver, Hayle leaned back in the booth at Denny's, decided on the Grand Slam, and laid the menu down. Yvonne was obviously wired about some development and chomping at the bit to spill all as soon as he'd arrived in Santa Fe. He'd convinced his sister he had to eat first. "Now what's up?"

"Well, you remember Schultz has been investigating this Ross Stewart guy, thinking he might be the stolen McCreath boy? They've confirmed it. Even more interesting, the grownup boy has started to remember stuff."

"Get out." Hayle inserted a derisive tone into his voice. "How did they find out?"

"DNA. Remember that baby tooth of Gordon's they sent to the Denver crime lab? Proof this guy is not Gordon's son. Then they did a paternity test with the McCreaths and Ross Stewart. The McCreaths are his parents."

Crap. I don't need this. Now what should I do? "Have they figured out yet what happened to the real Ross Stewart?"

"I don't think so. For all they know he's still out there."

"What's he remembering?"

"Just childhood stuff about his parents and brother." She wiped a tear from her eye. "It's so touching, a reunion after so long."

"He hasn't remembered anything about the kidnapping?"

"I haven't heard anything about that. I thought you'd be more excited. I think it's wonderful after all this time."

"Yvonne, I don't even know these people. Was that all your news? I thought you were going to tell me something interesting."

◆ ❖ ◆

That afternoon, Hoot walked along the Pecos River near his home. The light snowfall they'd gotten last night had mostly melted, and the river flowed quietly along. He came to a boulder lying back away from the icy water and sat. Wow! Even though he'd expected it, his world had just been jolted into a new reality. The paternity test results showed a probability of more than ninety-nine percent that he was a child of Andrew and Lynn McCreath.

Hoot had spent part of the day with Cliff and with his parents, learning more about his new family. He wouldn't tell his kids until school was out for the holidays, giving them a chance to take it all in before Matti went back.

His name was John McCreath, not Ross Stewart. His children had grandparents, aunts, uncles, and cousins. It was a lot to take in. Even his birthday was different. Well, that wasn't true, but he'd always thought he'd been born on August 9, 1983, but he was actually born on February 11, 1985. He wouldn't be thirty-four on his next birthday, but thirty-two—again!

He thought of the real Ross, whose birthday he'd been celebrating as his own. Pete told him they'd already been investigating the missing Ross even before confirmation arrived that Hoot was Johnny.

He went back to his musing. What would he do about his name? He and Melody had talked about it. Hang loose for a while, he'd decided. People could call him Hoot. Eventually, the police reports might help get all the legal paperwork out of the way. His and

Melody's marriage license. The kids' birth certificates. Social Security numbers. A whole raft of legal paperwork. What a hassle. The bureaucracy would get it right—over time.

His phone rang. The number wasn't one he recognized. He answered.

"You told." The words stretched out in a loud whisper. Then the call ended.

Damn. Was this a stupid prank?

A shudder went down his spine. A sliver of doubt crept into his mind. Had he done the right thing?

He zipped his jacket higher and turned away from the river, the mood of the moment shattered. The water, now foreboding, seemed to echo the whisper. You told. You told . . .

PART II – YOU TOLD

CHAPTER TWENTY-EIGHT

Skyla and Anton's wedding day—December 17—had finally arrived. In a small room of the Presbyterian church in downtown Santa Fe where she was getting ready, Skyla pulled off her engagement ring. She smiled as she touched the spiderweb turquoise comets bracketing the center diamond. The night Anton had given it to her had been the highest point on a rollercoaster week, which had careened from despair to joy. She held the ring against her lips before tucking it safely away in a wee pocket for that purpose until it could join the wedding ring Anton would soon place on her finger.

Melody came in, her red curls swept back and caught with a burst of tiny satin roses and dangling seed pearls. Happiness shone from her face.

Skyla greeted her with a mock complaint. "Hey, it's the bride who's supposed to look like she's on cloud nine, yet you have that look."

Melody pulled her into a hug, careful not to disturb makeup or hair. "Your radiance makes mine a pale imitation. Is Krista here yet?"

"She and Karen are getting a bite for us to eat. I love it. A daughter to stand up with me on our wedding day. Anton will get teary-eyed when he sees her." Her own eyes misted over. "I miss my brother. I wish he could have been here."

"He'd have been the best man. And he'd probably have concocted a scheme to have drones overhead, dropping flowers or something on the congregation."

Skyla wiped away a tear as she laughed. "Don't give Anton or any of his crew ideas. Now what's up? You have good news."

"Don't tell anyone yet, but the results of the paternity test are back. It's official. Hoot is Cliff's brother. He and his parents have decided to let the news out tomorrow."

"I knew it! I'm so glad we won't have to tread lightly around Hoot when Pete and Cliff are there."

"Me, too. Hoot seems a lot lighter in spirit—like a load has been lifted from his shoulders."

"Do your kids know?"

"We'll tell them tomorrow. They wouldn't be able to keep it secret today."

"As soon as Karen comes back, you can help me get into my dress." Skyla moved to where it was hanging and touched the white-on-white lines of elvish embroidery on the heavy silk fabric.

"You two are such Lord of the Rings fans, but that elvish look is perfect for you."

"I wondered for a while if this fitted medieval style with a pointed waistline was going to work, or if it would draw attention to my baby bump."

"Skyla! You're pregnant? Why didn't you tell me?"

"I just did." Skyla laughed. "You know my history. Anton and I hardly dared say anything or tempt fate too early. It's too precious."

"When's your baby due?"

"May. We haven't told Krista yet. I'm sure Karen knows, but no one else."

"Has Anton seen your dress? It's gorgeous."

"He hasn't, though I'm sure he has a good idea of what we're up to. Maria, Karen, and Wilma not only made my dress, but they told him exactly what kind of vest he had to get for his tux. Then they

138

whisked his vest away and did all the embroidery on both. He hasn't seen the elvish tiara I've made either."

"I could help you with that now."

Skyla sat in front of the mirror, arranged her long, wavy hair, then lifted the delicate concoction of silver filigree, beads, and seed pearls over her brown hair.

"Shades of Arwen, with a smidge of Galadriel," said Melody as she arranged the intricate back to fall just right. "At first glance, this appears to be a luna moth design, but there's— Skyla Bjornson! You sneak. You did it. Most will see the moth. But if you look at it a different way, it's a Norse dragon!"

Skyla laughed in delight.

"It's brilliant, absolutely brilliant."

Anton stood with Cliff and Sam at the front of the church, looking out over the congregation of friends. His mother had just been seated in front with Dom. He saw all the Circle Sleuths, the crew from his company, Drone Tech, some from the forest service, and a good-sized contingent from Pecos National Historical Park where Skyla worked.

Melody walked down the aisle, and then Krista. His firstborn, confident and happy, turning into a beautiful young lady. There was a new babe on the way, too.

As the organ began the glorious *Trumpet Voluntary*, Anton blinked to clear his eyes. The moment he'd dreamed of was here. Skyla, radiant in her long dress, elegant in a medieval style, came toward him.

Then she was by his side, her extraordinary eyes shining with joy. He savored the moment, reached out his hand, touched the filigree in her hair. His fingers dropped to her wide neckline, and he felt the drag of the embroidered silk fabric against them. He smiled and winked.

Then he took her hand and turned to the minister. At last, vowing before God and the world they had chosen to live with each other in marriage, as long as they both shall live.

After they'd exchanged the rings, they drew close for their first kiss as husband and wife. As his lips left hers, he opened his eyes. So lovely. Suddenly he pulled her back and kissed her again, open-mouthed, ripe with the promise of all that would come later. They held each other as she laughed softly, happily. Chuckles rippled throughout the congregation.

Then the organ trumpets began their triumphant sound. She took his arm, and they started down the aisle.

♦ ❖ ♦

Pete watched the happy couple while they moved among their guests. The reception in the church fellowship hall was winding down. He liked this kind of event, short on pretension, big on genuine enjoyment of the company, delicious food, and music with memories and melodies that you didn't need earplugs for. Pete and Akiko had indulged in their bit of dancing. Slow dances and some of what he called shake-it-loose dances.

He smiled at Akiko, rested his arm on the back of her chair, and lightly caressed the nape of her neck. She leaned subtly toward him and smiled back.

Hoot and Melody left the dance floor to come to their table. Hoot poured himself some coffee and settled back in a chair next to Pete. Melody and Karen left to help Skyla get changed. She and Anton were postponing their honeymoon trip until later. Christmas with family and friends would come first.

Dom sat on the other side of Akiko. It's an oasis, Pete thought, a pleasant interlude in the journey of life. How nice it was to be away from his work for a change.

Hoot laughed at something Dom said, before looking toward his ringing phone. As Hoot answered it, Pete saw his face change. The levity left. His eyes shut briefly, and when he opened them, Pete saw a haunted look of despair.

Pete put a hand on Hoot's arm as he lowered the phone. "What is it? Did something happen?"

Hoot swallowed. "A voice, a whisper."

"Who was it?" asked Pete.

"No idea who. They said, 'You told. Now those you love will pay.' Then they hung up. Just like before."

"Before? When?"

"Wednesday afternoon. I thought it was some prank."

Pete held out his hand toward the phone. "May I look? We'll try to find out about the number."

Hoot handed his phone to Pete. "My number is private. How'd they get it? Who would do something like this? The kidnapper is dead, gone. Why?"

CHAPTER TWENTY-NINE

Hoot tried to push the threatening phone calls to the back of his mind and deal with the day-to-day reality of his newly discovered identity. His family deserved to bask in the joy of reunion. So much had been stolen from them. This would not be spoiled.

Still, he felt the world was spinning out of his control, leaving him with a sense of unease.

He and Melody had talked for a long time about the best way to tell their kids. On Sunday afternoon, in their family room with just the four of them, Hoot said, "Your mom and I have a story to tell you. Matti, I need Koda to help."

Matti ran to fetch the toy. When Hoot settled Koda on his lap, he took a deep breath. Matti and Bonnie, always ready for a story, looked at him expectantly. Melody smiled encouragingly. Well, here goes.

"This Koda was mine when I was little. You remember the man with red hair who we met at Anton's house who looked at you so funny?"

"Yeah," said Matti. "He was scary at first, but he was nice the day we baked ginger cookies."

"He was watching you that way because you look so much like I did when I was your age. It turns out I'm his brother. We were separated, and there was an accident. I was lost and couldn't find my way home again. He is your Uncle Cliff. He kept Koda for me all those years. And now, I've found him and my mother and father again. They are your grandparents. They want very much to meet you."

"But we already have a grandma," said Bonnie.

"Families are sometimes complicated," said Melody. "She's your great-grandma. Most kids have more than one set of grandparents."

"That's where Grandpa Dwight and Grandma Marilyn come into the story," said Hoot. "They thought I was their grandson, Ross Stewart, who was coming to live with them. Everybody in that faraway town thought that."

"Why did they think you were him?" asked Matti. "Couldn't they see you weren't?"

"They hadn't seen Ross for four years. Children change a lot when they're little. Just think how Bonnie has changed in four years."

"Four years—she wasn't even born."

"I be four on my birthday. When's that, Mommy?"

"January tenth."

"How come you didn't tell them, Daddy?" asked Matti.

"You've heard me talk about the plane crash," said Hoot. "I hurt my head, and it took away my memory. Seeing this toy helped. When your Uncle Cliff showed it to me, I started to remember."

Melody smoothed the hair away from her daughter's eyes. "Tomorrow night, you'll get to meet them. Your grandma and grandpa are coming for dinner."

"There's going to be lots of hugging and crying," said Hoot. "Don't be surprised. That's what reunions are all about. They cried, and I did, too, when I met them after such a long time."

"Why did you cry? Were you sad?" Bonnie's eyes were big with wonder.

"Sometimes people cry when they are really happy," Hoot said. "Feelings get too big to stay inside."

"Yuck," said Matti. "Crying. And hugging. Do they have to hug me?"

Melody laughed. "They'll hug your daddy first, I bet. He was once their little boy."

"If you don't want hugs, I'll take them, you little rascal." Hoot tickled his son and smiled at the giggles. "I need all the hugs I can get."

"This Christmas will be very special," said Melody. "We're going to be at your new grandma and grandpa's place. There will be cousins to play with, too."

"What are cousins?" asked Bonnie.

Melody sighed. Hoot laughed and grabbed a piece of paper and one of Bonnie's crayons to show them what a family tree was like. When he was done, Melody said, "Keep that drawing. I've a feeling that we'll want to refer to it again."

As Hoot handed Koda back to his son, he thought again of the vicious whisper in the threatening phone calls. "You told." That feeling of an unseen evil gnawed at his insides.

Pete said he'd try to find out where the calls had come from. While Hoot wished it was only a prank, he knew it wasn't. He realized how isolated his home was. How Matti sometimes walked home alone from school. His children, so young, vulnerable. How could he keep them safe?

Ever since the news of the happy reunion had broken Sunday, the press had been hounding Lynn and Andrew. The Santa Fe and Albuquerque Monday papers had the reunion news splashed all over their front pages. So far, the media hadn't tracked down John McCreath, but they knew it wouldn't be long.

"Did we escape them?" Lynn examined the interior of their borrowed car which sported tinted side and rear windows. They'd exchanged cars with a friend out of the public eye in their church's underground parking garage. They'd expected the attention and had prepared for it, having a spokesperson, and plans like this already in place.

Andrew glanced in the rearview mirror as he merged onto the interstate heading toward Pecos. "I believe we did. They'll catch on to that trick soon enough, but for now, we're okay."

Two more grandchildren, thought Lynn as they traveled to meet Hoot's family. Ten days ago, she hadn't even known about them. Matti was already seven, the oldest of all her grandchildren. Bonnie—almost four. She'd missed out on so much.

What a Christmas this would be. A gift of family.

But the years apart brought challenges. "Andrew, there's something I'm wondering. I'm picking up tension from Hoot. I know we just met him, in a way, and so we don't know what he's like normally. On one hand I see him as joyful, open, and loving. But he's also strung like a piano wire. Is it anxiety? Pressure from the press and public?"

"He's been body-slammed. Everything's changed. He needs time."

"Thank God for Melody. I feel a steadiness in her that will help him adjust."

"Almost there," said Andrew as he turned off the interstate.

"The closer we get, the more excited I feel. But Marilyn . . . Our coming brings her world, as she knows it, to an end."

"Or to a new beginning. I was thinking of her, too. The flip side to finding our son is that her grandson is now missing. They didn't even know Ross was gone."

"Such a long, hard journey ahead. Her son's betrayal was so cruel," said Lynn.

As soon as they stepped inside Hoot's home, Lynn hugged her son, and then Melody. When she released Melody, her eyes saw the boy.

"Oh, my God." The red, curly hair, big blue eyes filled with uncertainty—surely the years had been swept away, and this was Johnny! She'd seen Matti's picture, but nothing prepared her for how much he was like Johnny. Tears filled her eyes, and she sank onto a nearby chair. Suddenly the child rushed forward and threw his arms around her neck. She wrapped him tightly in her arms and couldn't stop her sobs.

"It's okay, Grandma." He leaned back and patted her cheek. "You can cry. Daddy said you would."

Andrew knelt by them. Matti pulled away from her and went to his grandfather. Bonnie came close, ducking her head, blue eyes peering shyly at her through a fringe of red hair. How precious.

"Are you my grandma?"

Lynn nodded and suddenly found herself in another embrace. She looked up, taking in the moment. Feeling the sweetness of her granddaughter's hug. Her son, her daughter-in-law, Andrew with their grandson. She eased back from Bonnie.

Standing near the kitchen, a white-haired woman waited. Her face was wet, and quivering lips seemed to be trying to smile.

Hoot drew her forward. "This is my grandmother, Marilyn."

Lynn rose and went to her, putting her arms around her to hold her close. "I'm so glad to meet you."

"Oh, my dear, what must you think? I'm so sorry."

"You're Johnny's guardian angel." Lynn set her hands lightly on Marilyn's shoulders. "It was agony missing my son. But when he couldn't have us, God gave him you and Dwight to watch over him. You loved him, gave him a home, and raised him to be a fine young man. That should make you proud."

Andrew stood next to them. "We shall always be grateful to you." Then he smiled. "Like it or not, Marilyn Stewart, your family just got bigger."

After dinner was over, Hoot watched Andrew pick up a bag, left by the door. Two packages, wrapped in bright paper, peeked out of the top.

"These aren't Christmas presents," said Andrew. "They're for all the time."

He handed one to Hoot and one to Melody. They opened them to find GPS kid trackers.

"I love these. What a great idea," said Hoot. The fact that he could actually do something to keep his kids safe pushed back against the lingering fumes of past evil.

"They didn't have these back when you were little," said Andrew. "It's an excellent invention."

Matti and Bonnie examined their trackers. Matti's blue one looked and acted like a wristwatch. He put it on and was soon proudly telling them the time.

"Matti's tracker can receive and call out to limited numbers," said Lynn. "Andrew can help you program it later."

Bonnie's lower lip bunched up as she looked at the simple boxy shape of her tracker. Uh-oh, thought Hoot, trouble's coming. He knew she'd like the red color, but she clearly felt Matti's was better.

"This one fits on your shoe," said Lynn. She demonstrated by unlacing one of Bonnie's sneakers and threading the lace through the tracker before securely tying the shoe again.

"What's mine do?" asked Bonnie, looking over at Matti's with a frown on her face.

"These trackers mean your mommy and daddy can find you if you get lost. They send signals to their cell phones."

Hoot reached out to Bonnie's tracker. "Have you ever seen that green gizmo on Twitch's collar?"

Bonnie nodded.

"That's a tracker. He wears that because Anton loves him and doesn't want him to get lost. Yours is like Twitch's, but people get to wear shoe ones, not collar ones."

Hoot saw another way of distracting Bonnie. "I saw photo albums in the bag Grandpa brought. Do you want to ask him if we can look at them now?"

The two photo albums were from before the kidnapping. With Hoot sitting in the middle of the couch, his parents on either side, each with a grandchild on their lap, they looked eagerly through the photos. Melody and Marilyn sat nearby.

Hoot found a photo of himself carrying a large, long-haired, gray cat. "Smoky! I'd forgotten him. He used to sleep at the foot of my bed." He looked up with a smile at his mother.

She blinked rapidly and smiled back. "His name *was* Smoky. That was his favorite spot."

Finally, after they had been through the albums, Matti slid off Andrew's lap. "We have albums, too, from when we were little. I'll get 'em."

"Pick just one, Matti," said Melody. "Save the rest for another time."

"Where did the name Matti come from?" asked Lynn when he returned, clutching a fat album.

"I got to be named after Matti in *Koda and the Sami*."

"That was always your favorite book," said Lynn, looking in surprise at Hoot. "Do you suppose subconsciously you were beginning to remember?"

"Can't tell you," said Hoot. "I do know that book was always important to me."

"They couldn't name me Jussi after the book," said Bonnie, "because I'm a girl."

"That book's about me," said Matti. "I'm the hero."

As Hoot watched Bonnie's face after her brother's statement, her initial mutinous expression cleared. She tilted her chin up. "Girls don't do dumb things wike Jussi. Slide down a hole and can't get out. Girls are smarter than that." She went back to turning album pages.

Hoot looked at Melody. "Where does she get this stuff?"

Melody just shrugged and smiled.

Hoot touched his daughter's hair. Then his hand covered the new tracker on her shoe. He closed his eyes. Pray God they would never actually need to see the trackers in action.

He felt little fingers lifting up his eyebrow and opened his eyes to see Bonnie bending close to his face with a mischievous grin. He smiled back at her.

CHAPTER THIRTY

Tuesday, December 20. The calendar on Pete's desk caught his eye as he leaned back and contemplated the twist of the threatening phone calls.

He looked up at a rap on his door.

Cheveyo Loloma, one of his detectives, stood there. "Lieutenant, got a minute? I've run into a snag with the tribal police."

"Come on in." Pete liked how Cheveyo worked with the different agencies. His broad understanding of the various cultures and his quiet attention to detail kept potential problems from growing.

When Loloma left, his cell phone rang, and he glanced at the screen. "Marilyn, what can I do for you?"

"Do you want more of Gordon's papers?"

"Sure. We still don't know what happed to Ross."

"I have two boxes. Hoot's going into Santa Fe today and can drop them off."

Pete went back to his paperwork and began jotting down notes.

"Andrew McCreath, line one," Yvonne's efficient voice broke Pete's concentration.

"Andrew, how can I help you?"

"I got a call this morning from the *Friday Stories of Hope* TV producer," replied Andrew. "They want to devote their show the thirtieth of December to John's reunion with his family, just ten days from now. I said I'd talk with everyone and get back to them tomorrow. The media circus is in full swing."

"How do you feel about their offer?"

"I've worked with them before in my position with Families of Missing Children. They're reasonable enough, but I want some say in how it's handled. This show has great potential for helping others. We'd like to talk with you this afternoon."

"At your house?" asked Pete.

"It'd be better if we could meet away from the TV trucks and reporters," said Andrew. "They've dug in."

"I can find us a room here," said Pete. "The press will move on as soon as the next sensation hits."

Melody sank gratefully back into her couch cushions with the phone to her ear. "Hoot just left for the meeting about the TV program."

"Cliff, too," said Lou. "Is the media camped out by your house?"

"A few. Honestly, I'll be glad when they're tired of us. I knew it was coming, but that didn't prepare me for the reality."

"I know," said Lou. "I like having another sister-in-law, though."

"Me, too. I think the circus is getting to Hoot. He jumps every time the phone rings. This morning he yelled at Matti for playing out of sight. He's usually more mellow than that."

"Cliff's given up walking Gandalf. Poor dog."

♦ ❖ ♦

At the appointed hour, Pete welcomed Lynn, Andrew, Cliff, and Hoot into a small conference room.

"We're asking for guidelines into the scripting," said Andrew. "First, we want to protect our families."

"I don't want my children mentioned or on camera," said Hoot. "Marilyn, either. I don't want anything to reflect badly on her."

150

"We shouldn't have Melody, Lou, Erin or her husband, or any of the children on camera," said Andrew.

"You'll want to give your organization time to get across their goals;" said Pete.

"Absolutely," said Andrew. "I'll speak to the board tonight."

"One goal," said Lynn, "is to let other families with missing children know they're not alone."

"I'd like to emphasize," said Pete, "how critical the first forty-eight hours are and how important it is to involve the community. The positive publicity from this happy ending may stimulate a look at other cold cases."

"That's good," said Andrew. "Let's organize this and get it down on paper."

When they finished and were collecting their papers to leave, Hoot said, "If Gordon hadn't been killed, how did he think he could keep control over me in the future? Even if he threatened me every so often, wouldn't I have found a way to say who I was? Dwight and Marilyn loved me. I never felt bad vibes from them. I don't think Gordon thought that through well."

"I don't know, Hoot," said Pete. "He had tremendous control over you. He could have harmed your family at any time, as far as you knew. That power was all his."

Hoot's phone rang, and he froze for a second before he answered. Pete glanced sharply at him. The expression on Hoot's face told him immediately. Another threat.

Hoot handed the phone to Pete, who looked at it, grimaced, and jotted a few notes down in his notebook. "What did he say this time?"

"Same thing," Hoot said. "You told."

"Same thing! What's going on?" asked Cliff as he sat down in his chair again.

"Hoot, I know you've told Melody and your grandmother," said Pete, "but do Lynn, Andrew, and Cliff know?"

"Not yet. I'm grateful for having my family back. *I am.*" Hoot's voice began rising. "It's just that my children are being threatened, and I don't know how to protect them. I'm sorry. This whole happy reunion thing has plunged Melody and me into hell." Hoot leaned forward, put his elbows on the conference table and covered his eyes with his hands. He whispered, "I'm sorry."

Lynn looked shocked.

Cliff jerked upright. "Bloody hell!"

Andrew spoke urgently. "That phone call? Please tell us."

"Hoot, may I?" asked Pete.

Hoot nodded and leaned back in his chair. "I'm sorry."

"You've nothing to apologize for," said Pete. "Hoot has been getting anonymous phone calls, all about the same as this one. They say, 'You told. Now your family will pay.' Then they hang up."

Andrew let out an expletive and banged his fist on the table. "Bastards!"

"Why would somebody do such a horrible thing?" cried Lynn.

"Pete, can't you figure out who it is and stop them?" asked Cliff. "Trace the calls?"

Pete snapped his eyes to him. "Don't you think I've tried? I suspect it's a burner phone."

"Do you suppose . . . we should cancel out on the TV show entirely?" asked Lynn. "Not do it at all?" The room was quiet as her words sank in.

Pete's gaze swept the faces around table. Confusion and sadness. No one said anything, they just looked lost.

Pete closed his eyes, seeing the possibilities from the inspirational show dissipate like smoke. *Damn the caller.*

Then he heard a soft voice break the stillness.

"No."

Pete opened his eyes.

"No," Hoot repeated, his voice stronger, his eyes glistening. "Who wins then? As much as I'd like it all to go away, the pain will never stop until they're caught, and until we face them." His voice shook. "I've had enough—enough of living in shadow and fear."

"Of being a victim," said Cliff. "Of lacking power."

Hoot nodded.

Andrew reached out to Hoot's shoulder. "We need a plan."

"Amen," Pete said.

"Could we draw the bastard into a net?" Andrew asked.

"Maybe we could make this TV program work in our favor," Pete said reflectively. "Using great care."

"What we say and do will be seen by millions," said Lynn.

"Hope is the lifeline of many families caught in this web," said Andrew. "What we do has a ripple effect."

They settled back, opened their notebooks again, and began going back over the material, looking for ideas, for nuances, for ways of articulating things that might make a difference. A plan to entice the caller into a trap where he could be apprehended.

CHAPTER THIRTY-ONE

Hoot's mind wandered away as he and Melody, Lou and Cliff, Sam and Farah met at Books and Bearclaws amid the hustle of last-minute, Christmas-Eve-morning shoppers. Their great plan was still coming up empty. They'd left the meeting last Tuesday after his emotional outburst with nothing definite in mind. Just a vague idea that he could somehow trap the caller, using himself as bait. The deadline for airing the show marched closer and still—nothing. They'd bought a little time by convincing the production company they needed to film the last segment as late as they could to "accommodate current developments" in the case. He shrugged. Whatever those were!

Hoot supposed it was a risk, being here in public view, but they couldn't stay cooped up all the time without getting squirrelly. They found a table next to the play cube where the Koda and Sami merchandiser sat almost empty. The plush rabbit caught his eye.

"Have you heard Bonnie's hints about wanting the rabbit?" he asked. "She told me the other day Foxie was lonely."

Melody rolled her eyes. "She's told everybody. I think Lynn has already gotten one for her."

"What kind of a rabbit is that?" asked Farah.

"Snowshoe rabbit," said Hoot. "Big feet. Smallish, black-tipped ears."

"I don't think they have snowshoe rabbits in Lapland," said Cliff.

"What kind of rabbits do they have?" asked Sam.

"Mountain hares," said Cliff.

Sam picked up one from the display and looked at the tag. "It says rabbit, not hare."

"Listen to you," said Lou, laughing. "Arguing over species in a children's fantasy book? You've got a little gnome-like critter that rides on the back of a snowy owl, and a fox that makes northern lights. Give me a break. It can be any kind of rabbit you want it to be—even a make-believe one."

"You do have a point." Sam set the rabbit back.

"If I were the illustrator," said Lou, "I'd choose the species that appeals to kids—especially if you want to sell lots of them. The snowshoe rabbit was a good choice."

"Hare," said Melody.

"What?" Lou started laughing again.

"It's snowshoe hare, not rabbit." Cliff leaned back with a smile.

"It's a fantasy," said Sam. "If I say rabbit, man, that's what it is."

"Rabbit Man? Where did the man come from?" Farah asked.

Sam had a mischievous grin. "Don't know. Just hopped into my head."

"Rabbit Man. Give me a break," said Cliff.

Hoot sucked in a breath and frowned.

"What's the matter?" asked Melody.

He shook his head. "Nothing. Just a shiver going down my spine."

"Speaking of shivers, here come the paparazzi," said Cliff. "Shall we go?"

CHAPTER THIRTY-TWO

Humming along with "Silver Bells" Karen looked at the bins of fresh arugula, kale, and spinach at the Saturday Santa Fe Farmers' Market. She bought some and put them on top of the carrot bunches in her produce bag. She moved past the potatoes, mushrooms, and fragrant soaps, stopping at the dried herb and strawflower wands.

She spotted a dark-haired woman sniffing a sage bundle. Karen smiled. "Akiko, I thought it was you."

Akiko waved the sage at the display. "Aren't they pretty?"

"I'm addicted to lavender," said Karen. "I always have it in my weaving studio."

"I love it, too," said Akiko. "but for now, I want something that will release scent near our soaking tub."

"This time of year, it would be great to have a hot tub," said Karen. Akiko had such a pretty smile, she thought.

"In Japan, it's a great pleasure to sit in a hot bath, to talk, and relax. Pete and I have followed that custom here."

"Are you coming to watch the TV program with us on Friday?" asked Karen, as she picked up a lavender wand.

Akiko's smile disappeared, and her nostrils flared. A moment of silence stretched just long enough to make Karen uneasy.

"Pete hasn't mentioned it, but of course I am," said Akiko. "I'm assuming everyone's coming?"

"*Uff da*. Isn't that just like a man? Even Lynn and Andrew McCreath are coming. It should be quite a celebration."

"I must be going. Merry Christmas."

Karen returned the greeting and watched as Akiko left the pavilion without stopping to make more purchases. That cheerfulness was feigned. "Did I just get Pete in trouble? I hope not."

"Who's in trouble?" Dom appeared at her elbow, carrying two cups of coffee and a small bag of pastry. "Want to split a chocolate-chunk scone with me?"

"I'd love to." She took one of the coffees and told him about the exchange with Akiko.

"Pete probably hasn't gotten around to telling her yet," said Dom, licking a scone crumb from his lip. "I wouldn't worry about it."

◆ ❖ ◆

Late Monday night, Hoot slouched on his couch, watching TV. Their Christmas tree lit their front window, though they'd opened all the packages yesterday at his parents' home. What a Christmas celebration that had been. A gift of family.

Bonnie had gotten her rabbit from her grandparents. At the moment, Rabbit peered out from under the decorated branches of their tree. Bonnie said he liked it there. Foxie still reigned in Bonnie's heart and was tucked into bed with her. The rabbit would have his day, but not yet.

Hoot still brooded about what they would do at the meeting tomorrow. Their great plan was still nonexistent, and time was running out. Another headache flirted with his mind, but he didn't stir himself to go for the ibuprofen. Maybe if he closed his eyes, the headache would go away.

Melody stretched out beside him, snuggled under a blanket, her feet propped on the coffee table. She spoke, but he didn't hear her words. An image struggled to form, frightening him. He heard himself pant and turned his face away from the shadowy figure.

He was coming . . .

"Hoot?"

His eyes opened. "Huh?"

"What's the matter?"

"Sorry. I saw him. At that door in my mind."

"Another memory?"

"All that talk about Rabbit Man. It's been haunting me. I remember . . . someone else. In the plane when we left Santa Fe."

Melody sat up and turned to him. "My God. A second kidnapper? Could he be making the threats?"

"Rabbit."

"What?"

"He had a red mark. Reaching up from his neck. Like rabbit ears. I watched. Lying there."

"Lying where?" Her hand was warm as it covered the cold clamminess of his own. She drew her blanket over them both. "Close your eyes. Think. What do you see?"

After a few moments of silence, his voice came out soft and hesitant.

"A man. I was lying on the seats behind him. I couldn't move. Tied. He wouldn't help. I was crying. The plane made a constant droning noise. When the sun started to go down, inside the plane the light turned red. It shone on his neck. Those two ears reached up onto his face. Much darker red. He was Rabbit Man. Not soft and cuddly, but evil. Mean."

Hoot swallowed hard and opened his eyes to look at her. "I watched him the whole way. Before we landed in Denver, he looked back at me. Said again if I *ever told* anyone what happened, how he would hurt my family. Over and over. And he laughed. *He laughed.* I knew I could never tell. I didn't want my family to be hurt and die. I never saw him again after Denver . . . but I knew he would do it." His voice dropped to a whisper. "Melody, what have I done? Our kids are in danger."

"Call Pete. Right now."

"Melody, look at the time."

"It's the right time to call. Pete wouldn't want you to wait. This is important."

Chapter Thirty-Three

"I thought you should be included on Hoot's plan, Hiram, since it may play out in your jurisdiction." Pete smiled at the older, gruff state trooper as they walked through the labyrinth of halls the next day on their way to Chief Grover's conference room.

One of the New Mexico State Police offices was in Pecos, and, in an oddity of bureaucracy, they looked to the state police as their local law, and thus to Hiram Brower.

"I didn't know if I'd be able to make it," said Hiram. "Holidays always land us with a heavier work load."

"Too much alcohol and stress," said Pete, "and no lack of stupidity."

Hiram snorted. "You can say that again."

Pete admired the trooper. He looked innocent and benign, but his kindly brown eyes under those shaggy gray brows didn't miss a thing. Pete had already filled him in and had made no secret of his misgivings about the sketchy details of Hoot's plan.

He pushed open the conference room door. The others were already there—Chief Grover, Lynn and Andrew, Cliff, Hoot, and Sam. They plunged into the heart of the matter with Hoot's memory of the second kidnapper, Rabbit Man, and their plans for the revelation during the TV program.

"It's a long shot, this idea," said Grover. "Not the most efficient plan."

"I have to do something," said Hoot. "Most of my life has been affected by his threats. If you have a better idea, say it."

Whoa, that was a challenge, thought Pete. Hoot's eyes locked with Grover's in silence.

Finally, Grover sat back in his chair. "I'm just expressing concern. We've no specific details, just anonymous threats from a burner phone. This has the markings of a misdemeanor more than a felony and stretches into an indefinite future. It will be damn hard to protect innocent lives under such vagueness. How do we use our personnel and tax money wisely here?"

"I see this plan as only one part of our tactics," said Pete. "We'll be investigating this dirtbag from other angles, too."

"The likely outcome is that it will stir up a hornet's nest after the broadcast," said Hiram. "Protection is something we should be prepared for." He looked at Grover from under his bushy brows. "Dollars are important, but so is our moral responsibility."

"Let's tackle the protection first, then," said Andrew.

"Hoot, you're going to be sick of us wanting to know where you and your family are all the time," said Grover. "But that's key to your safety."

"Document everything. Log all calls," said Pete.

"Get used to calling us with what's happening, even if you don't think it's significant. And don't think you're a bother. I'd rather be bothered than miss a clue." Hiram's brows drew together. "Hoot, I'd like you and me to sit down with your boss. There's good folk working at the forestry office. They can help."

"How about Matti's teacher and his principal?" asked Lynn.

"I can talk to them. No more walking home. They have to know who's picking Matti up," said Hiram. "It's excellent your kids have trackers."

"Since we don't know this kidnapper's mind and what he will do," said Sam, "I think we ought to know about the schedules of Hoot's parents, Cliff and his family, and Marilyn, too."

"We aren't even positive that the caller is this second kidnapper. Could be a nutcase getting his jollies and presenting no real threat," said Grover.

160

"Are you willing to take that chance?" asked Pete.

Grover shook his head. "Let's get this down on paper."

Together they crafted a protection plan which would be coordinated through Grover and Hiram. Grover arranged for Hoot to record his cell phone calls.

"I've worked with many families in crisis," said Andrew. "We should make conscious choices as to what facts the media gets."

"Pecos is a small town with an overactive grapevine," said Hiram, "but you're right about filtering what the world at large gets to hear."

"If you know how that grapevine works," said Grover, "use it to your advantage. That community might circle the wagons around one of their own."

CHAPTER THIRTY-FOUR

Anticipation filled Pete as he arrived at the Bjornsons' to watch *Friday Stories of Hope* with the Sleuths, out of sight and reach of the press. The script, coordinated between law enforcement and the production company, included a final update with Lynn, Andrew, and their two sons, filmed two days ago. The Bjornsons, at Pete's suggestion, had invited Hoot and his family, including Marilyn, to spend the night after the gathering to watch the program.

As Pete walked to the door, he saw a large Christmas tree dominating the front window. Traditional Scandinavian candle holders held light in the other windows. A nice tradition, he thought, from a country where December daylight was scarce.

Inside an air of festivity and a feeling of energy radiated from the group in the family room. Karen greeted Pete with a smile.

"Akiko had other plans tonight," Pete said. "She sends her regrets."

"Oh, she's already here. She came with Lou and Dougie." Karen waved her hand in their direction.

"What?" Pete recovered quickly. "I misunderstood her then." He looked over at Akiko. She met his eyes and raised her chin a notch before turning back to her conversation with Farah.

He closed his eyes briefly. Why did he keep doing this to himself? You'd think he'd know better after so many years. It was just that he'd been shaken to his core when he'd heard about Cowboy and his wife.

Yet trouble always followed his assumptions that it was good to keep Akiko separate from anything involving work. He'd hear about his stubborn German protectiveness, and he had it coming. Several times the words had been on the tip of his tongue to tell Akiko about the gathering, but he'd kept mum. Obviously, she'd heard about it from someone else.

He sat down by Sam and accepted a glass of wine.

"Twitch, where's your collar?" asked Anton.

Bonnie looked up from where she was playing with the dogs and pointed to where it lay, still connected to his leash. "That thingy is too hard for my fingers to do."

Anton sighed and put Twitch's collar back on. "The show's starting."

The program flew by, crammed with pathos and hype for the amazing reunion. Pete was dismayed at the few minutes allotted to programming. Commercials from the sponsoring DNA company, Climb Your Family Tree, and other advertisers had nabbed seventeen minutes of the hour.

The first part told the horrifying story of the kidnapping and, gave a come-on for the reunion. They showed Lynn and Andrew and then switched to Hoot at his home, sitting on the couch in a rather pensive attitude. The cameraman, evidently admiring the puzzle box sitting on the table, had briefly focused on that box with its carved wooden hand. Then they went to a commercial break.

"Where'd the box come from?" asked Pete. "It's very unusual."

"It was in the things I've been looking through," said Marilyn. "It was Gordon's."

"Hoot brought it on Thanksgiving, and we tried to open it," said Anton. "It's a puzzle box. We got the first level open, but haven't figured out the rest."

"I love puzzle boxes," said Pete. "I'll ask Hoot to show it to me. There's a German company that makes really challenging ones."

His attention returned to the TV as Lynn and Andrew talked about the importance of support for families, and then his own screen-time talking about the investigation and the community working together.

The happy reunion followed, before the interviewer began asking questions of Hoot. "What triggered your memories?"

"It began for me when I met this guy at a festival." He motioned to Cliff, who told the rest of that bit.

Hoot said, "Sometime after that, Detective Schultz, who'd been on the case from the beginning, met me. I couldn't remember anything before the plane crash. The couple I believed were my grandparents were expecting their grandson to be delivered to them. Everyone just assumed I was him. I grew up believing it. The doctors said I had amnesia from the crash."

Hoot reached out to touch the hand on the puzzle box on the table in front of him. "I felt like this creature was in my mind, trying to get out. Memories started to come, just flashes at first. In time, I may remember more."

Finally, they reached the last segment—the update filmed just Wednesday. The interviewer turned to Hoot. "Have you remembered anything more about the kidnapping itself?"

"I remembered the other man on the plane."

The interviewer appeared startled. "Two kidnappers? But wasn't there only the pilot on the plane with you when it crashed?"

"The second man only went to Denver. He wasn't on the plane the second or third day."

In the Bjornson family room, Pete watched the faces around him. Some knew what was coming, but most didn't.

"When I was grabbed, there was another man in the car. They said stop screaming, or they would kill my family and hurt me. In the plane, they tied me up on the seats behind the pilot."

"A second kidnapper! Pete, did you—" Anton stopped.

Pete held up a hand. "Listen!"

The interviewer asked, "Would you recognize this other man now? That was twenty-five years ago."

164

"The image is fuzzy. I remember staring at the guy's neck—a dark red stain like two rabbit ears reaching up onto his face, a birthmark, I suppose. I thought of him as Rabbit Man. Don't know if I'll remember more."

"What is the most amazing thing to you about your story?"

"My parents never gave up looking. I can't imagine their feelings, not knowing, looking for years, no closure. Yet they went on and supported other families. Me—I was just a kid, growing up in a home where I was loved, going to school, having a normal life. I had no idea."

A commercial break allowed a torrent of comments from the gathering. Anton's cut to the quick. "Pete, did you know about this memory? Do you know who the second man is?"

"Haven't identified him yet. We're hoping this program brings him out in the open."

Then the show closed with Lynn and Andrew talking about hope and its importance. Andrew said they'd always kept the light on, thinking that it would someday light their son's way home. The camera went to the only outside shot they'd done—that of the porch light at the McCreaths' home. As they watched, the light went out, and the screen faded to swiftly moving credits.

"Wow," said Karen. "I'm impressed, but concerned as hell. If he's still on the loose, you might have just painted a big target—"

Farah interrupted. "Kids, do you want to help me make whipped cream for the pie?"

"I wanna help." Bonnie jumped up from playing with Twitch. Farah enticed Leyla, Bonnie, and Matti into the kitchen. Krista followed, but sent a worried look back at her dad.

Pete's eyes flicked to Akiko. She was quiet, her dark gaze intent on him.

"I wanted to do this," said Hoot. "We can't live this way. That man is evil and *must* be caught."

Anton turned off the TV off and looked again at Pete. "I'm assuming you have Hoot's back covered?"

"You know it. The PD and the state police."

Karen frowned. "When you suggested Hoot and his family stay over tonight here, that wasn't just for convenience, was it?"

"No." Pete glanced around. "You can all help. Keep your eyes open. Tell us if you feel something isn't right. Now we wait."

"And watch," said Sam. He looked to the kitchen and smiled as the kids focused on whipping the cream, the noise of the mixer Farah held an audible shield to the worries expressed in the family room.

Pete enjoyed the pie and coffee, biding his time before he could talk with Hoot.

"Have you remembered anything more?" asked Pete, as he and Sam finally got a chance to pull Hoot aside. They walked down the hall to where more electric candles raised in triangles softly lit the window near Karen's studio.

Hoot shook his head. "I feel like I'm standing on the edge of a cliff in a strong wind. I didn't appreciate just how nerve wracking this would be. Not knowing when, or even if, evil will pounce again. I hope I'm right that their target will be me, not my family."

Melody came in sight, a serious look on her face.

"Let us know if you remember anything more," said Pete. "We'll check in with you regularly."

Melody slid her arms around Hoot. He dropped a kiss on her hair before lightly rubbing the scar on his head.

Pete's brows drew together in concern as he watched the couple. How could he protect them against such an amorphous threat? "Sam and I will double down in our investigation. I can't help but think there are more answers in those boxes of papers."

Then he heard sounds indicating the party was breaking up. "People are leaving. I'd better see if Akiko is ready."

He hurried down the hall to find her holding a sleeping Dougie while Cliff helped Lou with her jacket and the diaper bag. "Angel, I didn't see your car. You can ride with me and save the kids the trouble."

"It's no trouble," Akiko said. "My car is at their house." She adjusted the blanket over the baby and left.

CHAPTER THIRTY-FIVE

Stunned by what he'd seen, Vassily looked wide-eyed at his wife, calmly knitting as she sat in her recliner and watched the end of *Friday Stories of Hope*.

"Such a heartwarming story," Yvonne said. "Hard to imagine it happened in Santa Fe. I mean, you expect things like that in New York, but not here. That kidnapper must have had a birthmark like my brother's. I'm glad they're able to treat port wine stains now. I know it always embarrassed Hayle. He was much happier when he had it removed."

She came to the end of a row and took a sip of tea.

Vassily still hadn't said a word. That brother of hers was a kidnapper! If she had half a brain, she would know it, tell her boss, and solve that damn case she fantasized about.

He remembered that week back in 1991. It was the last time that pilot had stayed with them. Hayle had traveled with Gordon on hunting trips. They often flew from Denver, stopping over in Santa Fe, and then went on to the White Sands area for oryx hunting.

Hunting wasn't Vassily's thing, though those beasts were impressive—awkwardly long horns to handle. He didn't know what happened on that last trip, but there had been a dust-up with the taxidermist Gordon always used. He'd gone out of business or something and left them high, dry, and owing them a ton of money.

Then Hayle had called from the airport where they'd left Vassily's car. Said he'd have to pick it up from there. Something had come up and they had to get back to Denver immediately. Damned inconvenient, interrupting his schedule like that. Months later, when Yvonne asked her brother about Gordon, Hayle said he'd crashed his plane and died.

"Would you like anything from the kitchen, dear?" Yvonne set down her knitting and picked up her cup.

Vassily couldn't believe she didn't get it. "No." In amazement, Vassily watched her leave. The whole damn thing had gone right over her head. If she knew, would she snitch on her brother? Interesting question. Probably. Her illusion of her great detective-self was more motivation than love for her brother.

That slimy bastard. Hayle had been using her. He only wanted to see those papers to know what the cops were up to.

Would Hayle pay to keep him quiet?

What could Hayle do? Complain to the cops about him?

He'd start off small. See how it went. Let him know he knew. Vassily would never tell if . . . if Hayle treated him well. Maybe a couple hundred a month.

Or a week. Vassily began to formulate his plans.

A thousand miles away in an unremarkable motel in a small, sleepy, rural community, a man turned off the TV.

Finding that program had been a stroke of luck. Forced to watch what the local networks carried rather than cable channels, he'd been idly flipping back and forth, lamenting the rotten choices, when suddenly, he'd happened on Schultz's face. The man hadn't changed that much. Hair was thinner and receding. He was still a cop.

Funny, that kidnapping had been more than twenty-five years ago. If Schultz was interested in cold cases, he'd give him a cold case challenge.

He went to his pickup and came back in with a road atlas. Things were looking up.

◆ ❖ ◆

Spending a quiet evening at his mansion near Denver, Wit turned another page of the novel he was reading, tuning out his wife's TV program.

"Didn't you used to have a similar box, dear?"

His wife's cultured voice pulled Wit from the world of deception and intrigue on the pages of his thriller. "Box? What are you talking about?"

"Look. On TV. I always thought it was appalling with that hand trying to get out." She shuddered dramatically.

"What are you watching?" The image on the screen of that distinctive zebrawood box sent all thought of his book catapulting from his mind. *That damn puzzle box!*

Could there be another like his? His father had said there wasn't.

Did it still hold his secrets? How could he be sure?

He swallowed against the burning, sour taste in the back of his throat and rubbed his knuckles against his breastbone. The book slid off his lap, losing his place, to lie forgotten as he watched the rest of the program.

Not now, after all this time. His life was going so well. His daughter's future would be brilliant, reflecting well on him. His son-in-law-to-be was intelligent, cunning, and ambitious enough to chart a run toward the White House.

Now that wretched box with its secrets could ruin everything.

Was there any way he could get it back? He simply must.

Why had he ever put anything in there? But it had been the only place he'd thought of at the time. His wife was in and out of their safe daily. The box should have worked for a few days, until he'd had a chance to get to the bank, secure what he wanted, and destroy the rest.

And then it had been stolen.

CHAPTER THIRTY-SIX

The New Year's holiday brought company to Vassily's household. With excitement tinged with fear, Vassily watched Hayle from his recliner as football games clogged the airwaves. He knew Hayle was chomping at the bit until Yvonne could go to work again and find out what the detectives were up to following that show with its bombshell revelation. He got up to fix another round of drinks.

Vassily handed his brother-in-law his glass and sat down again. Sounds from the kitchen told him Yvonne was preparing dinner. "I heard something Friday. Remember that kidnapping case Yvonne was obsessing over? I could help her solve it. Seems there was a second kidnapper. I know who it is."

Hayle flicked a glance at him before taking a sip of his scotch. "Don't tell me she's got you hooked on that nonsense. I thought you were smarter than that."

"The doctor did a good job on your port wine stain, didn't he? Can't even tell there used to be an ugly rabbit-like shape on your neck halfway up your cheek."

As Vassily watched, his brother-in-law's jaw muscles tightened.

Hayle cleared his throat. "There's some scarring, but I was fortunate. Kids are lucky now. Stains are easier to treat when you're young."

"Except the technology wasn't there yet when you were a child. Funny thing, technology. Technology got me laid off just before I'd worked long enough to draw my full pension. I miss that income." Vassily noted the rigidness in Hayle's posture.

"What's that got to do with Yvonne and her kidnapping?"

"Don't play stupid. You and Gordon used my car to kidnap that boy. You left it at the airport. Here's this kid, all grown up, remembering a fellow with a rabbit-shaped birthmark. I could tell Yvonne what I know. She could solve her case, or—" Vassily looked down into his glass, swirling the scotch around. He took a deep breath. "Or you could help me make up that missing income."

"She would never turn me in."

"No? Perhaps not. But would I?"

He met the steely gaze of his brother-in-law. The line had been crossed.

"You should think long and hard before you say any more."

"My plans are always made with a great deal of deliberation." Vassily raised an eyebrow. "And with great care regarding contingencies."

Hayle blinked. "The difference in your pension. What are we talking about? I might be able to help a family member . . . for a while." He looked at Vassily. "Especially if I can study those papers your wife brings home. Mutual aid is always agreeable, don't you think?"

Vassily glanced at the clock and set his empty glass down. "It's four. Let's walk."

◆ ❖ ◆

Wit couldn't remember a more horrible New Year's weekend— nothing sparkled and festive banquets may as well have been sawdust. On Monday, Wit went to his downtown office, cancelled his appointments, and tried to rein in his panic. He had to get that box. No hint of it could ever reach his father-in-law, his family, or even the public.

Two pillars supported the empire Wysocki shared with his father-in-law, and both prospered better because of the reputation they had cultivated—successful, and noisily benevolent in charity. Initially, real estate development provided the financial underpinning, but recently, their political consultation firm had blossomed under Wit's passionate leadership. Grooming candidates for success paid well, and he exulted in his role as king-maker.

Wit went online to research the TV show, the kidnapping, and the reunion. He found out the young man lived near Santa Fe.

There was only one thing to do—send somebody to retrieve the box. Certainly, he'd have heard something if the people on TV had managed to open it. He had the key to the second layer anyway. That gave him hope his secrets were still hidden. In the TV program, the box was just sitting on the coffee table. The household was not, by any stretch of the imagination, sophisticated and didn't strike him as the kind of place that would even have a security system.

Wit leaned back in his chair, thinking about whom he could send. In the old days, Wilcox could have pulled off a stunt like this in his sleep. But lately, he was losing his edge, overlooking important details, and more than once, requiring somebody to clean up the mess he'd made.

He'd like to send Jed, but he was still on another assignment. On the other hand, how difficult could this be? Wilcox would have to do.

He flipped the switch to talk to his secretary. "Tell Wilcox to come by this afternoon. I have a job for him."

CHAPTER THIRTY-SEVEN

Pete turned on his office lights to augment the weak sun of the day after New Year's.

"*Mein Gott*, Sam. A second kidnapper." He moved a box of Gordon's papers to the round table. "Those first phone calls were made even before it was known locally that Johnny had been found. Why now after twenty-five years?"

"Must have inside knowledge somehow. Do you suppose it's someone who knows the Stewarts or the McCreaths?" Sam opened his laptop.

"Rather that, than a leak from within the PD."

"Pete!"

"I don't like the timing. Let's organize this box better. Catalog the names and dates that aren't standard-type bills."

"You sort, I'll document. What box number is this?"

"Four. We'll do five later," said Pete. "What happened to the damn car? Two men were on the flight to Denver. No rental cars turned in. No cars abandoned. *Ach du lieber*, is there a third person?"

"Someone picking up the car as a friend might not have known what was going down."

Pete nodded and moved a stack of photos out of the way and started rifling through the papers. "There's a lot here about Gordon's hunting trips."

"Will those be useful?"

Pete shrugged. "He has trips organized into packets—eight of them in this box. One trip per packet." He looked at the names of the hunters. No repeats. "Gordon was either charismatic or he fished the society pages. Even I recognize some of the names."

"Like who?"

"Cullen Barlow. Well-known defense attorney. Bruce Flannery, who, if I recall, made his fortune developing ski resorts. Last packet is Wit Wysocki, a big-shot real estate guy. Dabbles in politics, too." He opened the first packet. "Contracts, arrangements, invoices, envelope of photos. *Mein Gott*, even notes about delivery. This one has a redelivery date to hang properly."

"Chart the trips," said Sam. "Look for patterns." They worked through two packets and started the next.

Pete scanned the third packet. "Interesting. A guy named Hayle came on this trip. Why does that name sound familiar?"

"We met a Hayle in Denver."

"The former cop." Pete scribbled a note. "Stonewalling."

"You think?"

"I don't believe in coincidences."

They worked for a while longer. "So far, three of three packets have dates for delivery and redelivery. Why didn't they get it right the first time? You'd think they'd have learned."

"Or gotten a new taxidermist." Pete opened the next packet, glanced through it, and skipped ahead through all eight. "Every packet has two delivery dates."

Sam sat back from his charting. "Intentional?"

"Has to be. Deliver. Won't hang right. Redeliver. I'd love to get my hands on one of those trophies. Sam, hand me the papers with that taxidermist's information. While you catalog these packets, I want to check something."

Pete got on the internet, then made a few calls.

"Sam, listen. The taxidermist was busted just before Johnny was kidnapped. Convicted of receiving stolen goods. He reset stones, sold the new pieces, and gave a cut to the thieves. Wouldn't surprise me if Gordon used that service."

"Where's this guy now?"

"Dead."

Yvonne knocked on the closed door and entered. "I wanted to say congratulations on the TV show. Have there been any new leads since it aired?"

"Thanks, Yvonne." Pete ignored her question.

Yvonne picked up the files in the out-box and left, leaving the door open behind her. Pete watched as she stopped at the filing cabinet and began working on the stack.

"What do we do now besides shuffling papers?" asked Sam. "Just keep our eyes open for indications that the second kidnapper is nervous?"

"Not much, is it? I want you to examine all the photos from these boxes, looking for someone with a birthmark or port wine stain on their neck and face. Why did we ever let Hoot do this? I'm afraid time is not on our side."

"We should look at Gordon's friends again," said Sam. "Only someone close and trusted would share secrets this size."

"We'll have to visit the old geezers again. See if they recognize anybody in the photos, but I don't think we'll go back to Isaacson's precinct."

Pete laid some more old bills on the "not-interested" pile, then got up and shut his door. "There's a bad taste in my mouth from the Denver folks in all of this. The stonewalling, being tracked. I keep coming back to a comment one of the geezers made—about Gordon and his cop friend. And now the name Hayle again. What if that cop was somehow involved in the kidnapping? What if he doesn't like old memories being stirred up?"

"I've an idea," Sam said. "All the cops that were possibly involved in the stonewalling who were the right age—Oliver, Commander Isaacson, Cannon, and Hayle? Can we get their police academy photos to show to the geezers? Those pictures would show them as they were when the geezers met him."

Pete sighed and shook his head. "Why didn't I think of that? I'll have Yvonne get the photos." He went back to his sorting. "*Scheisse*! Just remembered. Stanley said he had one of Gordon's trophy heads."

"You don't suppose?"

"*Ja*, I do.

♦ ❖ ♦

Early Tuesday morning while visiting his sister, Hayle made a point of getting up early to talk with her in private before Vassily arose.

"I saw that TV program about the kidnapped boy and your boss. I bet he's happy." Hayle kept his voice calm. "What did you learn yesterday about what's going on? Does that Stewart guy think he can identify the kidnapper?"

"Stewart is remembering more. I brought home notes from yesterday to study. I even copied a picture of Stewart's children, not that it will help solve the case. Such darlings. Wouldn't it be exciting if Schultz was able to make an arrest soon?"

"Oh, yeah. Real exciting."

Yvonne shot him an annoyed look. "I don't like your attitude. You've never given me the credit I deserve. Look, I don't have to tell you anything if you're going to be such an ass about it."

"I didn't mean it like that. I like talking with you about it. Where does this red-headed guy live? Santa Fe?"

"No, he works for the forest service in Pecos, lives on the east side, I think, not too far from the Pecos River Cabins. Maybe I shouldn't tell you that. Anyway, you're not involved in the case." She let out a peal of laughter.

"You're right."

Yvonne sprinkled the crumble topping on the coffeecake she was making and put it in the oven. Then she turned to Hayle with a frown. "I've been wondering something. Schultz asked me to get your picture and a couple others from the police academy. Why's he interested in you?"

"I've met Schultz. I've talked with him. He's not interested in me." Hayle straightened the silverware on the table. "Does he know I'm your brother?"

176

Yvonne set the timer. "I don't think he knows anything about my family, except that I'm married. He's going to ask a witness if they recognize any of those people in the photos."

"Really? Who is this witness?"

"Somebody in Denver. He's going to make another trip there in a few weeks."

"I won't say a word to anyone. It's just idle curiosity on my part." *Interesting, though. I think it might be time to tighten the screws. I don't want any more memories popping up.*

◆ ❖ ◆

"Sir?"

Pete looked up from where he was helping a detective in the bullpen with search-warrant wording to find Yvonne standing at his elbow.

"There's a call for you. Mrs. Stewart, line one."

Pete selected the line on the detective's phone.

"Marilyn, how can I help you?"

"I was wondering if you'd looked in those last two boxes yet that Hoot delivered to you. One of our recent photo albums might have gotten there by mistake. Bonnie had been looking at it. She said she put it back, and we just realized we hadn't seen it since. It has a red cover and likely would be on top."

Pete walked into his office. In box five, he found it immediately and picked up his own phone. "It's here. I'll set it on my desk and make sure you get it back."

"I'm just glad to know where it is."

He flipped through the album to confirm that it was recent, before turning his mind back to the detective's search warrant. He made a few suggestions, then left to meet the forensics team at a crime scene.

As he was finishing there, midafternoon, his cell phone rang. Hoot Stewart.

"Hoot, any more calls?"

"I was wondering if I could show you something. I just got it in the mail, and frankly, it scares me."

"I'm almost through here, and then I'm heading back to the office. You can meet me at Books and Bearclaws."

As soon as Pete arrived at Books and Bearclaws and spotted Hoot waiting in the coffee area, the pallor of his skin told him the young man had another headache. Pete sat, and Hoot held out an envelope. Pete put on gloves before taking it. Plain envelope—available at any office-supply store. He looked at the postmark—Santa Fe. Yesterday. He opened the flap and removed a folded, four-by-six index card. Printed with a black marker, it said, "You told. I know where you live."

"Ach, no," said Pete. "We'll see if we can get prints from this. Has anyone besides you touched it?"

"I showed it to Melody," said Hoot, "but she didn't touch it. We thought of fingerprints. Do you think this is the same person who called at the wedding?"

"Very likely," said Pete. "They have the phrase, 'You told,' in common. I'll have forensics check. Bad move on the part of the perp—brings in the postal inspector. Makes it a federal crime. I'll let Hiram know."

CHAPTER THIRTY-EIGHT

Scheisse! Pete knew he was in the doghouse. Akiko was cordial, but frosty. Hadn't been so noticeable with all their kids home for New Year's, but it was evident now. Gone were the loving touches, the warm laughter. Where they normally had done things together, she was off doing something else. She was there at night lying by his side, but miles away in their queen-sized bed.

Saturday night, while running with Beowulf, Pete tried to think back over the past week. She hadn't said anything. Children in Japan were taught to avoid conflict, but that had seldom stopped Akiko. Her parents had instilled an unusual independence in her.

Jogging along, he forced himself to look at what he'd done. It had been an idiotic idea, thinking he was keeping her safe by not including her in the gathering. He knew damn well she would be upset. This had come up again and again in their marriage.

But those images he'd seen from North Dakota sent a shock wave through him. That beautiful home obliterated to splinters. Gone. Cowboy and Arlene. Down-to-earth good people—gone. He'd read the reports from the investigation. The authorities were stymied—saw no reason for such violence.

A cold thought shuddered down his spine. He didn't allow himself to dwell on it, but he feared his being badly injured or killed in the line of duty. The thought of danger to his family because of his job was even more abhorrent.

Technically, this TV gathering had been work-related—the culmination of a long case, or that's what he told himself. He jogged on, from long practice noting his surroundings with one part of his brain, and cataloging the movement of the cars as he turned onto Paseo de Pedro for the last blocks before home.

Sunday morning, Pete awoke at four o'clock and couldn't get back to sleep. He lay there brooding, watching the darkness give way to pre-dawn light. His eyes wide open, he waited until a decent time to get up, his mind working out his best strategy to make things right between Akiko and him.

Akiko tensed when Pete entered their bedroom Sunday night after his jog with Beowulf. He carried a tray with two glasses of the gewürztraminer she'd seen chilling in the refrigerator earlier. Their Airedales padded in behind him, jumped up on the bed and flopped across it.

She looked up from where she'd been reading in one of the two upholstered chairs by the window overlooking their back yard. The drapes were pulled against the cold. She was dressed in a kimono-style robe, a favorite of hers. He set the tray down, doffed his jogging clothes, and put away the gun that he almost always carried with him when he went out.

Well, she thought, he'd reached the point where he wasn't able to tolerate the wall between them. By the time he tied the belt on his own bathrobe, she had begun to sip her wine.

"Angel, I'm sorry I didn't tell you about the gathering last Friday."

She watched his jaw flex, waiting for him to finally spit out his excuse.

"I wanted to keep you safe."

She rolled her eyes. "This was an invitation to watch a TV program. Even our infant grandson was there. I saw red when Karen talked to me. I was embarrassed."

"I don't want my work to put you in danger."

She leaned forward in her chair. "Peter Alarik Adalwulf Schultz. That wasn't your work."

His head jerked up, and his gray eyes grew stormy. "Stop. Don't call me by all my names like I'm a disobedient child. You know that pisses me off."

"I'm already pissed off. When were you going to tell me about it? How did you plan to explain when I heard about it from everyone else?"

"Akiko, I—"

"How many times have you told me that we would face troubles together, and you would stop trying to be the long-suffering sacrificial shield keeping your little woman safe?"

Pete shut his eyes and took a deep breath. "If only you would see reason."

"Peter, I am not some submissive wife. You knew what I was like when you married me. Don't shut me out. You said you weren't going to do it anymore."

He looked down again. She saw his Adam's apple move as he swallowed. When he raised his head moments later, his eyes held an agonized expression.

"I know, Angel. But then we heard about Cowboy." His voice was tortured. "He was gunned down and left to die. Their home was blown up. It wasn't natural gas. That was a bomb that killed Arlene. A deliberately placed bomb."

She looked at him in shock. The seconds ticked away as she searched his eyes. "That's what set you off again, isn't it? You never told me about the bomb."

He shook his head. "I'm sorry, okay? I just . . . I need you, Akiko. The thought that you or one of our kids might be in danger because of who I am and what I do. It *scares* me."

Akiko met his gaze.

"I feel that, too, Pete. Every time you walk out that door, I know it might be the last time I see you. I've lived with that fear since we began dating. None of us, no matter what we do in life, is guaranteed that we will be safe. A speeding car, a heart attack, or an idiot with a gun. We aren't going to be safer just because one of us tries to shield the other from life. Together, Pete. You promised."

◆ ❖ ◆

Pete looked at her. Feisty. Such a complicated woman. Clad in cherry red, so vulnerable looking with a tendril of still-black hair escaping down the smooth skin of her neck. He knew she was right. He took a deep breath.

"I know." Hell, he thought Lou had been the one to tell her. It was a surprise to find out Karen had spilled the beans. No wonder Akiko was angry. Being made to lose face only added insult to injury.

He heard her reasoning-with-him tone. "You don't know the deaths of Cowboy and Arlene had anything to do with his work. He'd just won an election." Her voice began to frost over. "Or is there something else you've kept from me?"

"No, there isn't. The investigators don't seem to have a clue yet as to who did it or why."

Akiko was silent, eyes downcast as she pleated the hanging sleeve of her robe. Finally, she looked up, moistening her lips. "Why did you not want me to go with you?"

Pete heard the pain in her voice. "I . . . I've been asking myself that. When the Circle Sleuths began, they really did meet to help us solve cases. But we've become friends. I was too stubborn to acknowledge the change. I'm a dummkopf."

She smiled at that, leaned toward him, and covered his mouth with cool fingers.

He captured her hand and went on. "I hurt us by keeping you out of an important part of my life. Both of us need the nourishment of this group, and they need both of us. I'm just realizing how much."

The silence stretched between them again. He held her hand lightly, rubbing his thumb over her fingers. Sometimes a cross-cultural marriage could be hard.

Hell, marriage, period, was hard. His German background, where facing a problem head-on was the norm, often ran into problems with Akiko. Japanese culture seemed to favor indirect confrontation. But he found Akiko to be a baffling, unpredictable combination—culture mixed with her own strong feelings about how man and wife should relate.

He'd said he was sorry, but knew she needed more than words. Until he showed her, the rift would still exist. He was impatient to fix it now.

Suddenly he knew what to do. He slid off his chair to his knees in front of her, laid his hands over hers and put his forehead on their hands in her lap. "Akiko, I need to be cleansed—to make a clean beginning again for you. Will you help me?"

"Will it happen again?" She pulled a hand away to raise his head.

He studied her eyes in the widening quiet. "I hope not, but I know you've heard that before. I may need reminding. It's hard for this leopard to change his protective spots."

"I know. I love this leopard—even when I want to shake him."

He grinned. "Shake me until my spots rattle?"

"Only just." She raised one eyebrow. "I suppose we should see if your spots wash off. Lava soap?"

Pete winced. "If you must."

Her laugh was sultry as they rose, and she led him toward the shower. God, he'd missed that laugh over the past chilly week.

"I got some lavender-lemon soap the other day. I'd rather use that." She glanced up at him. "And I think it's only fair that you wash me, too."

Somewhere between the lathering and the washing, the caressing and the rinsing, he noticed her glow was back; her dark eyes held a playful glint. He smiled in satisfaction. Their closeness had returned, but words were only temporary. He'd have to back them with action.

As they left the shower and stepped down into the hot water, the eyes of the large stone polar bear lying on its tummy by the soaking tub seemed to follow him through the fragrant rising steam. He handed Akiko her wine, then reached for his own, but paused, frowning at the innocent look of the bear. He picked up a fluffy, white towel instead and draped it over the bear's eyes.

Akiko laughed. "What're you doing?"

Pete picked up his glass and settled back into the water, relaxing into the heat. "Ahh, Angel. He's way too young to see this part."

CHAPTER THIRTY-NINE

Wit Wysocki leaned his head against the brown leather of his chair. Only a week since New Year's? The time dragged interminably. How many times had he heard it said that if you wanted something done right, do it yourself? But he'd paid Wilcox good money to retrieve that box.

It was a good thing Wilcox was dead, or he'd kill him. Fool! He'd told him there was a carved hand on the box, even showed him a picture. The idiot got the wrong house, stole the wrong box, but then got caught stealing guns and landed in jail. Well, the devil had him now. Most convenient heart attack he'd ever heard of.

What now? Did he have to go himself?

Even as he thought it, he rejected it. He shouldn't have to dirty his hands. That's why he paid people and paid them well. This time he'd send Jed.

After being buzzed into the mansion's study, Jed faced the mogul across his desk. A jitteriness marred Wysocki's usual calm elegance.

"I have an assignment for you. The pay is big, but it has to be done quickly." Wysocki gave him a picture of a creepy box with a hand on top. "This box was stolen from me long ago. It belonged to my father and has great sentimental value. Get it back, but do not mention my name in connection with this."

Wysocki shoved a large envelope across the desk. "This has a copy of a TV show. It will show you that box and tell you what you need to know about the fellow who has it. He lives by the river in Pecos, a one-horse town near Santa Fe. He's been in all the news—a long-lost child kidnapped years ago."

"How do you want me to get it?"

"You figure it out. Wilcox was supposed to, but he went to the wrong address and didn't follow directions. Blew it."

"I hear Wilcox is dead. Heart attack."

"So they say. Damn fool." Wysocki handed him a glossy folder. "Spin them a yarn saying you represent a developer. Make an offer that is worth their while—you don't have to follow through. Find the box. Buy it, steal it, whatever, just get it."

He handed him an envelope, fat with bills. Jed's eyes widened as he fanned through the denominations.

Wysocki smiled. "That's half your pay, but your expenses will have to come out of it. The rest will come when you deliver the box to me."

Driving through the night toward Santa Fe, Jed wondered how he would ever get out of this stinking web. He wasn't proud of what he'd done since he started working for Wysocki. At first, he'd been grateful—a well-known, sought-after mover and shaker in Denver's political world. A steady job, no more catch-as-catch-can jobs.

It hadn't taken him long to see through the facade. He'd been hired because he was desperate, willing to do most anything, and looked the part his employer wanted—belligerent demeanor, muscular build. Desirable in event security—a fancy name for enforcer. Lately he'd been assigned more and more bodyguard stints for family. And now this task. Something was going on, making Jed uneasy.

He was close enough to Wysocki to see the ugly underbelly of the real estate mogul and knew the philanthropic image hid a soul as dark as Jed's own father's had been. Worse even. Jed's father had been a pathetic, mean drunk, who lashed out in anger. Wysocki's actions were deliberate, clothed in a saccharine, religious veneer, which confused and squeezed his victims until they had no way out except to give in to his demands and succumb to his control.

Already, Jed felt himself slipping into darkness, doing things he hated, treating people like shit. For what? To make enough money to break loose and do what he really wanted to do? Every passing day nailed the lid tighter on the coffin of his dreams.

What if this was his last job for Wysocki? Could he disappear and start again? The thought tempted him.

◆ ❖ ◆

In Pecos, Jed scoped out the situation, finding out Stewart worked at the forestry office. Jed showed up there near closing time to discreetly follow him home, parking a distance away. With binoculars he could see what he needed.

The sun would soon slip behind the mountains on this raw January day. Stewart parked in his driveway, and suddenly a little girl with flying red hair ran out, happy and smiling. A little boy, older than the girl, followed. The man in the forestry uniform swung the girl up in his arms. She pulled off his stocking cap, revealing bright hair, and pulled it down over her own head, where it sat lopsided. She put her arms around him and hugged him. She wasn't wearing a jacket. The man tugged his own around her as he carried her toward the house. He looked down and smiled, taking the hand of the boy.

This guy had it all. Beautiful children, cared for, loved. He had a job Jed dreamed of. Jed lowered the binoculars and closed his eyes, thinking of little Annie, his sister. She'd been about the same age. Her hair had been kind of a honey gold, not red like this child's. Instead of running toward her father, she would shy away, cowering if he should reach for her. When had their father ever cared if a child of his might get chilled and wrap his jacket around them? When had he ever laughed with them and hugged them?

Jed couldn't think of a single time.

◆ ❖ ◆

Hoot panned the group around the table with his phone, capturing Bonnie's birthday party—just family, including his mom, dad, and grandma. Melody had made Bonnie's favorite baked pizza-pasta even more special by using snowflake-shaped pasta and adding lots of pizza-topping ingredients. His camera caught Bonnie picking out a snowflake covered with stretchy cheese with her fingers, holding it up triumphantly, and then popping it in her mouth with a giggle.

The doorbell rang, and he looked at Melody. "We expecting anyone?"

She shook her head. He hoped it wasn't more press. He walked past the big pile of presents waiting on the coffee table and peered through the peephole.

A stranger. Damn, he was carrying a portfolio. Hoot didn't see a camera. He opened the door to find a smiling man about his age or a little younger. A black SUV was parked behind Andrew's car.

"Good evening, my name is Jed Hawkins. I'm wondering if I might talk to you for a bit."

"We're busy right now." Good grief, this guy's eyes weren't even meeting his, just trying to peer into the house past his shoulder. Hoot shifted slightly to the left.

"This won't take long."

"Why are you here?"

"I represent a developer who is looking to build a resort along the Pecos here. He's prepared to make an excellent offer."

"Look. You're interrupting our evening. We're not interested. Good evening." Hoot started to close the door, then looked down. "Do you mind moving your foot?"

"I'd like to at least give you the information." Jed smiled and pushed onward with a warm voice. "It's a really good offer. Just let me step inside in the light where I can show you the brochure."

"Not. Interested." Hoot looked down. "Your foot?"

"You'll be sorry, sir."

The smooth voice began to grate on Hoot's nerves. "It's not my foot that will be caught in the door. Or are you threatening me?"

"Of course not. I'm just saying you'll love this offer." He slowly moved his foot.

"Good night." Hoot shut the door firmly and turned the deadbolt with an audible snick. Through the peep hole, he watched the man turn and go to his vehicle. "I hate pushy salespeople. We need a security screen door. It'd be nice to talk through it and still have a locked door."

"I would like that," said Melody.

"He may not have been a developer," said Andrew. "Reporters use that ruse."

"I wish they'd give up."

"Daddy, can you eat? Mommy says I can't open my presents until everybody is done."

"Sorry, Bonnie. I'll eat."

CHAPTER FORTY

Pete adjusted his light gray sweatpants over the bulge of his holster, pulled on his jacket and lightweight gloves. He patted his pocket, double-checking to make sure he had his flashlight and a clean-up bag. He thought about the route he would take tonight. It was good to vary his routine, and he always let Akiko know his intentions.

He kissed Akiko's cheek as she rinsed out their coffee cups. "We'll head down the street and around by the school. Love you."

"Love you, too."

"Come, Beowulf." He clipped the leash on his dog.

The night was clear and cold. Pete glanced around as he closed the door behind him. Streetlights showed no one out and about, no cars moving, not even on the larger cross street by their house. He turned left at the sidewalk and began jogging.

Suddenly, car headlights approached from behind. Halfway registering that the lights seemed wrong, the thought of Dom's being hit from the rear flashed through his mind. He glanced over his shoulder. *Scheisse*! A car coming on the wrong side of the street! A hand holding a gun emerged out the driver's window. No—not now!

Instinctively, he dropped the leash, extended his arms, and leaped, dropping his shoulder into a diving roll, over evergreen bushes into the rocks and small stones behind them. Midair he saw a flash and heard a shot.

"Down, Wulf. Stay!"

More shots. Pete drew his gun and fired at the car from behind his cover. The car passed him, the driver still shooting. Pete fired again and saw the hole appear in the back window. Then he rolled, not wanting the muzzle flash to give away his location.

A sharp bark. A blur rushed the car. Pete held his fire. *More training, Wulf. When I say stay, I mean stay.*

In horror, he saw the arm pointing back toward his dog.

Then there was a loud crunch as the distracted driver drove up on the curb and the side front fender hit a large landscaping rock. The shot went wild. The car wobbled, corrected, and accelerated down the street. A broken section of bumper fascia scraped along until it was caught by the tire and spun off into the road. The car rounded the corner of their loop, tires squealing.

Beowulf stopped. "Come!" Pete bellowed. The dog turned and ran back to him, leash trailing.

Pete grabbed his cell phone, pulled off a glove, and called 911. He kept to the shadows, keenly aware that the bastard might come around for a second pass. As he talked with dispatch, he rubbed his hand above his eye. Was he sweating? His hand showed dark streaks in the streetlight. Blood. The lava rocks had done a number on his head. He sat back on his heels, cried out, and landed on his butt.

The calf of his left leg burned with hot fire. Blood stained the ravaged material of his sweatpants and dripped on the red lava rocks he sat upon. "I'm hit," he told dispatch.

He heard sirens. He heard Akiko's frightened call, saw her running to him, and reached out a hand as she dropped to her knees beside him. Blood ran freely from his scalp. Soon several patrol cars arrived with red and blue flashing lights. An ambulance followed. Beowulf growled at the first patrolman to reach his side.

Akiko took the leash of the trembling dog. "Beowulf, it's okay. Leave it."

The first responders took over. Neighbors started to venture out, alarmed by the shots, sirens, and police cars. One part of Pete's mind launched into detective mode as he handed the officers his gun.

"It was a dark sedan, four-door. Maybe a Honda Civic. It hit a boulder and left a piece of the bumper on the road." Pete pointed. "I hit the rear window. Saw the hole. Driver shot with his left hand. Get the word out now. Get the forensics guys to look at the broken bumper piece he left behind. See if they can determine the make and model."

"We're taking you to the emergency room, Lieutenant."

"They're keeping me overnight for observation," Pete grumbled as Sam and Chief Grover came into his hospital room. "What are you doing here? It's close to midnight."

"They know you," the chief said. "If they let you go home, you'll never rest. You'll be directing the investigation from your bed. What's with the bandage on your head? Bullet graze?"

"Nothing that spectacular. Adrenaline kicked in. Don't know if it was old instinct from combat training or Rick's parkour training, but when I saw that gun, I went into a diving roll over the bushes. Didn't tuck my head right and banged it on the rocks. I tell you, landing on lava rock hurts a hell of a lot more than grass or foam pads. I don't recommend it."

"So, you didn't get shot?" asked Sam. "I heard you did."

Pete flipped the blanket back to show the bandages on his calf. "Just grazed. Nice little furrow. Must have got me when I was heels-over-head. Almost got my shoulder, too. The fabric on my jacket is all shot to hell. Thought Akiko was going to spit fire when she saw that. Funny, I didn't feel any pain until I saw blood. Did you stop by the scene?"

"You bet we did," said the chief. "Forensics is still there. No sign yet of a car with the missing bumper piece or a back window with a bullet hole."

"They collected a few surveillance videos," said Sam. "I wish New Mexico required front plates. It would increase chances of getting the license number."

"Did you see the plate?" asked the chief.

"No. I was focusing on Beowulf and the guy with the gun."

"Any idea who it was, or why they'd shoot at you?"

"*Gott im Himmel.* No telling who carries a grudge. I'd scrutinize those who just got out of the slammer."

"Did you get a look at the driver?"

"They were in shadow. Must have been waiting for me across Paseo de Pedro. The headlights shone at an odd angle, lighting up landscaping differently. I thought of what happened to Dom, and I dove. Heard maybe eight shots in all. All I could see was that hand out the window extending farther than he could have if he were shooting with his right hand. I quit firing when Beowulf charged. I've never seen him chase a car before. The guy was looking back at Wulf, and his car hit a boulder."

"What he did will let us identify the car," said the chief. "We'd better let you get some sleep. You know the routine, just a formality, but you'll be on administrative leave for a few days. You're going to feel like crap anyway. Take it easy, Schultz."

Pete lay quietly, reflecting on Akiko and Rick's brief visit earlier. His son had given him a cocky smile when Pete told him about his less-than-perfect parkour roll. Gave him a hard time about not turning his head the way he was supposed to, about practicing, and who was it that ended up in the emergency room? Smart-mouth kid.

Should have been a printer. Lay out documents on the computer. Chug them out on machines. Never have to take work home with you. Even if you got something wrong, they would hardly come gunning for you.

Cowardly to attack from behind. Already he was itching to find out who and why. They'd tangled with the wrong guy this time—every officer in Santa Fe would react to an attack on one of their own.

Now he had bruises all over, swelling, a headache, and protesting muscles. His arm was sore where they'd given him a tetanus shot. He turned on his side, wincing as the movement jarred his calf. He'd seen the wound in a mirror the doctor had held for him. Nasty looking. Probably the doc wanted to impress upon him that this wasn't just a scratch.

Pain, he could handle. Death could easily have found him tonight. Taken him from Akiko, from his family.

He felt a pressure behind his eyes.

Mein Gott. So hard. If only he knew how to keep them safe.

CHAPTER FORTY-ONE

After the rebuff by Stewart, Jed went to his next plan—peeking into their house at night. Maybe he could spot the box that way. It had been horrible timing on his part to crash a birthday party. He'd recognized the room from *Friday Stories of Hope*. The pile of colorfully wrapped packages had been sitting where the puzzle box had been during the TV program. With any luck, they'd have put it back there now.

Well past midnight, he returned to the Pecos home and parked his car nearby.

Looking in someone's window in the deep of night like a common Peeping Tom? Yet here he was. According to Wysocki, it was the folks who lived here who were in the wrong—it wasn't their box.

The temperature hovered just above freezing, giving a frosty squelch to his steps as Jed stealthily walked around the house in the pale moonlight. The closed blinds and curtains brought a frown. Wait! One window showed faint light. With luck, the table with the box could be seen from that window.

He crept closer, the fog of his breath coming and going. He peered into what looked like a child's bedroom and stepped to the side for a better view.

Squeeek! A rubber ball squashed under his foot. *Jesus!* Without thinking, Jed kicked at it in annoyance, and it squeaked again as it sailed off across the yard. *Damn it all to hell!* If they had a dog, that would wake it up.

In the light from the hallway, he saw a small figure sit up in bed and look toward him, brushing tangled hair from her face. For a moment, his muscles froze.

Then he ducked down and ran, hoping to get away before the child raised the alarm. No lights came on; nothing seemed to change. Jed slowed, breathing a momentary sigh of relief when he reached his SUV.

He'd come back again. There must be a way to get in and get the box.

♦ ❖ ♦

"Shadow Man was wooking at me wast night," said Bonnie before taking another bite of toast.

"Who's Shadow Man?" asked Melody. Her stomach was sure feeling off this morning. She wondered if she had a touch of flu, but discarded that thought in favor of another. The signs were right, and the feeling was familiar. If she were not mistaken, there was another little one on the way.

Matti taunted his sister. "There are no monsters, silly."

Bonnie looked at him, chewing her toast carefully. Then she shook her head and took a sip of milk. "I saw him. He must have comed out from under my bed and gone outside."

Melody pulled herself back from her reverie. "Tonight we'll shine a light under your bed before you go to sleep to chase all the monsters away. That'll take care of any old shadow man." She smiled at her daughter, then turned to Matti. "Do you want cheese in your sandwich today?" The mere mention of food left her in dread.

"Peanut butter and honey," replied Matti, "and an apple. And carrots. And chips."

"Pack a wunch for me, too," grumbled Bonnie. "I wanna go to school."

"You're not old enough, silly," said Matti.

"Yes, I am."

"Are not. You're just a baby."

"I not a baby. You are," she screeched, throwing her crust at her brother before bunching up her lower lip in a stubborn look.

This was all she needed, thought Melody as she intervened, quickly steadying Bonnie's rocking glass of milk. "That's enough. We don't throw food. Matti, stop teasing your sister. Use your inside voice, Bonnie. You aren't old enough for school. But we'll pack you a lunch, too, and we'll take it to Grandma's and eat there."

Hoot came in, ready for work in his forest service uniform. "What's all this ruckus I hear? Matti, come and help me make the lunches. Bonnie, drink your milk before you spill it. Give your mother a break. Melody, why don't I make you some tea, and you can go back to bed for a bit. I have time enough to get these rascals ready for the day."

"Thanks, ginger tea, please, and crackers. That sounds wonderful."

He sent her a questioning look, took her gently into his arms, and tilted her chin up to look into her eyes. "You okay?"

He would know now. Ginger tea was a dead giveaway. She smiled up at him. "Yes, *very* okay. I—" Then suddenly she put her hand to her mouth and pulled away to flee the kitchen.

CHAPTER FORTY-TWO

Melody called, "Goodbye, Grandma," and followed her daughter down the steps after their lunch with Marilyn. Bonnie jumped in a series of little hops to the hedge that divided their yard from Grandma's. How would she ever convince her daughter that she should take a nap? Once in their own yard, Bonnie ran toward a bird foraging on the ground, prompting it to fly up to a clothesline post and let out a series of harsh squawks.

"Look, Mommy, a boo bird."

"Yes, it's a Steller's jay. It is blue."

"I fly." Bonnie began flapping her arms and circling the yard.

Laughing, Melody ran after her, and near the house, caught up the giggling imp in her arms. The bird flew away into the trees at the back of their property, where the Pecos River flowed.

"It flewed away."

"Back to its nest." As she set Bonnie down, her eyes dropped to the dead marigolds in the flowerbed by the house. Large boot prints showed where some of the brown plants had been crushed into the mud. She looked up and froze. This was right under Bonnie's window!

What the hell? Shit! There had been a man?

What was a man doing outside her daughter's window? She was so used to Bonnie and her stories of monsters under the bed that she hadn't taken her seriously at all.

The threatening messages—that danger suddenly became real. Wait—maybe those were Hoot's tracks. How could she tell?

They went inside, and she bribed Bonnie—just a *little* nap. Then she called Hoot to tell him what she'd seen. "Did you go back there?"

"Not since the first snow, that I remember. Call Hiram Brower, just to be on the safe side."

In a little while, a state highway patrol car pulled up. Melody recognized Hiram, with his bushy eyebrows. She went out, showed him the tracks, and told him about Shadow Man. He checked all the windows, looking for more tracks and signs that might indicate somebody tried to get in. He did a plaster cast of the print. Then he went over and talked with Marilyn, and checked all of her windows.

"If you see anything else suspicious," he said, "call immediately. Don't alarm your daughter, but tell her that if she sees another monster, to come and get you right away. Don't wait for morning."

Melody smiled. "Thank you. She'd be okay with that." There was something about this kindly man that imparted confidence.

"Seriously, don't hesitate to call 911, or me, or both, if you'd rather." He handed her his card. "I gave one to your husband, but you need one. I'm going to call Sam Martinez and brief him. We should be able to get to the bottom of this soon."

She nodded and watched him drive away.

After work, Hoot listened as Melody told him about Hiram's visit. Then he went out with a flashlight and looked at the tracks for himself. He was concerned. No, more than that—frightened. Another headache flirted with the edges of his mind. The door in his head might be open, but in the dark beyond, evil still lurked.

You told. You knew what would happen. Now your family is not safe.

When Sam returned to the bullpen after checking with forensics about the scene where Pete was attacked, he was just in time to pick up Hiram Brower's call about Bonnie's shadow man.

"Couple of things on my mind," said Hiram. "I didn't see any sign that he tried to gain entry. It could be related to those calls and letter that Hoot got or something else entirely."

"Have you had other similar complaints in Pecos? Is there a Peeping Tom in the area?"

"The only other complaint was last Wednesday. Some old slimeball from Colorado broke into a house on the other side of the highway that crosses the Pecos. He stole a jewelry box, some guns, and such. Wasn't very clever. We nabbed him."

Sam's ears perked up. "Still in custody?"

"Had a massive heart attack in his cell the day after. Died."

"Son of a gun."

"My troopers are still checking on Hoot's periodically. Second thing—I'm concerned about Pete. How's he doing?"

Sam updated him about Pete's injuries.

After he hung up, Sam headed for Pecos to see Hoot.

When he got there, Hoot took him around to Bonnie's window, where the powerful beam of Sam's flashlight lit the tracks.

"It scares the hell out of me that someone is threatening our children. Dang. It makes me want to put bars on the windows."

"Any home repair or yard people around?"

Hoot snorted. "You're looking at the maintenance department. I think it has to do with those threats."

"Keep your eyes and ears open."

Hoot nodded. "Come on in."

Inside, Marilyn asked, "How's Pete? We heard he was shot."

"They grazed him, and he's pretty sore. He's on administrative leave for the present. Fire at somebody, and that's what happens."

Marilyn frowned. "I have one more box of papers and photos for him to look through. I suppose it can wait."

"I can take it for you," said Sam. "No problem."

"Do they know who shot him?" asked Hoot.

"Not yet, but we'll find out." Sam frowned. Too often lately he was saying that. They needed answers.

♦ ❖ ♦

Sam called Pete at home about the box. "Do you want me to swing by or just take it to the office tomorrow?"

"Come on by. It'll take my mind off my aches and pains."

When Sam arrived at Pete's home with the box, Akiko showed him into the family room where Pete was resting on the couch, his legs up. A pair of crutches leaned within his reach.

"Have a chair." Pete hissed in a breath as Beowulf jumped up on the couch and plopped down by his leg. "Not there, Wulf. Move down a little. Move."

Beowulf obliged.

"Just put it here where I can reach it. Maybe I'll start tonight."

Akiko came in with coffee for them both and gave Pete a look. "I heard that."

"Or maybe tomorrow. Thanks, Angel."

Sam took a sip of the hot brew and looked at the scabs and bruises on Pete's scalp. "Son of a gun. Anybody'd think you landed on your head, man."

"That was the problem. It's looks worse now than last night. When Rick saw me, all he said was, 'That'll teach you to tuck your head when you roll.' No sympathy at all. I suppose I should be glad it didn't happen a couple of doors down. Their yard is full of cactus."

"Ouch. How's the leg?"

"Hurts like the devil. The doc said the third day would be the worst. I'm pleased, actually, about having this box to go through. I hate sitting and doing nothing. What'd you find out?"

"I knew you'd ask. You're not supposed to be working."

"I don't need to be mollycoddled. It was my leg that was hit, not my brain. Tell me."

"Well, from the bumper piece that was left behind, they know it was a black 2014 Honda Civic. It hasn't been found. The body shops, car dealers, and the windshield places have been alerted. No word yet. They've been through the surveillance videos—yours and a neighbor's on Paseo de Pedro. The car had been waiting for you across the street."

"How about the bullets and casings?"

"No surprise there. Eight shots. Nine millimeter. You were lucky, Pete."

"I know. But it's difficult to hit a target while shooting with only one hand."

Pete's phone rang. "Hi, Chief."

As Sam watched, a smile lit the older man's face.

"Good. Thank you, sir." Pete hung up. "They finished their inquiry and cleared me to come back. I'll go in tomorrow for a few hours."

"I'm thinking Grover also told you to take it easy."

Pete nodded. "Work isn't going to go away just because I'm not there. I'd rather keep up."

"Is our Denver trip still on?"

"Sure. Those seminars involve a lot of sitting anyway. I'll be fine."

"What do you think of contacting Hayle while we're there and asking him some questions?"

"Can't justify questioning him yet. All we know is he was a friend of Gordon's and went with him on hunting trips. Frankly, I don't want the man spooked by knowing of our interest."

CHAPTER FORTY-THREE

Friday afternoon, Pete limped across the bullpen to greet an officer who handed him the day's mail. "About time. Usually we get it by ten. What happened?"

The officer shrugged. "You're looking pretty colorful—black eye even. How're you doing?"

"Probably a good thing I'm not out interviewing people."

Pete flipped through the mail. He pulled out one envelope and left the others for Yvonne to deal with. "NamUS," he read. "Wonder if this is about Ross Stewart?" He slit the envelope open.

A match! Unidentified juvenile found by San Antonio Police in 1991. Texas? How'd Ross get there? Finally, some closure for Marilyn. He read through the letter, found the name of the officer in charge, and called him.

"Hell, that was a long time ago when I was a rookie," said the San Antonio officer. "Let me look up the files, and I'll call you back."

While he waited, Pete went through the notes he'd made about the maternal grandmother, Winona's mother. The information listed in Gordon's address book had been uselessly outdated. After a lengthy search, he'd discovered she lived in an assisted-care facility in San Antonio. Her husband was dead. He'd tried to talk with her, but the only thing of sense she'd said was that Ross had gone to live with his other grandparents.

The San Antonio officer called back. "This juvenile showed up in our records only when his body was found, August 1991. He was dirty and unkempt. Officers searched the neighborhood. Nobody knew who he was. Finally somebody thought to ask Old Bessie, a homeless lady—part mother hen, part Fagin—who collected runaways and throwaways into a loose-knit family of sorts."

"Did you learn anything from her?"

"She said she heard he took sick with a high fever and died. Said she'd talked to him a few times. My translation of that—she'd been looking out for him."

Pete was jotting down notes. "The boy was from Denver. Were you ever able to find out how he got to Texas?"

"Bessie said he told her he used to live in Colorado, but went to Corpus Christi with his grandparents. He didn't like it there. They sent him back with a guy who stole his money and ran off. I'm afraid that's all I can tell you."

"Thank you. Appreciate your help." Pete shook his head as he hung up the phone. This news would bring Marilyn more distress.

He should drive to Pecos now, but sure didn't feel like it. Maybe he could talk someone into driving him. What a comedown.

When he got home, he discovered Akiko giving Krista dog grooming lessons in their large utility room, which served as a dog room. Karen had kicked back in the family room with a book.

Akiko greeted Pete with a kiss. "I made a fresh pot of coffee and was about to offer Karen some. We just got started on Shadow."

"Coffee sounds good. Especially if I can put my feet up for a bit."

Karen looked from the open family room into the kitchen. "I can pour the coffee. You do look a little worse for wear, Pete. Have they caught the gunman yet?"

"Not yet. I do have some interesting news though." Pete showed them the letter from NamUS and told what the San Antonio officer said about Ross.

"What's NamUS?" asked Karen.

"Stands for National Missing and Unidentified Persons System." He propped his legs up on the couch in his family room. "*Ach du lieber.* I'm not looking forward to driving to Pecos."

"But you'll go anyway, won't you?" asked Karen. "I know you. This child is Marilyn's grandson. It's the decent thing to deliver the news in person. Would you like me to drive you? They won't be done dog grooming here for quite a while."

Akiko smiled at them. "I heard that. Take her up on it, Pete. Then I won't have to worry about your overdoing it." She left to join Krista in the dog room.

◆ ❖ ◆

Pete and Karen found Marilyn at her home in Pecos. Pete gave her the letter and told her what he'd learned.

"This was not the result I hoped to hear," said Marilyn. She closed her eyes and rocked back and forth slowly. "But it's not unexpected. Better to know, than wonder."

Karen made Marilyn some tea. They waited while she sipped.

"I'd like to go to San Antonio," Marilyn said, "to talk to Winona's mother while she's still with us. I would like to talk with that policeman, too." She looked down at her hands, smoothing her wedding ring. Finally, she raised her head. "If I could, I'd like to make arrangements for Ross to be moved to the cemetery where Dwight is buried and where I'll be someday. It's the right thing to do."

She put her hands over her eyes, and Pete heard quiet crying. Karen moved to sit next to Marilyn and put an arm around her.

"Marilyn," she said, "I'd be happy to go with you to San Antonio. We could fly there, do those three things, and fly back the next day."

"You'd do that?"

"Of course. We'll do it soon. Maybe next week."

"Oh, my dear. That would mean so much to me."

Before he got back in Karen's car, Pete limped to Hoot's house and told them. As they drove away, Hoot went into Marilyn's house.

CHAPTER FORTY-FOUR

On Monday, mid-January, Pete and Sam tackled the sixth banker's box. It included a letter from the taxidermist to Gordon. "This is interesting," said Pete. "This must be Wysocki's trophy according to the date. He says the head will be ready for pickup at the end of February in 1991. Says the hunter should be pleased."

"Probably a code, meaning that Gordon will be pleased. Smart enough not to put anything incriminating in print."

Pete's phone rang. "It's Hoot."

"I just got another letter. It's horrible."

"Sam and I will meet you, and I'll call Hiram. Do you know Pepper's, that truck stop just off the interstate?"

"I know the place. See you there shortly."

When Pete walked into Pepper's with Sam, he spotted Hiram waving at him from the farthest-back booth along the windows overlooking the big rigs dotting the parking lot. Pete sighed. A distance that wouldn't have fazed him at all last week looked a lot more daunting when one had just graduated from crutches to cane.

A dark-haired waitress chatted with truckers sitting at the long counter while she cleaned and filled salt-and-pepper shakers. "Just coffee, please," Pete said as he limped past her.

Hiram waited until she brought the coffee and returned to the truckers. "Heard anything more from the postal inspector about the first letter?"

"Not a word," said Pete, tracing the blurry, earth-toned stripes on his pottery mug.

Soon Hoot came, a worried look on his face. He held another envelope, similar to the first. Pete put on latex gloves and looked at the postmark. As he expected, Santa Fe.

The single sheet of paper had a copy of a photo of Matti and Bonnie. Pete figured it might have been taken about a year ago. A big black X slashed across each smiling face. The printed message under the photo said, "You told. Say goodbye to your kids."

Pete looked into Hoot's anguished eyes. "*Mein Gott*. Do you know this photo?"

Hiram put on gloves and took the paper from Pete. His frown caused his bushy brows to meet as he examined the image.

Hoot sat back and rubbed his temple. "It's from a trip that we took to the Spring Festival at El Rancho de las Golondrinas last year. I took it myself."

"Who had access to it?" asked Pete. "Is it displayed on your desk at work or something like that? Did you put it on a social media site? Email it to friends?"

"Never displayed. We've never done much with social media, especially with photos. I don't recall emailing any of that batch, and Melody didn't either. I printed off a set on photo paper for Grandma. She's not very savvy with computers. She likes old-fashioned photo albums."

"It would help considerably if we knew how someone got it," said Pete.

After Sam and Hiram had examined it, Pete tucked it away, protected, into his portfolio. "I'm afraid that we won't find prints on this one either. Whoever did the first one wore gloves."

"Have you told Melody and Marilyn?" asked Hiram.

Hoot nodded. "Damn, I'm tired of being the victim. I want this over. I don't even know who I am anymore."

Pete put a hand on his shoulder. "You are an extraordinary young man whom I'm proud to call friend. Even as a six-year old, you had the strength to survive what would have destroyed others. Your resolve in not telling to keep your family safe was remarkably courageous. Now you've taken the initiative to draw out this scumbag. I look at you, and I don't see a victim. I see a warrior protecting his family."

"Don't let the bastard get you down, Hoot," said Sam.

"I'll brief our troopers in the area," said Hiram. "They're still swinging by periodically."

CHAPTER FORTY-FIVE

Pete and Sam's Denver flight left before dawn on Wednesday, January 18, for part two of their Interviews and Interrogations Seminar. They arrived just in time to get checked into the hotel before the first of the day's three intense sessions began.

Pete paused with Sam in the hotel lobby that evening. Marble floors, interrupted by carpeted areas and fat upholstered chairs, stretched past the desk toward the restaurant and bar. This was a rarity, he thought. No worries about being called out for violence and mayhem. He could relax and enjoy these moments with his peers.

A man in his forties with closely cropped, curly hair approached Pete.

"I finally remembered why you looked familiar and not just from last November. Weren't you on TV recently? About a kidnapping cold case? Awesome work." He shook Pete's, then Sam's hand. "Detective Aznar, Phoenix PD."

Pete introduced himself and Sam. "It took a community to bring that one off. I'm hoping that success sparked some interest in cold cases elsewhere."

"It certainly has for us. Can I buy you fellows a drink?"

The gleaming wood bar dominated the space between two muraled walls with frontier themes and was surrounded with places to sit and talk. Conversations buzzed, punctuated by laughter.

Aznar was full of questions on cold case investigations. Pete listened as he shared his frustrations. "It's difficult to reconstruct what happened. Memories are bad. Some records and notetaking are piss poor. Witnesses move or die."

Pete nodded. "Picking up anything from this seminar?"

"Not about that, but it's been helpful to see all of the interrogation approaches laid out the way he's done. I can see where it'll help."

"That detective from Dallas certainly challenged him on the "inflating or deflating ego" tactic," said Pete.

Aznar turned to Sam. "I thought sparks would fly, but he made some good points. What did you think?"

"I'm just learning. Most of my experience has been patrol. If I understood him right, he was talking about putting the suspect down saying he couldn't have done the crime because he was too dumb, or on the other hand, telling the guy how smart the crook was to pull it off, making him want to brag about it."

"It's a good thing we have a dozen other approaches in our bag of tricks," said Pete. "What works on one, won't on another."

Aznar drained his glass. "One topic of tomorrow's agenda—best ways to get admissible confessions—that I really want to hear. It's very hard to keep the suspect from using their right to lawyer up."

"What's been your experience on numbers waiving rights?" asked Pete.

"Somewhere around half. Surprises me, actually, that any do."

"We're probably between fifty and sixty percent." Pete moved his leg, winced, and picked up his cane. "Sorry, guys. I need to get this leg up. See you in the morning."

◆ ❖ ◆

"This was definitely worthwhile," Pete checked around their Denver hotel room after their morning session and closing luncheon. He unplugged his computer cord, secured it in his case, and rescued his cane from a doorknob.

Sam checked the bathroom and stowed his last belongings. "I'm looking forward to my next interrogation. The body language review was great."

"I learned some new tricks, too." Pete looked at his watch. "Glenn should be waiting for us. We're meeting the four geezers at Stanley's house this afternoon. He's recovering from surgery."

"Good. I love those characters."

Pete's trained eyes took in Stanley's single-story, brick bungalow as he, Sam, and Glenn entered. The home had a comfortable but tired appearance, the furnishings fading in years like their owners. He wondered if Stanley and his wife were originally from Britain. On a shelf near the wide archway into the dining room, a Beefeater teddy bear sat in his jaunty red uniform with a white ruff. On the wall above it, hung a print of vintage planes flying over a landscape with a cathedral prominently silhouetted against the sky.

Glenn had warned them that Stanley was slow in getting back his energy. He was seated in a sturdy recliner with a walker parked nearby. Floyd and Paul came in from the kitchen, carrying a tray of coffee mugs and a red-tartan container of Walker's shortbread.

"We're still working on the case involving Gordon Stewart," said Pete as they sat in Stanley's living room. "I have his old address book. I was hoping you could flip through it and see if any of the names sparked memories. Then I have some photographs and want to know if you can identify people." He started with photos of Gordon's wedding party.

When Floyd got them, he pointed at the groom. "That's Gordon. I'd forgotten how bright that hair of his was." He pointed at one of the groomsmen standing near Gordon. "This one looks kind of familiar. Danged if I know why. It's been a long time."

"That there was his cop friend," said Stanley when he got the photo.

In the sixth and last banker box from Marilyn, Pete had found a picture of the Beaver plane with Gordon standing by it with two men. He knew these guys would get a chuckle out of it.

"Gawd, Stanley. That's you. Look how long your hair was," said Floyd.

Stanley smiled. "Pretty dapper, wasn't I?"

"Hey, Paul, the other guy is you," said Glenn. "I could tell by your—"

"Shut your face," growled Paul. He touched the plane gently. "Sweet little lady."

Next Pete passed around the photos from the police academy. He'd included a couple of anonymous cops as well as the ones they'd met.

"Here he is again," said Stanley. "Hayle. That's his name. I remember now, when I saw those two, a song used to run through my head—'Hail, Hail, the Gang's All Here.' He hung around with Gordon. He was there the day we got reamed out for putting that stag head in the loo."

"Do any of the others look familiar?" asked Pete, pleased with the reactions to Hayle's photo. The four studied the other photos and passed them around again. Stanley squinted at them and frowned. All four shook their heads.

"Too long ago," said Paul.

Pete noted that the address book had completed its round. "Any names jump out at you?"

"Found myself in there," said Stanley. "Makes sense, since we had adjacent bays."

"The guy we paid our rent to was in there," said Paul. "Other than that, nothing." The other two shook their heads.

"Gordon kidnapped that kid, didn't he?" said Glenn. "My wife and I saw that TV show."

"I was afraid of that." Stanley's pale blue eyes were watery, his face a picture of discouragement. "To think I actually saw the boy. I'm sorry. I thought it was his own kid. Wish I'd known. What happened to his real son?"

"We found out—"

Pete interrupted Sam. "Stanley, how could you have known that kid wasn't his? We're still looking into what happened to Gordon's son."

"Don't be taking that on." Floyd put a hand on his friend's arm. "Only hindsight is twenty-twenty."

"If I remember correctly," said Pete, "you had one of Gordon's trophy heads. Would it be possible for us to examine it?"

"Sure." Stanley brightened a little. He got shakily to his feet and led the way with his walker into a cold garage, Glenn and Paul guiding his steps. He pressed the remote to open the door. Outside light revealed half of the space taken up with boxes and furniture.

"Sorry about the mess, guys. The missus and I moved here out of a much bigger house. We ran out of room before we ran out of stuff. Then she got sick, and I don't get as much done as I used to." He waved to the once-proud head hanging over the tool bench. "There he be."

"That sucker is huge," said Floyd. "It's a shoulder mount."

"I can see why your wife wouldn't let it in the house, Stanley. It's all chewed up by mice." Glenn shuddered as he used a broom to brush away dusty cobwebs from the stag's antlers.

"Would it be possible for us to take a look at the back?" asked Pete.

Stanley nodded, plainly curious.

"Sam, you and I seem to be the most able-bodied here," said Glenn. "Want to help me?"

Sam nodded and reached up to grasp an antler.

"Yowza!" Glenn jerked back and let go as a mouse jumped to his arm and off, scampering away to hide behind boxes. Sam, unprepared for the sudden change in weight, lost his grip. The head bounced off the tool bench and thwacked to the cement. The mount was knocked loose from the plaque, sending dust, fur, and other detritus wafting into the air.

Floyd sneezed. "Stanley, this is gross. You ain't *never* going to want this in your house. Look, half the fur is chewed off. Mouse dirt. It's disgusting."

Stanley peered down. "You're right. Chuck it. Darn. I guess I'll have to set a few mousetraps now. Where is the cat when you need him?"

Pete spoke up. "Since you're going to get rid of it anyway, do you mind if we look inside? See the space where the back is breaking off? Is that how they normally make these things?"

Glenn picked up a crowbar. "Somebody put their foot on it." He pried the plaque the rest of the way off to reveal a large empty cavity.

Pete ran a finger over the extra set of screw holes on the plaque and exchanged a look with Sam.

Floyd glanced from one to the other. "What are you thinking? That stuff could have been smuggled in there?"

"Quite possible. Could Gordon have used it that way?" asked Pete, leaning on a box and taking the weight off his leg. Sam snapped some photos of the head and cavity with his phone.

Stanley snorted. "If he thought he could make a buck by cheating or stealing, he would."

"Use a buck to make a buck?" asked Floyd with a grin.

"How deeranged," said Glenn.

Pete grinned. "Deer's no smoke without a fire."

"Deer you have it," said Sam. "Bringing in stolen goods under the radeer."

Pete looked at him in surprise. Puns weren't usually Sam's thing.

"Stop," said Stanley, leaning both hands on his walker. "You're awful. I ain't laughed this hard in a long time."

"Okay," said Pete. "Buckause you said so."

Floyd groaned.

"This buck stops here," said Glenn as he hefted the trophy head off the floor. Floyd opened the garbage toter lid and they tipped the head in with a resounding clunk.

"Whatever it was, it was years ago, and Gordon's dead," said Paul as the laughter died down. "That there head ain't telling no tales."

"Most heads don't have tails," said Floyd with a grin.

"Haven't you ever heard of pigtails or ponytails?" Paul's face lit up as he scored his point.

"Don't start," said Stanley.

Later, on the plane, Pete said to Sam, "Sorry to interrupt when you started to tell them what happened to Ross. I still think there's somebody else involved besides Hayle, if he *is* the second kidnapper."

"Certainly not one of those four?"

"Chances of that are extremely slight. No, there are too many unknowns here in Denver. This octopus has too many tentacles, reaching, feeling, hiding in dark corners waiting to latch onto an innocent passerby. Any one of those old geezers might say something unknowingly to the wrong person. We don't want that."

"Interesting the stag head holding its secret that long," said Sam. "That compartment had to be how Gordon was transporting stuff right under the noses of the hunters. He and that taxidermist were definitely in cahoots."

Friday evening, Pete answered his door to find Karen and Dom on his front steps.

"We just dropped Marilyn off after our San Antonio trip," said Karen. "We thought you'd like to hear how it went."

"Taking her was extraordinarily kind," said Pete. "What did you learn?"

"Not much from the PD, but Marilyn was able to make the arrangements to have Ross buried in Montana."

Pete smiled. "Good."

"The grandmother was ga-ga—that was Marilyn's observation," said Karen. "Her mind wandered in and out, even though the nurses said she was having a good day. We gleaned what we could from her rambling. Such a bitter woman."

"Why did they take Ross in the first place?"

"To *save* him. She called Gordon a liar and accused him of cruelty to Winona and Ross. All those accusations about drugs she said were lies."

"Out of touch with reality," said Pete.

"I watched her when she was telling Marilyn all this. She ducked her head, looked out over her glasses, and bragged they had outsmarted Gordon. They snatched him during the Christmas break and traveled all over Texas and the south in their Airstream. Gordon didn't know where they were. She said they called him by payphone periodically until spring when he said he'd get them thrown in jail if they didn't bring Ross back."

"That must have been about the time Gordon tried to get money from his parents," said Pete. "Without the kid, he wouldn't get it."

"Poor little fellow," said Dom. "Just a pawn."

"I'd wondered why he needed to kidnap a child."

"Evidently when the novelty wore off, the months on the road in a confined space with Ross became very difficult," said Karen. "They got back to Corpus Christi, I'd guess in April, but were heartily sick of each other."

"Did Ross run away?"

Karen shook her head. "His grandmother complained he was ungrateful for wanting to go back to that evil man. He didn't appreciate what they tried to do for him."

She looked at Pete. "This is so sad. The old lady said Ross told her he'd met a nice fellow who was going to take him back to his dad. Marilyn was aghast. She couldn't believe somebody would send a child off with a stranger and said so. Things got really contentious in our visit then. The grandmother got all huffy, said she'd met him, and so he wasn't a stranger, and he was very nice looking, like that made a difference. She gave Ross cash so he could pay his own way on the trip."

"*Mein Gott*. A recipe for disaster."

"She planned to tell Gordon, but she put off calling and then heard about the plane crash, Gordon's death, and that Ross was injured. Obviously, she believed he made it to Denver and had flown with his dad to Montana. That was all we got out of her. She didn't even ask about him now. Marilyn was really upset by our visit and didn't tell the old lady the rest of the story."

Pete shook his head. "Understandable. How did she end up in San Antonio?"

"They moved there from the coast after their home was flooded by Hurricane Bret in 1999."

"How's Marilyn doing now?" asked Pete.

Dom took Karen's hand. Karen laced her fingers with his, sniffing a few times before looking at Pete. "We talked a long time. It's incredibly hard for her, but I think she'll be okay. Dom and I will keep in touch."

"Any closer to finding that second kidnapper?" asked Dom.

Pete rubbed his forehead tiredly. "I'm worried."

Chapter Forty-Six

"Oh, good," said Krista as she took her hot chocolate from the barista at Books and Bearclaws. "The window seat is open. Usually on Saturday mornings, it's taken." She and Leyla moved quickly to the table in the bay window, which looked out on a one-way street with cars parked next to the sidewalk and a narrow, planted area.

Outside the window, among a few dormant shrubs, a whimsical, bronze sculpture of a bear holding a mug sat affixed to a rock. Drizzle beaded up and dripped from his sleek finish.

From this coveted spot, Krista and Leyla had a good view up and down the street and of the large, landscaped park across from them. Krista looked back at her dad, who was just joining Sam and Pete at a larger table near the books.

"I like it here, even when it's misty mid-January," said Leyla as she laid her jacket on the seat beside her. "There's Dom parking his car." She pointed down the street to the left.

"Have you thought of any more acts of kindness ideas?" asked Krista. "I wish there was something big we could do."

"Wilma had a good idea. She remembered being frustrated when she lived in Chimayo, having no big grocery stores. So now she and Marilyn are taking some of the old ladies to the grocery stores here once a week."

"Hoot just got here." Krista pointed up the block to the right. "See? Next to that white car."

"There are a lot of white cars. Sam says people like them because they reflect the heat in summer."

"Phooey. Hoot didn't bring the kids with him." She and Leyla waved as Hoot came in and took his place near Dom in line. Krista sipped her chocolate and resumed watching.

"Look at the little birdie," said Leyla. "He's perched on the bear's nose. He's all fluffed out to keep warm. That would make a cool drawing. I'll have to remember that."

Krista giggled. "You could make the statue look cross-eyed at it. That'd be funny." She watched a lady with three leashed dogs struggle to open her car while hanging on to her furled umbrella. "Look at that lady. She's got standard poodles."

"Where?" Leyla swiveled on the window seat to look.

Krista pointed to the left. "On the corner, right next to Dom's car." They watched as the lady and her dogs went past their window. "I think the rain has pretty well stopped now."

"It's busy today," said Leyla, setting down her cup. "A pickup got her spot already."

As they watched, a man got out of the pickup and took a backpack from his truck. He slung the pack over his shoulder and looked down at his cell phone.

"He's got sunglasses on," said Krista. "Looks goofy with a stocking cap and a big, fat, red jacket. It's not like he's in bright snow."

"Maybe the glare bothers him. Are you done with Cliff's new book yet?"

The man came toward them, eventually passing their window. "Finished it the day after I got it," said Krista. "We talked about the extra stuff he put in the back on kidnapping. I think it was his best ever." She frowned, looking down the street.

"What?"

"That man with the backpack. He just stopped by Hoot's car. That's funny. He's just standing there looking around. Now he's bending down."

"Maybe his shoe came untied," Leyla said as she turned to look. "He's going now." She sipped her chocolate. "I'm not quite done with Cliff's book yet. I have maybe five chapters left. Don't tell me how it ends."

"Let me know when you're done." Krista frowned.

"Now what's the matter?"

"The man must've forgotten his backpack. Look. You can see the corner of it under Hoot's car."

"Are you sure? Maybe he forgot to pick it up when he tied his shoe. Do you see him?"

Krista looked up the street in the direction the man had been heading. "No."

"There," said Leyla, pointing to the left. "He's way back there already. He's going into the Mexican restaurant kitty-corner from his truck."

"I hope nobody steals his pack."

"Should we tell our dads?"

Krista sat up straight. "I know—I've been looking for an act of kindness. I'll get the backpack and put it back in his truck. It's not raining now. He'll think he lost it, and he'll be so happy when he finds out that it was there in his truck all along." Filled with glee, she slid off her chair, looked over to where her dad was laughing. "I'll be right back."

She walked quickly outside to where the backpack lay almost entirely under the car. How did it get so far under? Hoot wouldn't even see it, she thought, and he might drive over it. She knelt and tugged it toward her. Wow, what was in there? Rocks? Lots of books? It was heavy.

She stood up and looked toward the restaurant, but didn't see the man. She picked the pack up and started back toward his pickup. She shifted the weight to free a hand to wave at Leyla in the window.

Something clanked inside. Didn't sound like books. Maybe he was a rock collector. Would they make that kind of noise? Still no sign of the man.

At his truck, she went to the driver's side, grunting as she hoisted the backpack over the edge of the cargo area. She tucked it where it would be safe, undercover as best she could, by the side of the pickup and the toolbox. It might get a little damp if the drizzle came back, but not nearly as wet as it would have lying in the street. Then she ran back to Books and Bearclaws.

"You did it," said Leyla. "That was a brave thing to do, helping a stranger like that."

Krista was pleased with herself. "It was heavy! I was glad I didn't have to carry it longer than a block. He'll be so surprised. He'll wonder how it got there."

They looked out periodically, but the man never appeared.

Dom stopped by their table. "I'll see you both tonight. Anton has invited us all for dinner."

Krista stacked the empty mugs. "Everybody's getting ready to go." Hoot waved at them as he left.

Pete stopped by their table with a smile. "You lucked out getting this window seat."

"We did. What'd you get, Daddy?" asked Krista, spotting the bag in his hand.

"Some books I ordered. Skyla mentioned this new book, so I picked it up for her. And then there's one with an odd title. Akiko said you'd like it."

"Is it about Airedales?"

"*Terrier Grooming Chart Book.*"

Pete laughed as Krista eagerly snatched the bag and took out the spiral-bound book. "With Shadow, Scherzo, and Twitch to practice on—"

Kaboom!

The building shook with the force of an explosion. The panes in the bay window shuddered, and Krista heard breaking glass. Her

221

father's arms grabbed her, and she was swung in front of his body. He stumbled, and they both went down to their knees, his back to the window. Around them, they heard screaming. Car alarms started to blare.

Sam landed next to them with Leyla in his arms.

"Was that a bomb?" Leyla's voice was high-pitched and frightened. "Is it war? Are they dropping bombs here now? Will Mama be okay?" She clutched at Sam.

"What the hell?" Anton rose to his feet. "What was that? Jesus, something's on fire." Heavy smoke blew past the window, filling the air with an acrid smell.

"Sam," cried Pete. "Let's go." He turned and headed for the door, yelling, "Stay inside, folks! Stay away from the windows."

Sam put his hands on Leyla's shoulders. "Sweetheart, it's not war. Mama will be okay. You stay with Anton." A tortured expression crossed his face. "Oh, my God. Dom and Hoot just went out there!"

Krista blinked away frightened tears as her hand fumbled for Leyla's, giving it a comforting squeeze. Her daddy pulled them both close, and she leaned into him. He was so big, so strong. He'd keep them safe.

CHAPTER FORTY-SEVEN

Anton watched Sam and Pete head for the door, phones to their ears. A few customers had rushed out, gawking toward the left end of the block, hugging their arms against the chill. Anton heard Pete tell them to get back inside until they'd determined it was safe.

His command was punctuated by another explosion from the same location, this one significantly louder. The building shook again. One of the baristas screamed as a window shattered. It was enough to bring the customers rushing back in, some of them crying.

"Did you see?" one said. "It looked like a car on fire at the end of the block."

"Is this a terrorist attack?" asked another.

Anton was stunned. Dom had parked at that end of the block. Was he okay? Ash and light debris still fell. The air was hazy with the smoke. Anton guided the girls deeper into the bookstore. With the advantage of his height, Anton glimpsed Hoot through a front window, running up to Pete and talking with him briefly before coming inside.

Anton beckoned Hoot over to where they stood. "Did you see Dom? He left a few minutes before you did."

Hoot's face was pale. "He drove by just as I was getting into my car. Why would a vehicle explode like that?"

Anton closed his eyes in relief at hearing Dom was safe.

"From what I saw," Hoot said, "it was a pickup truck at the other end of the block that blew up. The explosion went off just as I started my car. Gosh, stuff flying all over. Pieces everywhere, some still burning."

Already Anton saw a firetruck heading the wrong way down the street, followed closely by another. He heard more sirens in the distance and saw a patrolman driving past, sirens wailing and lights flashing.

"I'll call Dom. Make sure he's okay." As he listened to the rings, he saw a patrolman block off the intersection next to Books and Bearclaws with crime-scene tape.

"Hoot, a pickup truck?" As Krista's frightened voice got his attention, Anton put a comforting hand on her shoulder. She turned from Hoot to him.

"Daddy—"

"Not now, Krista. Hi, Dom." He told him what had happened and asked if he was okay, then he hung up and said, "He heard the explosion, but didn't have a clue what it was."

"Daddy, I have to tell you something."

Sam came back. "Anton, can you take Leyla home with you when they let everyone go? I have to be here."

"Sure. Was anyone hurt?"

"Was anyone in the truck?" asked Hoot.

"So far, the only injuries we've seen are from flying glass. Nothing serious. I've got to get back." Sam smoothed Leyla's hair away from her face. "We're all okay, honey. You'll be safe at the ranch."

Anton felt a tugging on his sleeve. "Daddy, it's important." Krista's voice pleaded.

"Krista, can't it wait?"

"No, Daddy. Listen! I think that's where I put the backpack."

"Backpack? What backpack?"

"We saw a man park his truck at the corner of the block and take out a backpack. He came down here to where Hoot's car was. He bent down to tie his shoe or something. We looked away for a bit, but then I saw the backpack was still there, kinda under the car. The guy had gone back through the park and was going into the Mexican restaurant. I thought I could use it as my act of kindness. I went out and picked it up and put it back in his truck so nobody would steal it, and he wouldn't lose it."

"Holy—" Sam's expression was sharp as he looked at Krista. "Hang on! Hoot, can you keep folks back from us a bit. Anton, girls." He turned away from the curious onlookers to a back corner and called Pete.

"Pete. 10-33! Bomber may be in the Mexican restaurant. Krista, Leyla, can you tell us what he looked like? What he was wearing?"

As the girls told Sam their story, he relayed it to Pete.

Anton felt the blood drain from his face. Backpacks and explosions had disastrous connotations that scared the hell out of him. "My God, Krista, you picked up a stranger's backpack?"

She nodded her head, as a little sob escaped. "I thought it was the kind thing to do." She wiped her sleeve across her face.

Sam's urgent voice brought Krista's eyes back to him. "Where exactly was it?"

"It had slid under Hoot's car."

"My car?" Hoot turned to Krista away from the curious folks, giving her a look of incredulity.

Sam sent a look to Hoot and Anton. "How far under?"

"Quite a ways. I couldn't think why he would leave it there on purpose." Krista began crying in earnest. "I just wanted to do something kind."

Anton drew her into a hug. "You did, sweetheart, you did. But don't you ever do anything like that again. You see a backpack or package where it doesn't belong, tell a grownup or call the police."

Sam stepped away, still talking to Pete. In a few minutes, he was back. "They're searching the restaurant for someone matching that description. Pete's got someone collecting the footage from the surveillance cameras in the area. Where are you guys parked?"

"Will they let me past the crime scene tape?" asked Hoot.

"We're in the parking garage, a block or so from here," said Anton.

Sam looked up as a couple of patrolmen came into the bookstore and headed toward him. "They won't let you move your car, Hoot. It's a crime scene. Pete thought the safest thing for you to do is to go with a patrolman to the station. A detective will take your statements there. You can get your cars later. I'm coming, too."

Hoot looked at him sharply. "Safest?" He didn't say more when Sam motioned with his head to the girls.

"Is it possible that this might have been aimed at Hoot?" asked Anton.

The three men exchanged looks. Sam nodded. "Very possible."

Hoot sucked in a breath. "I don't want to believe it, but I'm afraid you may be right. Should I take my family to a motel?"

"I think," said Anton, "that you, your family, and Marilyn, should come and stay with us until the trouble blows over. Come now. Immediately. We don't know what they'll do next."

"We can't bring our troubles—"

"We've plenty of room. You'll be safe. We've a good security system. It would be very hard for whoever is doing this to find you."

Sam nodded. "It's an excellent idea, Hoot. Farah, Leyla, and Wilma stayed there when they were in danger. I'm glad Anton suggested it. Is thirty minutes enough time for Marilyn and Melody to grab what they need? I'll call Hiram. He and his troopers should be able to guard the place while they pack."

"Wow. That quick?"

Worry showed on Hoot's face as his eyes met Anton's. Finally he said, "I admit it would be a load off my mind. Not only for security, but emotionally, too. Melody is pregnant. Knowing somebody was standing outside Bonnie's window frightened us to death. Yes, we'll come, but just—"

"For as long as it takes. We'll enjoy having you." Anton took out his phone. "I'll call Mom."

Karen's invitation was instant and enthusiastic. As Anton put away his phone, Hoot called Melody.

Sam turned to the girls. "We're going to the police station. Hoot will go with us."

Leyla picked up her jacket. Anton retrieved their books from where they'd fallen on the floor near the window seat. His mind churned as they followed the patrolmen out the door. Already he saw reporters gathering by the crime tape, hoping to get some eyewitness sound bites for the news.

In the backseat of the patrol car as they were whisked away, he held Krista's hand firmly, needing the physical connection. He couldn't believe his daughter had come so close to being killed.

His eyes strayed to the red-haired man in the front passenger seat. It suddenly hit him. If not for Krista's act of kindness, this day would have ended in an unbearably cruel manner.

◆ ❖ ◆

When Anton arrived at the police department with Krista still holding his hand, he followed the others down narrow corridors and through several locked doors to a room with cubicles and desks. A large, more private office lay beyond the cubicle area, with windows both to the outside and to the inner area of the detectives' bullpen. Sam showed the girls his cubicle.

"You have pictures of Mom and me," Leyla said.

"You're my family. I like to look up from my work and see you." He smiled at her and smoothed back some curly tendrils of light brown hair that had escaped from her braids.

While the girls tried out his swivel chair, Sam beckoned Anton and Hoot back out of the girls' hearing. "Hiram is on his way to your house, Hoot. The state troopers will escort them to the ranch." Anton glanced at the girls. They had rolled a chair from another cubicle into Sam's space and sat watching them with big eyes.

Then Anton's attention went to a Hispanic woman entering the room, dressed neatly in blazer and slacks. Her smile was warm and friendly.

"This is Detective Ruiz," Sam said. "She usually does our interviews with children."

The woman's rapport with kids was good, thought Anton, as he watched her draw them into conversation. She had obviously been briefed on the situation.

"Would you like to be present when we talk with Krista, Mr. Bjornson?" she asked.

"I insist on it."

"If you'll follow me, we'll talk with Krista first." Detective Ruiz led Anton and Krista down another hallway and into a pleasant room where several teddy bears perched on the chairs.

"I know you've already told Detective Martinez about what you saw and did," said Detective Ruiz, "but it's important that we hear it again and record it."

Anton listened as Krista launched into her story, telling about the man, what he looked like, and why she moved the backpack.

"What did the backpack feel like when you picked it up?"

"It was heavy. And it clanked."

"Clanked?"

"Yeah, a metal sound, like when you move pots and pans around and nest them in each other. I thought of unzipping it and looking, but that would have been rude. It wasn't mine, and I shouldn't be snooping."

Anton closed his eyes. My God. She worried about snooping? She could have been killed!

"You have a good memory for details. How do you remember so much?"

"I'm always looking for stuff to draw. Lou—she's my drawing teacher—is teaching me how to observe. And I like to read mysteries. Cliff's books always talk about how to see and remember things."

Anton smiled. His daughter never ceased to amaze him.

◆ ❖ ◆

My God! What on earth is going on?

Her mind in a whirl, Melody pressed end on Hoot's call. Calling from the police station? She could hear the strain in his voice. Pack

228

for a week? In a half hour? Troopers were coming and would escort them all to the Bjornson ranch for their safety. *Their safety?* When he left this morning, everything was fine.

Hoot said they'd be staying at the Bjornsons' for several days. He would call Marilyn next, as she would be coming, too. He certainly had some explaining to do, but for now speed seemed to be called for.

"Matti, Bonnie, listen carefully. Daddy just called and said we are going to stay at Anton and Skyla's house for a few days. Won't that be fun? But we have to pack what we need quickly."

"How come, Mommy?" Matti's blue eyes looked up at her.

"Well, ah—" *Good question.* "The city is going to be doing work, and they have to shut off our water and electricity. We'll come back when they're done. Right now, I need both of you to go to your rooms and choose five outfits for the days we'll be there and put them on the bed. You each get to pick five toys and three books to take with you. Can you do that? Then I'll help you pack."

"Is Daddy coming home?" asked Bonnie.

"I'll have to pack for him," said Melody. "He'll meet us there."

He'd said he wanted her to bring the puzzle box. She grabbed that first, so she wouldn't forget it, and put his uniforms and other clothing on top of it. For her and the kids, casual clothing would do fine. Laptops, phone chargers, tracker chargers, toothbrushes, shaving kit. She'd never done such a quick job of throwing stuff together. Medications, vitamins, shoes, socks, pajamas, underwear. She was flying.

The kids were slow about their choices. She threw what they'd chosen into suitcases and added some more. Bonnie insisted on her princess outfit. She didn't have time to fight that battle, so in it went.

A state trooper knocked on her door, and she sent him over to help Marilyn and to make sure she'd remembered to pack her prescriptions. By that time another trooper had arrived. Marilyn's car was loaded and waiting.

"I want to see you with your jackets on, hats and mittens, too," she called to the two wide-eyed children. A quick glance told her that Matti had on his tracker, and Bonnie still wore her sneakers with hers. The officer carried what she'd collected out to her car and stowed it.

Thermostat, lights, lock the door. Thirty-eight minutes. What wasn't packed, they'd have to borrow, buy, or do without. Then they were buckled in and on their way with police cars escorting them front and back.

All the while her mind was in turmoil. What had happened? What kind of a bad movie had she landed in? Why did they need an escort? She turned on the radio. Breaking news was all about a bomb going off in downtown Santa Fe.

What was the world coming to?

Chapter Forty-Eight

"I have to go home today and pick up Bonnie's fox," said Hoot as he joined Anton in the Bjornsons' breakfast room the next morning. "I don't think I can face another night like last night. Just when we got Bonnie to sleep, she woke up crying for Foxie again. That child has a one-track mind."

"When you pack that quickly, you're bound to forget things. We can lend you what you need," said Anton. "But sorry, no Foxie."

"Melody made a list. She didn't even think about my uniform stocking cap and jacket. I'll need those tomorrow. It should be okay if I pick them up, shouldn't it?"

Anton hesitated. "It's not for me to say. Whoever is out to get you knows where you live. I don't know if they might conjure up an ambush. Ask Pete when he gets here. He's coming this morning."

When Pete arrived, Hoot explained the problem.

"I'll take you," said Pete. "Hiram's troopers are keeping an eye on your house."

When they arrived at Hoot's home, Hiram was there, with a couple of state police cars. "*Ach du lieber*," said Pete. "Something happened."

Hiram met them. "Somebody broke in. Must have been just after we checked the last time. I'm afraid it's a mess."

"How about my grandmother's place?"

"No sign of disturbance there."

"We came to pick up some items Hoot needs," said Pete.

"You can go in with us, but let us retrieve the items for you. If anything's missing, let us know."

Hoot stopped inside the front door. "Dang! Mess is an understatement."

The coat closet stood ajar, everything from the shelf thrown out onto the floor. He moved into the kitchen and dining area. Cupboard doors were open, and items pulled out on the floor. Boxes of cereal and other foodstuffs had been haphazardly moved around. Down the hall, he saw linens and towels heaped on the carpet.

Even in the kids' bedrooms, drawers had been emptied on the floor.

"Dang. It's too much. They were in our house. Messing with our stuff."

Hoot stood in Bonnie's room, taking in the chaos. He rubbed his head and took a deep breath. Panic started to rise, and his eyes drifted shut. *You told. Say goodbye to your kids.* He felt an encouraging hand on his shoulder, squeezing gently. He looked over to see Pete's gray eyes on him, full of concern.

"Hoot, your family is okay."

Hoot nodded, took a deep breath and then another. He focused on the room again. *We can get through this.* Pete's hand stayed on his shoulder, reassuring, strong. *I'm not alone anymore. I'm not six years old.*

Seconds ticked by. "I'm sorry." Hoot paused, looking for the right word. "I'm overwhelmed. Violated somehow."

"It's natural to feel that." Pete's calm voice steadied him. "But there's no danger here now."

Hoot forced himself back to the list in his hand. "That's the fox my daughter's been crying for," he said, nodding toward the toy on the bed. An officer handed it to him. He took it gingerly. "I almost—" He swallowed and tried again. "I feel like I should run it through the washer before I give it to Bonnie. Like whoever was here left everything dirty." He turned quickly and left Bonnie's room.

"Hoot, can you tell if anything's missing?" asked Hiram as they stood in the master bedroom.

"How, with this mess?" Hoot felt more in control now that they had left Bonnie's bedroom. "It's crazy. What were they looking for?" He pointed at a heap from one of the drawers. "Look, Melody kept some extra cash with her underwear. The money's still there."

"Hiram, have you ever seen a break-in around here like this?" asked Pete.

Hiram shook his head. "Right after you were shot, we did have one where some perp broke in. I told Sam. Along the Pecos, but on the other side of the highway. Stole guns and stuff. Wish Colorado would keep its riff-raff. We have enough of our own."

"Colorado!" Pete's voice was sharp.

"Yeah, somebody named Wilcox from Denver. Why are you so surprised?"

"Denver keeps popping up in this case. Did you arrest him?"

"We did. Retrieved the stolen items. But he had a heart attack a few days later. He didn't make it."

Hoot collected more of the items on his list. Then he watched Pete, quietly turning in the middle of the room, studying the mess.

"Hiram, did you notice it's the big drawers that have been dumped? The small drawers aren't touched. Same in every room. Valuables, even money, ignored." Pete rested a hand on the back of a chair and took the weight off his leg.

"You're right," said Hiram. "Look at the boxes from the closet shelves. The lids are off, but contents aren't disturbed."

"I'd say they were looking for a particular, good-sized item. They ignored places where it wouldn't fit."

"Question is," said Hiram, "what were they looking for?"

"Why now?" asked Hoot. "Do you suppose this was the same person with the backpack bomb?"

"It's strange," said Hiram. "You get threatening calls, letters. Somebody looks in your windows during the night. A man puts a bomb under your car. They trash your house, looking for something, but don't appear to take anything."

"All except the calls began after the TV show," said Pete.

"What did the film footage show?" asked Hiram.

"We were in the living room." Hoot led them back. "The cameraman was set up over there." He pointed.

"Look around you, son," said Hiram. "Picture what the camera would have caught. Is any of that missing?"

Hoot looked around, cataloguing the furnishings in his mind. He looked at the coffee table. "The puzzle box was here then, but Melody took it with her yesterday. It's at the ranch. I hoped Anton and I would get a chance to make the key and open it."

"How big is this box?" asked Hiram. "And what's it made of?"

"Big enough to hold a six-pack of beer." Hoot made length and height motions with his hands. "Made of wood with a carved hand on top."

"The jewelry box Wilcox stole was wood," said Hiram. "Had roses carved on it, but it was nothing special. I'd think there was a connection, except the guy died before this break-in."

Pete looked at Hoot. "I'd like to be there when you open that puzzle box. That second kidnapper might be interested in the contents. After all, it was Gordon's. And Colorado? You know what I think about coincidences."

Hiram nodded. "I don't get it. To put a bomb under his car? That wouldn't get them their puzzle box."

"More and more I'm convinced that some answers to this case lie in that box," said Pete. "You might consider using force to open it."

"I'd like one more chance at opening it properly. Maybe Anton can make the key tonight."

"How about if Sam and I come out tomorrow afternoon then?" said Pete.

"If we can't reproduce the key by then," said Hoot, "we'll break it." He frowned, looking at the mess. "You don't suppose they got the wrong house? That this isn't about me at all? Or maybe the wrong car was targeted with the bomb?"

"You forget, the bomb didn't go off until you got into your car," said Pete. "They must have been watching."

One of the investigators called to Hiram from where she stood in the kitchen. A cupboard door and several drawers beneath it were all open. "Look at this." She pointed to several spots of what looked like blood. "This is speculation, but the intruder may have looked at the upper cupboards first, not bothering to shut the doors. Then they opened the drawers below. You can tell because there are items that are consistent with drawer contents placed on top of cupboard contents. I think they might have come up under this open door and banged their head. They might not have realized they were bleeding until some of the blood had been covered by other stuff they pulled out."

"Good work," said Hiram. "Head wounds bleed like the devil. When the culprit is caught, that will identify them."

Hoot surveyed the kitchen and sighed. "Heck, I just about forgot what I came for. My jacket is still in the front closet. The hat is there on the floor." He checked his list. "Melody is going to come unglued when I tell her about this. I hope whoever bashed his head on our cupboards did some serious damage. They dared to enter our home. Frigging cowards."

◆ ❖ ◆

On Sunday afternoon, after Pete had gotten home, Sam stopped by. They sat in the Schultzes' family room, bringing each other up to date on the bombing, the break-in, and the plans to open the box the next day.

"In the men's room of the Mexican restaurant, they found that red jacket and the stocking cap," said Pete. "He knew they'd be looking for them. You'd have to know downtown would have security cameras."

"Did anyone at the restaurant see him?"

"Not beforehand, and it was chaos there just across the street," said Pete. "Lot of broken windows. Debris raining down. People fled screaming."

"What happens now?" asked Sam.

"We're done gathering evidence and interviewing witnesses. ATF will shoulder the rest. FBI will fill in where they can."

"Damn it, Pete," said Sam. "This frightens me. We almost lost Hoot yesterday."

"I know. Why did we ever let him try to draw this scum into the open? The man can't feel safe until we catch this second kidnapper. The only good thing about this bombing is that it gives us present-day actions to investigate. Poking about in the past looking for friends of a dead man—damn frustrating."

"I have hopes for that puzzle box," said Sam. "I remember it being in plain view on the TV program. It's tied to Gordon. Has to be important."

Pete nodded. They sat in silence for a few minutes.

Then Sam looked at Pete with a somber expression. "I learned something yesterday. My daughter will never be an ordinary American kid. She carries a history—her flight from a war-torn country. She's never actually witnessed a bombing, but she's heard talk and seen pictures on TV. Her father was killed by a bomb dropped on their home. When she heard that explosion and cried out to me—the fear that war had found her—that look on her face shattered me. I realized that fear will always be a part of her."

"How does that make you feel?"

"I can't take that fear away from her or from my wife. I talked to Farah and Leyla a long time last night. We've got to be the kind of people who make a difference, who help people get along and respect each other."

"I believe you're right about the fear always being there," said Pete. "But you can also stress the hope that brought her mother to this country. The vision is still valid, even if it gets clouded over for a little while. That hope sends us into the future with a positive attitude. There's power in that, Sam."

"Yeah, Karen and her light on a hill." Sam slumped back in the couch, running his finger over the design on his coffee mug. "Do you suppose Krista has realized the magnitude of her act of kindness yet?"

"When Melody hugged her and thanked her for saving Hoot's life, that did it. Never saw her eyes as big and blue. Sheer wonder."

CHAPTER FORTY-NINE

Yvonne heard Vassily leave for his walk and looked at her watch. Four o'clock on the dot. Since Hayle had left earlier that day, the time had flown. She'd have to get cracking on dinner. God forbid that dinner wasn't ready exactly at five. She never got time just to sit and work things out. Damn schedule wouldn't let her concentrate.

The pork chops were in the grilling machine, and the potato water had started to boil merrily. Just enough time left to microwave the veggies. She glared at her ringing phone and checked the number.

"Hayle, are you all right? Where are you? Did you have an accident?"

"For God's sake, Yvonne. I'm fine. I stopped to have coffee in Raton. I wondered if I left the book I was reading there. Can you check? It's by Stephen King."

She hurried into the guest room. "It's here."

"Just keep it for me."

She heard some dishes clatter over the phone. "Where did you say you were?"

"In Raton. I was sleepy, so I stopped for coffee."

"You shouldn't be driving when you're tired."

"Yvonne, stop worrying. I'm only three and a half hours from home. I'm fine now that I've had my coffee. Would it help if I called you when I got home?"

"Yes, then I can go to sleep and not worry."

"Whatever."

She heard a car door slam and the sound of an engine starting. "Bye." The call ended.

She hurriedly set the table and turned on the news. She dished up the potatoes and veggies and covered them. She turned off the griller. Vassily would fuss if everything wasn't hot enough. She sat at her place and straightened her napkin. Her attention was caught by the newscaster talking about yesterday's bombing. Tomorrow should be very interesting at work. How neat it was to have an inside look through police eyes.

Her thoughts drifted off to how she might find clues, when the weather came on. Weather? This early? Usually that came later— my goodness. Vassily wasn't home yet and the news was almost over. Damn. The food would be cold. He didn't like it when it was reheated in the microwave. If she called him, he'd yell at her for being a worry wart. She fussed another ten minutes, then called anyway.

No answer. She'd never hear the last of it if he missed *Jeopardy*.

Yvonne looked out the front door and brooded about what to do. She'd go after him. No matter what, he'd complain. With a last frown at the table, she found a flashlight, put on her jacket, and started for the door. Damn. She'd have to use the microwave. Men!

One good thing—he hadn't varied his route in six years. He only changed it then because some neighbor had a barky chihuahua he detested. Dog was probably dead and gone by now. Phooey, the neighbor was probably dead and gone, but would he change his mind? No way.

Oh, dear. What if he'd gotten in trouble by using his slingshot and hit something he shouldn't have? Would he have gotten into a fight? Then she remembered seeing his slingshot on the table by his chair and felt better.

Her flashlight lit the path ahead of her. She didn't like walking alone in the dark. Too many horror stories abounded at work about what could happen to ladies. She zipped her jacket higher and marched along trying to look confident. Where was he?

At the halfway point on his route, she spotted a dark shape lying on the path.

"Vassily?"

She ran toward him. He lay on his left side, slumped over face down. She shook him slightly, calling again. He didn't answer. She turned him over, then stopped with a cry. His leg looked odd. Was it broken? She whipped out her phone and called 911.

◆ ❖ ◆

In a visitor's lounge in the hospital, Yvonne sipped at a cup of cold coffee. She made a face, set aside the coffee, and glanced at her watch. The doctor had been by to see her about an hour ago. They were taking Vassily to surgery—it was his head they were most worried about. To tell the truth, she hadn't noticed that injury at first. But when she saw him again before they wheeled him away, she'd been shocked by the bruising on the right side of his head.

Her phone rang about nine thirty. Good—it was Hayle, calling to let her know he'd gotten home.

"Vassily fell when he was walking. I think he broke his hip. He's in surgery now."

"Oh, no. How awful. Did he tell you what happencd?"

"No, he hit his head, too. He hasn't been conscious at all." Tears trickled down her cheeks. It was so good to hear her brother's comforting voice.

"You hang in there, sis. Keep in touch. Call if you want somebody to talk to. Even if it's in the middle of the night, I don't mind."

CHAPTER FIFTY

The Bjornson home was quiet as Anton left his workshop late Sunday night. The 3-D printer still hummed away behind him, working on a third key. The puzzle box was locked away.

When he came into the bedroom, Skyla was still awake, reading her new book. "I wanted to talk to you about an idea. What do you think of our selling my old house to Hoot and Melody? It has all the security stuff you installed. There's even suitable land for Marilyn's trailer on the lot."

Anton smiled. "I'd been thinking about that, too. Would they like the idea?"

"Melody always loved the house, and it's closer to the elementary school."

"We could bring it up by saying we thought we'd get it ready for sale."

Skyla closed her book. "Let's ask them tomorrow."

Pete looked at the message waiting for him at his office Monday morning. Yvonne wouldn't be in today. Her husband had fallen and was in the hospital.

He called her. "Yvonne, how is he?"

"Oh, Lieutenant, he still isn't conscious. He broke his hip. They said he hit his head, too, and has a concussion or something. I forget what they called it. My mind isn't taking in all those big words right now. They did surgery last night."

"What happened?"

"I suppose he tripped when he was walking. I'm sure he'll come out of it soon, but it worries me."

"You take the time you need with him. We'll muddle on through here."

"I'm sure I'll be back in a few days."

As Pete hung up, he thought it would be good to stop by and see her later.

Chapter Fifty-One

Late Monday morning, Yvonne broke her bedside vigil and went home for lunch. While she was there, she searched for their insurance papers. Vassily, an accountant, had always paid the bills. Yvonne liked his doing that. Her mind was not particularly mathematical. She thought he'd mentioned some kind of insurance that would pay extra if he were injured and couldn't work. She should look and see if that was still good.

She snapped the light on in her husband's office. The sight of the neat, orderly room brought tears to her eyes. She stood still for a moment, remembering the pale, quiet form of her husband hooked up to all those machines helping him get better.

She crossed to the file cabinet where he put the paid bills. It was a funny feeling opening the drawer, like she was trespassing. But she had to do it. He wasn't able. She flipped to the folders marked Insurance. Goodness. Such a lot of them. Cars, Disability, Health, Homeowner's, Life, Special Supplemental. She pulled out the Disability folder and flipped through it. That looked promising. She laid it on top of the file cabinet. What was this other one? Special Supplemental?

Pulling that one out, she closed the drawer and sat down at Vassily's desk with the two folders. The Disability one seemed to be what she remembered. Statements, filed by date, noted with check numbers. She opened the other one, expecting paid bills from some company, instead finding a small notebook with Vassily's tiny, crabbed handwriting with dates, notes, and amounts.

May 9-17, 1991.
    Hayle and Gordon Stewart stayed with us except for one night at White Sands.
    They used my car for "business" in Santa Fe.
    Hayle phoned me at 5:00 p.m. on May 17.
May 17, 1991.
    McCreath boy kidnapped in late afternoon.
    Gordon had gotten an urgent call from Denver, and had to fly back immediately.
    I should pick up my car at the airport.
May 19, 1991
    Gordon killed when his plane crashed on a lake in Montana. His "son" survived.
March, 2006.
    Hayle began treatments to get rid of his port wine stain.
December 30, 2016.
    TV Show ran. Second kidnapper.
    Rabbit birthmark on neck.
January 11, 2017.
    First of weekly cash payments made.

Her brows drew together. What did this mean? Did Vassily think her brother was involved in the kidnapping? Ridiculous. That couldn't be true. Payments?

She looked back at the dates on the first page. Hayle had visited more often recently. With a sickening feeling she glanced down the column of dates and figures. All corresponded to Hayle's visits.

Could her brother be the kidnapper?

Vassily knew? Was he blackmailing him?

She didn't know these men at all.

This case—it was one she'd pored over and even discussed with them—mostly Hayle. She let out a cry of dismay. He hadn't been helping at all. He was snooping! Trying to find out what the police knew.

Her breathing turned to audible pants, and then sobs as she took in the depth of the betrayal. How they must have laughed at her. Her husband. Her brother. The shame!

God, what was she to do? Maybe there was some mistake. Maybe she wasn't interpreting this correctly. She would ask Vassily. More tears welled in her eyes. It would be a long time before she'd bother him with this. He had to wake up and get better.

She wished there was someone she could go to, to find what it really meant. Vassily would certainly be annoyed if she asked her brother. He'd laugh at her for being silly and misunderstanding. Maybe her boss? Would the lieutenant be able to shed some light on it? She wouldn't tell him about her studying the case, just that she'd found this and was concerned about what it meant—which was all true. She took a deep breath. She'd stop by the police department on her way back to the hospital. She'd feel better sitting by Vassily when she had an explanation.

Pete was going over case notes with Sergeant Ruiz at the table in his office when he saw Yvonne at his door, clutching a folder in one hand and her purse in the other.

"Please stay, Sergeant." He rose and opened the door. Yvonne's eyes were red, like she'd been crying, and she was uncharacteristically disheveled. "Yvonne, news on your husband?"

"I'm on my way back to the hospital. He wasn't awake when I left." She thrust the folder at him. "I was hoping—" A sob rose and then another. "I don't know what this means."

Sergeant Ruiz put her arm around the sobbing woman and guided her to a chair.

Pete sat and glanced at the first page, then the second, his eyes widening in surprise. He looked up at Yvonne. "Who is Hayle?"

"He's my brother. He lives in Denver."

"Your brother! Where did you find these?" He slid the papers across the table to where Ruiz read them quickly. Her brown eyes grew big as they met his in wonder.

"This was filed with all our insurance policies. What does it mean?"

"What do you think it means, Yvonne?"

"It looks like my brother helped take that boy, and it looks like Vassily was blackmailing him. But I don't want that to be true." Her lips quivered. "I want . . . I want you to tell me I'm wrooong." Her voice trailed off in deep sobbing.

"Where is your brother?"

"He was visiting us this weekend, but he left early Sunday afternoon to go back to Denver."

Mein Gott. Pete's mind raced. The cop friend and the fellow Gordon did the hunting trips with. Hayle was already on his radar— he must be the second kidnapper!

"Does he know about Vassily's accident?" asked Pete.

"Yes, he called when he got home about nine thirty Sunday night. I told him then."

"I'll look into this and find the explanation for it. And it would be better not to mention any of this to your husband or brother. You don't want to upset your relationship and find out later there was a different meaning entirely. Do you agree?"

"Yes. I'd rather not have this between us." Yvonne managed a weak smile. "I knew you would know how to handle it."

"Thank you for your trust. Right now, I think it would be good if you had someone with you at the hospital. The people you work with—we look out for each other." Pete looked at Ruiz. They'd worked with each other for more than a decade. He felt confident she'd know exactly what he expected of her. "Sergeant?"

"I'm happy to come and sit with you," said Ruiz.

"Oh, thank you, I've been feeling so alone. No one I could talk to." Yvonne stood. "I'd like to go now."

Sergeant Ruiz put a hand on Yvonne's arm. "You need to be there for your husband. We'll be glad to stay with you. Police are family. You don't need to worry about being alone at night."

Ruiz gave Pete a thumbs-up sign as they left.

He looked down at the papers in his hand. *Heilige Scheisse!* For years he'd wondered what happened to the car the kidnapper had used to take Johnny. Here was the answer. Right under his nose all this time.

Had Vassily's fall been helped by someone, maybe Hayle, out to do him harm? The longer the site of his fall sat unguarded, the more any evidence it contained would be compromised. It was crucial that someone visit the site. He couldn't get away, but he knew just the person.

He found Cheveyo Loloma on his way back from a court appearance. This detective of Hopi ancestry was expert in processing crime scenes. If anybody could read the signs and figure what happened, it would be Cheveyo. He'd have him talk with the medics who responded to Yvonne's 911 call and check it out.

CHAPTER FIFTY-TWO

When Pete stopped by the hospital, he found Yvonne and Ruiz in the waiting room outside intensive care.

Yvonne looked up, smiling tiredly.

"He's still not awake," she said. "I know broken hips are scary and sometimes people die, but Vassily isn't even sixty yet, and he's healthy."

"Have they told you anything?" Pete asked.

"The doctor's supposed to talk to me, soon. Oh—this might be him now." She rose to face the man in scrubs in the doorway.

Pete and Ruiz started to leave.

"Oh, please," said Yvonne. "Stay with me. Doctor, this is my boss, Lieutenant Schultz, and my friend, Detective Ruiz."

The doctor nodded to them, then faced Yvonne. "Your husband is strong, Mrs. Novak. It's a good sign he made it through the surgery last night."

Pete listened as the doctor told her how critical the next few days would be. He watched Yvonne's face as she tried to absorb what the doctor was saying.

"You may sit with your husband now, Mrs. Novak, but he will not know you are there."

"How long does it take before his hip will heal, and he can walk? He's not going to like being laid up."

"I'm more worried about his head."

"Oh, I didn't . . . He hit it when he fell."

The doctor hesitated. "It could have been that, or it could have been a seizure that made him fall, or someone may have attacked him."

"Oh, that wouldn't be it. He still had his wallet and his money."

While Pete waited, Yvonne implored Ruiz to come with her to see Vassily, and they left.

◆ ❖ ◆

Pete stopped the doctor before he could leave and handed him his card. "Doctor, may I ask a few questions?"

"Are you asking as a policeman?"

"I am. In your professional opinion, what could have caused his head wound?"

Concerned brown eyes met his. "You suspect there may have been foul play?"

"It's a possibility. I don't think this has occurred to Mrs. Novak yet, and she doesn't have to be told. But I believe it is important to keep him under watch. Someone may intend further harm to him or to his wife."

"That changes things. I can help by restricting visitors. Can I assume that Detective Ruiz is also here in a professional capacity?"

"You may. We'll try to have someone from our department with Mrs. Novak at all times."

The doctor nodded thoughtfully. "His head wound. Like I said, it could have been from the fall, especially if he fell on something that rose from the surface. Or it could have been caused by an attack of some sort. Not something big and blunt like a bat, but something small and deadly. Possibly a hammer, or a rock, even the end of a walking stick."

"Could it have been caused by an object thrown or projected at him somehow?"

The doctor's keen eyes met Pete's. He seemed to choose his words carefully. "I must admit being puzzled by the severity of the wound on his right temple. It didn't seem logical that falling would have resulted in such a forceful impact. That is a vulnerable spot on the skull, but even so, whatever it was caused a depressed fracture, resulting in the subdural hematoma. Lying there for more than an hour didn't help. Even more odd, the wound isn't on the side he'd fallen on. I can't say with any certainty what happened, but it seems compatible with a small object hitting him with force. Don't jump to conclusions, though. His fall could have been caused by a seizure of some sort, or just that he stepped wrong on an uneven surface."

"Thank you. I appreciate your candor."

As the doctor walked down the corridor, Pete remembered his own doctor's appointment to take the stitches out of his calf.

Pete hoped that he could get back to Beowulf's training soon, and was gratified at his doctor's assessment of his leg's healing.

When he was through, he stopped back at the ICU waiting room to see a subdued Yvonne talking with Ruiz and another police-woman he recognized as being from the traffic division.

Yvonne looked up. "The department is being so kind. Ruiz has offered to stay the night with me."

"Right now, Officer Rosales will stay with you while I pack an overnight bag and pick up my car."

"I can give you a lift," said Pete.

As he left with Ruiz, he told her what the doctor had said. Then he frowned. "Elena, I wish I could, but I can't authorize this kind of overnight overtime."

"Pete, I know you're thinking about budgets and costs. Forget it," said Ruiz. "We both know it's important to monitor the situation. Yvonne works with us. It makes sense for friends to step in and support her."

"I wasn't aware that you were close."

"Stuff it. I'm not asking for overtime. I'm telling you that I'm doing this on my own. Don't argue. This way I can spend the night sleeping in a bed rather than being on duty in a car out in the cold. As a friend, I can learn much more."

"If you witness anything, will we run into trouble with some defense lawyer?"

"If I do see anything, it will be handled properly."

"What do I tell Grover?"

"That you have an extraordinarily efficient and compassionate staff." She flashed a smile at him.

"Elena, thank you."

Then he headed home to pick up Akiko and head to the Bjornsons' ranch.

After Ruiz ate a light meal with Yvonne at the hospital cafeteria, she followed Yvonne home. She looked around the neatly kept home, curious about this woman who didn't fit in well. The living room was arranged with two recliners—each with its own end table—a big-screen TV, and a couch with a coffee table in front. It was obvious which recliner Yvonne used. A knitting bag was leaning against the side of the chair. A stack of mystery novels, a notebook and pen, and a candy tin sat on the table.

The other end table was uncluttered, except for a square coaster lined up evenly with the edges and a slingshot. Ruiz picked it up. "What's this?"

"Vassily saw my brother hitting soda cans with a slingshot. So, he went to some sporting goods store and got one. Said he was going to surprise him by showing him what he could do. I think it's kind of stupid myself. Whoever heard of a grown man with a slingshot?"

Ruiz agreed with Pete's suspicions that foul play might be involved, especially in light of the blackmail scheme. Could this have been what the attacker used?

"Let me show you our guest room. I really appreciate your being here. I'm not used to being by myself at night, and I'm so worried about Vassily."

"It's not a problem, Yvonne. I'm glad to help. Excuse me, just a moment. I have to make a call to my friend. We were supposed to have dinner tonight."

Elena stepped outside and called Pete about the slingshot.

Chapter Fifty-Three

Hoot carried the puzzle box as he, Marilyn, Karen, Pete, Sam, and Skyla followed Anton into his office.

"We made three keys to try," said Anton, setting them on his desk.

"It's amazing what this man can do with a computer," said Hoot, playfully saluting Anton. "That CAD program totally lost me."

Pete, seated next to Hoot, pointed at the box. "May I?"

Hoot handed him the box and watched as he ran his hands lightly over the carving and the smoothness of the wood.

"I haven't seen it in person before," said Sam. "I hope we can open it without damaging it."

"Very impressive workmanship," said Pete. "I'm torn. I love it, but if it holds clues to who's out to harm you, Hoot, well . . ."

"The keys are all a little different in the detail on the notches," said Anton. "The first one we made is gray, the second salmon. The black one is third."

Hoot took the box and manipulated it to open the first level. It was a little awkward with the lid not being able to come all the way off, so he adjusted the box on his lap to support it. He inserted the gray key into the holes on the next level and twisted it slightly, first one way, then the other. Nothing.

Anton handed him the salmon key. This time he felt give when he twisted it, but nothing opened.

The circle of people inched closer as Hoot picked up the last key. The room was quiet enough to hear their breathing. Marilyn folded her hands and brought them to her lips. Anton held up his crossed fingers.

Hoot inserted the black key and twisted it to the right. Nothing. He twisted it to the left and was rewarded by a few clicks. Suddenly he felt the cover move on his lap. Holding on to the key and the carved wooden hand, Hoot lifted the unit of lid and first compartment floor away and handed it to Anton. The box rested on Hoot's lap with a new layer showing.

Anton held the cover unit and turned the key back and forth. As he did, little pegs came out of the thick floor and retreated again. "Clever," he said, turning the key again.

"Come on!" complained Karen. "You can figure out the intricacies of the design later. What's in it?"

All craned forward to look into the box. Lying within was a bag made of what appeared to be chamois leather. Hoot lifted it out and opened the drawstrings. Pete picked up a magazine and held it under to catch the contents. A glittering heap of red and white spilled out onto the flat surface.

"Ye gods and little fishes!" said Skyla.

Pete flicked a glance at Sam. "Hoot, don't touch it. Use pencils to hold it up."

Sam handed Hoot a couple of pencils, and he elevated the necklace for all to see.

"Talk about bling!" said Karen. "Diamonds. Lots of them. And if those rubies are real, they have to be worth a fortune."

Marilyn put her hand on her cheek. "Look at the size of those stones."

"Marilyn, have you ever seen this before?" asked Pete.

Marilyn shook her head, eyes wide with wonder. "Never in all my born days."

"Why didn't you want me to touch it?" asked Hoot.

"Just precaution. Fingerprints," said Pete. "If Marilyn has never seen it, it may have been stolen. Those red stones might have prints.

They're big enough. A piece like this has to have a history." Then he frowned.

"Everybody. I'm deadly serious about this." Pete met the eyes of each in turn. "It appears someone, maybe that second kidnapper, is very interested in the contents of this box. The car bombing may have been meant to harm Hoot. I'm asking you all not to say a word. We don't yet know if there are other secrets in this box."

"Is there another compartment?" asked Karen.

"Must be," said Hoot. "It's deep enough."

"Sam and I will check out the necklace tomorrow," said Pete. "As soon as possible we need to delve into that bottom layer."

The panel which now made the floor of the box had a beautiful marquetry pattern. Hoot passed it around the circle, with each trying to puzzle their way to the next, and hopefully, final layer.

"Everybody will be here soon," said Karen. "I don't think there's time to figure it out now."

"Wait! There's a little hole in the floor," said Hoot. While they examined it, Anton picked up the section that had been lifted out. On the bottom of it was a little peg about an inch long.

"I think this peg fits there." Anton tried to put the box back together, then frowned. "Now there's something in the way. The peg won't go in."

Hoot fiddled with it for a while. "What say we leave it in two parts until we have time to figure out the next level. How soon can we get back to it?"

"Tilt it again like you just did, Hoot," said Sam. "I didn't hear that noise before."

Hoot moved the box and heard something moving back and forth.

"Tomorrow should be our deadline," said Pete. "It's important to get to the bottom of this—literally."

"Tomorrow's fine for you all to come back again," said Karen. "Let's put a piece of painter's tape over the black key to keep it in place."

Pete picked up the necklace with the pencils. "Anton, do you have a manila envelope?" He busied himself, starting the chain of evidence on the envelope, noting all who were present and the date, before sealing the chamois bag with the necklace in the envelope and tucking it into an inside pocket in his sports jacket.

Anton and Hoot carried the two box parts out to the workshop to lock them away. Then they all gathered in the family room for a buffet. Melody, Diego, and the kids had come home. Dom came with Leyla, Farah, and Krista. The noise level grew as the dogs came in to greet them.

Pete patted the bulge in his jacket. He'd be glad to stop by the police department on his way home and get the envelope into the evidence locker. Though he'd hate to destroy the box, he was adamant that one way or the other, tomorrow they'd uncover the secrets of the puzzle box.

CHAPTER FIFTY-FOUR

Jed entered his Santa Fe motel room and shut the door firmly. Another early morning trip to Pecos with nothing to show. The state police still had the Stewarts' home under surveillance. What the hell was going on?

His phone rang. He kicked back on the bed, checked the number and braced himself to be yelled at.

"Do you have my box yet?" Wysocki's angry voice blasted his ear.

"No, sir, not yet."

"What the devil is taking so long? It's January 24 already. Is this task too much for you?"

"No, I can do it. Tried the realtor thing, no sign of that box you wanted. The wife doesn't have a job. She's home all day."

"Can't be home all the time—has to do shopping and errands. Find a time when she's not there and break in."

"Already did. I turned the place upside down. No box. Every two hours police come by. Why? What haven't you told me?"

"I don't know anything about that. Don't give me excuses. Just get the damn thing. You produce results, or else. Put pressure on them. Get a bargaining chip. Squeeze them until they hurt."

A cold chill went down Jed's spine. "What exactly are you suggesting, sir?"

"Snatch one of them. Shake them down. Give them a taste of what will happen if they don't turn over my box." Wysocki hung up.

Jed's heart sank. He wished he'd had the forethought to record this conversation.

He found it unbelievable that Wysocki didn't know about the place being under surveillance. Jed had no intention of being caught with his pants down in a trap. Angry and disgusted, he grabbed another pillow and stuffed it behind his back.

What could be so important that you didn't care who got hurt? The more he thought, the worse he felt.

Secrets. He wished he knew more of Wysocki's. Should he turn the tables on him? Use the tactics his employer had taught him? No one forged their way to the top, as this mogul had, without a trail of figurative bodies. Bodies that would still be there, even with his boss's devilish talent for hiding them.

This box had been missing for twenty-five years. Wysocki had been in his early twenties, married, with a baby. What was he hiding?

How would Jed find out?

He fired up his laptop. One of the corollaries of being well-known and wealthy was the information abounding on the internet. Wysocki had been born and raised in Pueblo. Jed decided to head back up the interstate and start digging.

On Tuesday morning while Pete checked out leads and wrote reports, he had forensics check the necklace for fingerprints.

Then he and Sam began in earnest to unearth the history of the ruby and diamond necklace.

"Isn't there a list of stolen pieces we could check this necklace against?" asked Sam.

"There is, but it won't go back far enough. Likely an insurance company paid off any claim long ago. Let's start with a jewelry-appraiser friend of mine. He'll be able to estimate the value and give us some guidance."

Soon they were being buzzed into a small office in an old part of town where a little wizened man met them. The eyes of the appraiser widened when the necklace tumbled out of the envelope onto his black velvet tray. "Jumpin' jailbirds, Lieutenant. Where did you come up with this piece?" He proceeded to examine it closely.

"It's magnificent," he said as he handed it back to them. "I don't know if I've ever seen anything of this quality. I'd say it's probably worth close to two million."

Sam whistled.

"How would you recommend we go about finding where it came from?" Pete asked.

"I'll take photos and write up a technical description for you. Check with the major insurance companies and maybe Lloyds of London. I'd say they'll run it through a jeweler's clearinghouse group for lost or stolen items. Keep the real thing in your safe. A distinctive piece like this has to have been appraised, insured, and likely reported stolen. If that's the case, you're going to make some insurance company very happy."

CHAPTER FIFTY-FIVE

Late Tuesday afternoon, Pete and Akiko arrived at the Bjornsons' home. Sam, Farah, and Leyla came soon after. Pete felt the anticipation grow. Tonight they would wrest the remaining secrets out of the puzzle box.

"We have some exciting news," said Hoot. "Skyla and Anton made us a deal on her old home, too good to pass up. We'll be moving there soon."

After an early dinner, Skyla, Farah, and Akiko began baking cookies with the kids. Sam, Anton, Dom and Karen, Marilyn, Hoot and Melody slipped away to Anton's office where the box waited.

Hoot picked up the part of the box that still held secrets. He passed it around for each to have a try.

Marilyn took it first. "I don't see any hinges. Are you certain there's another layer?"

"We're only about two-thirds down in the height of the box," said Anton. "There's the noise of something rolling. Definitely another layer."

When Pete got it, he pressed on the marquetry panel, massaging it, feeling the give from side to side.

Sam took it next. "There's also some flex on the very bottom of the box where the little legs are."

"Can you move that marquetry floor at the same time you move the very bottom?" asked Dom.

"That's really awkward to do," replied Sam. "It's too deep. Can't get your hand on both the inside floor and the bottom at the same time."

"I hear something rolling as you tip it side to side," said Dom.

"Why couldn't we hear that in the beginning?" asked Karen.

"See that little peg on the bottom of the layer we lifted out?" said Anton. "That went down into this hole." He pointed to it. "It kept the ball from rolling."

"Sounds to me like there's more than one ball." Dom held the box near his ear, slowly tipping it back and forth.

Eyes followed the box as it passed from person to person. Pete wondered who would be the one to figure it out.

Hoot picked it up, held it bottom side to his chest and tilted it back and forth. They heard a new sound. "Something happened. Was that a ball dropping?"

The balls clicked as they rolled. Finally, they heard another drop. Hoot manipulated the panels again, balancing the sides of the box on his lap.

"Since that second ball dropped, the bottom has more play," said Anton.

"This is super annoying," said Karen.

"I don't want to break it," said Anton. "Maybe if I—"

Suddenly, the marquetry level popped up. He lifted it out carefully.

Pete peered down. A tray of dark wood divided the compartment into three sections. One section, only wide enough to fit the balls, was empty. In the middle section, two wooden balls now moved freely. The biggest and last section held what looked like rolled-up papers.

"Don't touch any contents without gloves in this layer." Pete took several pairs of latex gloves from his pocket. "It may be important. We don't know yet."

259

"There's a hole in the cross piece between the skinny section and the middle section," said Hoot. "That's what allowed the balls to roll into the middle section of the tray."

"Now you can move the dark tray a little farther back and forth. It's connected to the bottom. When we were feeling the play on the bottom of the box, this tray was moving, too."

Pete put on gloves and pointed to two shiny metal spots in the divisions of the tray next to the skinny section. "What are these?"

"I bet they're magnets," said Anton. With gloves on, he picked up a polarized magnet lying on his desk. "I thought this might come in handy." He held it over one spot and then the other on the dark wood. "Oh, yeah. I can feel the attraction from one circle. The other repels it. Look. If I hold the magnet very loosely over the repelling one, it pushes it right out of my fingers. Very clever."

"Does the marquetry panel have any?" asked Dom.

"I think it has to," said Anton, picking it up. "Just one on each side. I think I know how this works. When the balls are in their initial skinny compartment, they keep the lid aligned with the attracting force magnets. When the balls go into the middle compartment, there is more play in the bottom. Then when you wiggle it, it comes into alignment with the repelling magnet, and the lid literally pops up."

"Come on, you guys, stop with the mechanics. I want to know what's in it." Karen pointed at the papers.

Pete cautiously picked up the papers. As he did, they uncurled some, and a tissue-wrapped item fell out. He left it where it lay on the table and carefully unrolled the brittle papers partway. The inside document had a fancy border and proclaimed in Old English script to be a Nevada marriage certificate, issued in 1984 for a Tonya Abrerro and a DeWitt Wysocki.

"Wysocki!" Pete's eyes met Sam's. *The hunter, Gordon's client.*

The rest of the papers were letters. Pete carefully unrolled the envelopes enough to read addresses. There were several to Tonya: one each from Wit Wysocki, Jane Phillips, and Bob Norton. Another was addressed to Wit from Tonya.

Pete looked at Marilyn. "Do these names mean anything to you?"

"Not a one," she said.

"I know the name Wit Wysocki," said Karen. "It's an unusual name, but there could be more than one. The one I know is a realtor in Denver. He also has a firm which supports political candidates. But it must be someone else, come to think of it. I'm sure his wife's name is Monica. I don't know them well —just enough to say hello, but we've been at some of the same nonprofit functions."

Pete set the papers down and they curled again on their own. "I'd open them and read them, but they appear to be quite brittle. I'll have forensics copy them, so we can read them safely." He unwrapped the tissue carefully and discovered a heart-shaped locket. He opened it to find a photo of a smiling couple. He held it out for Marilyn to see.

She shook her head. "I've no idea."

"Karen?" asked Pete as he held it for her.

"I can't tell if that's the Wysocki I know. This couple is very young."

Wysocki, thought Pete. We'll have to compare this photo to the hunting trip photos. He closed the locket again, and tilted the tissue to study the chain. Rusty stains marked the ends where it had been broken. The tissue had little stains of the same color. Pete shot a glance at Sam who nodded almost imperceptibly.

"Marilyn, do you mind if I take these items and find some answers?" asked Pete.

"Please do. They've no meaning to me."

Pete felt eagerness rising within, and the gleam in Sam's eyes told him of the excitement he must be feeling. Solid evidence from which to extract information! Was that blood on the chain, and whose was it? Were these connected to the Wysocki from Denver? Who were these letter writers, and what did they write? How did the box end up with Gordon? Pay dirt at last.

Anton handed an envelope to Pete, who wrote on it, signed it, and printed his name. One by one, eight names and signatures were written on the envelope. Then Pete placed everything inside and sealed the envelope.

"It's so quiet," said Sam. "More than once I was ready to take Diego up on his offer of a crowbar."

"I sure hope you'll be able to tell us the rest of the story, Pete," said Dom. "The mystery has only deepened."

"I'm looking forward to solving this one, too," said Pete.

With Anton's help, Hoot put the puzzle box back together. Sam documented the process with photos on his cell phone, step by step.

"It's really well-made," said Hoot. "First there is the wheel-box puzzle that gets you into the first layer. There you find the key that lets you into the section where the necklace was. And last is the mechanism with the balls that must be maneuvered to get you to the bottom layer. Wow."

Karen touched the little pin on the end of the box. "Did anyone ever find out what this little pin does?"

Dom smiled. "I told you, but you didn't believe me. Its function was to mystify you."

"Diego was right. That is mean," said Karen. "Anyhow, I think it's time we joined the others. I smell cookies baking."

"Coffee?"

"Yes, Pete." She laughed. "For you, always. It's your life blood."

CHAPTER FIFTY-SIX

Pete rubbed his hands in anticipation as he sat down at his desk the next morning. Now that everything was moving at breakneck speed, a little prioritizing was in order.

First, he started the forensic team on the puzzle box contents, lifting fingerprints from the papers and making copies of the documents so he could read them. Processing the suspected blood stains on the locket chain and tissue was crucial. He'd heard nothing back yet about the fabulous necklace, but that wasn't surprising—it had only been yesterday.

Then he let the chief know about the contents of the box. Grover was able to tell him that Wit was the nickname used by DeWitt Wysocki, the prominent Denver citizen. Grover quickly confirmed that Wysocki had married Monica in June of 1988.

Pete conferred with Agent Sloughman of the ATF. Nothing yet of any startling import. Evidence had been documented and collected from more than two square blocks. That was now in the hands of the ATF team.

He called Ruiz. With the help of some female patrol officers, they had worked out a schedule so someone would always be with Yvonne. Vassily was strictly monitored by hospital security. Ruiz wasn't a doctor, but she found Vassily's hold on life to be much more tenuous than the optimistic Yvonne was willing to admit.

And now Hayle was connected to the kidnapping, very likely to the threats against Hoot and his family, and possibly to an attack on Vassily. He was also a person of interest in connection with the bombing.

Pete left a message for Cheveyo to report on what he found at Vassily's accident scene as soon as he could.

Having cleared the way for what he considered top priority, he turned his attention to Hayle. Neither the postal inspector nor the FBI had anything new on the two mailed threats. Hiram hadn't anything new on the break-in either.

Pete printed Hayle's name in the middle of a blank page, and drew a small circle around it. Then he made other circles surrounding the first, labeling them, Second Kidnapper, Bombing, Phone Threats, Mail Threats one and two, Attack on Me, Denver Stonewalling, Shadow Man, Necklace, Attack on Vassily, and Ransacking Hoot's Home.

He drew a line connecting the Second Kidnapper circle to Hayle. Then he began making notes near each labeled circle with what he knew about Hayle's possible motive, means, and opportunity.

Pulling another sheet of paper toward him, Pete wrote Wysocki's name in dark caps and scribbled some notes. Could he have been involved? How? Or was he only a victim with his own problems?

But there had to be two people involved. One couldn't be in two places at once.

He was itching to get his hands on the copies of the papers in the box. He didn't have all the answers.

On a third sheet of paper, he jotted down the dates indicating when Hayle had been in Santa Fe according to Vassily's kidnapping notes.

Pete took off his glasses and rubbed his hands through his hair. Then with a tissue, he polished his glasses while thinking about the circles.

The phone call at Anton's wedding. Hayle could have done that with a burner phone.

Denver Stonewalling. Possibility. Pete had met Hayle there. The motive wasn't clear. Even if Hayle wanted to impede the investigation, why would Isaacson be involved? Strange.

The first threat by mail, postmarked Santa Fe, January 2. Easily. Pete connected that circle to Hayle's circle.

Now this was interesting. The world at large didn't know about Hoot's being Johnny until after the TV program aired on December 30, though local news had been abuzz since December 18. The threatening calls had started earlier. How did they know what was unfolding? Did Denver have anything to do with it? What were the connections? Isaacson? Hayle? Cannon?

The second threat by mail, postmarked in Santa Fe on Saturday, January 14. Check. Well, maybe. How the hell would Hayle have gotten a copy of that photo? Connection with only a dotted line.

Shadow Man had looked into Bonnie's window very early on the morning of Wednesday, January 11. That date wasn't in Vassily's notes. But that might only mean Vassily hadn't known he was in the area.

Was that Hayle looking for the box? Did he know what it contained? Pete needed to hear back from the insurance companies about that necklace.

The next was a longshot. The attack upon himself. Didn't see a motive. Hayle's schedule didn't jibe. No line.

Bombing. Opportunity? Bingo. Hayle was in town. He'd talk with the ATF folks about that. Motive and means were sketchy. He'd never heard that Hayle had any affinity for explosives. That one got a question mark. He'd ask Yvonne about Hayle's activities that weekend.

Ransacking Hoot's home. Still in the area. Now that was cool— they had DNA from that person. If Hayle had been after that necklace, that'd be a good motive. How could he get Hayle's DNA to make a match? Connection.

Attack on Vassily? Yvonne said he was on his way back to Denver when that happened. Question.

Where did that leave him? The evidence against Hayle as the second kidnapper seemed pretty circumstantial. No credible eyewitness. Hoot did remember what he assumed was a birthmark, and Hayle had had such a mark. But port wine stains were not that rare, and, while it indicated possibilities, it proved nothing. On the other hand, Vassily's notes, which looked to be basis for blackmail, gave credulity to Hayle's being the kidnapper.

Forensics called. His copies of the letters and papers from the box were ready. On his way back to his office, he asked Sam to join him. Sam closed the door and sat down at the round table with his laptop.

"Pete, remember you asked me to go through the photos from the boxes looking for any showing a birthmark?"

Pete nodded. "You didn't find any."

"I went back and looked at the ones we know are Hayle. He never turned that side to the camera, even in his academy photo."

"Let's see what we have," said Pete, spreading out the copies. "First the marriage license. May 16, 1984. Sam, I need you to start two documents. The facts we learn and a to-do list. For the list, get a copy of the license for Wysocki's marriage to Monica in 1988. He went to high school in Pueblo. See what you can find out about Tonya Abrerro. Is she still alive? See if there any records of an annulment or divorce. See if you can get verified photos of Abrerro and Wysocki from the late eighties, early nineties, and have forensics compare them with the locket photo. We'll give forensics the shots of the hunter with the oryx kill from Gordon's records, too."

Then Pete organized the copies of the four letters and their envelopes by postmark, which were all in 1991.

Jane Phillips – Chit-chat about lunch and shopping. Bragging about boyfriend.

Bob Norton – Nothing except he was on business in Oklahoma. He was very, very bored, and he missed her very, very much and would see her when he got back. Love and kisses.

Tonya to Wit – Pete read this one to Sam. "I was in Denver the other day and drove by where you and your little ladybird live. She's filthy rich. You have a damn mansion. You expect me to be happy with a crummy apartment? Unless you come up with a whole lot more, I'm going to tell the world you're a bigamist, that your precious baby girl is a bastard. If I divorced you, I'd probably get half of what you have. Since I'm so nice, ten thousand should last me for a while."

"That's an explosive threat," said Sam. "Wysocki wouldn't want that known."

"Wysocki has strong reason to go after that box." Pete said before reading on. "Otherwise I'll sell my story to the newspaper. I'll show them our marriage license and my locket with our wedding picture. They'll give me a whole lot of money."

Pete picked up the next letter. "This is from Wit to Tonya. He says for years, you have liked the arrangement we've had. You've done really well out of it, getting hundreds every month without lifting a finger. You know I can't afford to bring this all out in the open. If I am involved in any scandal, I don't get any of my wife's money. If you threaten me, you'll get the same back."

"Lovely people," commented Sam.

Pete continued to read. "I can come up with the ten thousand, but only in exchange for our letters, our marriage certificate, and that locket, too. I'll meet you at our spot at the reservoir at four o'clock on Wednesday, March 15. Don't be late. It's damn cold there in March."

They got to work researching Wysocki and Abrerro and then compared notes.

"Tonya Abrerro died on March 15, 1991, an apparent suicide," said Sam. "Supposedly jumped off a cliff at the reservoir in Pueblo and drowned. Take a look at the autopsy report." He tapped a box on the form documenting a wound found on Tonya's neck. "I'm thinking that could be consistent with a chain being violently removed."

"What else?" asked Pete.

"Blood alcohol content of point-zero-nine percent." Sam picked up another paper. "This is from the police report. Her purse was found at the top of the cliff. Contained a half-empty bottle of whiskey. Wallet had picture of Bob Norton. Scrawled across it, the words, 'Sorry, I can't take it anymore.' It was thought to be her writing. It was consistent with how she signed her name with a little heart. Her car was parked near the base of the path up the cliff."

"We don't know if there was any DNA material kept of Tonya's," said Pete. "But forensics has already indicated that it was blood on the locket chain in the puzzle box. The prosecutor may want to reopen that case. And it doesn't stop there. Bigamy, certainly, when juxtaposed to the letters. It all points to a possible murder charge. Strong motivation to keep the box contents secret."

"A lot of this evidence is circumstantial," said Sam. "A good defense lawyer would have a heyday with both what we have on Wysocki and what we have on Hayle."

Pete nodded. "We need to keep both Hayle and Wysocki's involvement in this to ourselves until we have run everything by the chief. I'll go talk to him and get his advice on how to proceed. Denver and Pueblo are going to have to be involved eventually. We're sitting on a powder keg. You can't tell who might unwittingly let something juicy slip, and we don't want any nosy reporters snooping around getting in the way."

"If it's okay with you, I'd like to start making notes for our interview with Hayle. Shouldn't we be doing that soon?"

"Indeed. Good call, Sam."

CHAPTER FIFTY-SEVEN

On Thursday, Pete's cell phone rang at seven in the morning.

"It's Elena. Sorry to bother you at home. Yvonne wanted me to call. Late last night the doctor called and said we should come without delay. Vassily died about three thirty. Never regained consciousness. Just slipped away. Yvonne's sleeping now."

"Tell her she's in our thoughts and prayers, Elena. I'm so sorry."

"I told her I'd stay with her through the funeral. I hope that's okay. Such a lonely person. Her life centered on her husband, her work, and her brother. She's a lost soul, Pete."

"I'm glad you're staying, for her sake and also for her protection. Vassily's death may be ruled a homicide yet. I don't feel right about Hayle being alone with her."

"She still hasn't allowed herself to think about that blackmail folder. She's very uneasy when Hayle calls, and she's dreading being alone with him. She was fussing about his staying here. I gave her the excuse that while I was here in the guestroom, he'd have to go to a hotel. He should be here by Friday afternoon."

The next morning, Friday, Pete rested his elbows on his desk and tented his fingers, bringing them to his lips. His brows drew together as he looked at his notes on his computer. The coroner had not been willing to rule Vassily's death accidental. He could now officially launch a homicide investigation.

Sam came in, and Pete joined him at the round table.

"Regarding Hayle," Pete said. "Vassily's murder is priority. And if Hayle killed one person to avoid paying for the kidnapping of Johnny, might he have put the bomb under Hoot's car? Made the threatening phone calls and sent the letter? Ransacked his home?"

"Do you think he might be the one taking pot shots at you?" asked Sam.

Pete snorted. "Going after the detective in charge of a case is a bit of a stretch." He got up to pop a cup into his coffee maker. "We need to plan our case."

"Should we bring in Yvonne for questioning today?"

Pete shook his head. "Hayle is supposed to arrive in Santa Fe this afternoon. I'd like to pull Yvonne and Hayle in at the same time on Saturday morning. That would lessen any opportunity they have to talk together, though Ruiz is doing a good job of monitoring." He picked up his coffee and sat. "Plenty of time to get our warrants in order. Ruiz has gotten a ton of information from Yvonne, just by being kind. They talked about Hayle's visits. Ruiz even asked her if she ever talked about the kidnapping case with Hayle. Normally Yvonne was open, but that made her evasive."

"Which probably means they did talk about it," said Sam.

"I'd say so."

"Hayle must believe he's gotten away with it," said Sam. "Has it even occurred to Yvonne that Vassily was murdered?"

"I don't think so," said Pete. "She believes Hayle was halfway to Denver when Vassily fell. One goal of our interview should be to separate Hayle from his cell phone and check it out. We should also keep any beverage container Hayle discards for his DNA."

"Remember our conversation with the cop from Phoenix at our seminar? How do you think Hayle would respond to the inflating ego approach?"

Pete grinned. "He's cocky enough. I'm also hoping that if he feels confident, he won't think he needs a lawyer."

"Won't he know that we can find where he made the calls from?"

"Perhaps, but he wants to be seen as cooperative. I imagine he's proud of his plan to convince his sister he was far away. Remember, Hayle left the police force before much was known about cell phone technology and digital forensics."

"If what we believe is true, and he has a burner phone," said Sam, "would he have used that to make the calls?"

"No, he has to be able to point to those calls on his own phone to prove his alibi. Ruiz said Yvonne recognized the number when he called. This afternoon, I want to visit the site where Vassily was found."

"Certainly you don't think Cheveyo missed something?"

"No. He's the best," said Pete. "I want to experience that site personally. When we interview Hayle, if I can put him in that setting, make him remember how it looked, smelled, sounded, and felt, he's going to think—this cop knows I was there. He knows what I did, and he'll begin to feel the crumbling of the cliff he's standing on. He'll feel the tension that won't go away until he admits it."

When the rest of the team had assembled, Pete and Sam shared what they'd learned.

Pete looked at Cheveyo. "What were you able to discover at the site?"

"It's too bad we didn't know earlier it might become a crime scene, Lieutenant. Any defense attorney worth his salt is going to question anything we find. It's bad enough it was unsecured for more than twenty-four hours, and at the mercy of the weather. John Q. Public has been all over it."

Ruiz looked up from her notebook. "Yvonne said her husband walked the same route, same time, every day, weather permitting, always going the same direction. What's more, when her brother was in town, he accompanied Vassily. It's an acknowledged fact that he knew the trail. Proving he was on it wouldn't help us."

"Still, I'm convinced it will be useful," said Pete. "When we question him, what we find may prod him into giving up information to us."

"It's a longshot," said Sam.

"Well, then we'd better just hope that he confesses and doesn't lawyer up."

"Pete—"

"I have every faith that the four of us will leave no stone unturned in preparation." Pete met the eyes of each. "Cheveyo, what do you have?"

"The path where he'd fallen was pretty smooth. Nothing to trip on. Nothing sticking up to smack your head on.

"Anything that seemed out of place in this setting?"

"Not really. I found several roundish rocks about an inch in diameter along the path there, but they're not uncommon. I did pick up all that were in that area. Got seven, I believe."

"No steel ball bearings that some folks use for slingshot ammo?" asked Pete.

"No. I thought of that, and made a point of looking."

Pete nodded. "How about a possible hiding place to lie in wait?"

Cheveyo grinned as he handed Pete some photos. "He picked a good spot. Screened by bushes from the trail. An adobe wall shielding him from any neighbor's vision. Something was lying in wait for our attacker, too."

"What was that?" asked Sam.

Cheveyo's grin grew broader. "Goatheads. Some of the nastiest weed seeds on the planet. Even though the plant is dormant, those little sputniks from hell were in abundance. Wouldn't surprise me if they'd be in his shoe soles. I did pick up several and I got some soil samples in case they're needed."

"Mother Nature's medieval caltrops," said Pete. "The scourge of dog paws, bicycle tires, and running shoes. I hope they got him. We can bait our trap with that knowledge and see if he falls for it. Let's wrap this up. Motive? The blackmail scheme makes it highly likely Vassily was attacked by Hayle. Means? We know Hayle uses a slingshot, and that's the likely weapon of choice. Opportunity? That we haven't determined. Yvonne said Hayle was almost halfway back to Denver when Vassily fell. We haven't even tried to verify that."

Pete turned to Ruiz. "Have you picked up any more information about Hayle?"

"He'll be here this afternoon. Yvonne is in a dither, torn about seeing him."

"Stick to her like glue when he comes. We don't want him alone with her."

"How about the search warrant for the burner phone and his cell phone?" asked Sam.

"Already in process. It's for his car and his hotel room in Santa Fe. Elena, as soon as you know where he's staying, let me know."

CHAPTER FIFTY-EIGHT

"How's it been going?" asked Pete the next morning, looking away from his office window where rain dripped steadily as Ruiz hung her wet jacket on the coat tree and put her umbrella in the stand. So much for not working on Saturday. This couldn't wait.

"Hayle is clearly frustrated by my presence. Yesterday afternoon when he arrived, he did the supportive thing with Yvonne while she dealt with the undertaker. After that, whenever he brought up Vassily's name, she just said she didn't want to talk about it."

"And this morning when the officer came?"

"Hayle had arrived in time for breakfast. The officer said that both Yvonne and he should go to the station. Said Vassily's death was a possible homicide and the police needed to clear up what happened. Yvonne was upset. I had her ride with me. She's waiting in the little room where we put family members."

Pete greeted Sam as he came in. "Hayle is already in the gray room. I spoke briefly with him, told him I thought we could clear this up without too much trouble. I may have left him with the impression that we wanted to clear his sister of any involvement, and that we were sorry, but we thought we should talk with her first, since she is under a great deal of stress."

"You *may* have left that impression?" Sam smiled.

"I certainly tried."

♦ ❖ ♦

Pete looked at the distraught woman sitting in the chair in the pale green room. Sam sat opposite her with a notepad.

"Yvonne, we were very sorry to hear about Vassily."

Yvonne smiled a teary smile. "Elena has been wonderful. I don't know how I'd have gotten through this without her."

"I'm sorry we had to drag you and your brother down here today, but we have some questions about Vassily's death."

"The officer said it might be homicide?" She looked bewildered. "Certainly it was his fall that k-killed him."

"Let's get the formalities out of the way. This won't take long."

Pete said it would all be recorded and proceeded to get her name and other information into the record. "Yvonne, we're not holding you for anything. We're just trying to find out what happened. You are free to leave at any time."

"I want to help. If someone harmed my Vassily, they need to be caught and punished."

"Tell me about Saturday and Sunday before Vassily went for his walk. Everything, even if it doesn't seem important to you."

Hesitantly, and then more animatedly, Yvonne related how that weekend had gone until the moment she called 911.

Pete frowned as he listened. Timewise, it didn't seem like Hayle had opportunity to be involved with the bombing or the break in. "What kind of a mood was Vassily in when your brother left?"

"Good. Maybe even better than most days."

"Your brother was a policeman at one time, I believe. Do you enjoy comparing notes about police work?"

"It was long ago that he was a cop. He was only interested in talking with me because Vassily wasn't very supportive of my work. I think I would have made a good detective."

"Hayle encouraged you to talk?"

She nodded. "He was interested in that kidnapping . . . Oh, dear. I try to put it out of my mind, but those papers of Vassily's . . ."

"You can't forget them, can you?"

"Lieutenant, do you think my brother might have helped take that poor little boy?"

"What do you think, Yvonne?"

275

"I'm afraid. It looks very much like he did." Yvonne looked down at her hands in her lap, nervously twisting her wedding ring. "And if he did . . . Oh, Lieutenant, I wondered if he hurt Vassily. But he couldn't have. He was in Raton when Vassily fell. It's so confusing."

Pete opened his portfolio and pulled out a photocopy he'd made before he'd returned the red album to Marilyn. It showed Hoot's kids standing next to a wooden-wheeled oxcart at Rancho de las Golondrinas. There was no good reason for Yvonne to ever have seen it. "Have you ever seen this picture?"

Yvonne smiled. "Oh, yes. It was my favorite— Oh, dear."

Here we go. She knew about it? Did Hayle? How the hell?

"Yvonne, when and where did you see it?"

Yvonne seemed to shrink in her chair.

"Yvonne?"

"I looked through that red album in one of the banker boxes. I was all done with my work." She looked up with wide eyes. "It was on my own time."

"One thing has puzzled me," said Pete. "How did the person responsible for the threats get access to that picture of Hoot's children. Do you have any idea how that happened?"

Yvonne bit her lip and remained mute.

"How did your brother get the picture?"

"It's so precious. It inspired me. I would look at it and think of how I could help solve that mystery. I thought that if I studied the case, maybe I'd discover something no one had thought of. If I could do that, people might look at me differently and see someone who mattered, not just some dime-a-dozen secretary."

Pete spoke in a quiet, measured tone. "How did he get the photo, Yvonne?"

"I copied it. Took it home. I looked at your notes and thought about the case. I kept the notes hidden. But then, Vassily probably knew where my folder was. He must have showed Hayle."

Pete sat up straight. Was nothing sacred? "Yvonne, you copied my notes from confidential files and smuggled them home?"

"I knew I wasn't supposed to, but I was doing it to help!" She sat back in tears.

Pete looked at Sam and put the picture back into his notebook. "When Sergeant Ruiz takes you home today, you will give her every shred of notes that you took. Everything. All of your comments, all papers that have anything to do with the work of the police department. Everything. Do you understand?"

"Y-yes. What's going to happen to me?"

"I don't know, Yvonne. I just don't know. We're done for the moment. I'll get Sergeant Ruiz."

At the door, Pete looked back before following Sam out. Yvonne was slumped in her chair, her arms wrapped around herself. Closed eyes, red nose, and tears running down her face. A more perfect picture of misery he'd never seen, but he wasn't feeling too happy either. He closed the door quietly behind them.

Ruiz came out of the control room.

"Did you see?" asked Pete. Fury began flooding his veins.

She nodded.

"Take someone with you to stay with Yvonne. Get everything and bring it back. Interrupt us, even if we're with Hayle, and we'll see what's there before going further. Sam, if you'll brief Grover for me, I'd appreciate it. I need a few minutes, and then we'll review our plan for Hayle and get started."

In his office, Pete slammed his portfolio down on the round table. Pens flew off the edge and rolled away. He'd never felt more like punching his fist through the wall.

Anger against Yvonne. Betrayed by one of his own. She'd crossed a line, and he couldn't repair that damage.

Anger against himself. He'd failed. One of his own, and he'd been clueless. How could he have let it happen?

He sat, leaned back in the chair, and took a deep breath. He had to calm down. Couldn't face Hayle wanting to punch someone.

More deep breaths. Slowly he tamped down his anger. He did blame himself. Later he'd have to look at how this happened and what would stop it from happening again, but now was the time for Hayle.

Relax. Calm. Focus.

He zipped open his abused portfolio as Sam came in. Best redemption now was to nail Hayle so convincingly a defense lawyer wouldn't have a prayer. Focusing on his training, his experience, and the notes of his team, he found the cool methodical puzzle solver deep within himself. Scanning their notes, he nodded his head, feeling anticipation grow as the last few minutes ticked away before he and Sam would sit down with Hayle.

CHAPTER FIFTY-NINE

In the gray interrogation room, Pete swept his glance over Hayle, leaning back in his chair, one ankle crossed over his knee. Cocky bastard, almost eager.

Sam sat across the table. Pete sat in a rolling chair between Hayle and the door.

Pete began. "Sorry to make you wait so long. This has been a very difficult time for your sister."

"She would never do anything to harm Vassily. The thought is absurd. At least I hope." Hayle's laugh was snarky.

"We'll try to clear this up quickly. First, formalities. A recording is being made of this interview. You are not under arrest and can leave at any time."

Hayle nodded. "Whatever. I want to help my sister."

Pete ran through the questions for the record. "What do most people call you?"

"Hayle. Ever since high school, most have just called me by my last name, even my sister."

"Occupation?"

"I own my own business, Curtail Security and Investigations."

"What does your company do?"

"Security for craft fairs, conventions. Also, we track down cheating spouses and people that have skedaddled, owing money."

"Hayle, what is your understanding about the purpose of this interview?"

"I guess there's been some idea that somebody caused my brother-in-law's fall. What did Yvonne say? I wasn't here when he fell."

"I understand you were visiting with them last Sunday afternoon?"

"Yes, but I was well on my way back to Denver before Vassily took his walk."

"I'm told Vassily was a creature of habit, and that you sometimes walked with him?"

Hayle laughed. "You could set your clock by Vassily. He walked at four on the dot. I kept him company when I was in town."

"Can you tell us if he had any confrontations with people along the way?"

"Vassily didn't usually chat with strangers." Hayle looked down at his nails. "Of course, there was that one guy with the chihuahua. Vassily hated dogs, especially ones that crapped on the trail."

"Did you ever meet this man?" Pete held his pen poised over his notebook.

"I don't know his name. Lived along the trail. Adobe house, blue gate. Lots of cactus. Vassily stepped in his dog shit once and yelled at the man. Dog wouldn't shut up. Yap, yap, yap. The man looked like he was from Mexico, about five foot six, maybe two hundred pounds, mustache, black hoodie and jeans. Cowboy boots."

"Vassily got into an altercation with this man more than once?"

"Yeah."

"Do you remember where his house was?"

"No."

Pete jotted down a note. "On the first half of the walk or the homestretch?"

"Don't remember."

"Think. You're walking with Vassily. Was his house on the right or left as you walked by?"

"Don't remember." Hayle shrugged. "Do you think that Mexican-looking guy mighta thrown something at Vassily?"

Pete kept his expression schooled. *No one had said anything about throwing something at Vassily.*

"Walk me through what happened Sunday."

"It was pretty normal. I left after lunch."

"What was Vassily's mood like?"

"He's usually kind of a sourpuss, but he was in an okay mood."

"How about Yvonne?"

"You're not thinking she had anything to do with it? I mean, they've had their moments, but she loved him."

"Their moments?"

"He controls her. Meals on time, things arranged just the way he wants them."

"Let me ask you something, Hayle. Do you think this was something your sister could have done? This was a well-planned attack. No witnesses. Nothing traceable, like bullets fired. Whoever did this was smart."

"She could never have pulled anything off this brilliant."

Pete sighed. "Just thought I'd ask. It was clever." He turned another page in his notebook. "What time did you leave on Sunday?"

"Musta been between one thirty and two. Yeah, that's right, because I called Yvonne from Raton about four thirty."

"Hayle, it would help your sister if we could verify that call. Did you call her house phone or her cell?"

"House phone."

"Perhaps we could pinpoint the call? Your phone has a history— right? It records when you made calls? That may help clear her and you of any possible involvement."

Hayle smiled as he handed his phone to Pete. "Sure, have a look."

"Thank you, Hayle. I'm not a tech expert. If it's okay with you, we'll just hand it over to someone who can check the history. I appreciate your cooperation. Verifying that will help immensely."

As Sam took the phone and left, Hayle looked after him with a slight frown. "They won't muck it up, will they?"

"Of course not. You'll have it back shortly."

Pete turned another page in his notebook. "Did you ever hear Yvonne talk with Vassily about police cases?"

"Never. He didn't take her work seriously."

"You and she share an interest in investigation. Did you ever talk about cases with her?"

"Absolutely not. She might not be that bright, but she's a professional. She kept her lips zipped."

"Oh, but she said . . . Never mind." Pete looked at his watch. "We're going to take a short break. Can I get you a coffee?"

"Aren't we going to be done soon? It's lunchtime."

"So it is. We'll spring for a hamburger then. Cheese? Fries?"

"Uh, yes."

When Pete and Sam came back in with the burger, Sam handed Hayle's phone back to him. Hayle looked at it suspiciously, checked to make sure it worked, then put it in his pocket.

"Did your tech guy find the calls?"

"Yes, he was able to confirm both of them."

Hayle relaxed, smiled, and took a bite of his cheeseburger. Ketchup oozed out and dripped on his shirt.

"Hayle, where were you on the night of January 10?"

"Hell, I don't remember. What day of the week was it?"

"Tuesday."

"I had an event. It's a week-long winter fair that we do security for every year. I like that one, so I always schedule myself."

"Can someone vouch for you?"

"Hell, yes." Hayle laughed. "Commander Isaacson was moonlighting for that event."

"How about the weekend Vassily fell?"

"You know I was here that weekend and that I got back to Denver Sunday night. I went in to work the next day. You know, that was a hell of a weekend to visit Santa Fe. Couldn't do anything downtown. Some crazy fool set off a bomb. You got a problem in this town, bro. Murders, explosions."

Pete turned a page in his notebook. "What was the relationship between you and Gordon Stewart?"

"Gordon Stewart? The pilot? Are you asking if we were into anything kinky together?" Hayle laughed.

Pete sat, face calm, eyes focused on him. The laugh trailed away.

Hayle dipped a few fries into ketchup and stuffed them into his mouth. "I knew him, not well. We went on hunting trips together, that's all."

"Tell me about the wooden box with the carved hand."

"I don't know nothing about a box."

"You saw it again recently when you were watching the TV show about the kidnapping. The boy mentioned a second kidnapper, one with a rabbit-shaped birthmark on his neck."

Hayle's eyes showed white for a brief millisecond. "I didn't have anything to do with a kidnapping. Yes, I had a birthmark on my neck. Lots of people have them. I had it removed. What's more, I never saw this TV show. If the kid said that, he's making it up. He was only six. How could he remember? Anyhow, didn't see it. I had an event that Friday night."

"Interesting. Is that when it was on?"

Hayle made a face and took another bite of his burger. He wiped mustard smears off his chin. "Yeah, Vassily told me about it and said it was Friday. I'm not into crime shows."

"The wooden box was on the table in the TV show."

"With a hand?" Hayle reddened, quickly bit off a mouthful, and chewed. "The only time I might have seen a box like that was when Gordon stole one."

"You did see it. Tell me about when Gordon stole it."

"We were visiting this guy's house. Gordon took it. He'd do stupid stuff just to see if he could get away with it. Life was a lark. Anyhow, that was a long time ago. He's dead."

"It's a good size box. How did he get it out of there without the owner noticing?"

"I honestly don't remember."

"You know exactly where he hid it."

"How would I know that?"

"We'll talk about that later. Gordon kidnapped that child. What was your part in that adventure?"

Hayle stuffed more fries into his mouth and slurped his drink. "It was all Gordon. I never laid hands on that kid." Hayle leaned forward. "I thought we were here to talk about Vassily. I don't like these past history questions."

"You'll see how it is tied to Vassily. Stick with me, Hayle."

"Whatever." Hayle leaned back again. "Do you think Vassily had something to do with the kidnapping?"

"Do you think he might have? Why did Gordon take the child?"

"He needed money. His parents said they would give him forty grand—if he would give them custody of his kid. They went through lawyers all legal-like. The papers were signed, everything was ready, but his wife's parents snatched the kid."

"Why didn't he go to the police and get him back?"

"No time. This taxidermist in Texas had reset and sold some jewelry of Gordon's. Owed him big time. We went down there to collect, but just before we got there, the cops took that bastard down and put him away. Left Gordon high and dry without either the money or his jewelry. He had to do something—he didn't know where his in-laws were. Maybe he saw this kid in the paper—dead ringer for his son."

"What paper was that?"

More fries disappeared into Hayle's maw. "I said he *could* have seen it. Jeesh. Don't you guys listen?"

"From what I've heard, Gordon was a pretty impatient guy. A kidnapped child would draw a lot of unwanted attention. What did Gordon do when the child wouldn't stop crying?"

"Slapped him. Kid needed slapping. He wouldn't stop screaming."

"So, you did see him take the child?"

Hayle set the rest of his burger down. "Yes. No. Whatever. What if I did? Gordon was my friend, but I had nothing to do with taking that kid."

A knock sounded on the door, and an officer handed Pete a note. Pete stood. "If you'll excuse us for a moment?"

Pete and Sam went into the control room where Ruiz waited with Yvonne's papers. Pete glanced through them quickly, shaking his head, and muttering in German. When he came to the copy of the photo, he swore. Sam glanced away from the monitor which showed Hayle leaning back in his chair, licking his fingers, and not looking too chipper.

Pete turned to Ruiz, Yvonne's photocopies in his hand. "I know you have compassion for Yvonne, but I cannot tolerate this. I will not have her back in the Santa Fe PD."

"She has betrayed a sacred trust," said Ruiz. "She's not a sworn officer, but that's no excuse. I'm with you. I'd charge her."

Pete poured himself coffee from the thermos on the desk. Ruiz had managed to surprise him. He sipped slowly for a few minutes. "What happens might depend on her cooperation in her brother's trial. The two people she cared most about—both betrayed her. And now, by her own action, she's cut herself off from her workplace. Gone. Kaput."

"Let's go read this scumbag his rights," said Sam, "and hope to God his cocky attitude will keep him from lawyering up."

When they entered the room, Sam resumed his spot. Pete set his portfolio and coffee mug on the table, but remained standing, a folder in his hands. He faced the man in the corner chair. "Hayle, I have in this file the results of our investigation into the kidnapping of John McCreath on May 17, 1991. The results show that Gordon Stewart, aided by you, Curtis Hayle, took the child from the playground to the airport, in a black 1988 Ford Escort. From there, Gordon flew you and the child on a de Haviland Beaver plane to Denver. The results indicate that you have not told us the complete truth about your actions on that date. I am placing you under arrest for the kidnapping of the child, John McCreath. You have the right to remain silent." Pete finished the Miranda rights.

Hayle jerked back in his chair, anger on his face. "Gordon took that kid. I had nothing to do with it."

"I'm sure that the heavier weight of guilt lay with Gordon. Let's see if we can find the truth of what happened that day."

Pete sat in his chair. "You and Gordon took wealthy clients on big game hunting trips. He always used the same taxidermist to mount the trophy heads. This fellow had a sideline, resetting the stones from stolen jewelry, selling them and splitting the money with the thief. Gordon stole jewelry and other items from his hunting clients when he delivered the trophy heads. He smuggled them out of the hunter's homes using a built-in cavity in the trophy head. Gordon took away the mount to 'fix' it, brought it back, and hung it perfectly. On one of those trips, a carved wooden box caught Gordon's eye. It just fit into the mount."

"I don't know what the hell Gordon wanted that creepy-looking thing for," said Hayle.

Another knock sounded on the door. An officer looked in and handed Sam a note. Sam read the brief message and passed it to Pete.

Quickly glancing at the message, Pete resumed the story in a soft, confident voice. "On Gordon's last trip to New Mexico, the taxidermist had been arrested. You borrowed Vassily's car and made off with the look-alike child. You had Vassily pick up his car at the airport. The child thought of you as Rabbit Man because of the port wine stain on your neck. He lay in fear on that flight to Denver, told by both of you, repeatedly, that his father and brother would be killed if he told anybody who he was."

Pete watched as Hayle picked up his napkin and blotted at the ketchup stain on his shirt. Then he wadded it up and set it on the table.

"What good is the word of a little kid dozens of years later? It's a fairy story. It never happened."

Pete smiled. "The story doesn't end there. Your sister wanted to be taken seriously as a detective. She brought home notes from the case. She talked about it, and you encouraged her. Why not? It told you what was going on. You became worried when the child began remembering. You decided to ratchet up that old fear, and so you began making threatening phone calls. Then you escalated to sending threats through the mail. One of those had a picture of two children which your sister had copied."

"That's a bunch of—"

"Not at all. You see, we got a search warrant for your car and your hotel room. We found the burner phone you used for the threatening calls. The type you own keeps records of calls, all your digital history."

"I think—"

"You didn't want that old kidnapping to resurface. I am charging you additionally for the murder of Vassily Novak." Again Pete read him his rights and then paused.

Hayle's mouth opened in surprise, and he jerked back in his chair. Hot denial burst from his mouth. "Bull! I couldn't have done anything to Vassily. I was halfway to Denver. Your tech person verified that."

"You did make those calls, Hayle, but your four thirty call was made from Santa Fe and the other one from near Trinidad, Colorado."

"That's a lie."

"Cell phone towers show where the calls were made. We know your brother-in-law had figured out what happened back in 1991 and had started to blackmail you."

"If you just let me say one thing—"

"Hayle, hold on for a minute. You see, the important thing right now is for us to understand the circumstances that led you to attack your brother-in-law."

"I—"

"Vassily was breaking the law by blackmailing you. You couldn't allow that. This man was bleeding you dry. He was destroying your life."

"I would never do anything like that. And I would certainly not hurt my sister."

"You never would have done this if there was another way out. I know you must have tried to make him see reason."

"Vassily was laid off recently. Those bastards let him go just before he reached retirement and got his pension. Sure, I've given him money lately, because he asked me to help out. If you've found any money from me to him, it was just that. A gift."

"Hayle, I hope that's true. It just makes my point that you found yourself frustrated by the situation."

Hayle's posture had slumped. His head was down. Pete rolled his chair closer to Hayle, close enough so their knees were almost touching. He leaned forward, and Hayle looked up.

"It's hard, isn't it? I know how difficult it has been for you to keep a secret of this size inside for so long."

Hayle was listening. He began to blink rapidly. He sniffed loudly twice.

Sam quietly moved the tissue box closer. Hayle grabbed some and blew his nose.

"I'm glad to see those tears, Hayle. You know why? Because they tell me you are sorry this happened. You're sorry you did this, aren't you Hayle?"

Hayle bent his head again in defeat.

Pete's voice droned on. "You knew there was no end in sight. Your relationship with the sister you love would get worse and worse. You saw no other way out of the terrible situation."

Pete's eyes caught Hayle's. "Did you plan this attack or did you decide that afternoon? I think it just happened on the spur of the moment, didn't it? You got to the point where you couldn't take it anymore, didn't you?"

The man in the chair nodded.

Pete allowed a tone of pleasure to enter his voice. "Good, Hayle, that's what I thought all along. I'm going to ask you to tell me the whole story of what happened. It'll be good to have this all straightened out."

Pete glanced over at Sam, who was sitting quietly. Neither of them wanted to spook Hayle.

With short questions, Pete drew out the story.

"After the rock hit Vassily, what happened?"

"He fell, never said a word, just lay there. Then I called Yvonne and started home."

"If he hadn't died, would you have tried again?"

"He had to be stopped. You said it."

"That rock hit Vassily with a tremendous amount of force. You could have made a great pitcher, or did you use something to help?"

"A slingshot."

"There was blood on the rock lying beside Vassily. Was it his or yours?"

"Musta been his." Hayle glanced down at his fingers. "How could it be mine?"

"You had a run-in with goatheads while you were waiting. We saw the area. Full of the nasty little things."

"I knelt on one. Sucker went way in. When I went to pull it out, it got me again."

"So, your knee was bleeding, and your finger was bleeding."

Hayle looked away from Pete and shifted in his chair. He shrugged. "Maybe it was my blood."

"Maybe?"

"Yes, damn it, that damned goathead got me good."

"What did you do with the slingshot?"

"It's in my car. In the glove compartment."

"Hayle, in a few minutes we will have a copy of what's been said here for you to sign."

A defeated Hayle nodded. He didn't look up.

At the Bjornsons' later, Hoot felt his body sag in relief at Pete's words, all the starch gone from his spine. "Thank God. You got him." He took a deep breath, let it out, and grabbed Melody's hand. "We're safe," he whispered.

Melody threw her arms around him. He held her fiercely for a minute, then turned to Pete. "Do Cliff and my parents know?"

"Sam is giving them the news as we speak."

"Can we go home now?" asked Melody.

Hoot grinned at her. "Why not? No more threats."

He looked at Pete. Rather than the agreement he expected, Pete was frowning.

"What aren't you telling us?" asked Hoot.

"Some threats are gone, but questions remain. Who was Bonnie's Shadow Man? Who ransacked your house? And who the hell planted the bomb under your car? I don't believe that was the second kidnapper. We still have more investigating to do. Don't go home while that deadly dirtbag is out there."

PART III – DARK SHADOWS REACHING

CHAPTER SIXTY

Near midnight, Akiko opened her eyes as Pete turned over in bed yet again. He was obviously troubled. Maybe she could help. At this rate neither of them would get any sleep.

She rolled toward him and put her hand on his chest. "What's the matter?"

"Maybe I should get up for a while."

As he started to sit up, she held him back.

He relaxed back with a sigh. "Sometimes it's hard to shut out work. I'm sorry. Should have been a chef. Can't bring that home with you."

"Would it help to talk?"

"This isn't the time or place, Angel."

"I think maybe it is. I know I've tried to keep work talk out of our bedroom, but sometimes it's important."

"I can't."

She laid her head over his heart. "We can talk about ideas without violating any confidentiality."

"I screwed up. Not about the case, but . . . people." He played with a strand of hair on her nape. "It's just . . . Somebody broke the rules, and I completely missed the signs. I could get written up for this."

"That doesn't sound fair."

"It may not be fair, but that's how bureaucracies work. It was on my watch. I'm the leader, and it comes back on me."

"Karen, Dom, and I talked about leadership the other day. Dom said he admired your style. You have a way of seeing within people, of finding their potential gifts, and building a strong team."

"Dom said that? About me? That's an honor coming from him, but my style . . . It failed this time."

"Your style is fine. Maybe the solution for you going forward is making everyone feel like they own the goal and that their contribution is respected."

"You make it sound easy."

"You say you *could* be written up? Be pre-emptive. First thing tomorrow, even if it is Sunday. Send a memo to your team. Strongly worded. Rules *will* be followed. You will not tolerate anything less."

"A little mandatory Monday morning training?"

She laughed, low-pitched and confident. "Think it'll work?"

"Angel, sometimes you can be annoying." Pete's hand caressed her cheek. "But you are also a gift. Practical, perceptive, positive."

Akiko heard him yawn. "Better?"

"Much." He settled back, keeping her hand tucked warmly in his.

A gift? Practical? Perceptive? Positive? A wife could live with that. She smiled into the darkness.

CHAPTER SIXTY-ONE

Pete looked at his watch as he stopped by Sam's cubicle. After four o'clock. "Sloughman from the ATF has called a meeting in the chief's office. They've had a breakthrough in their investigation. Hope it doesn't run too long. It'd be nice to eat with my family for a change."

Soon Pete, Sam, an FBI agent, and the Santa Fe Bomb Squad leader joined Chief Grover, Agent Sloughman, and another ATF agent at the conference table.

Sloughman opened his portfolio and started on his briefing, telling them they'd learned the pickup had been stolen a month earlier in Nebraska. The plate had been stolen from a vehicle in Albuquerque. "We have determined the pickup had two bombs. A smaller one, which had been in the backpack, and a larger one in the tool chest."

Pete nodded, remembering the second explosion.

"Bombers develop a recognizable pattern as they learn what works for them. They build their bombs the same way, using the same components and detonating devices. They develop what we call a signature. We have found the signature in this Santa Fe bombing identical to a so-far unsolved bombing in North Dakota. There the widow of a newly elected sheriff was killed by a bomb placed in her home."

Pete sat up straight. It was like he was seeing Sloughman in sharp focus through a long tunnel. "Cowboy Olson?"

"Why, yes." Sloughman's brown eyes widened. "Are you aware of any connection between the Olsons and the Ross Stewart targeted here?"

Pete closed his eyes and sagged back in his seat.

"What's wrong?" asked Sam.

Pete shook his head and swallowed hard. "That bomb might have been meant for me. Cowboy was my partner when I was stationed in Japan in the eighties. We busted a gang of our own military who was stealing weapons and selling them. My commanding officer was involved. He was court-martialed and sent to Fort Leavenworth. I remember being notified when he got out, maybe five years ago. Hell."

"Damn it, Schultz," said Grover. "You were shot at recently. Wasn't Olson shot and killed before their house was blown up?"

"Yes, he was," said Sloughman. "I need this guy's name."

"Uhhh. Torres was the last name. Seems to me his first name was a city name. Salvador? Santiago? *Ja*. Santiago Torres. That's it."

The agent entered it into his laptop.

"I'm confused," said the bomb squad officer. "Did this dirtbag put the bomb under the wrong car?"

Pete frowned. "Krista did say Hoot's car."

"But she knew about the threats against Stewart," said Grover.

"Lieutenant," said Sam, flicking a glance at Pete, "that day you were parked right next to Hoot. Your cars are similar, both white. This guy was watching from a block away, and couldn't use binoculars without drawing attention to himself."

"Even from that distance, would he mix up a young, red-headed man with me?"

"According to Krista, you and Hoot were already parked by the bookstore before the pickup took the spot at the end of the block," said Sam.

"She's the young girl who moved the backpack, right?" asked Sloughman. "Does she know cars? Could that be where the confusion came in?"

Sam chuckled. "She and my daughter could tell you every breed of dog and their conformation, but when I've asked what kind of a car someone had, they get that deer-in-the-headlights look. Both identify cars by color."

Pete heaved a sigh. "He must have been plotting revenge all that time."

Then it slammed into him, and he rose from his seat. "Akiko! My family. This guy is sick! Arlene Olson had nothing to do with Japan, and yet he killed her. Damn it."

He looked at Sloughman. "Akiko helped to bring him down. My wife, our kids, Cliff, Lou and the baby! I need to get them to safety. Now!"

"Sit down, Schultz," said Grover. "We'll take care of it. Is there a place your wife can go quickly? The Bjornsons' ranch, maybe?"

"I'll call her."

"Surely this Torres wouldn't have another bomb already!" said the FBI agent.

The chief already had his phone to his ear. "Don't assume anything. We'll send out a BOLO." He alerted dispatch with the information.

"Martinez, call Cliff and Lou," said Pete. "Get them out of their house."

Pete's hand shook as he waited for Akiko to answer. He cut off her greeting. "Angel, this is an emergency. Drop whatever you're doing, get Rick, the dogs, and get out of the house immediately. Go to the Bjornsons' house. I'll call you shortly. It was Torres, that guy from Japan who was court-martialed, who killed Cowboy and Arlene. Now he's after me and you."

"Rick is at the gym," said Akiko.

"We'll pick him up. Be safe, my angel. I love you."

"I love you, too. I'm on my way."

Pete looked at Sam. "Rick and Steve are at their parkour class. Can Rick stay with Steve tonight?"

"Sure. They ought to be through soon."

"Call them," said the chief. "I'll have patrol pick them up."

Pete called and waited for Rick to answer, drumming his fingers on the table. When it went to voice mail, he hung up and wrote a text message instead. After hitting send, Pete contacted Karen.

"Of course, you're welcome," she said. "We'll be watching for you."

Within minutes Sloughman had a picture of Torres on his computer. He quickly forwarded it to the chief, who added it to the BOLO along with an armed and dangerous, do not approach warning.

The chief was still issuing orders. "This guy needed transportation after he blew up his truck. We'll get cracking on any stolen vehicle reports and the car rental agencies in Santa Fe and Albuquerque. Concentrate on the twenty-four-hour period following the explosion as the most likely time. Circulate this photo among the motels and hotels, too."

The chief sent the picture to his printer. He picked up the image and laid it down by Pete and Sam.

Sam swore. "I've seen this guy. I remember that face and those intense, hooded eyes. He's been hanging around the gym!"

"Hold on," said the chief. "Dispatch just let me know the patrolman is at the gym. He was told the boys had already left. Then the officer showed the fellow at the desk the picture of Torres on his phone. Torres was there this afternoon, too. The guy at the desk didn't see when he left, but he's gone now. What route would they have taken? We'll have patrol find them."

CHAPTER SIXTY-TWO

At the end of their parkour class, Rick listened carefully as their instructor listed what practice exercises he wanted them to work on.

"Next week, we'll learn the tic tac," said the instructor, "where you run, push off a tree or wall to gain height, change direction, and go over an obstacle."

Rick watched the assistant give a demonstration before the group broke up.

"I like that," he said to Steve. They put on their jackets and picked up their backpacks.

The man standing at the refreshment area caught Rick's attention. He poked Steve's arm. "El Creepo's got his beady little eyes on us again." His skin crawled as he felt the staring. Whatever the old man with the fake black hair was up to, Rick wanted none of it. He looked up quickly to see the man's eyes slide away before walking off.

"Let's walk to my place," said Steve. "My mom can't pick us up."

They went outside. Chilly. Not much daylight left. Rick zipped his jacket higher and tugged on his gloves. "What do you suppose Creepo's problem is?"

"He never works out or anything. Just watches. Pervert."

The boys started walking, shoulders hunched against the damp cold. At the corner, Rick looked back, shrugged, and kept on going.

They cut across a parking lot, and he looked back again. "Is that black car following us?"

"I saw Creepo getting into a black car," said Steve. "Let's turn up this next street and see if he follows."

"Crap. He is. Let's turn on that one-way street."

As they turned, Steve looked back. "We're in trouble. He's still coming, even driving the wrong way."

They broke into a run. "At that driveway, go over the wall and get down."

They spun around the corner and sprang over the four-foot adobe wall. They landed in the dark cover under three Arizona cypress trees bordering a deserted backyard. They hid behind the prickly, stinky needles. The sun had set, leaving the dark house and yard in gloom.

"I don't like this," whispered Rick, pulling his phone out of his backpack and muting the sound. "I'm calling 911."

"He stopped," Steve whispered. "But even if he looks over the fence, he can't see us."

Rick grabbed Steve's arm. "Hang on. There's a text from Dad."

"Then I'll call 911," said Steve, getting his phone. "Read your text."

"Some guy's after our family. We're to stay at the gym. They're sending a patrol car to pick us up."

"Too late. Text him back." Steve's call was answered, and he began whispering to dispatch.

Rick's thumbs flew on his keypad as he hunched in the shadows. "What's Creepo doing? Can you see?"

"No. Still see his headlights though. What's that noise?"

"Sounds like a gate."

They peered through their cover at the adobe wall, built with a stepped arch over the gate. A bronze bell hung in an opening above.

"He's in the yard. Over by the garage." Steve quietly filled in the operator.

"We should get the hell out of here," said Rick. "Do you know where we are?"

"Not far from Acequia Madre. I recognize the house. Let's split up. See that oak? I'll climb up to the roof and cross to the garage. When I get there, I'll throw something to distract him. You go back over the fence again."

They quietly doffed their backpacks, told dispatch they needed to move, and put their phones in their pockets. Steve crept away. The man was looking behind garbage cans and under furniture covers on the patio. He came closer to Rick's hiding place.

Rick shrank further into the shadows and held his breath. Then there was a clang, followed by another, as a couple of Steve's stones hit the bell above the gate. The man spun around. Rick flung himself up and over the wall. The guy hollered and ran toward the gate.

Landing lightly, Rick found himself beside the black car, its engine running quietly, the driver's door wide open. Did he have time to grab the keys? The gate squeaked again. No! Rick turned and ran.

The man gave chase, his shoes crunching on the gravel. The next neighbor had a four-foot adobe fence with landscaping boulders in front. An old pine grew behind it. Easy. Rick dove over the wall under the low-growing branches. He tucked his head and dropped his shoulder, thankful for the cushion of soft needles as he rolled.

Two shots rang out behind him. One of them struck the adobe wall. Holy shit! Creepo meant business. A dog in the neighboring yard started barking like crazy.

Keeping low, Rick ran between the houses, coming out onto another small lane. A security bulb turned on, bathing him in light. Ahead of him, two eight-foot walls met in a corner. He heard the sound of pursuit behind him. Jeesh! Could he do it? Well, he had to. He ran at the corner, hit one wall with his foot about three feet off the ground, pushed off, pivoted, and grabbed for the top of the other wall. Yikes!

One hand got a good grip, but the other slipped, and he slammed into the unforgiving adobe. His fingers dug in as he struggled to maintain his hold, stretching the other arm up. Grasping with both hands now. Adrenaline pumping. Brace one foot on the wall. Puulll up. Muscles screaming, swing one leg up. Over the edge!

Just as a bullet thunked into the adobe.

Another tree stood next to the house ahead of him. He scaled the tree, bare of leaves, but sturdy under his weight. Around him, he could see lights coming on in houses, and more yard lights flashing on. He dropped down to the flat roof and pulled out his phone. In the distance, he heard sirens wailing. Running footsteps receded, a car door slammed, and an engine revved. Its noise faded as the sirens grew closer.

He was pretty sure he could stay put now. He didn't think he'd been seen getting onto the roof, and it was likely the sounds meant Creepo had fled. Heart pounding, he flopped back on the rough surface of the roof.

He texted Steve. "You ok?"

The message came back. "Ok. He's gone. Cops are here. Sam and your dad are coming."

Rick stood up, wincing as he rolled his shoulders. He went down the tree, out the front gate, and made his way back to where Steve and the cops waited. His dad drove up, parked in the queue of cars with flashing lights in the narrow lane, and ran toward them. With his father's arms tight around him, Rick pressed close. After a bit, his dad's hold loosened, and they moved apart.

He looked down at his hands, surprised to see his fingers scraped and bleeding. His dad brushed pine needles from his hair. Rick stepped back, and his knee gave slightly. His jeans were now fashionably torn. His knee stung and throbbed.

"Guess what," he said to Steve. "I did a tic tac. Over an eight-foot wall."

Steve grinned as he dropped their backpacks on the ground. "Awesome. And I snapped a photo of El Creepo's car and license plate."

Rick turned to his dad. "Who is this guy?"

"Somebody who has held a grudge ever since we arrested him in Japan. Now that he's out of prison, it seems he wants revenge. He's already killed my old partner and his wife. Now he's after us. I'll tell you more later. Now, I want you someplace safe. Your mother is at the Bjornsons' ranch."

"El Creepo shot at you," said Steve. "I heard. Did he hit you?"

"Shot at you?" His dad grabbed his shoulders and looked him up and down.

"He didn't hit me."

"Show us where you were when he shot at you," said Sam.

Rick led them back and helped them find the bullet holes. When he got to the eight-foot corner, his dad looked up at the wall.

"You went over that?"

"Very impressive," said Sam. "Pete, I'll take these two to my dad's ranch in Pecos. This guy would have no way of knowing about it. Good security there. You don't even need to go back to your house. Steve can lend Rick anything he needs."

His dad nodded and put his hand on Rick's face and studied him. Rick felt an intense burst of love. His dad whispered, "*Geh mit Gott,* my son, go with God."

He threw his arms around his dad. He hung on, only reluctantly letting his arms slide away when they turned to go.

As he got in Sam's car, he looked out the back window at his father, standing there, still watching him. When Sam drove around the corner, Rick faced forward. His eyes stung.

Surely his dad would be okay? Nothing would happen to him? They'd catch that guy?

"*Geh mit Gott,*" he whispered.

Pete drove through the well-lit gates at the Bjornson ranch, feeling satisfaction as they slid smoothly shut behind him. Somebody at the house had been watching. He drove up the long, winding drive, past the corrals and the alpaca pens. When Sam had driven away with Rick, Pete had called Akiko and said they were both safe. Now, here she was, with Karen and Dom, waiting for him near the door.

He got out of the car, and she flew into his arms, backing him against the car with the force of her greeting. They clung to each other in silence.

Pete took a deep breath of the cold, crisp air with the scent of piñon smoke from the chimney. Through the bare branches, he could see distant twinkling lights of Santa Fe. The weight lifted from his shoulders. At this moment in time, they were safe. He took Akiko's hand, and they walked inside to where the Bjornsons and the Stewarts anxiously awaited.

◆ ❖ ◆

"Both of you must stay here, Pete, for as long as it takes to catch this guy," said Anton. "Akiko told us about him and his scheme in Japan. Your home is the first place he'd look for you."

While they were eating dinner, Lou called. She, Cliff, Dougie, and Gandalf were at the Martinez ranch where Rick and Steve were. She and Farah had patched up Rick's scrapes and bumps. They were fine. Not to worry.

After dinner, Pete excused himself and called Chief Grover to see if there were updates. He learned that patrolmen were watching his residence. So far, all was quiet.

"As soon as they got the license plate number from the truck wreckage," said Grover, "we had officers checking area motels to see if anyone had registered with that number. They found a motel where he registered under the name of Jason Miller. They have the room staked out, but he hasn't been back."

"That's the name he gave my cousin, Karl." Pete told Grover that story. "How about the license plate number that Steve Martinez got?"

"Stolen. Steve said the guy wouldn't know he'd taken the photo, so Torres might not feel the need to change it. Also, they found the Honda Civic with the messed-up front bumper and a hole in the back window where you returned fire. It was abandoned in an apartment complex in a visitor spot."

When Pete got back to the family room, he found most had gone off to put kids to bed and get ready for tomorrow.

"I've a room prepared for you in my wing," said Karen. "It's big; even with three dogs, you won't be tripping over them. I know you didn't get to pack anything. We have whatever you might need."

"Do you want to talk any more," asked Dom, "or just crash?"

"I wouldn't mind staying up longer," said Pete. "Especially since I'm sure the chief won't call me out tonight. I can safely indulge in a second glass of wine. How about you, Angel?"

"I'd like that."

Pete hissed in a breath as he put his feet up in Karen's sitting room. "When I saw Rick, I ran like hell toward him. My leg is telling me it wasn't ready for that yet."

"Are you okay?" Akiko's voice was anxious.

"*Ja*, just a bit sore. You know, I find it incredible Torres waited so long for revenge. Thirty years."

"That court martial is seared into my mind." Akiko sipped her wine. "I was watching him when he realized that his plan to incriminate Pete and Cowboy had failed—when that moment of awful truth hit him. He glared at us with such an intense look of hate. I remember being glad to be in a courtroom full of people and not alone with him. Before that he'd been contemptuous—looking down his officer's nose at the lowly enlisted men. How could they be the ones to take him down? The ignominy of it must have stung him deeply."

Akiko turned to Pete and put her hand over his. "This is something we will face together. I will not let this evil man threaten my husband and my children without a damn good fight."

Pete slipped a hand into her hair and studied her dark eyes, full of emotion. "My Avenging Angel . . . My love . . ." He sighed in resignation. "Okay. Together."

CHAPTER SIXTY-THREE

"Can we go home and pick up some stuff?" asked Akiko.

Pete considered her across the table in the Bjornson breakfast room. "I'll check with Grover. If the patrolmen are there, it might be okay. I need my vest and more ammo, not to mention changes of clothing." He sipped his coffee. "I don't suppose you'd give me a list of stuff you want, and you could stay here?"

She raised an eyebrow and said nothing.

Pete sighed. "I thought not. It was worth asking."

"We'll take Beowulf with us. He's good about noticing things out of the ordinary."

An hour later, Pete drove up to their house. The garage door opened, and he drove in. Nothing seemed to be disturbed.

The cop on duty came over. "It's been quiet," he said. "Grover had a couple of officers take fliers around the neighborhood last night with the dirtbag's picture. Nobody'd seen him. A couple of your neighbors seem to be out of town, like the guy behind you."

"He vacations this time of year." Pete unlocked the house door. "I told Grover we'd only stay fifteen minutes. I'll check with you before we leave." He and Akiko, followed by Beowulf, went inside.

"I'll get the stuff from upstairs first," said Pete. "Come, Wulf."

Once in the bedroom, he quickly changed shirts and put on his bulletproof vest. He got the other items on his list and grabbed the chargers for their phones and computers.

Downstairs Akiko had left a box on the counter next to his coffee maker. He added his items and looked longingly at the coffee maker, but there wasn't time.

"Is the box ready to go?" he called to Akiko.

"Yes. Don't forget Rick's computer."

Pete stowed the box in his car, and went back for the rest. Beowulf stood at the doggie door, whining. "What's the matter— Oh, it's locked, sorry." He unlocked the sliding glass door, and stepped out on the patio.

Beowulf ran past him. Halfway across the yard he stopped and looked towards the casita, posture stiff and bristly. He growled.

Pete drew his gun. With sharp eyes he surveyed the familiar surroundings. Nothing moved. Beowulf intent on the casita, disappeared along its side, nose to the ground. Cautiously Pete moved to the edge of the patio bordered by low shrubs, still clinging to their leaves, and Akiko's long planters holding the desiccated remains of her herb garden. Nothing. Seconds went by. He lowered his gun and turned toward the door. He'd get the patrolman to help check this out. Beowulf didn't act that way for no reason.

Suddenly a tremendous force propelled him forward, closely followed by the sound of gunshots. He hit the cement hard next to the planter, the breath whacked from his body, his gun skittering under a chair. He sucked in a deep breath and cried out at the pain of it. He couldn't move.

Akiko screamed an anguished "No!"

Torres advanced toward him, still firing. More shots thudded into the adobe and the thick glass of the door.

Beowulf had gone all the way around the casita. At full speed he grabbed the wrist of the gunman. The momentum jerked the man to his knees and sent the gun into the turf grass. Torres flailed, screaming as he tried to escape the strong Airedale jaws.

Pete rolled toward the chair, his fingers reaching for his own gun.

Holding an object high over her head, Akiko flew past him toward the screaming man. She brought her weapon down on top of his head. Pieces went flying. Water sloshed over the man, who struggled to get away from Wulf.

Whooosh. Akiko swung the object again like an ancient Japanese flail and bashed the angry, distorted face of Torres, this time sending him to the ground. Wulf shook the arm he held, biting deeper until the man lay still.

"Don't move!" The cop from the front came through the patio door, both hands aiming his gun at Torres. "Move away, ma'am."

Pete retrieved his gun and heaved painfully to his feet. "Wulf, leave it." Wulf dropped the man's arm, and backed away, his body stiff, his eyes focused on the prone man. Growls still rumbled deep in his throat.

Pete cast a quick look at his wife. Her nostrils flaring, chest heaving, wisps of dark hair hung over her face. She held the cord of Pete's coffee maker in her hands, the battered appliance at her feet.

Magnificent.

Sirens squealed to a halt, car doors slammed, and more police officers ran into the backyard. A cop quickly removed the gun from where it lay.

Another officer cuffed Torres. Pete heard the familiar words. "Santiago Torres, you are under arrest. You have the right . . ."

Beowulf's savaging and the impact of the coffee maker left Torres with blood running from his wrist, nose, and mouth. Defiant, he spat out a tooth and glared at Pete. "Why aren't you dead? I was certain I put that bomb under your car. How did it move? It should have killed you. I shot you. You were hit. This can't be real. Why aren't you dead?"

Pete put an arm around Akiko and brought her close. "Because the angels are on our side."

Akiko looked up at him. The cord fell from her fingers. "He hit you? Pete?"

She ran her hands over his chest, then went around to his back. He heard a soft cry as she found the hole and the deformed bullet caught in the layers of protective vest. He let out a cry of pain as she flung her arms around him. Sobs of relief shook her body as she clutched him.

Standing there, he whispered, "Angel, my angel."

CHAPTER SIXTY-FOUR

The next morning, Pete was back in his office, a little worse for wear. They'd insisted on his going to the hospital to be checked out after Torres had been brought down. He was bruised from his collision with the cement, and the large, angry-looking purple area over the cracked rib from the bullet impact quickly taught him to lean back gingerly in his chair.

Sam knocked on his door. "Somehow I knew they couldn't keep you overnight."

"Being home with Akiko and Rick, a good night's sleep, and a visit from Lou, Cliff and my grandson—that was the best medicine. I'm a lucky man. Except . . ." Pete put his hand over his heart. "My birthday-present-coffee maker gave up its life for me. I'm in awe of the sacrifice."

Sam laughed. "Shall I compose a heroic lament in its honor?"

"Not necessary." Pete grinned. "Akiko already replaced it. She said she wasn't sorry she'd ruined it on that ugly face."

"Brought down with a coffee maker." Sam tsk-tsked.

"And a dog. Don't forget Beowulf."

A day later in Pueblo, Jed scanned his notes. His search of the Pueblo newspaper archives for articles with Wysocki's name had borne fruit.

He began with his college years when Wysocki had come into the sphere of the business tycoon who eventually became his father-in-law. His career shot up like a meteor. He reinvented himself and left Pueblo for good. His parents died about the time of his marriage. Wysocki inherited their fortune, though it paled in comparison to the one he'd married into.

Jed dug back further to high school years. He pored over yearbooks, forming a picture of what young Wysocki was like. He studied photos and charted his associations and friends.

Two individuals began to stand out from those years—Tonya Abrerro, cheerleader, and Bob Norton, football jock. He started digging into their lives and following trails with one goal in mind—contacting them and getting to know the real Wysocki.

Tonya's trail came to a distressing early end, a suicide in March of 1991. Jed tried to access her autopsy and the police reports, but failed.

With Norton, Jed was more successful. The guy still lived in Pueblo. He was able to arrange a meeting with him for the following day.

When they met, Jed pegged Norton as someone who lived in the faded glow of past achievements, never accomplishing much after his glorious high school football career. He'd settled for a position in his father's business and coasted along in life. Norton's muscular physique had turned to flab, drifted to his middle, and ballooned. Signs of dissipation marked his once handsome features.

Through flattery, sympathy, and a few scotches, Jed coaxed the story of Wysocki from Norton. At first Norton basked in the "I knew him when" and bragged about their exploits. Then Jed worked Tonya's name into the conversation and watched Norton's face fill with bitterness and regret.

"Wit used people. Climbed over them to get to the top, then forgot them. I loved her, you know, but she always said she'd marry Wit. Bastard strung her along. I never told Tonya, but Wit said his parents didn't like her and if they married, he'd lose his inheritance.

When he left Pueblo, I started dating Tonya, and I believe we would have gotten married. Then, when I was away on business for my dad, they said she took her life. Cops had non-stop questions, made me prove I was in Oklahoma where I said I was. I still don't believe she did it."

"You don't believe she committed suicide?"

"Never. I don't know what happened that night, but the last time we talked, she had big plans. She was going to be rich. Never saw her happier. Somebody must have pushed her."

Jed's phone rang. "Sorry, listen, I've got to take this call and get going. You've been a big help. Let me buy you one for the road." He signaled the bartender and left some bills on the table. Before he went out the door, he looked back at the morose man cuddling his scotch.

He answered the call, from another employee of Wysocki's, wondering what they wanted. Was this a subordinate pushed into giving him more bad news?

"Hey, Jed, I don't know what you're doing for Wysocki, don't need to know, don't wanna know, but watch your back. He asked Jorge to take on the job, but Jorge turned him down."

"Jorge! He's bad. He likes hurting people. Why would Wysocki jeopardize his reputation by involving him?"

"I don't know what's stuck in his craw. Sometimes Wysocki gets a little dodgy, but this time he even scared me."

Jed finished the call and went back to his car. The secret had to be huge. Back then Wysocki's empire was just beginning. What would threaten it? What he didn't want his boss or wife to know?

It was time to get back to New Mexico and find the box. He was afraid of what Wysocki would do to the family if he didn't. He thought of his sister, Annie, sweet, trusting he'd take care of her.

He couldn't let that happen. Again.

♦ ❖ ♦

On Friday morning, while Pete and Sam were working at the round table, Grover came by. "I came to tie up some loose ends for you. First, Torres had been holed up in your back neighbor's outbuildings for a few days, Pete. The car in Steve Martinez's picture was hidden under a tarp. He'd started collecting what he needed to build another bomb."

"Mein Gott. So close. Akiko and I'll have to thank the ATF folks for their quick work."

Grover nodded. "Secondly, after you and I talked with the Denver chief on Wednesday, he got in touch with Pueblo. There's now a quiet investigation beginning into Wysocki. They'll open the Tonya Abrerro case again."

"The press will have a heyday when that hits the fan," said Pete.

Grover heaved a sigh. "If Wysocki gets arrested, he'll lawyer up immediately. His attorneys will pick apart everything police do to try and unravel it. Of all the sleazeballs I never wanted to deal with, this guy tops them all."

Pete's eyebrows rose in surprise. "At one time I thought you admired him and his work."

The chief shook his head. "I've socialized with this man and worked with him on campaigns for our union's candidates. He's a clever man, wily like a fox. My only word of caution is, don't be suckered into believing him. The man will be whoever he needs to be to get whatever he wants."

"I've heard him described as a chameleon."

"Eh? A chameleon?" said Grover. "That fits. Lastly, you might want to know what's going on with Isaacson."

"Isaacson!"

"Because of your interest in Hayle, the Denver chief was poking into connections with Hayle's security business and the moonlighting cops from Isaacson's precinct. He uncovered a can of worms."

Pete let out a bark of laughter, then winced.

"Suddenly Isaacson decided to take early retirement. He still might face charges when it all settles. It looks like the city was supplying off-duty cops to work security for Hayle's company. The clients were billed for the time, and the city was reimbursed. That would have been fine, except they were billed for twice as many cops as actually worked. Because of Hayle's convoluted schedules, creative records, and different check-in points for security, no one had any idea who else was supposed to be there."

"Bet you a dollar to a doughnut that Hayle will squeal on him, or vice versa," said Sam.

Pete glanced at his phone. "It's Hiram checking in."

"All's quiet at the Stewart home," Pete said after he talked with him. "I told Hoot it wasn't safe to go back yet. No more threats, and now no bomber, though I'm convinced, more than ever, Wysocki is behind the search for the puzzle box."

"Wysocki wouldn't soil his hands with that kind of dirty work," said Grover.

"True," said Pete. "But he would hire someone."

"Farah and I, Hoot and Melody, Anton and Skyla are going to finish cleaning and moving stuff out of Skyla's old house tomorrow," said Sam. "Marilyn is going to be at her house with the kids. She's making lunch for us. We'll be in and out. Should be all done by mid-afternoon."

"Keep your eyes open," said Pete.

CHAPTER SIXTY-FIVE

Saturday, and already February, thought Hoot. Where had January gone? He and his family were still living with the Bjornsons. Right now the kids were with Marilyn at her trailer, while Melody and the rest were on their way back to Skyla's old home. For the past hour, Bonnie, Matti, and Twitch had been racing all around his and Marilyn's yards. He hoped Bonnie would be tired enough for a nap.

The checkout line ahead of him at a Pecos dollar store moved ahead as he mentally reviewed his list: light bulbs, garbage bags, and the main reason for this trip, shoelaces and a vacuum cleaner belt. The vacuum cleaner had attacked one of Bonnie's sneakers, sucking up the lace and wrapping it around the roller, putting the shoe in a death grip and filling the air with a burned rubber smell. Yuck. When Hoot had left, she'd been complaining about it feeling 'woose' because of the shortened jury-rigged lace.

He felt good about their decision to move to Skyla's house. He hadn't realized before how big her home was, having been in only a few of the rooms. Bonnie and Matti could still each have their own bedroom, and the master suite was bigger than theirs was now. He didn't feel at ease in their old house after the break-in. It was somehow alien.

Hoot left the store with his purchases and started on his next errand.

◆ ❖ ◆

Jed approached the Stewart home on foot, leaving his SUV down the narrow lane in a pullout. He'd driven by a few minutes earlier and discovered no vehicles parked at the house. He hadn't seen any nosy state troopers today, either. The coast seemed clear. If he could give Wysocki his box and tell him to shove it, he'd feel great satisfaction.

The door was locked, as he'd anticipated. He picked the locks and let himself in. The mess he'd made turning the place upside down hadn't been cleaned up. A pile of flattened boxes sat on the floor. That surprised him. Were they planning to move?

He took a quick glance into each room. In the master bedroom—unbelievably—the creepy wooden box sat in the open on the dresser. He grabbed a pillowcase from the bed to put it in and turned to leave.

He heard the front door open and light, running footsteps in the hall. Through the bedroom door crack, he saw the little red-headed boy go into his room. Silently, Jed left through the outside door in the master suite. Ducking low as he passed the windows, he peered around the corner to the front, expecting to see the rest of the family.

Instead, there was Wysocki sneaking in the front. What was he doing here? And where had that kid come from?

Alarm filled Jed. What would Wysocki do when he saw the boy?

Making a snap decision, Jed followed Wysocki in through the front door and called, "What the hell are you doing here?" Maybe the kid would hear him and hide.

Wysocki laughed. "I'm taking matters into my own hands. You're an incompetent fool."

"I'm curious. What is so urgent about finding that box now? Sentimental value, my ass. What secrets of yours does it hide?"

"How dare you? Mind who you're talking to. It's mine. I don't care if it's full of chicken feathers. It was your job to get it. You've no say now."

"I do have a say. Your secrets are coming to light. You had something to do with Tonya Abrerro's death, didn't you?"

Fury flooded the man's face with red color. "Damn you. You have the box. How did you open it?"

"Guessed right, didn't I?" He held up the pillowcase. "Here's your damned box, and I didn't need to open it. You taught me to dig up dirt on people. I just gave you a taste of your own medicine. You have a black soul."

Wysocki grabbed the pillowcase and looked in. "You're a dead man, Hawkins."

"Something happens to me, the world will know what you did. I quit. Do your own dirty work. But I swear, if you harm this family, I will go to the law and tell them what you've done. Your empire, built with lies—"

Sounds at the door interrupted him. Spinning, his mouth agape in horror, Jed saw the little girl Annie's age, wearing a red cape, push open the door and walk in. A dog followed, bristled, and placed himself between the two men and the girl.

"Who are you?" A frightened voice preceded a white-haired woman inside. "Get out. You don't belong here." She moved quickly to the phone and punched in numbers.

"Get out," she repeated, then put the phone to her ear. "Help! Two men—"

Wysocki darted toward her to grab at the phone. The dog intervened, growling and showing a mouthful of strong teeth. Wysocki aimed a kick at him. The dog latched onto his pant leg, tearing the fabric before retreating with more growling and barking.

A little whirlwind with flying red hair ran at Wysocki, hitting his leg with her fists, and screeching, "Stop it! Don't you hurt him."

Wysocki grabbed her up in his arm and swung the pillow-cased box at the dog. The girl's screech rose to ear-splitting as she pummeled and kicked him. One of her shoes went flying. Wysocki dropped the box and slapped his hand over the girl's mouth.

"Don't hurt her," yelled Jed, grabbing for the girl.

"Put her down," the woman screamed. The phone dropped and slid across the floor as she tried to rescue the child.

Wysocki shoved her into Jed, making them both stumble and fall. The old lady went down hard and lay still. Then he yelled as the girl bit down on his finger. Wysocki dropped her and shook his hand, sending red drops spattering against the wall.

"Gonna get Daddy." She scrambled to her feet and ran out the wide-open door, the dog chasing after.

The blood in Jed's veins turned to ice as the little boy appeared in the hallway behind Wysocki, clutching his box of Legos, his blue eyes wide with fright.

"Run!" Jed yelled, struggling to rise.

The boy dropped the box in a burst of skittering Legos. At the sound, Wysocki pulled a gun and spun around. Jed launched himself at Wysocki to grab his arm. He heard a deafening blast near his ear and felt himself hit the floor. Wysocki loomed over him.

Jed saw the child screaming, but heard no sound. Through half-closed lashes, he saw Wysocki grab up the pillowcase, and lunge after the boy to drag him by the arm out the door. Then pain smote him like a firestorm, all-consuming, before blackness swept away the fiery agony and claimed him.

CHAPTER SIXTY-SIX

Hoot left the forestry office and tossed the mail and messages on the car seat, glancing at the sky as he closed the door. He wouldn't be surprised if it snowed later.

His phone rang, the distinctive ringtone he and Matti had chosen together. He answered only to hear his child sobbing uncontrollably over a strange background noise, like a loud hum, almost a roar. "Matti. What's the matter?"

"Daddy, come get me."

"Matti, where are you? What happened?" More crying. "Slow down. I can barely hear you."

"Bad man took me. In his car. In the trunk. Daddy."

"Who took you?"

"Don't know. It's scary in here. Dark. I wanna go home."

"Listen to me, son. You're going to be okay. We'll find you with your tracker."

More sobbing.

"Where's Gramma?"

"She fell. He shot the other man. Then he grabbed me. Daddy, please come get me."

Shot? The other man? Good God, what was going on?

"I'll come and get you. I'm going to have Mommy call the police, and they'll be coming too."

"He's going fast. Ow. It's bumpy." More crying.

"Matti, you did just right to call me. We'll find you soon, son. We'll get you home. Where is Bonnie?"

"Man scared her. She and Twitch ran away."

Hoot started the engine. "Listen, Matti, I'm going to put you on hold for just a minute to let Mommy know. Then I'll get back to you."

His finger hesitated over the hold button. How could he break that connection to his son? Like thrusting a dagger into his own heart, he pressed it.

Melody answered on the third ring. "Hi, Hoot, we—"

"Melody! Call 911. Matti called me on his tracker. He's been kidnapped."

"No! Kidnapped?"

"Melody, listen to me. Go home. Marilyn's been hurt. I'm headed there now. Understand? I've got to get back to Matti."

"Not Matti. No!"

Hoot heard a hubbub of distraught voices, then Anton's voice on the phone. "Sam's calling 911. We're going back to your place right now."

Hoot switched back to Matti. "Okay, Matti. I'm back. Tell me what's happening. You're doing fine, son." Hoot pulled to the right as a state trooper screamed by him. He saw it turn on the road near his home. Quickly following, he got there just after the trooper did. More police cars pulled up after him.

"Hang on, son, I have to tell the policeman."

Quickly he told the trooper what was happening as they ran to the door. He stopped just inside. The first troopers were kneeling by a man, lying on the floor, his head and back covered with blood. Bonnie and Twitch were nowhere to be seen. Another officer was bent over Marilyn.

Hoot saw an officer pick up their house phone from the floor by the couch and heard him talk to the 911 operator, saying they were there, before pressing the off button.

Melody appeared, tugging at his sleeve, her eyes wide and anxious. "Matti? Bonnie?" The others were close behind her.

He shook his head, pointing to an object near the downed man. Bonnie's shoe with the jury-rigged laces and her tracker.

Hiram walked in, his normal easygoing gruffness replaced by efficient authority. As Hoot quickly briefed him, Melody gave Hiram her phone so the police could follow Matti's tracker.

"Matti, I'm on my way with the police," said Hoot.

"Quickly," said Sam. "My car."

Hoot faced his wife and gently put a hand on her face. "Melody, my love, look at me."

She raised frightened eyes to his.

"We will find them and bring them home. We will." He held her gaze until she pulled him to her fiercely and nodded.

Then, glancing at Marilyn beginning to stir on the floor, attended by medics, Hoot ran to Sam's car.

◆ ❖ ◆

Melody's mind was in a whirl. As Hoot left, she closed her eyes and took deep breaths. She had to be strong for her kids. To have Matti and Bonnie separated and both in danger—her heart was torn apart.

She saw a medic came in with a gurney and lower it near Marilyn. Where could Bonnie be? Focus on her daughter. She picked up Bonnie's shoe from the floor and ran to Marilyn's house, calling for Bonnie. Anton, Skyla, and Hiram followed. No sign of her little one.

Anton picked up Twitch's leash from the floor near Marilyn's couch. It was still attached to his collar with his tracker. He let out an anguished cry. "Why didn't I ever show her how to undo his leash? Damn it." He put the leash and collar in his jacket pocket.

Hiram cleared his throat next to her. "Melody, come with me to search your house. Your friends will search your grandmother's house with another officer, then they'll look outside."

Quickly she and Hiram went through her house. When they got to the master bedroom, she noticed at once the box she'd just put there this morning was gone, and that one pillow, missing its case, lay on the floor. Hiram relayed that information to those tracking Matti.

Even before they'd finished searching, Marilyn and the gunshot victim had been loaded into an ambulance and driven away. Both were showing signs of coming around, but neither one was fully conscious yet.

She followed Hiram back to Marilyn's trailer, where the others had no luck in finding Bonnie.

Hiram reached out to Melody. "Now you and I will sit down and put together what we need to get them back."

Melody looked at him, startled. "But I need to look—"

Hiram put his hand over Melody's shaking fingers. "I know you want to look, but your most important job now is to provide information, and be here for them when they come back. Do you have recent pictures of your children?"

"Sure. On my phone, but they're using it to track Matti."

"Pictures," said Anton. "The Christmas ones with the reindeer. Here—they're on my phone, too."

"Bonnie's wearing the same thing today," said Melody.

"These two," the trooper said, choosing the photos. "Send them to me. We'll get them out on social media and put them on fliers. Volunteers will have them shortly to hand out."

The troopers began talking about an Amber Alert. Another trooper came in to tell Hiram that the kid and dog tracks all over the properties would make it difficult to track the girl.

Melody heard Anton calling her name. She focused on him and Hiram again.

"Melody, do you want me to call Hoot's parents and Cliff?" Anton asked.

"I've already notified Pete," said Hiram. "He's the detective on call this weekend. I told him to go ahead and call Hoot's parents."

"Good. I'll call Cliff," said Anton.

As he spoke with Cliff, he looked questioningly at Hiram. "Do we have bloodhounds coming?"

"No such luck," said Hiram. "We called. Once again, they're on another search."

"Cliff is coming with Gandalf. Maybe he can help." Anton hung up the phone. "Hiram, you said you heard on the 911 call that Bonnie was going to get her daddy. I'll take a few volunteers with me and walk to Skyla's old house. It's not that far, and she knew he was there."

"Good idea," said Hiram. "But would she know the way?"

"I don't know," said Melody, "but try."

"I have to do something," Anton said. "I have to. If I'd shown her how to do the latch . . . Bonnie and Twitch have to be together. If you need me, call."

CHAPTER SIXTY-SEVEN

The GPS showed Matti on Highway 50 heading in the direction of Santa Fe. Hoot was thankful to see Sam's ordinary-looking detective car had lights and sirens. As Sam and Hoot turned onto 50, an ambulance sped by them toward Hoot's home.

Hoot's leave-taking of Melody had been so abrupt, so painful. But their friends were with her. In the car, Sam relayed a message from Hiram. The search for Bonnie had begun, they were coordinating with the Santa Fe PD, and a highway patrol helicopter would be looking for the kidnapper's car. The puzzle box was missing.

"Matti, we're coming. Hang in there, son. You're doing fine. The police are tracking you, too."

Crackle, crackle. Then silence.

Hoot looked at Sam in horror.

"Call him again, and keep trying," said Sam. "You know what coverage is like here."

Soon Hoot heard his son again, his cries even more frightened. "I can hear you now, Matti. Our call might drop again, but we'll get connected. You're doing fine."

"I'm scared. I don't wanna be . . . all grown up before I . . . find you again."

Sobs made Matti's words hard to understand. Hoot bit his lip, and tears welled in his eyes. "I know you're scared, son. But I didn't have a tracker. My parents had no idea where I was. I can talk to you. We can follow the car you're in on my phone. We will get you back."

Sam was relaying information on his radio. Hoot saw the marker on Matti's app turn from 50 onto I-25 and start toward Santa Fe.

"I was hoping he'd turn that way," said Sam. "Better coverage. More cops."

"Matti, I'm going to turn down the volume on your ringtone. If we get disconnected again, I don't want the bad man to hear it. Do you understand?"

"Yes." Matti was a little quieter, the initial hysterical sobs now whimpers and sniffs.

"I'm proud of you, son. You're doing great. We're getting closer." Hoot looked at Sam. "How will we tell which car he's in if we catch up to him?"

"Pete updated me just now. The missing puzzle box clued him in that it must be Wysocki. He checked the airport and learned Wysocki's jet flew in this morning, and he rented a car. We're looking for a black Toyota. I have the license number."

Sam pointed to his own phone showing a GPS map, propped up where he could see it. There was a moving marker on it. "That's us. We'll know." Sam negotiated past several cars that had moved to the right and turned onto the interstate.

"He just blew by the next exit on I-25," said Hoot.

"He might go for the one after. Outskirts of Santa Fe."

Hoot kept talking to Matti and relaying to Sam what showed on Matti's map. Sam would then update the Santa Fe police. He glanced at Sam's phone. They were gaining, but his son was still so far away.

"Tell Matti to let you know if he feels the car slow down, turn, or stop," said Sam.

Hoot looked up in alarm and took the phone away from his mouth, so his son wouldn't hear. "Why? You don't think we can see enough on the app? That we aren't getting good feedback?"

"Feedback's fine. Matti needs to feel like he's doing something, like he has a little bit of control."

Hoot nodded and told his son he needed his help. Minutes passed, and then the dot left the interstate.

A quavery voice came to Hoot. "It got bumpier. And slower."

"That's good, son. Remember how sound changes when we drive on a gravel road?"

"Yes. Noisier."

"Tell me if it changes like that. Sam, he just turned left."

"Can't be familiar with the area. He's headed into a housing development."

"Daddy, we're going real slow. Turning."

"Good. That helps." Hoot looked at Sam's map again. "That bought us some time. He's turning around. Got into a cul de sac."

"Excellent. That little glitch helped the helicopter pinpoint him."

"He's back on the Old Las Vegas Highway. Now he's turning off."

"Daddy, a gravel road."

"I see you on the map, Matti."

"What? Can't hear you. Noisy."

Hoot spoke slowly. "We know where you are." He turned to Sam and spoke quietly. "Why is this guy headed off into the middle of nowhere?"

"I don't like it," said Sam. "We have to hurry. Patrol is closing in."

"Daddy, we're stopping."

"I need you to help me again, son. I need you to whisper now so he can't hear you. I'll keep on talking to you."

CHAPTER SIXTY-EIGHT

In his office at the Santa Fe PD, as soon as Hiram's call ended, Pete was filled with urgency. The aches and pains from his battle with Torres faded to the back of his mind. The last of Hoot's nemeses was now on Pete's turf, and he was ready.

He called Grover.

"I've been listening to the scanners. Be right there." Moments later Grover burst through his door. "Are you certain this is Wysocki?"

"I believe it. The puzzle box is missing from Stewart's home. Wysocki flew in and rented a car. A man, ostensibly with the box, has kidnapped the boy, stuffed him in his trunk, and is heading this direction. The child may have seen him harm his grandmother and shoot someone. Grover, I need you with me on this. Help me build an airtight case." Pete didn't waver under the chief's penetrating look.

Finally the chief nodded. "First responders relayed that according to his ID, the gunshot victim is Jerome Edward Hawkins. I'll arrange for guards at the hospital for him and the grandmother. They'll be there when the ambulance arrives. I'll coordinate with Hiram to get personnel into position to nail Wysocki. I'll notify the airport to hold his plane."

"Thank you, sir."

"What's your plan?"

"We've started the warrant. Now that we know the name of the victim, we can add that. Even though we might get by without it, I want a warrant to swab for gunshot residue on Wysocki's hand. And it's possible that his violent handling of the children left traces. I need his DNA legally, that car he's driving, the gun, and the box."

"Judge Hernandez is the magistrate on call," said the chief. "Get it ready. He'll give you your telephonic warrant."

"As soon as I get that underway, I'm going to see Marilyn and Hawkins," said Pete. He looked at his watch. He could be there shortly after they would arrive.

Pete found Marilyn in an alcove in the emergency room. The doctor said they planned to admit her. She was anxious to hear what had happened. She had no idea that Matti had been kidnapped, and Pete didn't enlighten her. He asked what she remembered.

"Matti wanted his Legos. He took the key and went ahead. Bonnie only had one shoe on. I helped her tie the one with the lace the vacuum ate. Then we followed Matti over."

"What did you see and hear?"

"There were two men there arguing. I didn't know who they were, maybe robbers. One had a pillowcase with something in it. I didn't see Matti, and I was frightened. I called 911. Twitch was barking. The older man kicked at him, and Bonnie was screeching. He grabbed her. I tried to get her away from him, and that's the last I remember. Please, tell me he didn't take her."

"Your 911 call brought help very quickly, and Bonnie got away before he could take her."

"That's a relief. My head hurts so."

As she closed her eyes, Dom and Karen arrived to sit with her. Pete beckoned them into the hall, and briefly updated them before leaving to talk with Hawkins.

Nearby Pete found Hawkins being treated for his gunshot wounds. Bullets had grazed his head, made flesh wounds on his upper back, and nicked his butt. He couldn't hear at all out of one ear.

"I'm glad you're here, Lieutenant," said the doctor. "He's been very agitated. He didn't want to take any pain medication until he talked to the police, but we gave him a sedative. It should be working soon."

"Mr. Hawkins, I'm Detective Schultz, Santa Fe PD. Can you tell me who shot you?"

"The little girl? Is she okay? And her brother?"

"What happened?"

"Went to get the box. Wysocki came."

"Wysocki? You're sure?"

"Yes. Old lady and the little girl came. Wysocki shoved the lady into me. Both of us went down. Then he grabbed the girl. She bit him and ran. When he pulled a gun on the boy, I grabbed his arm to stop him. He fired. Then I saw him grab the boy."

Pete looked at the young man. He was visibly distraught about the children. Anybody else would want to know if they'd caught the guy who'd shot him. This guy's first thought was the children. Did he have a family of his own?

"The little girl ran away," said Pete. "She's still missing. He took the boy. Police are following him."

"Bastard. Hope . . . hope she's okay . . ." His voice trailed off. "Feel . . . blurry." A tear ran down his face onto the gurney. "Find Annie . . . please."

"Annie?" Pete paused in closing his notebook.

Jed's eyes closed. Pete met the eyes of the doctor and turned to leave the room.

Who was Annie?

Wit slammed a hand on the steering wheel. Sirens—in the distance. He needed more time. Very few houses here. Lots of brush. He pulled to the side of the road and stopped. Had the law gotten onto him this quickly? He'd been careful not to draw attention to himself. Had the kid's crying been heard at a stop sign or something?

When the kid hollered he was going to tell his daddy and went toward the phone, Wit had nabbed him. Couldn't leave him to get help. He'd been desperate, not thinking. The only reason the brat still lived, was that he might be of use yet. A bargaining chip.

At first the screaming had gotten to him, and he'd turned on the radio to drown him out. Come to think of it, the kid hadn't been very loud since then. Crying sometimes, and talking to himself, all muffled by the trunk. Maybe he hadn't been heard.

But how would the cops know?

Maybe they were chasing somebody else.

He needed to get rid of the kid and destroy the evidence in the box. Burn it maybe, but first he had to grab that necklace, and get back to his plane. If he had to disappear, the necklace would finance his way.

Sirens, closer, now from both directions.

He got out, grabbed the pillowcase with the box, and swung it against a big rock twice, hearing the smashing of the wood. Then he dumped the ruins out and pawed through the wreckage, spreading it frantically.

A cry rose from deep inside his chest. Disbelief. Nothing. *It had to be there.* He shook the empty pillowcase. Jed lied. His secrets! Jed must have them. Where was the necklace? Where were the papers?

Wait! There among the splinters lay a black M-shaped key—not iron like his—with blue tape stuck to it. Maybe there was an identical box. Maybe his secrets were safe after all. The manufacturer lied. Another box. Had to be.

He looked up at the noise. A chopper hovered overhead. He ran back to the car and accelerated away in a spurt of dirt and gravel. Police cars from all directions blocked him. Nowhere to go. Fence rows. Banks. Gullies. Could he still get away? Use his gun? Ahead of him, cars blocked the road, doors opened, weapons pointed at him. Behind him. More of the same. Above him, the whump, whump of the rotor blades.

He couldn't hear anything from the kid in the trunk—at least over the noise of the chopper and still more sirens coming. He could always say he didn't know the kid was there. Fool kid must have been playing and got into his car when he stopped to ask directions when he'd been lost. He was trying to get to downtown Santa Fe, but took the wrong exit and made a wrong turn.

Let his lawyers figure it out. Didn't have to burn the stuff in the box. Hell—it wasn't even there. With any luck, Jed and the old lady were dead, and the contents of the box would never see the light of day.

Wit leaned his head back. A voice through a bullhorn behind him. "Police. Turn off your engine. Throw the keys out the window."

Chapter Sixty-Nine

Melody grabbed Skyla's arm as Anton left. The gray skies were growing darker. "She'll be cold and so afraid."

How could she bear it? Her babies. She rubbed her tummy gently. What kind of world would this baby be born into?

Skyla's eyes, full of understanding, met hers.

Lynn and Andrew came, and Melody flew into their arms and wept. Their faces said they were reliving the agony of Johnny's snatching. The mobile command trailer was now in their yard. Neighbors came. Strangers came. The troopers organized them into search groups.

Melody grew impatient with Hiram and his methodical ways. She knew he was right, but damn it, she just wanted him to hurry it up. She was frustrated in having to stay at Marilyn's house, not her own.

Hiram quietly said that her house was a crime scene. "If we are going to catch and convict the people who did this, we need to do it properly. We made sure Bonnie was not there. We'll stay here now."

Her babies.

Anton called from Skyla's house. They hadn't seen any sign of Bonnie or Twitch. He was heading back.

She sat next to Hiram, listening for progress on tracking Matti. The search for Bonnie had teams checking the river, up and down stream. How far could a four-year-old go, anyway?

Even though her friends and Hoot's relatives were there, they were just so perfectly understanding, sympathetic, and helpful, she wanted to scream.

◆ ❖ ◆

Hoot spoke to his son through the phone as he and Sam hurried toward the activity at the center of the flashing lights. The officers had relaxed their defensive positions and lowered their weapons. "We're here, son. It's time to yell real loud."

Ahead of them, a man in handcuffs lay prone on the ground. An officer finished reading him his rights. From the trunk, a child's voice screamed for daddy. Another officer picked up the keys from the ground and opened the trunk.

Matti reached up to the policeman, who lifted him out. Hoot shook Sam's hand off his arm and ran, swooped his son into his arms and hugged him fiercely. Felt the little arms around him, the warm, live body, pressed against him—a rush of relief.

"Hoot," said Sam, pointing to Matti's jacket. "We'll need this."

Hoot looked and saw smeared bloodstains on the sleeve where Matti had been grabbed. He slipped his child's jacket off, saw the blue watch on his wrist, and smiled. Should he turn off the power button, now that they had rescued him?

No. Let those waiting watch the progress of their triumphant return.

He looked at the piece of offal lying in the dust, proclaiming his innocence and demanding his attorney. As he walked back to Sam's car, he spotted the wreckage of the box, the broken hand lying amongst zebrawood splinters. No longer a gleaming piece of art, but broken in the dirt, like the man behind him. All that was left of those evil secrets and ill-gotten gains. Shattered wood, shattered lives.

Cold raindrops began to spatter against them. He shifted the weight of his son to one hip and pulled his own jacket over him. He caressed Matti's red hair and whispered, "I love you. Let's go home."

CHAPTER SEVENTY

Anton returned to Marilyn's home, walking past the press crowding the area outside by the command trailer and went inside where Melody and the others waited. Still no Bonnie. The nightmare of Krista's kidnapping and his helplessness overwhelmed him.

Skyla's phone rang. It was Hoot; he had Matti, and they were coming home. Melody turned into Lynn's arms, and they both wept again.

The search atmosphere had now changed from the initial chaos to controlled efficiency. The searchers had already completed one canvass of Pecos east of the river. Anton felt the river as an ominous threat to a lost child. Volunteers went door to door, checking every spot in which a small, frightened child might think to hide.

Anton warmed his hands on a cup of hot coffee. He looked at his watch. Not much time before daylight disappeared. Damn the shortness of the winter days! The waiting. Pure agony. He had to do something.

The outside door opened, letting in a blast of cool, damp air as Cliff arrived with Gandalf to a round of hard hugs.

One child safe, one still missing. "Bonnie," Melody sobbed, "Bonnie."

Skyla hugged Melody's shaking shoulders. Cliff pulled Hiram aside and spoke to him before catching Anton's eye and nodding.

Cliff knelt in front of Melody and took her hands. "I'd like to have Gandalf look for Bonnie. He's had some luck in tracking and trailing. If you could get me a piece of clothing with her scent on it—maybe her pajamas or underwear?"

"There's a pair of her pajamas under her pillow," said Melody, looking at Hiram, who nodded and left.

Anton pulled on his jacket again. As he stepped outside, light drops of rain hit him and he pulled up his hood. He looked back to see Melody standing in the doorway with Lynn. The ache grew within him. *Come on, Gandalf. Can you do it?*

Skyla came up beside him. He took her hand and watched as Cliff clipped a long lead onto Gandalf's collar. Several volunteers gathered. Hiram handed Cliff a bag and some tongs.

Cliff pulled the pajamas out of the bag. "Gandalf, find."

The Airedale looked at him, sniffed the fuzzy pink clothing, and began moving back and forth, nose to the ground. Finally, he seemed to focus, moving steadily out of the yard toward the road. The group of searchers followed.

Anton kept calling for Bonnie and Twitch. Gandalf crossed to the other side of the road and started moving swiftly. In about a hundred yards, he stopped, zigzagged back and forth, sniffing, before taking off across a field. Soon they reached a fence row, and he followed that. Then he stopped, sniffing at a break in the wooden fence.

"Look," Anton said, pointing. There, caught on a jagged sliver of wood, was a small tuft of red fibers. "Her cape is that color."

"Good boy, Gandalf," said Cliff, holding out the pajamas once again. "Find."

Gandalf led them across a second clearing toward some outbuildings. Cliff stopped him, and pointed. "Tracks." Dog tracks ran through a muddy, low spot. Beside them were a child's shoe print, and a short step away, a depression that looked like a small mussed-up footprint. It was a good sign they were together.

A chilly drizzle had descended. Sunset was near. How far could a small child go? Anton called again for Twitch. Skyla called for Bonnie. They crossed a yard and followed a driveway to a county road. The trail kept them on the road now except for periodic divergences behind bushes or trees.

"She's afraid," said Skyla. "I bet she's been hiding when she sees anyone."

Gandalf barked again. There, on the side of the road, almost invisible with caked mud, was a small sock. "Find, Gandalf, find," said Cliff.

This time Gandalf turned away from the houses and back toward the river. He forged ahead on his lead. Several times, Anton saw lots of dog tracks, but since they found the sock, he hadn't seen any child footprints. Was Twitch on his own now? What happened to Bonnie?

They were coming to the river and his heart sank. Surely, she wouldn't have gone there. Gandalf barked and ran toward something on the ground. Cliff followed. "A shoe," he called. "Is it hers?"

"It looks like hers," said Anton. "Hard to say." The small shoe was well-chewed and torn apart.

"Twitch," called Anton. No response. Just silence and the sound of the nearby river.

Cliff called Gandalf to him. "What happened here?" They searched the ground, looking for tracks that might tell the story. "Searchers have already been along the river."

As Cliff studied the tracks in the muddy ground, the expression on his face changed. "There's not one single footprint of a child anywhere here."

"I'm not certain," said Skyla, "but I don't think these are Twitch's tracks. See how Gandalf's tracks are kind of round? These are different—longer."

Cliff peered at the ground. "You're right. Let's go back to where we found the sock and try again. Maybe another dog took off with her shoe."

The group went back to the road, silently now, except for calling for Bonnie and Twitch. When they got back to the sock, Cliff held out the pajamas again. "Find, Gandalf. Find."

Gandalf zigzagged, leading them a little farther down the road. He looked back.

"Find," Cliff said. Gandalf put his nose to the ground and cast back and forth again. Suddenly he let out a little yelp and moved steadily ahead, his long lead taut. Cliff moved faster to keep up.

Anton and Skyla called again and again. They passed several houses. We must have come a mile already, thought Anton. "Twitch, come!"

Then he heard an answering bark in the distance. Gandalf began to run with Cliff, Skyla, and Anton following closely. The other volunteers trailed behind. They passed a house and saw in the weedy backyard, an old, abandoned doghouse. Gandalf pulled toward it, barking excitedly.

Suddenly, Twitch was there, jumping on Anton, barking and wriggling.

"Bonnie, it's Skyla! Anton and Cliff are with me."

"I'm here," Bonnie called, poking her head out of the doghouse.

Cliff dropped the leash and ran toward her, picking her up in his arms and hugging her close.

"Twitch and I didn't wike that man. He hurted us. I tried to find Mommy and Daddy, but I got wost."

Anton thought it was one of the most beautiful sights he'd ever seen—the little imp with tear-streaked, dirty cheeks, cobwebs in her hair, and old musty straw clinging to her princess costume.

She smiled at Cliff and patted his cheek. "Hi, Uncle Cliff. Hi, everybody."

In their room at the Bjornson's just past midnight, Hoot stood behind Melody, his arms surrounding her, as they looked out the window. He watched big fluffy snowflakes falling in the yard light, softly delineating the branches and wall tops. Pristine, fresh, and new. Behind them in the bed next to theirs, their children slept. Bonnie clutched her fox and Matti his dad's old Koda.

The snow muffled all sound from the outside, leaving the world a hushed cocoon. Let it snow, he thought. They were warm and safe.

Hoot smiled against Melody's hair. "I think the threat is truly gone now."

"It was so awful, Hoot, I never want to live through a day like this again."

"I know." He turned her in his arms, smiling down into her face in the dim light, chuckling as she stifled a yawn.

"Matti was so brave," she said. "And Bonnie, trusting in Twitch to watch after her. I was so proud of our children. Thank God for that tracker phone."

"Good night, Bonnie, Matti." He tucked the blankets closely around the sleeping children and whispered, "Good night, Foxie. Good night, Koda."

In bed, Hoot slid next to Melody and pulled her against him. He caressed the swell of her tummy. "How's Junior?"

"Junior's doing just fine. I think I felt some fluttering tonight."

"Already? Awesome."

They lay spooned together, watching the snowflakes drift against the light, before their eyes closed in peace.

Chapter Seventy-One

Sunday morning brought bright sun and blue skies to a sparkly white world and a lighthearted feeling to Pete. Two children brought home again. Though there was much work to be done to make sure Hayle, Torres, and Wysocki faced justice, they were behind bars. Hoot had no more threats hanging over his head.

Pete's planning had paid off yesterday. His officers came through with everything he'd asked for as far as the evidence against Wysocki. The media blitz of the moment was all about Wysocki's fall from grace. Yes, he'd lawyered up, but his legal team faced tough challenges if he were to get off.

Pete discovered Marilyn would be released and go back to the Bjornsons' ranch that afternoon. She would be well looked after there.

What would happen to Hawkins, Pete wondered as he walked toward the young man's hospital room. He sympathized with him. Gunshot wounds were not pleasant. Been there, done that.

"The children?" Jed asked as soon as Pete walked in.

Pete told him they were safe. Wysocki had been arrested and charged with kidnapping. More charges would be added.

"How did you happen to be at that home yesterday?" asked Pete.

"I went one last time to see if I could get that damn box. No one was home, so I picked the lock. Found the box, just sitting there. I took it, and then I heard the boy come in."

"How did you know who it was?"

"Saw him through the door crack," said Jed. "Then I went out the back, and heard someone else at the front. I expected it to be the family, but it was Wysocki."

"How do you know Wysocki?"

"I worked for him. He paid me to get the box."

"Then what happened?"

"I worried he might hurt the boy if he got in his way, so I followed him back in the front door. We argued. I was hoping the kid would hear us and sneak out the back. Then the old lady and the little girl came in with the dog."

"Did Wysocki tell you why he wanted the box?"

"He said it was stolen from him. His obsession about it made me wonder what secrets it held. Wysocki operates by digging up dirt on people and using that knowledge to control them. I used what he taught me and found out about this girl, Tonya Abrerro, in his past."

"What did you learn?"

"I found out they had something going, and I figured he didn't want his wife to find out. Then Tonya turned up dead. That was a little too convenient for me, so I dug some more. Talked to an old high school buddy of his."

Jed took a sip of his water. "I confronted Wysocki with that name, accused him of having something to do with her death. He went ballistic. Demanded to know how I opened the box. Right then, I knew she was part of his secrets. But I gave him the box. Just wanted to get the hell out of there and disappear. You don't cross Wit Wysocki and stay healthy. He might seem like a wonderful guy, but inside he's evil. I hope he ends up in prison."

"Had you been at that house before?"

Jed closed his eyes and nodded. "Yes. I'm not proud of it, but, yes. I broke in and turned the place upside down. Couldn't find that box."

"I'm glad you told me you were there. We have proof of it."

"You do? How?"

Pete gestured toward the healing scab on Jed's head. "When you came up under that cupboard door. Head wounds bleed heavily."

"If I cooperate with you, is there a chance that things will go easier on me?"

"I can't make promises," said Pete. "That'll be up to the prosecution. But what do you think?"

Jed smiled. "I think you need all the help you can get to bring down that SOB. I think I might have a chance."

"In the world we live in, cooperation means something."

Jed shifted in bed, grimacing. "The world I've been in too long sucks. I'd rather be in yours." He closed his eyes. "Sorry. These pain meds make me sleepy."

"Just as the anesthesia began to work yesterday, you asked us to please find Annie. Who is Annie?"

A deep sadness crossed Jed's face. "My sister. She was only four. The little red-headed girl reminded me of her. My old man was a violent drunk. He used to beat on us—my mother, sister, and me—until I got big enough to hit back. I tried to get my mother to leave him, but she wouldn't. Finally, I convinced her to leave, but when I was at school, they went back." He looked down, swallowed. His mouth twisted, and he shook his head slowly. "A few days later they were dead. He killed them. I couldn't save Annie, but that little red-haired girl—sweet, like Annie—I couldn't let him hurt her."

"How are Pueblo and Denver coming with their cases?" asked Pete as he and Grover talked Monday morning. The media did not yet know that Pueblo and Denver would soon add nastier surprises for Wysocki's lawyers.

"They looked at the information you gave them on the marriage certificate and confirmed it. Like you, they were not able to find any record of a divorce or annulment. His marriage to Monica in 1988 appears bigamous."

"Did they find out anything about that necklace?" asked Sam.

"They followed up on the information you gave them, and once Wysocki's name was associated with it, results speeded up. Wysocki reported the necklace stolen in January, 1990. The insurance company paid off his claim in January of 1991.

"That's interesting," said Pete. "If we go by the dates on the hunting trip packets, Gordon stole the box with the necklace on March 16, 1991, the day after Tonya Abrerro died."

"Well after the insurance company had paid up," said Grover. "Yet it was obviously still in his possession."

"Too bad they can't still prosecute," said Sam.

"Don't be so sure they can't," said Grover with a chuckle. "The Colorado legislature has been playing with insurance fraud statutes. It used to be that the clock started ticking when the crime was committed. Now, if I'm not mistaken, the limit might start when the insurance crime is discovered."

Pete smiled. "That doesn't hurt my feelings."

"How about the fingerprints on the box contents?"

"We've confirmed the photo inside the locket was of Wysocki and Abrerro," said Pete. "His fingerprints were on the locket, the marriage license, and the envelopes. His letter was the only one with his prints inside."

"We sent copies of all those letters to Pueblo," said Grover. "They are reopening the investigation into Tonya's death and will build a homicide case."

"Why did he keep that stuff?" asked Sam. "Why didn't he just ditch it in the first trash can he saw?"

"Maybe he hadn't read the letters yet," said Pete. "Certainly he thought he had more time. He must have been a basket case when he discovered the box was stolen."

CHAPTER SEVENTY-TWO

As Hoot and his family turned into the Bjornson drive on his birthday, he grinned at Melody. "This is weird. For as long as I can remember, I've celebrated my birthday in August. Now it's February 11, and it's my birthday."

Melody laughed. "You can always celebrate both."

"Two birthdays a year? Talk about aging rapidly. No, I don't think so. Usually when you have a birthday, you're another year older. But I'm not going to be thirty-four, I'm only going to be thirty-two. Now I'm younger than my wife."

She grinned. "Next year, you'll be a year older. Enjoy it, squirt."

"And I'll still be younger than you," he teased. "Forever."

Marilyn chuckled. "Somehow that doesn't seem fair. I could really use getting younger, and yet it's my grandson who is."

"There are a lot of cars here already. Wow. It's a good thing Karen offered to have the party here." Hoot parked near his parents' car. "Our place is chaos."

Bonnie jumped out and ran ahead to the door, head down, running smack into Anton, who was coming out.

"*Uff da*," he said, swinging her up in his arms. "Watch where you're going."

"I was looking at my new shoes," she said, holding up a sneaker for his inspection. "They have lights!"

"Do they?" Anton said, putting her back down. "Show me."

She ran around him, giggling, lights flashing with every step, and ran into the house, calling, "Look at my new shoes, everybody. Lights!"

Hoot followed her inside, a big grin on his face. "Too bad she's so shy."

"Lights, Karen," said Bonnie.

Karen bent down to take a closer look and smiled at Bonnie. "Lights. They're important. Let them shine."

"Pretty," said Skyla. "And you said it right."

"Auntie Lou said I'm not a baby anymore. I grewed up, and pretty soon I start kindergarten. Big kids say lights." She darted away to show off her shoes, followed by Matti, who was carrying Koda.

Lou chuckled as she and Cliff came forward. "We worked hard on that. Auntie 'Woo' really thought she could do it."

Cliff grinned. "What did you do?"

"I taught her some songs—first the melody using la, la, la. Then words."

"Genius," he said, dropping a kiss on her lips. "You work miracles."

After all the Circle Sleuths had arrived and Hoot had gotten all of his birthday hugs, he looked around with a smile, taking in the circle of friends and family.

In the living room, he saw Matti climb on a stool and put Koda carefully on a shelf out of the reach of the Airedales. He turned to Skyla. "Matti's talking to Koda now. Just think of all the secrets he's been privy to and the things he's heard."

Skyla laughed. "It's a good thing Koda hadn't belonged to Anton. He would have found out how to put a gadget in it and record all the secrets for everyone to hear."

"What a cool idea," Anton said as he came around with a tray of glasses. "How are Matti and Bonnie doing after their adventures?"

"Okay, mostly," answered Hoot. "Maybe a little more clingy now."

"As I remember," said Anton, "that goes both ways. After Krista got back, I didn't want to let her out of my sight, either. I've been thinking. There was that one moment when you were snatched. Your life changed drastically from that point on, but so did everyone else's. There was a before and an after, like the fulcrum on a teeter-totter. When Krista was kidnapped, her experience brought back the anguish of his missing brother to Cliff. Possibly without that, he would have done only what was necessary to get Krista back to us and not have involved himself in the ongoing search for those responsible."

"Cliff has such confidence, power," said Hoot. "I am in awe of my little brother."

"His power came after one of those before-and-after moments. The Circle Sleuths were formed out of that crucible."

"She saved my life, your daughter, or perhaps Pete's life," said Hoot. "That act of kindness—" He swallowed and wet his lips, pausing before finishing. "Melody and I still get choked up over it."

"Me, too," said Anton.

"Melody tells me you and Skyla will have another fulcrum moment—in May."

Anton's smile broadened. "True, and a couple of months later, I'm told, you'll follow suit."

Hoot nodded. "Will Skyla keep on working?"

"She's still deciding. She's talking about going back to school. Getting more archaeology classes, maybe even aerial archaeology. We've kicked around the idea of creating a new division in Drone Tech. I could provide the drones and the technical expertise. She, the archaeology. We might take on students. Maybe do conferences. Bringing diverse groups together with Native Americans, museum staff, archaeologists, and anthropologists, as well as the public. She's talking about writing a book that teaches respect for the ancient sites and that leads to a better understanding of the Ancient Puebloans. That's all down the road."

"That sounds really interesting," said Hoot. "I think you should bring in some government folks, too. They could use an approach like that."

"That's a thought," said Anton, looking up. "Here are two others who would add a point of view. They get into some of the most interesting discussions I've ever heard." He smiled as Karen and Dom sat near them with their wine.

343

"Anton's talking about what goes on in my studio," said Karen. "A necessary part of weaving is mind-numbing, repetitive work, like warping the loom or blending colors of yarn into small butterfly skeins. Dom has started reading aloud to me while I do that. It has launched us into some pretty good philosophical and even theological discussions."

"It has pulled the rest of us in, too," said Anton.

Sam came over and sat down by Karen. "I heard that your foundation is considering plans to base more search-and-rescue bloodhounds in New Mexico. Our dog-trainer guy was all excited."

"Two times in the past year or so when we've needed trailing dogs, the ones available have already been working elsewhere," said Karen. "That's fairly common. It stands to reason that this state could support four or five regional bloodhound groups. We're just lucky that Gandalf was available. Not to take anything away from Gandalf, but bloodhounds have much more powerful noses."

"How did Krista react to that idea?" asked Sam.

"I try to expose her to some of the different projects that we do. She likes the bloodhound idea. We've let her explore and evaluate some of the grant proposals we get. She's actually got pretty good sense."

"That doesn't surprise me. How did she do at the dog show you went to?" asked Sam.

Karen smiled. "Shadow now has points toward her championship. Krista and Akiko were so proud."

Hoot sighed. "Is it inevitable that our family will have an Airedale in our future?"

"If I know Bonnie, you will," Anton said. "She'll wear you down, and you know what? You won't regret it."

"It's interesting to hear you say that," said Karen, glancing at Anton with an innocent smile. "Because Krista told me she wants to breed Shadow after she gets her championship."

"Oh, boy," Anton said. "Here we go. I knew from the moment she chose a girl dog what was coming."

Hoot turned as Maria called from the kitchen. "Lunch is served. Get your plates and fill them up. Save room for birthday cake."

CHAPTER SEVENTY-THREE

A deep contentment filled Pete as he took in the circle of friends gathered around the Bjornson family room for Hoot's birthday celebration. The sun had long since set, and the dishes had been cleared away. Krista and Leyla sat at the counter between the kitchen and the family room, working on their sketching. They were like his daughter, Lou, living and breathing art, seeing, then translating to paper, capturing beauty, and somehow an essence— whether it be dog, person, or landscape. Their talents boded well for their futures.

His gaze rested on Krista. The journey of the Circle Sleuths had begun with her. Because of her act of kindness, the group was still whole, thriving, not mourning, and he was here to enjoy it.

Andrew and Lynn were settled on a couch near Marilyn, Wilma, Maria, and Diego. Matti snuggled against his grandfather's side. Bonnie, ensconced on her grandmother's lap, listened again to the familiar words of *Koda and the Sami* and carefully turned the pages at exactly the right place as the story unfolded.

Near the kiva fireplace, Sam played his guitar, finding familiar melodies for the group gathered around him. He had such a kaleidoscope of talent, making music come effortlessly from under his fingers. The voices around him blended in harmony. Farah, Anton, Skyla, Lou, Melody, Cliff, and Hoot. Their faces were all animated, all enjoying the music, keeping Sam busy with suggestions of what to play next.

Sam began playing "You Raise Me Up" and Lou and Cliff joined him, singing. Ah, one of his favorites. Pete's eyes went to Akiko, sitting by him on the overstuffed couch with their first grandbaby, asleep on her lap. Any portrait of the Madonna and child paled in his mind next to this vision of Akiko and Dougie. He reached out to smooth the baby's dark hair that never seemed to lie flat. Akiko raised her eyes to his and smiled.

Then, as Dom's voice caught his attention, Pete turned to him.

"I believe there is a story in me that needs to be told. I'd like to write a novel."

"What will it be about?" asked Pete.

Dom smiled and shook his head. "I don't know yet, but that conversation we had the night you told us about the Avenging Angel started me thinking. Right now, I'm just exploring ideas, characters, what motivates them, and what gets in their way."

"Is that where stories start? With characters?"

"I've been thinking about books that stay with me, long after the covers are closed. For me, I think it is the characters that make that happen. When the time is right, the words will come."

"Will it be historical fiction?" asked Pete.

Karen chuckled. "What else could it be with Dom? His characters and plot will be grounded in history."

"It could even be fantasy," said Dom. "We see ourselves in characters from another world. Other worlds have histories, too."

"He's even threatened to have dragons in his story," said Karen.

"But what kind of a dragon? A fire-breathing dragon of yesteryear? Or maybe a corporate entity, protecting its ill-gotten hoard of gold?" Dom paused to take a sip of his wine. "One thing I know. I want the story to lift the spirit of the reader. Give them hope."

"Whatever you decide," said Pete. "It'll be a book I don't want to miss."

"Karen, why dragons? Do you deal with dragons in your own life?" asked Akiko.

Karen looked at her, startled. "Interesting question. I suppose I do. In a practical way, our foundation tries to fight some dragons, set things right, promote what matters and help people relate to each other in positive ways. I suppose my weaving deals with dragons, too."

"That I believe, my heart," said Dom. "Weaving expresses your passion. You create something that touches people. You make light shine."

Karen smiled. "You deal with dragons every day, Pete."

"Dragons?" Pete quirked his eyebrows. "*Ja*, I believe you're right." He chuckled. "Sir Peter, the dragon slayer?"

Karen laughed. "It's true, you know. Ever since we met, it's been what your life was about. If your dragons are chaos, you are the fighter for order and justice."

A burst of laughter drew Pete's attention back to the singers on the other side of the room, where two red-headed brothers joked with each other. Together at last, but with so much of their lives apart. In the end, one couldn't go back. A childhood stolen was gone forever. The brothers would never get back the experiences they would have shared.

But they could move forward and learn from each other. Meeting as adults, knowing they had a bond and love. People who cared about them. The John McCreath in this room tonight wasn't the same person that John McCreath would have been had things been different. But who among them was? Choices had been made. Roads traveled. The future stretched into infinity. Many choices. Many consequences.

He felt his eyes growing wet. Akiko looked up at him. "What's wrong? What are you thinking?"

"Want to go for a walk with me, Angel? I think Beowulf needs to go out."

Akiko carefully transferred the sleeping six-month-old to Karen. They got their jackets, and led Beowulf down the hall past Karen's studio and outside.

They moved past Diego's and Maria's duplexes to the trail that led away from the house. Out of the range of windows and yard light, the stars seemed brighter. The Milky Way hung above them—all those souls, he thought, all the myriad stars. They walked hand in hand in silence. On his left, Pete saw the big boulders that made a perfect spot to sit and watch over the valley and the distant lights of Santa Fe.

"I was thinking just now," said Pete, "about this epic journey the McCreath kidnapping has been. Feeling just welled up in me. Watching Cliff and Hoot. It feels damn good to have helped bring about that reunion, to bring justice to those who caused the pain, to know they didn't get away with it."

"It's a credit to your leadership, Pete. The Circle all contributed, each in their own way. A team you put together."

Pete stopped and put a hand to her cheek. "And you, Angel. You remind me when I falter. It's together our work is best." He tugged her to a boulder and they sat close together for warmth in the cold, clear air.

"*Mein Gott*, Akiko, I have been blessed beyond belief. For years I have been envious of all those with nine-to-five jobs where they didn't have to take work home with them. I wouldn't have missed this for the world. Oh, my angel, no other job, no award, nothing could be better than this. All the work, all the digging. Johnny is home at last."

Tears ran down his cheeks. Akiko snuggled closer to him. His angel, a treasured, quiet presence, a center so necessary to his life.

"I've been thinking about retiring. But I'm not ready yet. I'm good at what I do, and the world still needs what I can give it. You're well acquainted with the toll on cops, the cumulative effect of all the evil we see, but the Circle Sleuths—friends chosen and cherished—they help me achieve balance."

Beowulf settled at their feet, warming them with his furry coat, pinning them in place.

"The dragons almost got me this time," said Pete, "but God was good. I survived."

"Each day with you is a gift," said Akiko, "a gift I never take for granted."

He squeezed her hand. "I feel good about this world. There are so many who care. I used to worry about what kind of a world we would leave for our grandchildren to face. But Dougie and the others who come will have good company. There's hope ahead. You and I, just think. Five children. How brave we were to bring them into such uncertainty. I'm proud of them. I'm proud of you."

They sat in silence until Beowulf scrambled to his feet, alerted by some unseen night creature. Pete stood, pulling Akiko into a hug, looking down into her face. She slipped her arms around his waist and laughed her familiar sultry laugh. God, he enjoyed that sound, just for him. He pressed her to himself, angling his mouth over his angel's, exulting in her eager response.

His hands rode the curve of her back upwards, slid gently over her shoulders, and lightly framed her face. His kisses became softer, playful. He felt her mouth move under his.

"I love you, Pete."

"Ah, Angel, I love you, too."

In his mind, the universe encircled them, bringing them into unity with the star-studded sky. The myriad stars twinkled and then grew steady, surrounding, flooding them with light and hope as they turned to go back to the Circle.

About the Author

Betty Lucke holds a Bachelor's degree in elementary education from Macalester College, St. Paul, MN, and the Master of Religious Education and the Master of Divinity degrees from Princeton Theological Seminary, Princeton, NJ. She has fond memories of summers worked in New Mexico. She lives in northern California with her husband and a Welsh terrier.

She is a co-founder of the Town Square Writers, a weekly writing group associated with the public library.

www.ingramcontent.com/pod-product-compliance
Lightning Source LLC
Chambersburg PA
CBHW070406260626
47161CB00001B/293